'Frank, funny, warm-hearted and wise. **I adored this**
celebration of making your own kind of music,
and dancing to your own beat.'
Simon James Green, author of *Alex in Wonderland,*
Noah Can't Even and *Heartbreak Boys*

'**I loved the fresh and original voice** of this coming of age
debut, approaching big themes with a light touch.'
Bookseller, Highlights of the Season

'A **hilarious and heart-warming** story.
I can't wait to see what Christine writes next.'
Aisha Bushby, author of *A Pocketful of Stars*

'**Warm, funny and hopeful** . . .
I didn't really want the book to end!'
A M Dassu, author of *Boy, Everywhere*

'A **fresh, funny, feel-good** story and a powerful
exploration of identity, friendship and family.'
. . . deshpande

ABOUT THE AUTHOR

Christine Pillainayagam is a writer and retail strategist, who lives in Kent with her young family and a collection of records, CDs and minidiscs (remember those?). A mild obsession with the Beatles and the desire to write a story that reflected her own experiences growing up as a first-generation immigrant led her to put that love of music and words into a book. *Ellie Pillai is Brown* is her debut novel.

A singer and songwriter, she also writes a blog: thelittlebrownbook.co.uk

ELLIE PILLAI IS BROWN

CHRISTINE PILLAINAYAGAM

Illustrated by Trisha Srivastava

 faber

For Dad.

In the words of Pink Floyd: wish you were here.

First published in the UK in 2022
by Faber & Faber Limited, Bloomsbury House,
74–77 Great Russell Street,London WC1B 3DA
faberchildrens.co.uk

Typeset in Mr Eaves by MRules
Printed by CPI Group (UK) Ltd, Croydon CR0 4YY

A CIP record for this book is available from the British Library

ISBN 978–0–571–36691–0

MIX
Paper | Supporting
responsible forestry
FSC® C171272

Printed and bound in the UK on FSC paper in line with our continuing
commitment to ethical business practices, sustainability and the environment.
For further information see faber.co.uk/environmental-policy

2 4 6 8 10 9 7 5 3

You can listen to the *Ellie Pillai is Brown* album by scanning in the link below and enjoy hearing Ellie's songs come to life!

There are song chapters throughout the story that reference specific songs on the album so we'd recommend listening to each song when it appears in the book, but it's totally up to you!

1

Going Down

1

A Girl Called Ellie

'Won't you love me?' she cried out to the man in the yellow mac.

My name is Ellie. Ellie Pillai. And these are the words I find myself writing over and over, whenever I have a piece of paper and a pen to hand. I don't know why. Maybe I believe one day I will find unrequited love with a fisherman from a 1950s poster, or one of those hipster types with an ironic moustache and a penchant for Scandinavian clothing. Whatever way you look at it, my subconscious is telling me that this man is going to be rejecting me, possibly even running away from me, with his mac flapping in the breeze like a giant yellow eagle. And I can well believe that to be true, because I'm the kind of weirdo that writes things like 'Won't you love me?' and 'man in the yellow mac' over and over again on my science test, scribbling the words in all different shapes and sizes, like the world's worst calligrapher. I suppose I am a little bit weird, but then, aren't we all, just a little bit?

2

But Your Face

I'm stood in front of the mirror, staring at my reflection, when I hear it. The Rolling Stones, 'Lies'. It's sort of brilliantly manic. A mash of guitars fighting each other over the sound of Mick Jagger screaming about lies and dirt and mouths and dripping.

I stare at my mouth and wonder whether it's possible to see actual lies. Whether they have a tangible shape, or feel. Whether the reason I don't feel hungry this morning is because my mouth is full of Dripping Dirt Lies and the fear of being Found Out, or whether my stomach's just churning at the thought of one of Mum's back-to-school lectures. Mick keeps intermittently screaming at me, as if that's somehow helpful, as if I didn't already know about lies and dirt and mouths and dripping.

Oh. God.

The guitars feel a bit like they're flying. Like they're soaring above me, and I'm watching them speed away like birds.

I study my face carefully, analysing every feature.

Skin – Brown.

Eyes – Brown.

Lips – Pinkish brown.

Nose – Small, sharp, brown.

Eyebrows – Black. Forming one long arc across my entire forehead unless rigorously plucked daily.

Me – Brown. Obviously.

I never used to think that much about the way I look. Because before high school, being small, brown and not exactly the same as everyone else was OK. It even once earned me a stalker (by which I mean a boy once asked me out, prompting my father to report him to the school as a stalker and potential serial killer). Before high school, being me seemed simple. Turn up, be yourself, go home, repeat.

But then it happened. The day I awkwardly turned up at a new school, my shoes two sizes too big. High school was just different somehow. The stakes so much higher. The expectation that you should know exactly who you are, and exactly what you stand for – as though I should have an opinion on topics as wide-ranging as: how tanned is too tanned (brown, according to Addy McQueen, is the 'wrong kind of tan'), or who's cuter, [insert random teenage Disney person] or [insert random faux Rock God]. I mean, if I had to choose, random faux Rock God – because at least he or she is imitating something I can remotely connect with. It's like I'm fifteen and I'm a personal brand now, instead of just a person. And my brand isn't the one you'd buy. It's definitely not the one you're posting on Instagram, expecting it to be followed by a million likes. It's more like the brand you get in the sale section of your mum's favourite shop, the one you don't really fancy, but it's there,

5

and seems like the sensible choice. And that's me really. Somewhere between invisible and not very cool. And usually, I'm OK with that.

But today feels different, and I'm not sure why. Maybe because it's the first day back at school after the summer. The year I start my GCSEs. And everything I've spent the last year and a half trying to hold together feels like it's suddenly and unceremoniously about to come unstuck.

I take out the kohl eyeliner, which has only ever succeeded in making me resemble a panda, and attempt to line my eyes. I'm going for French Girl Cool, but it's coming off more Bear Native to South Central China. However much I try, I just can't seem to master the art of this make-up stuff.

'ELLIE! You're going to be late!' Mum knocks on the door emphatically, causing me to lose control of the pencil.

'I'm coming!' I jump as she pokes her head through the doorway. But of course, Mum's wearing eyeliner, and of course, hers is perfect. Because Mum's face is perfect. Even when I know she's been up half the night working and generally proving she can Have It All and still be Better Than Me at everything.

'Do you need help with that?' she asks, frowning.

'No,' I say, turning back towards the mirror. 'I'll be down in a minute.'

As she leaves the room, I try not to let Mick Jagger get to me. Apparently, I'm a dirty Jezebel.

I nudge my foot against the Rolling Stones album and push it over in retaliation.

6

Mick responds by suggesting I go to hell. Which seems rude.

All right, Mick, I think, trying not to wonder how Mum gets those perfect sixties eyeliner flicks, when once again I resemble an animal with an insatiable appetite for bamboo. I take your point, OK?

So, I may have told a lie – and not just about the fact I don't need help with my eyeliner (obviously I do), but a different lie. A really tiny, *other* white lie (and why is it that even lies are white when they're a better version of themselves?). But Mick, I ask you – did you have first-generation immigrant parents, who were obsessed with your future, and your opportunities, and every infinitesimal decision you ever made, because it's not just about you, but all the generations that came before you, and the sacrifices they all made to get you here? Did you, Mick, did you?

I sigh in frustration and turn away from the mirror. Normally I love a bit of Rolling Stones. I love any and all music, and the way it transports me to somewhere else, to being some*one* else. But lately, it's like the soundtrack that's been playing in my head, for pretty much as long as I can remember, is getting louder, and brighter, and bolder, and more *visible* to me than ever.

Because even though I have a million and one vinyl records (which most people think makes me weird and strange and super old) I'm not actually playing any one of them right now, I just have the entire Rolling Stones camped out in my head, and Mick Jagger is shaking his hips and frankly looking a bit ancient to be trying these kind of moves, while the rest of the band plays intently beside him.

It's pretty much the strangest thing ever, when music starts playing in your head for no reason; notes popping up like springs that can't be suppressed, sometimes accompanied by the appearance of a brass band or string quartet, or on one particularly memorable occasion, a sixties girl group singing to my PE teacher during a game of dodgeball.

And I know we all have those moments sometimes. When we're listening to our favourite song, or just any song, any music – and suddenly, it's like you're in it. In the music, in the moment, part of whatever's happening with the melody and the lyrics, inextricably connected to it. It's just that's how I feel I'm living my life. In an album of those songs. Note by note. Like somehow those songs are trying to write my story. Like maybe those songs are my story.

So I can't help but give in to the thrashing of guitars and lightly pulsing drums as I stand up and start putting on my school uniform. Dancing around my bedroom to a song no one else can hear. Nodding my head to the music and mouthing the words to myself in the mirror, followed by some air guitar when Keith takes me to the bridge.

Lies, lies and more lies – yes Mick, I know.

But after that, I might get a bit lost. Somewhere between real life and the one inside my head. Because the next thing I know, Mum is stood behind me, hands on hips, surveying me mid air-guitar solo, as I dance to absolute silence.

'ELLIE. Ellie!!'

It's like the needle's been pulled off the record in my head. A sudden and abrupt interruption.

'What are you doing?' she asks, frustrated. 'It sounds like a herd of elephants up here.'

'Nothing,' I say, grabbing my school bag, embarrassed. 'I'm, er, going to school.'

And I attempt to ignore The Look.

'Ellie, Dad and I need to talk to you.'

'I can't. I'm running late.'

She sighs.

I run down the stairs and pantomime a Late Face to Dad, who looks up and waves before calmly going back to his paper, undoubtedly grateful that whatever Mum and I are on the verge of fighting over, we no longer have time to fight over.

And the last thing I see is Mum, stood in the hallway, her mouth curled around the words.

'But your face . . .' she cries, as I slam the door shut behind me.

3

The Lie, The Lie and the Panda Eye

I'm halfway to the bus stop before I realise Mum's 'but your face' critique isn't a commentary on my disappointing genetics but an observation about my panda eyes. I lick my fingers and rub at them, hoping I can get the worst of it off.

But like the lie I told a year and a half ago, the black ink is clinging desperately to my skin, growing like some kind of radioactive spider's web, or one of those beanstalks with a flesh-eating giant living at the top.

The Lie.

The Lie.

And the Panda Eye.

If only I could take it all back.

Except that I can't, and really, I don't want to. Because somehow it all made sense at the time. And it still makes sense. Even if it doesn't.

Oh God. I can't even explain it to myself, let alone my parents.

I rifle through my bag, and stare at the printout from the end of last year. My mock GCSE grades. A row of beautiful little digits that should range from 9 to 4 but include one big glaring 2, which is not the number of times I have rechecked my grade, just to be sure (that number is one million, four hundred and forty-two).

Drama. I got a 2 for drama. Which is a subject my parents have no idea I'm even taking. Mostly because they would consider it the equivalent of taking a GCSE in unicorn studies. Pointless and The Waste of a Good Opportunity.

And for Most People, this would be the tiniest of tiny white lies. An omission. Because whose parents actually care that much about one in ten subjects? Ten per cent of your overall GCSE grades (because look – I can even do maths!). A sliver of your future so small, you can forget all about it by the time they've forced you into doing a Law Degree. It's just, I'm not Most People – which my friend Hayley would say is a good thing – but it's easy to say that when you are.

In my world, taking drama and possibly, maybe, not being *entirely* honest with your parents about it = A Big Deal. And when you add a 2 into the equation, even Albert Einstein wouldn't be able to work out the level of my mother's rage ($2 = MC^2$ x rage). Because it's not the little rebellion I keep telling myself it is when I start sweating when questioned about my fake computer science report – it's The Rebellion. Capital R. The kind of rebellion that leads to being sent to St Hilda's School for Girls Who Must Be Watched, and having to wear an unflattering smock dress for the next two years while singing hymns non-ironically.

(Did I mention St Hilda's is a boarding school? Where you get woken up at the crack of dawn to do *mass* in *Latin*?)

And that's probably why the soundtrack in my head has started to feel so vivid lately. Like the songs are trying to drown out the voice that keeps saying THERE IS NO WAY OUT OF THIS. JUMP. JUMP. SAVE YOURSELF!!!

Because this year, I know I can't really hide it any more. I can't pretend I've got the day of my Parents' Evening wrong again, forcing my dad to park in an empty playground and ask the caretaker why the school's locked up, on the only day of the year my mother gets to interrogate the teachers as to why I'm just not good enough.

As I head towards the bus stop on the village green, I kick at the stones on the road; Mavis from next door eyeing me disapprovingly through her lilac curtains.

The truth is, my parents think I'm a terrible actor – and so they would never have willingly let me take drama. Not even unwillingly. Because the last time they saw me in a play I had one line of dialogue, and I was so nervous there was a bead of sweat forming on the moustache I'd bleached blonde in order to make it *less noticeable*. And I forgot my line and just stood there, staring at my mother, until Hayley '*Who Wants To Be Like Most People?*' Atwell nudged me so hard I fell over. And that's how my life is. A comedy of errors with a blonde moustache for effect. So, as you can imagine, my parents don't really believe that drama is a subject for me. Or indeed for anyone who wants to make a living, make a difference, be useful to the world.

I have tried in vain to ask them why they go to the theatre, or why they have favourite films. How it is that stories have the power to move them. But the logic and sheer poetry of it all entirely escapes them.

When I reach the bus stop, I kick silently at the kerb, my toe tapping out a tune only I can hear. There are lies, and there is Mick Jagger screaming at you about lies, when only you can hear it.

Because I know there is no way out of this now. The Lie is out there. Creating a web of disaster I can't avoid. But who could have known that any of this was going to happen? Not innocent Year 9 Ellie Pillai. All naive optimism. All blonde moustache and monobrow; hopeful for a different kind of Ellie Pillai somehow emerging and seizing control of everything, between then and now. I mean, I've seized control of my eyebrows and I've worked out that blonde is not a colour that blends into my skin tone – but other than that, I am very much in the spiralling out of control part of this After School Special.

I just thought at some point I'd tell them. That there would be a perfect moment, when defences were down and we were all sat quietly and non-judgementally somewhere, and I'd turn to them and say, 'So . . . about that computer science GCSE . . . the reason I don't know anything about algorithms and *pseudo code programming* (because I'm pretty sure pseudo code programming is Not a Real Thing) is that I'm not actually taking computer science, I'm taking drama . . . And I'm learning about how to approach a script by examining settings and stage direction and dialogue . . . but don't worry, because I got an 9 in the exam, and my teacher has compared me to a young Meryl Streep . . .'

I root around in my bag for my headphones and pull them on. That was the way it was *supposed* to go. But Mr Grange keeps giving me roles that are effectively mute, like he thinks I belong in the age of silent film. And as good as my written work is, it just can't pull up my technical grade. And there has never, ever, been a perfect moment, when defences were down and my parents and I were sat quietly and non-judgementally, anywhere, ever. Because judgement is the very fuel by which my family exists.

I readjust my headphones and put on the Cure, 'Just Like Heaven', because there isn't much in life that song can't fix.

Three months, Ellie Pillai.

Three months until the first drama exam.

Three months to become a confident, non-sweaty, teenage Meryl Streep. To become *that* Ellie. The one who's going to seize control.

I scrub at my face as the bus approaches over the hill. I just wish I wasn't giving myself this pep talk while visibly resembling a panda.

4

Boys Don't Cry

It's cold outside, but every so often, the sun breaks through the trees on the village green and dapples the light on the road. I close my eyes and offer up a silent prayer to any God: Christian, Jewish, Muslim, Hindu, Sikh – whoever's available and listening to the pleas of a fifteen-year-old girl in a little east England village – that Rex won't be driving the bus today.

Rex has a tendency to 'not see me' at the bus stop, like all my wishes for invisibility have finally come true. When he does stop, he's weirdly passive-aggressive, making me take my bus pass out of its wallet and examining my photo like I'm some kind of potential flight risk.

One day last winter he muttered something semi-aggressively at me along the lines of 'I suppose they've never even seen snow where you come from.' And I wanted to say, 'I'm pretty sure my neighbour Mavis, whose mobility scooter got snowed in for three days, forcing her to eat nothing but cornflakes for three meals a day, three days in a row, has seen and understands the concept of snow.' But instead

I found myself saying nothing, and trying to drown him out with the Cure, 'Boys Don't Cry', in an effort not to actually cry.

But even from here, I can tell it's not Rex. Because at this stage, he'd be getting faster: foot on the accelerator in an attempt to convince himself he was passing nothing but thin air.

As the bus grinds to a halt next to me, I examine my face in the glass. The doors shudder open, dividing me into two – like I'm leaving part of myself behind on the pavement. If only. And I can see today's driver is Alan, who is slightly less mean but appears to hate everyone indiscriminately, which, I have come to accept, is better than hating anyone specifically.

I thrust my pass at him and walk as fast as I can to the back of the bus. When I'm sat down, I pull out my notebook and try not to think about Mum's face. That look she gives me, like I'm nothing but a disappointment to her. Like I don't know anything. Then I take out the pen I keep in my bag for just such occasions, and scribble down the words that seem to be writing themselves.

You tell me how
You tell me where
You tell me everything
You tell me who I should be
You don't know anything

And this is one of the songs that I write. Music so much bolder than I am. Because sometimes the songs I hear in my head aren't just the ones that exist already. And when I'm writing, I feel the most myself I've ever felt. Like I'm channelling the version of me I want to be. That I could be, maybe, one day soon.

That Ellie.

Teenage Meryl Streep Ellie.

And just when I think I'm on to something, I hear my phone buzzing.

Jessica:
trousers or skirt?

It's clearly a trick question.

Ellie:
u look 💐 in everything.

Jessica:
k . . . still need an answer tho.

I look outside.

Ellie:
skirt 🌼

Jessica:

greta says 🌍 = climate change

Ellie:

who is greta?

JUST JOKING

🩳 then?

Jessica:

Ellie:

I agree

Jessica:

with w@?

Ellie:

w/e u say

Jessica:

why r u being weird & passive aggressive?

Ellie:

um. first. day. back. at. 🏫

Jessica:

will be gr8

And GHE is my best friend Jess's sometimes annoying nickname for me; meaning Glass Half Empty, when actually I'm not being negative, I just have a half-empty glass. As in, not abundantly overflowing . . . as in, not as full as hers is.

The bus stops right outside Jess's house, so every morning is a carefully calibrated timeline; nine minutes from the village green until I see her stood beside her gate. Sometimes, at a distance, I watch her walk indifferently from her front door – as if even the bus route was planned for her convenience.

And this is how most days begin. Jess and I messaging until we meet on the bus – then throughout the day, and after she gets off the bus in the afternoon, and pretty much until we fall asleep, repeat ad infinitum.

Jess is my closest friend. The Thelma to my Louise. An equation that doesn't make sense to anyone, sometimes not even me. She's the 'it' brand. The girl who saved me from social suicide by sitting next to me on the bus on our very first day of high school. Long, thick blonde hair and ice-blue eyes, limbs like a baby gazelle and a smile so white she looks like she should be in an ad for teeth whitening.

I remember asking her that day, sort of whispering it. Why

are you sitting next to me? Like, maybe she'd made a mistake, and thought I was someone else. And she just looked at me – like I had something on my face. It felt weird, and awkward, so when she asked me what I was listening to I just offered her an earphone (it was New Order, 'Blue Monday', an excellent song for the first day of any new thing) and studiously explained that this was the song I'd choose if I was driving a getaway car. And she said, 'What are you trying to get away from?' and I said, 'Life,' and she just laughed – like the worldly eleven-year-old she always seemed to be. And that was it. She was Thelma. I was Louise.

Wherever Jess goes, people look at her. Boys look at her. Girls look at her. Babies and grandmothers and gerbils look at her. Not necessarily in that order, but they all look. She's the most sought-after girl at school, and my job as her best friend is to organise all these boys and decide which ones are worthy of her attention. It's not a job I like to do much, mostly because it means I have all sorts of boys trying to talk to me at totally inappropriate times. I even had one shouting at me through a toilet window once. His name was James Godfrey, and he wanted to tell me he'd just been promoted to the A side of the football team (Jessica only dates A-siders). I wouldn't have minded, at least he wasn't stood right next to my face, examining my sideburns like most of them do – but I'd just started my period and wanted to put a tampon in, for which I was not, at the time, the foremost expert in my field.

Peering out the front of the bus, I can see her. Standing at the stop that is mere metres from her house. She's wearing a skirt, and it's possible her legs may be the length of my entire body. I stuff my notebook in my bag and try to shake off the strange feeling in my chest. I wish my legs looked like that. I wish any part of me looked like any part of her. Even Alan smiles at Jess, and Alan hates everyone.

I watch her stride towards me down the aisle.

'Hey, E,' she says, throwing herself down. 'What happened to your face?' she asks, eyes wide.

'Does it look that bad?' I ask, suddenly panicked.

'No, no . . . it just looks a bit . . . cakey.'

'Can you fix it?' I ask hopefully.

'Give me a minute,' she says, reaching into her bag and pulling out a yellow snakeskin purse. She finds a cotton bud and a bottle of water and dabs at my upper and lower eyelids. Then she takes out a green liquid eyeliner and draws two perfect sixties eyeliner flicks.

'Beautiful,' she says, running her thumb over my eyebrows. 'I'd kill for these brows. Here, you keep it,' she adds, thrusting the pen at me.

'Did you finish watching *Funny Face* last night?' she continues, now the serious matter of my actual funny face is dealt with.

'You know I'd never not finish an Audrey Hepburn film. Did you get to the end of the *White Album*?'

'I got as far as that song about pigs and I just couldn't go on. Can you listen to something more *this* century, please?' Clearly, my efforts to educate Jessica on the Beatles are not progressing as hoped.

'This decade has proved very disappointing.'

'What about the previous decade?'

'Still disappointing.'

'Stop being a snob, Ellie,' she says, rolling her eyes.

'I'm not being a snob. I just have one thing I do better than you. And it's music. Let me have it.'

'Whatever,' she says, crossing her eyes and falling back in her seat. 'So, come on.'

'Come on what?' I say, batting my new green-eyeliner eyes at her.

'Your Audrey Hepburn monologue. I know it's coming . . .' she says.

I pretend to be offended.

'Audrey Hepburn? Adorable, feisty, beautiful, smart Audrey Hepburn? Pretty much perfect in every possible way Audrey Hepburn?'

'Do you like Audrey Hepburn?' she asks sarcastically, miming a look of fey surprise.

'Well, so do you!'

'There's nothing to not like, is there? Yes, she's gorgeous. And delicate, but strong and funny and quirky. And her clothes. The clothes . . .'

'I knew you were a Hepburn lover.'

'I prefer Katharine,' she says flatly.

'It's a less obvious choice, but in some ways, that makes it more obvious. I'm sticking with Audrey.'

'Can we discuss something other than your obsession with either Hepburn?' she says resignedly. 'If you could put as much effort into speaking to real people, living now, as you do talking about 1950s Hollywood, then I'm pretty sure you could rule the world, E.'

'Real people? Living now? Yuck.'

She looks frustrated. The way she does when I refuse to have conversations about things that anyone other than her, Hayley and a few select people (read: people that listen to music made before 1995, and those who enjoy their films in early Technicolor) can join in with.

I guess it's just a hangover from when my family used to watch old movies together when I was little. A mishmash of Grace Kelly films and Fred Astaire dance numbers, stuff my dad used to watch with his mum when he was little.

Since I turned six, I've pretty much been convinced I was born in the wrong decade, in the wrong century, probably in entirely the wrong life. I knew it the moment I watched Judy Garland sing 'Over the Rainbow' in *The Wizard of Oz*, all melancholy sadness and too-tight pigtails, looking for somewhere else to be. I felt like Judy just got it. She got me.

And I know I've spent too many wasted afternoons watching Doris Day films, or pondering why Stella Kowalski didn't believe her own sister over that idiot Stanley. I'm not trying to gloss over the fact that a lot of the stuff I spend my rainy Sunday afternoons watching has no one that looks remotely like me in it; it's just if I had to think about that fact every time I look for the non-existent brown film stars, and non-existent brown rock singers, and non-existent brown reality TV stars *right now*, then I would probably never leave my house. Because I'm not saying that Bollywood doesn't count – but Bollywood doesn't count. Because we do live other places, with other people, other than ourselves. We are, as the racists like to say, everywhere. So, why aren't we actually *everywhere*? And these are the thoughts that keep me up at night, when I pore over the fashion magazines my mother is obsessed by, and I can't see *me*. Or her. Or anyone that doesn't look like either a Kardashian or Kaia Gerber. Both of whom are lovely, but not that achievable.

So, I stick to the mid to late twentieth century. Because at least it is what it is. Unashamedly. Although it means everything I grew up loving is seriously suspect. Mickey Rooney in *Breakfast at Tiffany's* is a deeply disturbing parody of a Japanese man – but then Audrey Hepburn singing 'Moon River', all mellow-voiced heartbreak, has to be one of the most beautiful moments in cinematic history.

But sometimes it feels like that's in everything. My dad used to read me *Peter Pan* – racist. I have read *Charlie and the Chocolate Factory* at least fifty times – racist. Dr Seuss has a seriously worrying take on gender norms (not to mention – occasionally racist) and in *Back to the Future*, Marty McFly was terrified of changing the future in case it made him gay. Are these attitudes worrying and highly disturbing? Yes. Should they be written out of history? Honestly, I don't know. How do we know where we've got to, if we don't know how far we've come?

It's just so complicated. And emotional. History and art. What's right? What we're supposed to like, and what we're supposed to separate from where it comes from.

Life is screwed up sometimes. And I don't know if, or when, that is ever going to stop. I just know it's stories that make me see things differently. That make me see things at all. And I find them in books, and songs and films. And they make me feel worldly, and well travelled, and knowledgeable, when really I live here, on the furthest corner of the earth from anywhere.

'So, what's new with the Pillai family?' Jess asks, attempting to steer me towards a different subject.

'Hmmm . . . Nothing very interesting . . . Granny thinks Aunty Kitty might be gay. Is that interesting?'

'Because . . . ?'

'Because she keeps introducing her to all these eligible young men, and she isn't interested in any of them.'

'How old is Aunty Kitty?'

'Too old to be set up by Granny.'

'Would it matter if she was gay?' Jess asks curiously.

'Well, no, obviously not. It's just Granny's a bit . . . old . . . and Tamil . . . and Catholic and you know . . . it doesn't *matter*, I mean, *I* don't think it does, but in my family, it would kind of *matter*. Not like matter so much you can't get over it, but like matter enough that it would be a *thing*. You know?'

'Not really,' Jess says, looking suddenly bored by the conversation.

'Anyway, she isn't. She just doesn't want to marry one of Granny's moustachioed lotharios.'

'You're being a bit racist, E.'

'Shut up,' I say, shoving her.

'So, how are you feeling about the exams?' she asks, suddenly eager, her eyes lit up. Because this is her favourite subject, and I do not lecture her on the abnormality of this – mostly because she wouldn't listen anyway.

'How does anyone feel about exams, Jessica . . .' The girl is sick. She is literally the only person, ever, to consider exam revision *fun*.

As my phone vibrates, I narrowly miss telling her this fact.

Hayley:

& the nightmare begins

another yr at the centre 4 disease prevention & control

Ellie:

🙄

'Ellie, are you listening to me?' Jess says, staring at me. 'Who are you messaging?'

'Hayley,' I reply, trying to keep the phone out of view. She sits back patiently, aware that a Hayley message is best responded to immediately. Before she grows annoyed/more annoyed.

Hayley:

u kno, the diseased nature of the ppl we are forced 2 spend our day with. the ones we try not 2 let affect the outside world

Ellie:

ur being weird. more than usual

26

Hayley:

w/e. addy mcqueen just left a vile comment under my vlog

Ellie:

w@ did it say??

Hayley:

Ellie:

w@ does that mean tho??

Hayley:

don't kno but h8 her & all her kind

'What's she saying about Addy?' Jess asks, craning her neck to look at my screen.

'Nothing . . .' I mutter.

'Why does she think she's better than everyone else?' she asks irritably.

'She doesn't,' I say loyally. Jess stares at me, unconvinced.

'Addy and Billy haven't had the easiest time of it, you know, Ellie.' And this, I have definitely heard before. 'You just have to get to know them. Give them a chance.'

I think about the look the McQueen sisters give pretty much everyone who isn't Jess, or equally beautiful or popular as Jess, and wonder how she doesn't see it. That it's not *other* people not giving *them* a chance.

'Not everyone has a perfect family, E,' she says quietly.

I can feel my breath catch in my throat for a second, because my family are many things, but perfect definitely isn't one of them. And Jess knows that. She knows how hard it's been. What we've been through.

'Sorry,' she says, touching my hand. 'I didn't mean it like that. I know your family isn't perfect.'

I put my head on her shoulder momentarily, then look down as my phone buzzes again.

Hayley:

sorry ... not had ☕ yet. cranky.

obvs don't h8 her. just think she & all ppl like her r shallow socialites who'll bottom out after high school. hpy monday!

Ellie:

k, cranky ...

I guiltily shove the phone into my bag, hoping Jess didn't get a chance to read that last comment. It's a thinly veiled reference to her, and I know it. Even though Jess is incredibly smart, kind and really not a shallow socialite at all, Hayley can't get over the fact she's friends with Addy McQueen. Addy McQueen who put toilet paper in her bag in Year 8 and booed her in the school play. And even though Hayley, being Hayley, literally made Addy cry when she explained how toilet paper was a perfect analogy for Addy's life, I know how much it hurt her; and given Jess is friends with her, I don't think she can see the difference between them.

'Anyway, this year isn't about any of that,' Jess says, squeezing my arm and ignoring anything she may or may not have seen on my phone. 'This year is the beginning of the rest of our lives, Ellie. GCSEs. A levels. University. Life! We can be anything we want.'

'And you're going to be a doctor,' I say proudly. She looks fierce and yet somehow vulnerable. She wants it so much. I can't imagine wanting anything as much as Jessica wants to be a doctor.

'That's the plan,' she says, squeezing my thigh. 'And you're going to be . . .'

'Unemployable?'

'Don't be silly, E. You're brilliant at loads of things. You just need to work out which one you want to focus on.'

'I didn't get seven 9s and three 8s in my mocks, so I probably won't have as many options as you do.'

'I know I can do better,' she says, frustrated.

'Ugh, why are we friends again?' I say, pinching her.

'Ow!' she laughs, wriggling away from me. 'Because you need to borrow my notes? Listen, Ellie,' she says conspiratorially. 'This is going to be our year. The year it all starts happening for us.'

'OK,' I agree all too readily. Because I want to believe it's possible. That this is the year things will start to feel different, less like something's missing. This is the year I'll stop pretending I don't exist. Either way, big things, exciting things, don't happen to people like me. They happen to people like Jessica. Special people.

The most exciting thing I'm likely to say when I get older is, I knew her, once.

I pull my notebook out and surreptitiously carry on writing, while Jess sits staring impatiently out of the window.

You tell me that I run
But what else can I do?

'Ellie,' she says, turning to me enthusiastically. 'We're here.'

I look out of the window at the mass of architecturally designed boxes before me. School. I tuck my notebook and pencil away in my bag.

Here goes nothing.

5

Jets vs Sharks

Like me, our school isn't exactly attractive. It's squat, square and something apparently architecturally interpreted as modern. Which basically means it's a group of concrete and wooden boxes, lumped together in something resembling a shape – which isn't unlike me either.

Despite going to university in London, or maybe because of going to university in London, my dad is not a fan of big cities, and this small one, in the far-flung corner of east England, is just the right side of cosmopolitan for him. Big enough to house a decent college and hospital, small enough to be surrounded by villages with populations in the hundreds as opposed to the thousands.

Outside of school, you could even call it pretty, the stuff of picture postcards with its pretty Georgian townhouses and dark, gothic cathedral. But there's also something weirdly static about it; a city in fear of change.

'Ellie. Why are you staring into space?' Jess asks, shaking me. 'We need to go inside, to the real people.'

Ugh. Real people.

Who wants real people when you can have Bette Davis and Elizabeth Taylor?

'Jessica! Jessssssss!' Billy and Addy McQueen. The Twin Problem. If the Salem trials were still a thing, these two would be burning on a pyre somewhere.

'Hey,' Jess says, leaning in to hug them both, as they all start walking in front of me.

'Ellie,' they sing-song over their shoulders at me. It's barely an acknowledgement.

Jess turns back to face me.

'Remember what I said, Ellie. The future. Now.'

But as soon as we step inside the building, it's not about the future or change, in fact, everything is steadfastly, obstinately, the same as always. Jess gets swept away to the cool girls' wall, and I'm left floating, flotsam-and-jetsam-like, in the middle of the hall.

'Ellie!' she beckons. 'Come here!' But it's like there's an invisible wall between us – a line I can't cross, like one of those electric fences you can't see, until your hair's standing on end.

And I watch as the world around me morphs into a movie set. And we divide up – Jets to one side and Sharks to the other. Jess is leaning against the wall, all nonchalant high-school glamour, rhythmically clicking her fingers, while Billy and Addy, stood next to her, start clicking their fingers too. And then Jess starts moving, still clicking her fingers, moving in the way that dancers do, all exaggerated limbs and little kicks, walking this way and that way, the three of them moving in a pack. And as they move, they're gathering their friends up, all the other Jets, absorbing them into their group, moving as one.

'*Beat it!*' they click at Jeffrey Dean, stood in their way. Because when you're a Jet, you're the top of the ecosystem, even if technically that sounds like a spot that belongs to a man-eating predator.

So Jeff starts gathering up his Sharks, absorbing all the not-so-cool kids into his group, until their pack stands powerful too. And I swear I can hear the entire *West Side Story* prologue music. *Da da da da da, da-da-da*, as they move towards one another. The Jets and Sharks circling one another – their rivalry potent and palpable. And then the bell rings, and Jess gives one final click.

The Jets disperse. The Sharks disperse.

And I'm just left in the corridor, wondering why this happens to me. Why the world in my head is kaleidoscopic and symphonic, when the corridor I'm in is an unsunny yellow in the tone of A flat.

Da-da-da-da, da-da-da, I hum to myself as I watch the teeny Year 7 minnows struggling against the current of students flooding the corridor. These minnows seem almost ridiculously tiny in comparison to the rest of us. Their blazers swamping their frames, their shoes two sizes too big, laced so tight they seem like flippers instead of feet. Oh, the injustice of parents who buy clothes designed to last all year, when our bodies are growing at a rate of knots, doubling in size every few weeks. We are a school of fish, some of us surviving at the top end, others of us at the bottom – compared to these minnows, I think, I'm practically a piranha. Catching sight of my reflection I adjust my opinion. Less of a piranha, more of a big fat cod.

And that's when I see him. A boy I've never seen before. And I'm not sure why he's suddenly a him. Why he suddenly matters, when I don't even know who he is. It's just for a moment that I catch him. Stood in a shaft of light, uncomfortable, eyes half shut. That look on his face that I feel my face sometimes makes, entirely unaware. For just a second, he looks up at me, a pair of earphones trailed around his neck. And it isn't anything really. Or maybe it is, I don't know. But I just keep walking, because that's what you're supposed to do, isn't it? Put one foot in front of the other, and attempt to avoid obstacles.

♡ Song 1 ♡

Intro, Verse, Chorus – Give Me a Minute

There's a song in my head, but I'm avoiding it. An intro that keeps playing over and over. I tell myself to be cool. Not to be that girl. The one who swoons over boys she's never even met, constructing some make-believe personality that renders them entirely perfect, when they're probably the least interesting person I will ever meet.

But the song is undeniable, the lyrics tripping over and into each other like a sixties girl group singing nineties pop.

Give me a minute, just wait right there

And here they come. Sashaying towards me, perfectly in sync, their matching sequins blinding me as they catch the last rays of autumnal light.

I need a minute, baby, I need a minute

6

Tra La Land

The sixties girl group follow me all the way through registration. I can barely hear Mr Gorley call my name with all of their *shoop*-ing and *woo*-ing. I shoot the lead one the side eye, but she doesn't take the hint.

> *You know, you know, you know*
> *You know what they say*

It's catchy. Simple and staccato. I can almost feel myself playing the notes when I sit in the music room at lunchtime.

'Ellie!' I turn at the sound of hissing, as Hayley throws a piece of screwed-up paper far too accurately at my head.

'Hi,' I hiss back, picking up the paper and wondering if there's anything written on the inside. It appears to be a picture of Timothée Chalamet, with the words *So Hot*.

'Did you see my vlog?' she hisses, gesturing towards my phone.

'Yes,' I whisper-hiss, turning back round again. I'm not sure why we're hissing. Mr Gorley is so engrossed in his fingernails we could be standing on our desks screaming at each other.

'So . . . what did you think?' she asks impatiently.

The voice is audible now. Less of a hiss, more of a question at an entirely normal volume.

'About what?' Mr Gorley says, seizing the paper from my desk suddenly and returning to his seat as though it's some kind of exciting new beach read. And this is a favourite pastime of his, to be utterly uninterested in everything, until something, usually at someone else's expense finally interests him.

'Mr Chalamet's quote-unquote "hotness",' he says, now looking bored by the contents of the note, 'or your little video?' he asks Hayley. 'If you want my opinion – which I am assuming you do as I have told you all to sit quietly – then I would say smug, if occasionally quite good, on both counts.'

'Sorry, sir,' Hayley says, rolling her eyes, and yet there is no hint of apology in her tone.

'What exactly is this "Bechdel test"?' Mr Gorley asks, his fingers closing in around the words.

'Well,' says Hayley. 'It's a measure of how well a film represents women. To pass the test, a film has to have at least two named female characters, having a conversation with each other, about something other than a man.'

'Sounds . . . political,' he says, bored.

'Glad to hear you're on board with the movement,' she says, deadpan. He ignores her as he shuffles through the paperwork on his desk.

'New timetables,' he says, standing to pass them out disinterestedly.

'Yesssss,' I hear Hayley hiss as hers hits the desk. I look down at the paper nightmare before me – Monday, lesson 1 – drama. At least it's not lesson '2'. The irony of that could possibly kill me.

The bell rings, and as we pick up our bags to leave, Hayley links her arm through mine.

'It's drama,' she says excitedly.

Oh God.

'So, how many subscribers did Tra La Land get to over the summer?' I reply, desperate to change the subject.

Tra La Land is the vlog Hayley started about two years ago. She does these on-camera film reviews using the Bechdel test – everything from *La La Land* itself to *All About Eve* by way of *Black Panther*. They're brilliant. Funny, and wry, and intelligent. Just like her.

'I'm at just over ten thousand,' she says happily. And then less happily, 'meanwhile, in real life, I still can't get twenty people to start a film club at this school. This place is *so* depressing.'

'Ten thousand. Wow!' I say, feigning an enthusiasm I don't really feel – because, you know. Drama. 'Who cares what people here think anyway?' I demand, partly on her behalf and partly on mine. 'Who wants to be like everyone else?'

I do, I do, I do.

I feel as transparent as a plastic bag.

'Thanks,' she says, squeezing my arm. Because as much as Hayley

38

comes off as unshakeably confident, she isn't. Not really. 'I've worked really hard to make my content stand out.'

'You can tell,' I say, nodding solemnly, while simultaneously attempting to work out how I can get Mr Grange to see me as something other than Girl Unable to Deliver One Line.

Mr Grange.

Ugh.

'So, have you heard about Mr Grange?' she asks conspiratorially.

I turn towards her, as though somehow she can read my mind. Praying she'll tell me his body was taken over by aliens, and he has no recollection of failing me at all.

'He's off this term. He's got shingles, or lupus, or something. We've got a sub.' And even though this fact is alarmingly close to being seized by aliens, I can't help but be thankful he isn't going to be here, looking at me, with a big fat 2 in his peripheral vision. A new teacher could be the answer to all my problems, or at the very least *some* of my problems. A new teacher might not forget I exist.

And I know I don't help myself much in that area, because sometimes it's easier to be invisible than it is to be different – but that's what I love about drama, it's the chance to play at being someone else for a while. For me, it's always been my therapy, which according to my mother (who *is* a therapist) is something we are all in need of in one way or another (so she would say that). I'm considering the scream variety. The type where you stand in a padded room and just shriek, banshee-like, until your voice gives out. Or maybe that's just a 1950s asylum. It's probably the place I'll meet the man in the yellow mac.

'How do you know all of this?' I ask suspiciously, even though I already know.

'The witch told me.'

'Hay, should you talk about your mother like that?'

'If your mother was the deputy head at your school, I'm pretty sure you'd think she was a witch too.' I nod nervously. Hayley's mum has scarily good hearing and a propensity to hand out detentions for no reason, other than that she feels like it. She is Hayley, in adult teacher form. But however scary she is, I know how close the two of them are; something I wish I had with my own mother, who doesn't seem to need me at all, who pushes me away whenever I need her.

We stand in line outside the drama studio, and all I can think is: be *that* Ellie. The one who isn't afraid.

'Nice hair, Mia.'

Hayley's head whips around to where James Godfrey, he of Tampongate, is stood leaning nonchalantly against the wall.

'Mia?' she says, her voice dangerously low.

'Uma Thurman, *Pulp Fiction*? Your haircut. It looks nice.'

Over the summer Hayley has had her hair cut into a bob with a neat blunt fringe. It makes her blue eyes seem almost piercing, as if she's looking right through you.

'Nice,' she says drily. 'Did you hear that, E?' She looks at me slyly. 'James says I have nice hair. Can you repeat that?' she asks, taking her phone out of her bag. 'I feel like I should be filming this for posterity. I mean it's practically a personal validation from Vidal Sassoon. Everyone! Listen! James says I have nice hair.' She rotates away from him, her sarcasm almost entirely wrung out. 'Thanks for the opinion, Godfrey, but it was entirely unnecessary and most certainly unasked for.'

I almost feel sorry for James. Except that I don't. Because he tried to trip me up on the bus once. Or at least, someone he was with did, and he didn't try to stop it.

When the studio door finally opens, Jeffrey Dean, who is always at the front of any queue, disappears inside. We follow him in, to where our new drama teacher is stood quietly to the side of the room, watching us all as we enter. She's no more than mid or maybe late thirties – the same age as my own mother – but her energy is entirely different, childlike even. She's small and incredibly pretty, with dark hair and intelligent eyes; but more than that – she's brown.

For some reason, her colour catches in my throat. I've barely ever encountered a non-white teacher before, and I try not to notice that, to think about it. But now the denial seems impossible, because she's standing there, looking at us, looking at me. Different, but not. The feeling is all at once both brilliant and embarrassing, drawing instant attention to my otherness. I stare at my feet, refusing to meet her eyes. But it's too late, she's already connected. And a spark flies, as an invisible thread passes from my heart to hers. She had me at hello.

'Good morning, everyone,' she says, walking to the centre of the room. 'My name is Mrs Aachara, and I'll be teaching you drama this term, or until Mr Grange is well enough to return to school.'

Her voice is rich and surprisingly deep, not at all what you'd expect from someone of her size; because she's tiny, birdlike, skin stretched over bone. She's wearing a tight white T-shirt that exposes a sliver of taut, toned skin, with black, wide-leg, loose-fitting trousers that stop just short of her ankles, and dainty pink satin ballet slippers. Her energy is overwhelming, despite her small stature, and I can't think of any other word to describe her but sexy. I know this, because I can see the boys in the class hanging on her every movement, watching her hair as it swings back and forth in long, thick waves.

'My favourite film is It's a Wonderful Life, because I am an incorrigible romantic. And I love the idea that all our lives are somehow connected.'

'Each man's life touches so many other lives,' I whisper. Because that's what Clarence Odbody, Angel Second Class says in that film.

'What was that?' she says, scanning our faces. 'What did you say?' she asks, staring straight at me.

'Each man's life touches so many other lives,' I say in the smallest voice possible.

She smiles, holding my gaze for just a second longer than feels comfortable.

'So,' she says, turning back to the class, 'now you know something about me, tell me something about you. Let's introduce ourselves. I know you all know each other, but I want you to imagine for a minute that you don't. Tell the class your name, and something about you that you feel is important to know. Imagine you're in a room full of strangers. What would sum you up? We'll start here.' She points at Hayley.

'My name is Hayley Atwell, and I basically am Elizabeth Bennet.'

'Right,' says Mrs Aachara, smiling. 'And who is Elizabeth Bennet?' she asks the rest of the class.

'She's the heroine in *Pride and Prejudice*,' James Godfrey says smugly.

'And who are you?'

'James Godfrey. And I basically *am* Edward Cullen. Dark, brooding, mysterious, irresistible to women . . .'

'. . . and a blood-sucking, energy-expending waste of time,' Hayley retorts under her breath. Because there are many things you can say about James Godfrey, but irresistible is definitely not one of them.

'And what do you think being Elizabeth Bennet really says about you?' Mrs Aachara asks, turning back to Hayley.

'That I know who I am. I have strong opinions, and I know what I want.'

'And I'm always right,' James mock-whispers, in what I imagine he thinks is a hilarious impersonation of Hayley.

She glares at him before adding, 'But I'm willing to be proved wrong. By sensible, intelligent, articulate people. You know, as opposed to vampires.'

James grins at her, while she gives him a look best described as withering.

And suddenly it's everyone else's go, and there's an honesty to these introductions that feels bizarrely personal – like we're finally agreeing to know each other after four years in the same school together. But as my turn to speak gets closer, I can feel my heart beginning to pound, thick and fast in my chest.

I am nothing more than a record, I think, playing at the wrong speed.

'And finally,' Mrs Aachara says, looking directly at me.

My teeth are sticking to my gums, my mouth completely devoid of moisture.

'My name is Ellie. Ellie Pillai . . . and . . . I'm brown.' The words come tumbling out of my mouth before my brain gets an opportunity to register them. It's the stupidest thing I've ever said out loud, but it isn't something you can laugh at. Am I trying to be funny? Honest? Self-deprecating? Nobody knows. Least of all me. James Godfrey looks at his shoes, and Hayley looks at me like I've fully lost my mind, which is, by this point, entirely possible.

It would be great, Ellie, if the thing Mrs Aachara could see in you was potential, not idiocy.

Ugh.

She looks at me, her eyes steely but non-judgemental, kind. And it's like I've said it for both of us. Made the pink elephant in the room grey, and something we can actually talk about. She smiles, a sort of half-smile. Like she's curious. Like I'm worthy of attention. And that isn't something that happens to me very often. Well, not really ever.

'That's interesting, Ellie. That sense of how we create our identity and who we are; how the way we look feeds into what we feel we can become. Thank you for sharing. It's actually a great way for us to start our new project.' She gestures to the rest of the class. 'This term, you're all going to be working in assigned groups to write, produce and direct your own play, about identity.'

Oh my God, she's saved me. She's managed to make my embarrassingly inane, pointless, stupid and obvious comment into something positive that won't destroy the rest of my high school career. It's almost like I never even said it, I think, as she divides the class into groups. Well it would be, if James Godfrey wasn't assigned to my group, and didn't spend the rest of the hour staring at my sideburns.

7

Ain't Too Proud to Beg

At the end of the day, I'm waiting for Jessica in our usual spot, the one on the right-hand side of the main exit where we can get the best view of Mr Green – the basketball teacher who is half man, half god – as he walks to his car. He likes to pull his hoodie down over his T-shirt just as he is about to leave the building, and if you're stood in exactly the right spot, for a split second as he lifts his arms to pull on his jumper, the material of his shirt rides up a little, snagging against his skin, exposing just a hint of lean, toned abdominal muscles; like a covert glimpse of Michelangelo's David.

I'm trying not to overthink the disastrous *brown is the sum of my entire being* comment I made in drama this morning. Because it isn't the sum of my entire being. Just one little bit of what makes me who I am. And I want to tell Jessica about it. I want to tell someone, anyone, who might try and justify it, and make sense of why I am so, painfully, weird sometimes.

'Hello, Ellie.' I turn at the sound of the voice, rich and deep, and emit a tiny smile, thankful she remembers my name.

'Hello, Mrs Aachara. How was your first day?'

'It was wonderful, thanks for asking. How was your first day back?'

'Um, yeah, fine.'

Awkward silence ensues.

'So, you're a Frank Capra fan then,' she says, her eyes twinkling.

'I love *It's a Wonderful Life*.' I blush. 'But I think *It Happened One Night* is probably my favourite.'

'Clark Gable fan?' She smiles knowingly.

I nod.

'Me too,' she replies. 'We must be kindred spirits.'

Did she just call me a kindred spirit?

'So, Ellie, I hope you don't mind me asking – but I was surprised to see your mock grade when I was reviewing Mr Grange's notes after the lesson. Did something happen at home last year, some reason you weren't able to give the class your full attention?'

I swallow, hoping the dryness in my mouth will disappear.

'Er, no. Nothing. I guess Mr Grange just thought it was what I deserved.'

She looks thoughtful.

'Somehow I doubt that. There's something remarkable about you, Ellie Pillai. And before you even think it, it has nothing to do with what you said about yourself earlier.'

I can feel my face, warm and strange, turning that slightly off shade of purple my dad says reminds him of some kind of flower, as if that's a compliment, and I, a human girl, wish to resemble a sprig of maiden's blush lilac.

'Don't be embarrassed, Ellie. It took courage to say that. And there's nothing wrong with being different. It makes us see things differently – and as a creative, that's an asset. Anyway, I expect to see far more from you this term.'

I attempt a winning smile, but fear it comes off more Serial Killer Face.

And just as she's about to walk away, the half man, half Calvin Klein model that is Mr Green waves at her.

'William.' She waves back.

He grins as she winks at me conspiratorially.

'He thought I was a student earlier. Turns out being short does have an upside. See you Thursday, Ellie.'

As she walks away, I check my watch again. It's 3.58 p.m. – where's Jessica?

I want to talk to her. I want her to be excited for me. I want her to see that someone like Mrs Aachara is noticing me, and it could be the beginning of something new and exciting – so she can do her best to be supportive, while secretly questioning the point of taking an arts subject at all.

Because for Jessica, school is about science. The science of life, the science of death, the science of technology, of the future, of change. Progress, she says, real progress, is scientific, not profound. Jess is a person of facts. A doctor in the making. Just not one of those doctors who talk about the power of the human spirit or alternative therapies.

And then, like a cosmic response from the universe, I feel a sharp, sudden poke in my ribs, and a backpack the size of a small dog comes dangerously close to knocking me out. A mob of overzealous Year 9s have discovered our view of Mr Green and are actively pushing me out of the way, falling over themselves to get the last look at him as he walks away across the playground.

With some difficulty, I try to extricate myself from their oversized bags. I have no idea why anyone, let alone a Year 9, could be in need of a bag this big, but every time I try to move I get blocked in by another backpack. I'm ineffectively moving in circles, continuously being jabbed in the face with a pocket or zipper. I look up, trying to find a way out, when I catch him, the boy I saw earlier, the one caught in the light, watching me – a look of amusement on his face like he's watching a clown trip over their shoelaces.

There's a riot of colour and sound in my head at just his mere presence, because that's what happens in there sometimes, like my brain is made of rainbows.

I try to feign imperiousness and push my way out, but it's hard when a pink furry keychain keeps slapping me in the face – and when I look up again, I see nothing but his back, his earphones in, transporting him somewhere else.

'So, I'll message you when I return it to the library next week?'

I turn at the sound of Jess's voice.

'Great. And you'll let me know what you think of it?'

And another voice, a non-Jess one.

'We should get together and talk about it.'

'Definitely.'

'Hi,' I say quietly. My voice appears to have shrunk to near nothingness, I'm not sure they've even noticed I'm standing here.

'Ellie!' Jess says, startled, as if we haven't met in this exact spot for the last four years. 'This is Elina. Elina – this is Ellie,' she says excitedly, pointing towards one of the most beautiful girls I've ever seen in real life.

Ugh.

Elina smiles hi at me.

I smile hi back.

'So, what are you two doing now?' Elina asks.

'We're getting the bus home. We live out in the sticks,' Jess says, looking to me for confirmation. 'I know it's hard to imagine, but where Ellie and I live, our closest neighbours are cows.'

'You really shouldn't talk about the Milnes like that, Jess. I mean, I know they think climate change is a conspiracy theory, but who are we to judge?'

Elina laughs. I think I just made the beautiful girl laugh, which is cool, but I now have nothing further to say. Possibly to anyone. Ever.

'OK, well, I'll see you around. Keep me posted on that book, Jess.'

Relief floods over me as I watch her walk away. I have no idea, at times like this, why Jess is even friends with me. Girls like *that* are supposed to be friends with people like Jessica. Achingly cool, beautiful people.

And I try to shake off that nagging little voice. The one that says: you're just there to make Jess look special. Because you're not.

'So, what was that about?' I ask meekly.

'We were both trying to take out *A Brief History of Everyone Who Ever Lived: The Stories in Our Genes* from the library just now.'

'What's that?'

'It's a book about genes, Ellie, the clue's in the title,' she says, tweaking my nose. 'That eyeliner really suits you. Anyway, Elina seems nice, doesn't she?'

'Um, yeah.'

'She's doing an art project on identity,' she continues, blithely unaware of how much I want to change the subject. 'Something about genetics, and the stories of our past.'

'Oh.'

So she's beautiful, clever *and* artistic. Her mother must be so proud.

'Anyway, she's just started Year 13 and she doesn't really know anyone yet, so we should hang out.'

I leave a conspicuous silence. Year 13s don't usually hang out with Year 11s, but then, Jess is Jess.

'So, how was your first day back?' she asks, taking my arm.

And then I tell her everything. All about the idiot comment I made, and how worried I am Mrs Aachara might think I was making some kind of racial statement about her. That I'm one of those small-town, racist brown people who think they're white, like my uncle who supported apartheid.

'She clearly likes you, or she wouldn't have spoken to you just now,' Jess says soothingly. 'Besides which, she called you special, so obviously she has excellent taste.'

I ignore the compliment.

'So, what's happening with Nancy and Ted?' I ask, linking arms with her. Jess's mum insists I call her Nancy, which I find terribly sophisticated but Jess claims is because Nancy doesn't want to feel old, or like she has a family, or any kind of real responsibility at all. Ted, her new boyfriend, is twenty-seven, which Jess hates, but I think is brilliant. If I looked like her mum, I'd definitely be dating someone fifteen years younger than me as well.

'Oh, I don't know. They're arguing. She's annoying.'

When Jessica and I first met, her mum and dad were still together. They were always fighting, but then they were always making up. They were two people who seemed to love each other senseless, yet somehow couldn't make sense of their love. Her dad is a really nice man, and even my dad, who hates everyone, has time for him and thinks he's a human being worthy of saying more than two sentences to. When her dad finally left, Jessica never even cried. She said it was for the best. That it would stop all the shouting and recriminations, that he would be happier, that they would be happier. He doesn't live far away, but he's with someone else now, and they have another child, a little boy Jess dotes on. I guess that's how Jess and I got so close. She used to come to my house when her parents were fighting. Now she does it when her mum is fighting with one of her boyfriends, or forgets to pay the gas bill and they end up without heating for two days.

My parents love her, because she's clever and polite, and for my mother she's the beautiful daughter she never had, the one she can dress up and talk to about boys and clothes and manicures.

Once I even caught them having a manicure together without me. I was walking past Laura's Nails with my dad, when for some reason I just happened to glance in. And there they were. The two of them. Side by side, unmistakably together, the nail technicians bent low over their hands, the masks they wear to avoid inhaling the chemicals beginning to ride up over their ears. Their conversation seemed intense, private, not a moment for sticking my face up to the glass and blowing raspberries like I wanted to.

I've never said anything about seeing them together, but then they've never said anything about it to me, either. And I like to bury things. Not in a creepy, weird way, just to compartmentalise them. Box them away so they're easy to find, or in some cases, lose.

Buzz.

Hayley:

how amazing is Mrs A? shame we've got the vampire energy suckr in our group but @ least we're 2together

And just as I'm about to send a reply that goes something along the lines of – yes, she is amazing, and yes, it's great we're doing this project together, and yes, together we will defeat James Godfrey and his sideburn-staring ways, Jess looks sideways at me.

'It's a message from Elina,' she says, holding her phone up excitedly. 'She wants to meet up after school tomorrow.'

She looks at me expectantly.

'If this is going to be our year, Ellie, we have to do things differently. Meet new people. Elina seems cool. I think you'd like her.'

'I'm pretty sure she's not remotely interested in anything I have to say.'

She brandishes the phone in my face.

'It says "would you AND ELLIE like to do something?" Come on, E. At least try.'

'Stop it, King, you are not wheedling me into this.'

I twist myself away from her and look out of the window, pretending to be moody and thoughtful, when the sound of a drum roll makes me turn. There's a pause before a gentle high hat comes in, followed by the Temptations, 'Ain't Too Proud to Beg'.

And suddenly, Jess is stood in the aisle of the bus, lip-synching to one of my all-time favourite Motown hits, playing it at full volume off her phone. She's cooing at me, her mouth set in perfect harmony to David Ruffin's raspy, joyous voice. Because she is refusing to let me go, no matter how much I might want her to.

I shake my head vigorously as she puts her hand out and tries to pull me up, simultaneously rolling her shoulders to the beat.

'I'm not too proud to beg, Eleanor Eve Pillai.'

And I can't help myself, even though I'm shaking my head and repeating the word 'no' over and over as I laugh at her hammy performance: because it's so infectiously joyful, with its bluesy piano and harmonies and horns, that I have to let her pull me up. And as the top deck is totally empty we start shimmying down the aisle.

'Come on, Ellie,' she coaxes. 'Come and meet Elina tomorrow. It'll be fun, I promise.'

'Oh fine,' I huff, because I am powerless under the spell of the Funk Brothers.

And we neither of us say anything more. Because there is nothing left to be said, only dancing to be done, in the aisle of the 44 bus. And I'm singing like I'm alone in my bedroom, harmonising and trying my best to pretend I'm at the Hitsville Studios, 1966.

That's when I hear the footsteps, and it's too late to avoid them: James Godfrey and his cronies – stood at the top of the stairs, staring at us, with grins so wide they could literally swallow me whole.

Oh my God, I think. Oh. My. God.

I die.

I am dead.

I am a living, breathing person that is no longer alive.

I can feel the blood rushing to every part of my face, so red I'm convinced I must be a tomato. Perhaps I'm morphing into one. A person-sized tomato.

They must have heard me singing. Warbling like some kind of deranged karaoke lunatic. Hitting the high notes, and jiving like I think I am an actual Temptation.

Oh. God.

Strike me down. Please. I will never live this down.

'Are you looking at something?' Jess asks their sniggering faces. And her five foot nine frame looks suddenly enormous. Like a supermodel. Legs up to her armpits. Her blonde hair framing her face, just like Katharine Hepburn in *The Philadelphia Story*, when she's stood against the fireplace, looking extravagantly, wastefully beautiful.

'Hi, Jessica,' one of them says brightly.

'Hi, Tom. There are no seats up here. Can you sit back downstairs?' she says, somewhere between imperious and apologetic.

'Sure,' he says. 'Are you going to Kelly's party next weekend?'

'Maybe,' she says.

'Maybe I'll see you there,' he grins.

'Maybe,' she says again. 'Bye.'

They troop back down the stairs of the bus, and as a final insult, I see James Godfrey turn to look up at me, his eyes surveying me coolly.

James Godfrey.

Brilliant. Just brilliant.

My phone offers up a pathetic buzz as we slide back into our seats.

Hayley:

> the energy suckr just messaged me abt the play. he wants to tlk abt his *ideas*

> how does he hav *ideas* yet, & how did he get my number???

That's right. James Godfrey. He of my drama group.

Brilliant. Just brilliant.

'Come on, Ellie,' Jess says, giggling. 'What should we listen to next?' And while I'm very happy to have an opinion about it, because left to Jessica we could end up listening to nothing but Cardi B – who is amazing, but on the twelve hundredth listen begins to wane – I can't help wondering what this scene would have looked like without her.

Like days of being followed around with people singing falsetto at me and mimicking someone holding a microphone.

'How about Cardi B?' I offer.

After all, she did just save my life.

8

In the Morning

I can hear the radio on in the kitchen downstairs, and I know Dad's turned it up extra loud; either because he's trying to force me to get out of my room earlier, or because he's pretending he's Mick Jagger again.

This is something my dad likes to do sometimes. To pretend he used to be cool.

I'm wired this morning. I keep thinking about Mrs Aachara, about how different things could be now she's here. And I want to be excited about it. I want to tell my parents she's noticed me, that she thinks I'm special, that maybe I'm not so bad at this thing I love.

But we don't talk about things like love. Or being special. Or how I feel. We don't talk about things at all. Just gloss over them, like we're embarrassed to feel at all. Even when we should. Even when it hurts so much, you can't breathe.

And it's not because they don't love me. I know my parents love me. It's just, their job is to provide stability, security, routine, The Best for My Future According to Them – and the love stuff, that's just innate in all that. It's a practical love; solid and reliable. A

58

paper-over-the-cracks love that pretends everything's OK, even when we know it isn't.

I just wish I'd never lied to them, because I feel sweaty and sick almost all of the time these days, and that just makes me wish I'd admitted defeat. That I should be learning about programming language theory, instead of the importance of vocal elements, because 'what am I going to do with vocal elements, when I can barely open my mouth in the first place?' (An actual *quote* from my mother, when we discussed the possibility of taking a drama GCSE, two years ago.)

Kill me.

And then, I realise, my parents are going to do exactly that. Followed by sending me to St Hilda's School for Girls Who Must Be Watched, whose uniform features a maternity-style smock dress that makes anyone who wears it look like they're trying to hide a pregnancy from a mean-spirited nun. Which is ironic for both a Catholic boarding school (them) and a virgin (me).

I walk downstairs, towards the radio, and do a mini warm-up in the hall, jumping up and down on the spot, shaking my limbs loose, my head bobbing from side to side, my mouth wide open, emitting a disgustingly slobbery *brrrrrrrrrrr* sound. This is how Mr Grange used to warm us up for drama, and if ever there was a time to pretend I was someone else, then that time is now.

The kitchen door swings open and Mum catches me stood in the hall, mid *brrrrr*, my face contorted into a brown elastic band.

'Ellie,' she says, annoyed. 'What are you doing? You're going to be late for school.' I try to shake my face out. It feels like it's frozen into some kind of strange primal scream shape. 'She's here!' she shouts backwards to Dad.

But Dad's lost in the radio, drumming his spoon on the side of his mug to Razorlight, 'In the Morning'; it's that intro, all off-beat drum rhythm, aggressive guitar and Johnny Borrell's sulky vocals, like a man who's just been told off by his mum.

You don't know what you've been doing wrong, Johnny? Join the club.

I loiter by the toaster and try to remain inconspicuous. Mum's sat down again drinking coffee, looking hipster perfect in high-waist flared jeans, platform sandals and a blue denim shirt, while Dad adds too much sugar to his tea. We're all tapping our feet, heads moving in tiny, blunt motions from side to side, matching the beat. And even as Dad's moving to sit, Mum's moving to stand, the two of them dancing around each other in perfect symmetry, like they're in some kind of music video. Toast being buttered becomes rhythmic and enthralling, like a production line set to guitar strokes and drum solos.

'Ellie,' Dad says over the music. 'Your mum and I have been talking. We think we should arrange a meeting with Mr Gorley. See how you're set up for this year.'

I'm starting to sweat. *Sweat: to excrete moisture in visible quantities through the openings of the sweat glands.* Because at times of crisis, my brain regurgitates only utterly pointless information.

'Errr . . .' I mumble. 'Can't you just wait until Parents' Evening?'

60

'That's not until November,' Mum says, her head still moving in tiny, blunt beats. 'That's too late, Ellie. If there's a problem.'

'Why would there be a problem?'

'I'm not saying there would be,' she says, rolling her eyes. 'It's just we haven't seen Mr Gorley in over a year now.'

Oh God.

Oh God.

Oh God.

'How many times do you want me to say sorry for that? I got the day wrong. I made a mistake.'

Mum sighs and looks at her shoes. Her hipster-perfect shoes. She looks so modern and cool, just like she always does – but she isn't. Because she's stuck in a time warp. Trying to recreate the world that she grew up in, where her parents controlled every single thing that she thought and said and did. So how can she look like that, but *be* like this? And I can't tell whether it's a sigh of annoyance or resignation at my ineptitude. I just know it's a sigh. The way she always seems to sigh when I'm around.

'Come on, Ellie,' Dad says gruffly, putting his arm around me. It's like he's seen the look on my face, and he just *knows*. 'You know how much I love visiting the school.' And I can't help but grin back at him, aware of how much my dad hates Parents' Evenings, or any kind of school social event that requires him to speak to people he doesn't like – which is most people. He once told me it's why he's a biomedical scientist. Something that requires working in a lab where he can speak to as few people as possible, ideally in code, about organisms and microbes.

'*Fine*,' I lie. 'I'll talk to him. But Mr Gorley is probably less prepared for this year than I am. I saw him marking papers in his car yesterday.'

Mum and Dad exchange a look.

'Maybe I should I call St Hilda's?' Mum comments pensively. 'See if we can get her on the waiting list? Kitty says the offer's still open . . .'

Aunty Kitty, my dad's uber-successful lawyer sister, lives in New York and makes more money in a week than my dad earns in a year. A while ago, she offered to pay to send me to St Hilda's – because apparently, I have potential (ugh), and Mum thinks I'm not living up to it at Bridgewood. Thankfully, Dad wouldn't force me to go when I said I didn't want to.

They exchange another look. One that seems to say, maybe we *should* reconsider sending Ellie to a place where she can learn a pointless, ancient language, and not know anyone, and wear a hat that doesn't fit her properly.

My heart feels like it's about to explode. And not in a Ryan-Gosling-just-got-caught-in-a-rain-shower-and-is-now-in-my-bedroom kind of a way.

Mmmm. Ryan Gosling. Caught in a rain shower. In my bedroom.

Focus, Ellie.

Think!

'I don't think that's necessary, Nimi,' Dad says, looking at Mum, while studiously winking at me – our Morse code for *Mum's overreacting. Do. Not. Panic.* Dad's not a good winker. He looks confused. Like his eyes are working against him.

Oh. God.

'I have to go,' I pant, suddenly panicked by the cracks appearing in my plan so early in the year. At least, I think I'm panting. It's hard to tell in this moment. Maybe I'm cool as a cucumber. Maybe I'm Keyser Söze.

'The bus is due in three minutes.'

It's actually due in twelve minutes.

'Can you speak to Mr Gorley then, Ellie?' Dad says, playing with the dial on the radio.

'OK,' I say through gritted teeth.

'We just want you to achieve your potential, Ellie,' Mum responds in a clipped tone.

'OK,' I reply robotically. Because the truth is, I'm not entirely sure what kind of potential my mother thinks I have. The potential to be found lacking. The potential to annoy her. The potential to fall flat on my face and embarrass her at the school play. Been there. Done that.

'See you later.'

'Don't forget to speak to Mr Gorley!' Mum shouts as I run for the door. But I know it's probably her who'll end up forgetting. She'll get deep into some interesting case at work, or having to 'tell the idiots at the big office how to do their jobs', and she'll forget she ever even suggested it. At least, that's what I'm hoping, and holding on to, like the door Kate Winslet's character was clinging on to at the end of *Titanic* (which, by the way, is a terrible film). It's just more likely I'll be the guy you get to watch drowning, his hand stretched optimistically upwards, as if trying to hold on to some shred of belief he isn't going to die.

You know what's worse? I don't even know how to swim.

And in that moment, Razorlight comes to a searing end. Apparently, in the morning I won't remember a thing.

The problem is, I remember everything. I just wish I didn't.

Note to self. Learn to swim.

9

I Know What Boys Like

It's the part of the day I've been dreading.

'Is she definitely coming, Jess?' I ask, my throat beginning to itch. I could swear the collar of my shirt is trying to strangle me. It's 4.02 p.m., and there is still no sign of Elina.

I check my phone again. Fifteen seconds have passed. Fifteen incredibly long seconds.

Hayley:

ru still around? wanna get ☕ & tlk abt the play?

I message her back quickly.

Ellie:

cn't – mtg someone with J

Hayley:

sounds … yuck

Ellie:

stop it H

Hayley:

i'm sure they'll be lovely. mcqueen sista lovely

'Who's that?' Jess asks, as I peer down at my phone again.

'Nobody,' I mutter nervously. 'Are you sure you said 4 p.m.?'

'Elina's got Mr Bishop for English, and you know how he goes on and on. She's probably just running late,' Jess says, matter-of-fact, not remotely capable of believing anyone could stand her up.

'OK,' I say, swallowing back the strange lump in my throat, my hands tapping at my side. 'Are you sure she knows *I'm* coming?'

'Ellie, I showed you the message. She invited us both. Oh. And I think she might be bringing her brother . . .'

She sneaks that last bit in, like she's hoping I won't notice it.

'Brother?' I say suspiciously.

'She's a twin,' she carries on, studiously looking in the opposite direction. And now it all makes sense. The hot twin brother and me, the decoy.

Ugh.

I consider messaging Hayley with this new information, but decide I have no interest in the response. 'Look, here they come now.' And immediately the Waitresses, 'I Know What Boys Like' starts playing in my head. Because as I look out across the playground, I'm watching it in slow motion. Elina, tall, striking and infinitely gorgeous, her head shaking from side to side, like she's in an advert for shampoo. And him. The boy from the corridor. The one who last saw me being attacked by a pink furry keychain.

And now the girl group, the one I've been trying to banish to the outer regions of my mind, are fighting with the Waitresses, a cacophony of discord, as they wave their 'go-go' arms at me, the intro to his song tripping lightly, over and over in my brain.

Give me a minute, baby, I need a minute

Dear Brain. Please stop.

And I try to pretend that I'm normal. The best friend, the not-so-smart or pretty one, but a solid 6 out of 10, 6.5 on a good day. Because I'm not here to compete with Jessica, just to complement her, to accent her finer points. And even though I think this entirely to myself, for a second I wish I was fully invisible. Like see-through, transparent-ghost invisible. Like I wish I could haunt this meeting, instead of actually attending it.

And with all my mind, I will the music to a stop. Because I feel like this is Not Normal. That hearing songs in your head, and screaming at men in yellow rain macs who aren't really there, is the sort of thing some would consider Too Weird. And if I was living in medieval times I'd probably have met my ending as a witch burning at the stake. But then, I probably wouldn't have been anywhere that concerned itself with burning witches. I'd have been picking tea leaves, or serving some maharajah in a palace somewhere.

Shut up, Ellie.

Stop talking.

And then I remember I'm not actually saying any of this out loud. Because I'm having a conversation with myself. In my head. With the people in yellow rain macs and a shimmery sixties girl group.

Why didn't I notice that Elina looks like a taller, more tanned Audrey Hepburn, in balloon jeans and a leather jacket? I bet Audrey Hepburn wore that exact outfit when she was filming *Sabrina*.

Shut up, Ellie.

Stop talking.

There is a name for this, and it is hysteria.

The boy without a name, the brother, is wearing glasses. The kind hipster kids wear, with thick frames that accent his green eyes and make him look like one of those Hollywood actor/model/musician types, but he's here, in this sleepy English city, surrounded by lumpy concrete boxes and people with farming accents. The earphones that seem permanently attached to his person are casually slung around his neck, and I can hear the distant, tinny sound of music still playing as they walk towards us.

'Hi!' says Elina, pulling Jess then me into a hug.

I wonder what he's listening to. I wonder if it's soulful and melancholy or slick and electronic. If he likes guitar bands, or girl groups, or Dixieland jazz.

68

Shut up, Ellie.

Stop talking.

'Jess, Ellie – this is Ash,' she says, waving her hand towards her brother. He presses pause on his earphones, the music coming to a sudden halt.

Start talking, Ellie!

Say something!

'Maharajah,' I mutter.

'What?' he says, staring at me.

Oh God no. What just happened?

Jess stares at me, as if trying to communicate something meaningful, like PLEASE STOP BEING YOURSELF.

'Nice to meet you,' she says, smiling. 'What do you guys want to do?'

'Let's get a coffee,' says Audrey Hepburn. 'I'm dying for some caffeine.'

I wish I was dying for some caffeine. The way Hayley and Jess drink it all the time makes it looks so sophisticated and cool. I just find it bitter and unpleasant.

I watch Ash as he stares at Jess intently.

'The Spoke is nice,' Jess says, looking down at her feet. I don't know why she seems suddenly nervous. She's one of the most self-confident people I know, mostly because I've never seen her care what anyone else thinks. But perhaps it's the way that Ash keeps staring at her. Almost rudely, almost obscenely. Like he's trying to figure her out. A puzzle he's not sure is solvable. I've seen boys look at her like this before. It's nothing new. Everyone wants to figure out Jessica Leigh King. Even me.

'Sure,' he says, barely taking his eyes from her face. 'Sounds good. Do you know if they have almond milk?' So far, I have contributed exactly nothing to this conversation. I'm suddenly a hundred degrees in temperature, my mouth as dry as a desert. I'm sure my face is wincing. The effort of trying to act normal seems suddenly, profoundly, too much.

'Are you OK?' Ash asks, turning his eyes on me fully for the first time. 'Would you rather go somewhere else?'

'Um. No. It's fine,' I say, trying to swallow down the driest mouth imaginable.

'Really? You look pained,' he says quizzically, with just the hint of a smile.

'Actually, I hate coffee,' I say, somewhat satisfied to reveal this fact. 'All those pretentious blends and flavours, five hundred kinds of milk. What's wrong with a cup of tea and a nice bourbon biscuit? When did we become LA?' And there I go. Defending the tea leaves I picked in a past life.

Audrey Hepburn laughs and links arms with me.

'So, you don't like almond milk then?' says Ash, smiling. I ignore the smile and try to pretend I have some moisture in my mouth.

'The Spoke has other things, Ellie,' says Jessica, her voice tight.

'Oh, right. Sure. The Spoke is fine.' I try not to register the irritated way she looks at me, and focus on picking up my bag.

'Love the bag,' Elina says, eyeing up my satchel. It's bright yellow

70

leather, sturdy and box-shaped – the sort of thing you see Cambridge spies carrying in movies. But the colour is off, a slightly acidic shade you either love or hate; a traditional English silhouette with a twist. Just like me.

'Thanks,' I say, not really sure how to respond to the compliment.

'You're a Beatles fan,' Ash notes, looking at the badges peppered down the strap.

'Ellie loves the Beatles,' Jess says, smiling fondly. 'I must have seen *A Hard Day's Night* at least a hundred times before my fourteenth birthday.' I'm so grateful for the reprieve that I stare at her, willing her to understand through some telekinetic connection that I am sorry for being weird, for screwing things up for her.

'Really?' says Ash, looking at me. 'I took you for more of a *Yellow Submarine* kind of a girl.'

'Too pretentious,' I say, not missing a beat. Jessica rolls her eyes, and the irritation is back. Ash looks at me strangely while Elina laughs again. It's a twinkle really, not even a laugh. She's shiny, like one of those oversized comedy jewels you see in heist movies. Her skin is creamy, with a hint of gold in it, her eyes a sharp, pretty grey with flecks of green so deep she looks almost otherworldly. Her hair is cut in the Audrey Hepburn crop I've only ever seen five women pull off – including Audrey Hepburn.

'Come on, Ellie,' she says, as Jess and Ash start walking away. From here, they look like the perfect couple, an advert for some kind of his-and-hers designer perfume. Every now and then, I could swear he turns around to look at me, a tiny smile playing at the corner of his mouth. Like I'm an amusement. A funny little dog they've picked up on the street, running at their heels, thinking it belongs.

'So, where did you move here from?' I ask, smiling at her.

'London,' she says lightly. 'Mum wanted somewhere a bit quieter, and as Ash and I are off to university next year, it doesn't really matter where we are this year. She got offered a job, and a week later, we were here.'

'Why would she want to leave London?' I ask incredulously. London with the O2 arena, and Brixton Academy and the British Library and the Actual West End.

She looks away for a second before replying quietly.

'Our dad died.' She breathes. 'We just needed a fresh start.' At this, her voice catches. Just a little tug, a tiny swallow really, not enough that most people would notice, but I can hear it, the tear caught in her throat.

'I'm so sorry,' I whisper. Because I am sorry. Because I know grief so intimately that its company has sometimes felt welcome to me. 'When my brother Amis died, my parents couldn't face the house either. My mum ripped out the bathroom a couple of weeks after his funeral. And after that it was the kitchen and the living room and eventually his bedroom, like she was trying to erase him or something.'

The moment I say it, I feel disgusted with myself, because I know that wasn't what she'd intended at all. She hadn't wanted to erase him. She just couldn't function, looking at all the signs of his little life as they continued to exist around her without him. But I can't think about that. About Amis, or Mum, or being sad.

72

'I'm sorry,' I say, suddenly ashamed. 'That was a stupid thing to say. My mum didn't want to erase my brother, any more than your mum wanted to erase your dad. I'm sorry . . .' I trail away. This isn't something I usually discuss with anyone. Not even myself. She takes my hand and squeezes it, saying nothing more.

'What A levels are you taking?' I ask, attempting to break what feels like it should be an awkward silence, but weirdly isn't.

'Art, biology and English,' she says proudly. 'Both Ash and I are hoping to go to St Martins next year. What about you? You're doing your GCSEs, right?'

'Yes. All the usual subjects, plus drama.'

'Ah, so you're a fellow artiste,' she says with a flourish, and I laugh.

'Hardly. I'm a . . . well . . .' And then I realise I can't finish the sentence, because I don't know what I am.

'What's your favourite part of the dramatic process?' she asks, as though somehow I've given her some intelligent, thought-provoking response.

'I don't know. I guess it's just interesting. Inhabiting someone else's space for a while. Seeing the world from a different point of view.'

'That's what great art is,' she says excitedly. 'It's feeling something and being something that the artist wants you to feel and see. It's power, and control, and it's also . . . you know, letting go.'

'Yes,' I continue animatedly, 'it's letting go, isn't it? That's what I like the most about drama, it's the chance to let go of one version of me, and embrace another.' And when I say it, it feels truer than anything I've ever said about it.

73

Talking to Elina feels easy. And sort of freeing. And Jess was right, she's into music. Not quite the same stuff as me, but she DJs, and she's really knowledgeable. And I'm thankful she's interested to get to know me, because Ash is busy firing questions at Jess, to the point Elina has to intervene and tell him it's not a job interview, but Jess seems happy to answer them. Happy to take his test. And I wonder whether this is what a date looks like. Like a quiz on subjugated verbs.

At 5.30 p.m., I stand up from my peppermint tea and look down at Jess.

'We should go if we're going to catch the six o'clock bus.'

'How about dinner at our house?' Elina asks, looking at Jess and me. 'I'm sure Mum wouldn't mind dropping you both home later. Or Ash can practise his driving . . .' she says, making a terrified face, while he punches her lightly on the arm.

'Well . . . ?' Jess says, looking at me.

'I . . . can't,' I stutter. 'I really have to, um . . . revise.' Jess raises her eyebrows.

'Jess?' Elina asks.

Jess nods her head at me. 'You should come, E. It's way too early in the year to be revising.'

'Says the girl with the set of perfect 9s.'

'And 8s,' she says tightly.

'Oh, I forgot about the 8s,' and my voice is supposed to sound fun and teasing, but it's coming out more sarcastic and bitter.

'Well, I can come,' she says, smiling back at Elina. And the fact she won't even look at me now makes me know I've disappointed her.

74

'OK, well, I'd better go,' I say, picking up my satchel. 'See you all tomorrow.'

'Let's swap numbers,' Elina says, looking up at me. We hand our phones around and tap in our numbers. Elina Anderson. Ash Anderson. As if either of them is ever going to call me.

On the bus home, I put my earphones in and try to find a song to distract myself. I turn on WhatsApp and type a quick message to Jess.

Ellie:

sorry, sorry, sorry

u kno, 4 being me

Ex

The thread stays empty as I tap into Spotify. I settle on Blossoms, 'There's a Reason Why (I Never Returned Your Calls)'. It's instantly upbeat, all synthesizer, guitars and heavy driven drum beat. The sort of song that makes you feel simultaneously joyful and introspective, all at the same time.

I walk off the bus feeling heavy and weird, until I feel the familiar buzz of my phone.

Jessica:

revising? @ least try & make ur excuse sound plausible!

Jessica:

but never be sorry 4 being u

Jx

If only, I think, I could take that advice.

10

Music Gets the Best of Me

There's only one place in the world I feel completely at home, and strangely it's not actually in my home. It's not because my home is unhomely, I love our home, it's just the music room at school has a baby grand piano – slightly battered and most definitely out of tune, but the kind of instrument that feels like a best friend.

I started taking lessons when I was six, and was so terrible even years later that my teacher claimed she was retiring, keeping only a few select students on – namely everyone, except me. It took a while to find the confidence to get back to it after that, but high school can be overwhelming sometimes, and this place was an escape, somewhere I could go to be alone, to think, to take the soundtrack out of my head and into the real world. In the chaos of a high school lunch hour, I found the music room, and laying my fingers down on the piano keys, realised I could suddenly speak its language.

The music teacher, who is ancient and often referred to by the less kind people at school as the Crypt Keeper and by the rest of us as Miss Mason, is so used to my presence, she sometimes even brings me tea. We're an odd couple, but we enjoy each other's company. Sometimes I leave the door ajar, just a little, and when I come out, she gives me tips on my speed, or a chord progression I'm working on. She often shakes her head and asks why I'm not in the orchestra, or why I'm not taking music. But music is a solo exam, not something you can do as an ensemble. And I'm not ready for that. Maybe I never will be.

On the bus this morning, Jessica was quiet. Distracted. I wanted to ask her about last night. Whether she was annoyed with me. Whether I embarrassed her. Whether she had a good time and what their house was like. I wanted to debrief with her, the way we always have, but she was serene and thoughtful, like she was debriefing with herself, and I wasn't invited.

Run, run you can fly
And leave this world behind

I'm writing a song. Sort of piecemeal. It's coming to me in sections – cadences and chords, the odd line here and there, like lyrics on the run.

I put my fingers to the keys and press gently. Then I let myself sing.

It's like primal therapy, like I'm screaming for my soul. And I feel free. And heard. Like the person I want to be. Like the person I could be, if I could just find the words.

I'm lost in the song, so I don't hear the door opening, don't see the long legs and green eyes as they lean on the doorframe, taking me in, swallowing me whole. But suddenly I feel them. Stop short. Turn around. But by then he's walking away. Walking like he's swaying to music that I can't hear. He of the permanently tinny earphones and accompanying sixties girl group.

Ash.

Jess's Ash.

11

There's a Reason Why (I Never Returned Your Calls)

On my way from maths, I try to wipe away the thin veneer of spittle Mr Potts left all over my face when he was trying to explain quadratic equations.

Note to self. Do not ask Mr Potts a question, unless at least three rows back.

As I wipe my face with my sleeve, I hear the sound of laughter so vile, it could only belong to one of two people: the McQueen sisters. Identically annoying.

That's when I spot Jess.

'Jess!' I shout up the corridor. And I never shout up the corridor. Ever.

She stops and smiles at me, but something in it feels frozen and unreal.

'Ellie . . . I have to run,' she says, motioning over her shoulder. 'We're late for maths.'

'Make sure you sit at the back,' I joke.

'Why?' says Billy indifferently.

'Mr Potts . . . you know . . . shield yourself.'

'He's so *gross*,' says Addy viciously. And I feel horrible, because that's not what I meant at all. Mr Potts is just old, and overenthusiastic about maths.

Jess smiles apologetically, as if to say 'what can you do?' And I think, I'll tell you what you can do, Jessica, stop being friends with horrible, mean-spirited bullies. Stop making them think their behaviour is OK. And it doesn't matter how many times she tells me that they're 'really nice when you get to know them', or that their lives aren't easy, because their parents got divorced at the same time as hers did – we've all been through *stuff*, it's just most of us don't need to make other people feel bad in order to make ourselves feel better. And sometimes I just wish she'd admit it. That it feels good to have a pack of lemmings following you around, telling you you're great. Even if you genuinely are great, and should know it without the evil lemming twins to confirm it.

'I like your eyeliner.' Billy gestures at my face. 'It makes your eyes look . . . better.'

Case. In. Point.

'What Billy means,' Jess says, whipping around to face her, 'is you look nice, E.'

'Sorry,' Billy says, ignoring Jess's irritated tone. 'I'm no good with words. I'm failing English – which is like, my first and only language.'

'It's fine.' I smile through gritted teeth. 'See you after school, Jess.'

'I'm not getting the bus tonight, E.'

81

'Oh.'

'She's going out with *Ash*,' says Addy, laughing and making a pretend kissing face. Jess blushes and rolls her eyes at me, as if we're in on the joke together, except we're not, because she hasn't told me anything.

'I'll call you later, OK, E?'

'OK.'

And I try not to think any more about it. That Ash, and Elina, and Billy and Addy, know something about Jess that I don't. My best friend. Who for some reason didn't want to talk to me today.

On the bus home, I try calling her, but she doesn't pick up, so I message her instead.

Ellie:

hope ur ok. sorry we didn't get a chance to speak 2day.

I want 2 kno everything abt last night!

call me!

Ex

And when 11 p.m. rolls round, and we still haven't spoken, I go to my room and stare at the ceiling, letting the sound of Blossoms, 'There's a Reason Why (I Never Returned Your Calls)' wash over me.

But if there's a reason she won't return my calls – what is it?

And how do I make it better?

12

The Fuzzy End of the Lollipop

Our play could be amazing, if everyone would just shut up and listen to each other.

The past couple of days, instead of hiding in the music room, I've been meeting Hayley, James, Andy, David and Lauren: the drama group. Or as I like to think of them: the people who'll have to nudge me until I fall over, on exam day.

It's nice spending time with different people, even if it does mean I have James Godfrey permanently positioned next to me while I try to eat a grated cheese sandwich with any level of elegance. We can't seem to agree on much, but Hayley's written a script, which could be really good – it's just everyone has an opinion on it, and none of those opinions are the same.

But I'm thankful for the distraction, because all of a sudden, Jess has been strange and unavailable, which feels weird and out of character and mean. I've tried calling her. Tried messaging her. She isn't ignoring me, she just doesn't ever seem to have time to talk. She's so busy, even she and Ash seem to be communicating through notes; the slips of paper piling up like endlessly romantic gestures in her bag.

They spent the entirety of lunchtime staring into each other's eyes in the hallway today, but when I asked if she wanted to come over after school, she made some terrible excuse about being behind on coursework, when Jess is never behind on anything, and he just stared at me over her shoulder, like I was a girl with a giant panda head – even though I have now mastered the art of the sixties eyeliner flick and no longer resemble a giant panda at all.

If I didn't miss her, I could even say not talking as much has been a good thing, because I've spent my time working on the script instead. But when I'm at home I have to be more covert about my editing. Not least because I'm overwhelmed with nausea at the web of lies that keep growing and growing, fed by some invisible force. So, I'm doing what any sane, rational human being would do in my place. I'm lying on my bed, watching *Some Like It Hot*, making notes on it, and throwing the pages under my dirty washing whenever I hear a creak in the hallway.

As good as it is though, there's something a bit static about this script. Like it has all the elements to be more than it is, but it's missing something. Something powerful. Because loss and fear and anger, they're written in the silence of things. In the unsaid words. And I know on stage you can't just sit there silently and hope the audience get it. I know, because I tried it, and it definitely didn't work.

Creaaaaak.

I hastily push my notes under a T-shirt on the floor.

'Ellie, there's someone here to see you,' Mum says, poking her head through the doorway. She opens the door wider, to reveal Jess stood next to her.

Side by side, the two of them are coolness personified; Mum in cowboy boots, red lipstick and a midi dress, Jess in Converse, a denim mini skirt and Blondie T-shirt. And together they're the perfect fit; Mum's dark yin to Jess's blonde, delicate yang – but where do I fit in all this? Me in my stained Stone Roses T-shirt and pyjama bottoms.

'Can I get you something to eat, Jessica?' Mum says, reverting to Sri Lankan host who must feed all guests needlessly.

'I've eaten, thanks, Mrs Pillai.'

I kick the T-shirt further under my bed, like a ticking time bomb that could herald an explosion of mismatched underwear at any given moment.

'How's school, Jessica?' Mum asks, refusing to take the hint: the hint being my eyes, bulging out of my head, and my heart, beating a million times a minute.

'Good. This is an exciting year for us,' Jess enthuses.

'Such a positive way to look at it,' Mum says, making eyes at me, 'to see the exams as an opportunity . . .'

Please don't say the word potential.

'. . . to fulfil your potential.'

Great.

'So, er, how's your script going, E?' Jess asks awkwardly, noting the look of horror on my face.

Mum's head moves imperceptibly towards me, as if her antennae have picked up a strange signal.

'What's that noise?' I splutter, panicked.

'What noise?' Mum asks suspiciously.

'The door?' I mutter weakly.

'I didn't hear anything?' Jess says unhelpfully.

'Maybe it's . . . something else then.'

I pick up the water glass by the side of my bed and take drastic action.

'AAAAAAARRRRRRRRRRRRGH!' I shout as the glass hits my big toe. 'MY FOOT!'

'Ellie!' Mum says, rushing towards me. 'Are you OK?'

'Stupid glass. Stupid foot!' I say, jumping up and down on the spot.

'I'll get you some ice,' Mum says, hurrying away.

'No, no, it's fine,' I call. 'I just need to sit down.'

'Well, sit down,' she says worriedly, guiding me towards the bed like an invalid; Mum freaks out if I get so much as a cold, because that's how it started with my brother. Feeling unwell.

'I'll let you know if she needs anything,' Jess says soothingly.

'OK, well, I'll leave you to it,' Mum says uncertainly.

'Mum, I'm fine. I just dropped a glass on my foot.'

'OK,' she says, looking at me closely. 'But . . . you're not feeling faint or anything, are you?'

'No, just clumsy.'

'OK,' she says again nervously.

'I'll keep an eye on her,' Jess smiles reassuringly. Mum shuts the door, looking slightly nauseous.

Oh God, why am I such a bad person? Stupid script. Stupid foot. Stupid Jessica. Showing up and pretending she hasn't been avoiding me, when the only thing she's paid any attention to is the fact I'm working on a script.

'What are you watching?' Jess asks tentatively.

'*Some Like It Hot*, sonny Jim,' I say, faking an American accent.

'Oooh goody.'

'Not too *last century* then?'

'Marilyn Monroe doesn't count. Obviously.'

I sniff, turning away.

'Don't be like that, E. I just want you to try some new things. Stop being afraid of everything.'

'I'm not afraid. And you can do whatever you want, Jess. I'm not stopping you.' But we both know that's a lie.

She says nothing for a moment, staring silently at the floor.

'I just want to *do* things, Ellie,' she whispers. 'I want to meet new people and have new experiences and try new things.'

'What do you mean, *new things*?' I ask accusingly. 'You mean, Ash. Because that's not new, Jessica. You and some hot guy is not a new concept.'

'Why do you have to be like that?' she says angrily. 'It doesn't matter what he looks like. He's nice. They both are. Ash and Elina invited us over the other night and you made up some terrible excuse about why you couldn't come. It's just fear, Ellie. You're just scared. And I don't know why that is, but I'm not. I'm not scared. And it's like you think I'm a terrible friend just because I want to do something that you don't.'

'So I'm holding you back?' I say just as angrily. 'From doing new things. From the life you want to have? So don't be friends with me then. Just keep on ignoring my calls, or forgetting to return them, or forgetting me, or whatever.'

I turn away from her, worn out by the argument. Worn out by myself.

She sighs, changing tack.

'You're my best friend, E. I'm sorry I haven't been around as much lately, but no, I don't think you're holding me back – I just want to move forward. I want it to be OK for me to want different things to you.'

She takes a step towards me and puts her hand on my shoulder.

'I want to move forward too,' I say quietly. 'I'm just not you, Jess. I'm not some smart, beautiful, perfect girl that everyone wants to be around.'

'But you are,' she says, shaking both of my shoulders. 'If only you could see how brilliant you are. Why do you think I sat next to you on the first day of school? Because you're cool, Ellie. You're interesting. Everyone knows it except you.'

'Please don't use the word potential,' I mutter accusingly.

'And I'm not perfect, E. Anything but.'

'Whatever, King. We both know you are. Other than your sometimes questionable taste in music.'

'Not everything made after 1995 is questionable,' she smiles.

I harrumph, settling myself back on the bed, as she sits down next to me. She nudges me and I press play.

And we sit there, sort of silently. The movie playing between us. Filling the gaps between our non-existent words. I want to tell her I'm angry. But it sounds stupid and childish, and I want to pretend I'm cool. Cool with all this change. Cool with her new boyfriend, and my seemingly less important role in her life. Because I, Ellie Pillai, am cool.

Then our favourite part of the film comes on, and I let Tony Curtis do the talking for me.

'What's the matter with you?' I ask, adopting a high-pitched American drawl, in an attempt to mimic Tony Curtis's character, Josephine.

She turns away from me dramatically, hand to her forehead.

'I don't know,' she shrugs. *'I'm not very bright, I guess. Just dumb . . .'* She lays her hand on her chest, the words coming out in one long, breathy sentence, as Marilyn Monroe's doll-like Sugar Kane.

'Then one morning you wake up, the guy is gone, the saxophone's gone, all that's left behind is a pair of old socks and a tube of toothpaste, all squeezed out.' At this she feigns squeezing a tube, with a hapless look on her face, and I can't help but laugh.

'So you pull yourself together,' she says in that sugar-baby voice. *'You go on to the next job, the next saxophone player. It's the same thing all over again. You see what I mean? Not very bright.'*

89

And then we say the last bit, our favourite bit, in unison, like it's the chorus of a song we could never get tired of singing.

'*I can tell you one thing – it's not gonna happen to me again – ever. I'm tired of getting the fuzzy end of the lollipop.*'

We lean into each other, cackling like a pair of old witches. And I wonder, once again, whether I might have been one in a former life. I've always felt a curious affinity with black cats.

'The fuzzy end of the lollipop,' she snorts. 'I love that line.'

'Are you sleeping over?' I ask, looking at the time.

'Is that OK?' she asks cautiously. And for some reason, for a second, she feels like a stranger.

I throw a pillow at her.

'No,' I say, staring her down. 'You might look like an angel, but your snoring is the exact opposite of how you look.'

A pillow hits the back of my head.

'I speak the truth!' I screech.

Feathers. Fly. Everywhere.

13

There Is a Light That Never Goes Out

I've agreed to go to the river with Jessica, Ash and Elina after school today. Mostly because I couldn't think of a reason not to. Or rather, this happened.

Jessica: Come on, Ellie. Ash and Elina think you're cool. You promised you'd at least try and get to know them.

Me: Errrrrrrrrrrrrrrrrr

So here I am. Attempting to match my pace to their ridiculously long legs.

'Did either of you see *Ocean's 11* last night?' Ash asks Jess and me.

'As in Frank Sinatra, Sammy Davis Jr?' I say, trying not to trip over my feet.

'As in George Clooney, Brad Pitt,' he says smiling at me. And for some reason, the smile feels patronising, and annoying.

'I prefer the original,' I say, in what I hope is a condescending manner but may just be coming out as a big, sweaty mess. Why do tall people walk so quickly? And why am I even saying that? I actually don't prefer the original, I think it's a big, sweaty mess – where Sinatra doesn't even sing. I mean, what's the point of Frank Sinatra, if he doesn't even sing?

Ugh.

I can feel my nerves skittering around like marbles inside of me. Why do I care what he thinks of me? Why do I care how pretty Jess looks in this autumn light, her hair creating a halo of perfect blonde wisps around her Bardot-esque face.

Ugh.

'Well, I like it,' says Jess, side-eyeing me. 'I mean, I think the idea of the first film is just cooler because it's a cool cast, but the remake is actually better, isn't it? Sharper dialogue. More likeable characters.'

I do everything I can not to fall over. Jess has never shown any interest in *Ocean's 11*, or any other film really. And now she's suddenly a film critic worthy of her own column in one of those uber-hipster magazines only five people read. How does she do that? How does she know the right words to say? I fear there may be glue in my mouth. It feels gummy and unable to function properly.

'I suppose it is directed by Steven Soderbergh,' I admit begrudgingly.

'Do you like *Sex, Lies and Videotape*?' Ash asks, looking down at me enthusiastically. And for a second, because I am a big, sweaty mess with marbles inside of her, I think I hear him say 'Do you like sex?' And I can feel my face turning purple as I look down at my feet, the word 'sex' repeating over and over in my brain, like that time in Year 7 when

Joe Whatley kept saying 'sex' to me on the bus, and I kept covering my ears like I thought I could get pregnant just from the sound of it.

'Ermmmm . . .' I mumble.

'You know . . .' he says, 'the film . . .'

'Oh,' I say, relieved, my brain suddenly rearranging the words into the correct order. And just as I'm about to attempt an intelligent critical review of Soderbergh's greatest work, I lose my footing on the bank, or rather, I don't lose my footing, I just walk straight off it, like I'm in one of those silent films with music playing over the top, and I'm just watching myself fall haplessly into the river while the screen reads 'Oops!'

Ash, Jess and Elina turn towards me in slow motion as I plunge into the water.

'I can't swim!' I shout, panic-stricken. But actually, I don't need to swim, because I've fallen off the bank where the water is less than a metre deep. As I hit the bottom, I can hear Elina struggling to stifle a giggle.

Ground, please swallow me whole. Water, please rise higher so I look less like I just screamed *I can't swim* while lying in a puddle.

Ash reaches down to pull me up. And even as he's fishing me out, like an old boot full of water, I can see him grinning, the laugh straining to make itself known, a smile playing at the corner of his lips, threatening to split his face open. But I can tell he's hiding it. Holding it back almost heroically, trying not to make me feel like a bigger fool than I actually am. And even though I literally wish I could fall to the bottom, like that guy in *Titanic* – his arm outstretched, waving goodbye to the world – I can't help but smile back.

I bury my head in my hands and laugh as he pulls me on to the bank, and listen to the sound of Elina and Jess's quiet giggles turn into full-blown guffaws. And all of a sudden, all four of us are stood on the bank, holding our middles and rolling around with laughter.

'Are you OK?' Ash asks, still laughing.

'I'm amazing,' I mutter between snorts, trying not to look hysterical. I can't even imagine how horrible I look in this moment, and so I decide not to even try.

'Oh, Ellie,' says Jess, wiping her eyes and trying to look sympathetic while still giggling.

'Take my jumper,' Ash says, pulling his fisherman's knit over his head and passing it to me. When I put it on, I can feel the warmth of his body, like he's still inside it with me.

'Should we sit down?' he asks kindly.

Jess settles herself next to Elina, their long skinny legs skimming the water, and I know she must want me to talk to Ash. To get to know him and see for myself why she likes him so much, because that's what best friends do. And while I'm glad of that, I'm also sat here soaking wet and smelling of stale river water.

'Are you sure you're OK?' he grins.

'I'm *fine*,' I grimace, trying to wring the water out of the bottom of my trousers.

'Can you really not swim?' he asks curiously.

'Pathetic, isn't it?' I ask, looking straight at him. 'I've got this weird phobia about it.'

'Phobias aren't pathetic. Fear is normal.'

'Well, I'm scared of swimming, riding a bike, the radio getting stuck on any channel that isn't BBC 6 Music, and walruses – are any of those things normal?'

'Walrus fear is pretty normal. I mean, they're scary. Although not as scary as ice cream flavours that aren't vanilla, chocolate or strawberry.'

'So, no cookie dough then?'

'I like the classics. There is nothing scarier than experimental ice cream flavours.' He holds my gaze.

'Ellie,' Jess says, throwing a piece of moss at me and narrowly missing my head. 'Put one of your playlists on.'

'Really?' I say, embarrassed.

'Ellie makes the most amazing playlists,' she tells Ash and Elina enthusiastically. 'She puts things together you would never even think about.'

Why is she gushing about me? Like she's trying too hard to make them like me. I want to pull the fisherman's jumper over my head, pretend I'm a crab and scuttle away.

'Play one,' says Elina the DJ. Oh God. Why is Jess doing this to me?

'Let's listen to something of yours,' I say, trying to appeal to her.

'I've already heard mine,' she says.

I pick up my phone and hope no one can see my hand shaking. I tap the screen and the sound of brass launches into the stillness as Marilyn Monroe starts crooning 'I Wanna Be Loved by You'. Satisfied, Elina turns back to Jess.

'Can I look?' Ash asks, putting his hand out for my phone. I pass it to him nervously. 'Do you make a lot of playlists?'

'Yeah . . . I don't know . . . I kind of find it soothing. Collecting things together that remind me of a moment or a mood.'

I don't even know where that came from. It's just, like his sister, he has this thing about him. Confidence, or kindness, or something else, something that makes it easy to talk to him.

'Me too. It's like little things always remind me of a song. A lyric, or a couple of bars of something – like there are moments when I kind of play a song in my head.'

I try not to gape at him. Because he's just described my life.

'Sometimes it feels like music is the only thing holding me together,' he says, staring into space.

'Anyway,' he says quickly, 'you probably think that's a bit weird.' He widens his eyes at the word, like he's part mocking me, part mocking himself. But he can't make it into a joke now, because it isn't. Because I get it, in ways I don't even know how to articulate.

'No,' I choke, trying to find the right words. 'I . . . I know exactly what you mean. It's like music is the only thing that makes any sense to me most of the time.' He stares at me, the moment a bit too intense for when your best friend/their girlfriend is sat metres away, and your trousers are giving off a mildly sewer-like smell.

'You might get what I post on my Instagram then,' he smiles. And it's like we've shared the code word to some secret club only the two of us know about.

'What kind of stuff do you post?' I ask, pulling his jumper tighter.

'Yesterday it was a drawing from my art project.'

'What was the caption?' I shiver.

'The girl with kaleidoscope eyes, from . . .'

'Lucy in the Sky with Diamonds,' we say simultaneously. He smiles. And if it wasn't for the fact that he'd just referenced one of the Greatest Songs Ever Written, by The Beatles, obviously – I'd find his stare quite disconcerting.

'Anyway, I love your playlist,' he says suddenly, scrolling through the songs on my phone. 'It's really eclectic. Sort of joyful, and sort of melancholy at the same time.' He looks at me and narrows his eyes thoughtfully.

'What's that supposed to mean?' I ask, somewhere between shy and defensive, fully shivering now, my wet trousers clinging to my legs.

'The Smiths and Gloria Gaynor, on the same playlist?'

'"I Will Survive" is a classic. And one of the best piano intros of any song, ever.'

'OK. Agreed. But next to the Smiths, "There Is a Light That Never Goes Out"?'

'Why not? I think it's one of Morrissey's most uplifting songs. They're both about surviving something. Being OK.'

He smiles at me. And here comes the sixties girl group again, doing their go-go arms around his head, dancing in a circle about him, like I'm in my very own musical. A musical for the delusional. For people who hallucinate girl groups when they're sat by a river, talking to boys with green eyes and smiles that make your heart leap like a dolphin being rewarded for a trick with a fish. In a minute, I'll probably make one of those weird dolphin clicking noises and start trying to rub him with my nose.

'That's an interesting way to look at it.'

'Meaning, weird. A weird way to look at it.' I pull at his jumper, which feels like it's part strangling, part hugging me, my words interspersed with involuntary shudders.

'Weird is good, Ellie. I like weird.'

'So I'm weird,' I say, irritated. 'Thanks for that.'

I stand up and collect my bag from the floor. It's suddenly bitter, my teeth beginning to chatter, my wet clothes sticking to me. And it's not a joke any more. I don't want to be weird. I don't want to be the girl that trips over the riverbank and ends up looking like a drowned rat.

'What are you guys talking about?' Jess asks, looking over at us. And I don't know why she looks so uneasy. Because even as I've been speaking to him, I can see he's been watching her. His eyes flickering from my face to hers, like a bird unsure of where to land.

'Me being weird,' I answer.

'Oh,' she says, standing up so she's chest to face with me, her eyes dancing nervously from Ash's face to mine.

'I was just saying to Ellie, I like weird,' Ash says, standing up next to me.

I can feel my face getting warmer. I consider throwing myself back in the river to avoid the embarrassment of spontaneous combustion.

'Am I weird?' Elina asks, from her position on the bank.

'Very,' he grins.

'Good,' she says, leaning back on her elbows and narrowing her eyes. 'The best people are.' She looks outrageously beautiful today.

98

Lounging on the banks of the river, like a tanned Audrey Hepburn playing the part of some Oxford boater, all wide-leg stripy trousers, brogues and a crop top. I feel suddenly grateful for having to wear school uniform until I'm in sixth form.

'Now, who wants to go to the Shelley?' she says, pulling herself up to standing. 'They've got this really interesting artist showing – very weird,' she says, smirking at Ash, 'and I need to show an interest if I want to get the internship I've been talking to them about.'

'I should really get home,' I say, staring at the ground. 'I'm freezing.' Because I don't want to look at him, and I don't know why.

'Come and meet us later?' Elina asks, turning her grey-green eyes on me. 'After you get changed.'

I try to imagine what I might wear to go somewhere as achingly cool as the Shelley, with someone as achingly cool as Elina, and my mind goes disturbingly blank.

'I can't . . .' I say slowly. And for some reason, Jess won't look at me.

But I don't have anything to wear.

And I don't know anything about art.

And I am not achingly cool and will never be able to pull off a crop top.

'I should get home too,' Ash says, looking at me, and I can feel the hairs on the back of my neck standing to attention, my wet collar clinging to me under his jumper.

Jess continues staring at the ground, her mouth tight.

'You have to come,' Elina says, looking at him. 'I need numbers. I want to look like I'm bringing people into the gallery. You too, Ellie.'

She smiles at me, and I can't help but smile back – she just has That Thing about her. Energy and confidence and beauty.

Ash sighs heavily and rolls his eyes, throwing his arm around Jess.

'*Fine*,' he relents. 'Come on, Jess. Elina's in one of her moods. We'll have to stick together if we're going to make it through this.'

'OK, well, I'll see you later.' I wave, as I walk away from them.

'See you later,' Ash calls. But then I turn back, unsure of whether I'm being clear or not. 'Not at the Shelley, later,' I mumble. 'Because, you know, I'm going home now, and I'm not coming back. Like, tomorrow, later. Or later in the week. Or, you know, never, later, whatever.'

Jess glares at me, her eyes wide.

OH GOD. Why? Why do words come forth in meaningless multitudes from my mouth? WHY?

Elina smiles and waves, while Ash knits his brows and stares at me, like a sculpture in a museum whose purpose you cannot fathom.

When I'm about halfway along the footpath, I hear Jess behind me, breathless.

'Or, you know, *never*, later?' she imitates, annoyed.

'Oh, I didn't mean it like that, Jess,' I say, trying to shake it off.

'E, come on,' she says, grabbing my arm. 'Come with us.'

'I'm soaking wet, Jess. And I smell like a drain.'

'So get changed and come back,' she says, her face hard.

'I don't want to, OK?'

'And there's the real reason.'

'Look, Jess, I'm not cool. I'm not someone these people want to hang out with. I'm *your* friend. Just someone they have to put up with.'

'Stop feeling sorry for yourself, Ellie. That's not true, and you know it.'

'It is true, Jess. That's the truth. Whether you want to accept it or not. They're your friends – not mine. So, go be with them. With *him*.'

'I just wanted you to *try*, Ellie. For once. Because it's important to me. I don't want to have to choose between you.'

'Well, maybe you have to,' I say spitefully.

She looks at me, her eyes angry. And something else. Something I can't quite read.

'Fine,' she says robotically. And I watch her walk away from me, my heart like a drum.

I trudge to the bus stop, and ignore the group of boys staring at the water dripping off my trousers.

'Wet yourself?' one of them sniggers.

My phone buzzes.

Elina:

come & meet us

3's a crowd!

Ellie:

that's the worst!

Ellie:

sorry, hav to go home & be berated by parents

Ex

Elina:

w@ did u do?

Ellie:

not sure yet, but *something*

Elina:

let's hang out again soon

I put my headphones on and wish I hadn't argued with Jess. Wish I'd kept my mouth shut. Wish I'd thought twice before asking her to choose. Who's going to choose me, I think, as the wind whips the stale river-water smell off my trousers and up my nose.

I pull my phone out, and tap at the screen, over and over, trying to find the right words.

Ellie:

sorry, sorry, sorry

u know, 4 being me

i'm not very bright, I guess. just dumb . . .

I put on the Smiths, 'There Is a Light That Never Goes Out' and listen to Morrissey's perfect falsetto; another fallen icon whose music I have to separate from his questionable opinions. He's singing about being young and alive, about love, and lights that never go out, no matter how hard you try to diminish them.

Then I pull at Ash's jumper, drawing it closer around me, as if it has the power to make all of that possible.

That night in bed, I check the glowing face of my phone for what seems like the millionth time: still no response from Jess. Finally, I give in and click into Instagram. I scroll through her posts and see a picture of Elina and Ash at the Shelley, their tall slim frames stood side by side, surveying a picture from behind. And then the eleven-year-old, Nancy Drew version of me takes hold and I check her account to see who she's following. @cellophane_flowers just posted a moody black-and-white shot of the sun setting over the river, captioned 'Where the light never goes out'.

I try to pretend I can breathe.

Note to self. Learn to swim sooner. Drowning is not inevitable.

14

Hanging on the Telephone

I push the door shut behind me and put my satchel down in the hall, my script held tightly under my arm, Blondie, 'Hanging on the Telephone' blaring out of my headphones. It makes me feel punk-rock, like I'm somewhere between out-of-control-angry and totally-in-control-cool.

'What's that?' says Dad, as I pull my headphones down and stare at him.

'What's what?' I say suddenly, realising my idiocy.

'That. Under your arm?' he says, pointing at me.

'Oh ... this old thing ... it's just something Hayley asked me to look at.'

'What is it?'

Why does Dad have to choose today to be nosy? He rarely cares about anything I'm doing. Not in a horrible way, it's just he's not one of those parents who's particularly interested in how your day's been or what you had for lunch, or if one of your friends has taken to completely ignoring your phone calls and avoiding the bus.

'It's a script she wrote. She wants my opinion.'

We walk into the kitchen, where Mum is sat reading what looks like work case notes; files on people's strange idiosyncrasies and plans on how to improve their behaviour, her hair in a topknot, her eyes lined like a sixties supermodel.

'Ellie, you've got enough work of your own to do this year without reading other people's scripts,' she says sharply.

BUT IT DOESN'T MATTER HOW MUCH WORK I DO, BECAUSE NOTHING I DO WILL EVER BE GOOD ENOUGH FOR YOU, I scream internally. I try to channel the thoughts direct from my brain to hers, but it doesn't appear to work. And in my head I'm in that padded room in a 1950s asylum, screaming out to the man in the yellow mac. Asking him to love me. Asking somebody, anybody, why my mother can't believe I'm capable of anything.

'It's for her GCSE, Mum. It's important,' I say sharply.

'Well, you've got your own GCSEs to worry about. I'm not saying it isn't nice of you . . .'

'What *are* you saying?' I breathe.

'It's not exactly your area of expertise, is it?'

'Nimi . . .' says Dad warningly. And there's that voice again, the one he uses when he's trying to keep things calm. 'It's nice of Ellie to help out a friend.' He smiles at me and squeezes my cheek; a move he seems to have adopted from my granny, both strangely comforting and weirdly painful.

'I never said it wasn't nice,' says Mum, sighing. 'I'm just saying, I would have killed to have the opportunities you have, Ellie.'

'You had opportunities, Mum.'

'What?' she says, looking up.

And somehow, a thought has escaped my mouth without me being aware of it.

'You,' I say, suddenly venomous. 'You *had* opportunities. You went to university. You have a good job. I don't know what you're always complaining about.'

'I'm not *complaining*, Eleanor. But I was in my late twenties when I did my degree. Married with a child and another baby on the way. I had responsibilities. Things I couldn't do. Do you really think I've done everything I could have done in my career? Do you really think I've accomplished all the things I could have accomplished, if my parents had believed I should have an education? Your dad paid for me to go to college, Ellie, he's the one that pushed me, believed in me. Opportunities passed me by, Eleanor, and I am not going to let that happen to you.' She's seething, her eyes lit up.

'So, we, your family, we just got in the way, did we? Of the things you *really* wanted to do?' I seethe back.

'That's not what your mum's saying, Ellie,' and there's that voice again. The Voice of Calm.

'It doesn't matter' I say, shaking it off.

'Nimi?' Dad says questioningly.

'It doesn't matter,' she says, staring into the distance.

And the heat in the room is gone now, as if we've poured ice on it. Frozen out our feelings, until we're no longer aware we have any.

'How was school?' she asks, looking up at me again.

And unfortunately, Mum is the kind of parent who wants to know how your day was, and what you had for lunch, and whether any of your friends have stopped talking to you – so she can offer you ten ways in which you could have done everything better.

'Fine,' I reply, looking away.

'How's Jessica? I haven't seen her here in a while.'

And now we're getting to the crux of the questioning, how and where is Jessica, because Mum is more concerned about her than she will ever be about me.

Should I tell her about the fact that Jess has completely stopped taking my calls? That ever since that day on the river, she's been stuck to Ash like a mollusc. That she won't even look at me any more. That the other day I overheard her listening to Elina talk about her art project, and enthusing about 'experiential art', without once giving the speech she offers to me whenever we discuss anything related to art or theatre or storytelling – because really, Ellie, how are you going to get paid to tell stories? Or that when I saw her yesterday outside Chemistry, she said she'd call me. But she didn't. Again.

'She's fine. She's got a new boyfriend.'

'I see,' Mum says sharply. 'What's he like?'

'He's fine.'

'Are you OK, *sina pillai*?' Dad says, ruffling my hair. 'You seem a bit . . . out of sorts.'

And I know he's only asking that because I questioned Mum – when we both know questioning Mum isn't a good thing. She gets quiet and distant, like her body's in the room with you, but her brain's somewhere entirely different. And I can see it happening even now.

And I know I shouldn't have said anything, nothing that might remind her of him. Of a time when he was still here.

But the truth is, I'm not OK. I miss my best friend. And I know I've upset her, I know I was wrong to ask her to choose, but she's never shut me out like this before, never just disappeared. I've apologised. Over and over. Voice notes and messages, and emails and song lyrics taped to the side of her locker. And she says it's 'fine'. But it isn't. Because she's gone, and I feel it. Like a phantom limb I keep trying to flex.

'I'm *fine*,' I say, kissing his cheek. He pulls me into his side and squeezes. And for a second it feels like he's part of me. As though if I could just stay right here, forever, then everything really would be OK. Me and Dad versus the universe.

Mum looks up at the two of us suddenly, and I can't really read her expression. Annoyance probably. Or disappointment. That's the usual one.

'Can I get changed before dinner?'

'Sure,' she says, still watching me quietly.

I put my headphones back on and imagine myself calling Jess again. I imagine the Blondie video for 'Hanging on the Telephone', with Jess as Debbie Harry, running around being incomparably cool in front of a black-and-white-striped background, singing directly into the camera, hands running through her hair. And Ash and Elina are there too, Ash wearing sunglasses and rocking a guitar, while Elina plays the drums. And me. I'm somewhere else. Waiting for a phone call, even though they're the ones singing about it.

There are no words for the level of ugh-ness this instils in me.

I throw myself down on the bed and shove the script in its usual place. At least I have an excuse if they find it now.

If they find *it* or if they find *out*?

Further levels of ugh begin to swirl around my brain, like black brushstrokes painting over details, blocking out colour and light and space.

I pull my notebook out of my bag and start writing down the lyrics that are running towards me. That don't belong to Debbie Harry, but belong to me.

Tell me if you're really there
I'm not feeling you
Tell me if you really care
Don't know if I'm sure
If you're there at all
Can you prove it?

And the next day, after James Godfrey's stationed himself next to me again, watching far too closely while I devour a cheese sandwich and interrogating Hayley on the 'motivation' for his character, I go into the music room and start picking out some new chords. A song is writing itself, for all the wrong reasons, but a song is writing itself nonetheless. And just as it starts to come to life, I think I hear Ash in the doorway, with his tinny, distant hum. But it isn't him.

In fact, every day I think I hear him, but there's never anyone there.

♡ Song 2 ♡

Intro, Verse, Chorus –
Rewrite the Story

I thought we had a story. A simple story, with a simple ending. The same, but different – Me + You.

But not all stories are simple, I should have known that. Sometimes stories just outgrow you – the way shoes and shirts and trousers do.

And the sound of rewriting me and you is crushed precariously between a ballad and a pop song. The sound of missing you, and missing us, and knowing that somewhere in all that missing, I have to find myself.

A Me Without You.

Tell me how not to be scared
Of losing you

15

Pink Moon

It's a weird day. This day is always weird, and I doubt it is ever going to get any better. I roll over and look at the clock, trying to adjust my brain. Every*thing* is fine. Every*one* is fine. This day is going to *be* fine.

When I had my obligatory counselling sessions after Amis died, the counsellor told me to try and reframe the way I was feeling; to think about what I had, not what I didn't have; why I was lucky, instead of unlucky. When you're nine, those kind of things don't really mean anything. I just wanted to talk to my mum. I just wanted her to hug me, and cry with me, and tell me it was OK to feel sad. But she was locked away from me. Locked in her own head. And I wasn't allowed to bother her, for fear of making everything worse.

Even now, six years later, it feels just the same. Because today is Amis's birthday. And Mum and Dad and I just breeze through it. We don't talk about it, although there's a cake sat on the side, just like there is every year.

'See you later, Ellie,' Mum says, leaning down to kiss me on the forehead. Her lips feel cool and soft and soothing, the way they felt when I was a child in bed with a temperature.

'Bye, Mum.'

I get the bus to school with a heavy, weird feeling in my chest, like someone's sitting on it and I can't really breathe.

My phone buzzes.

Hayley:

here if u need me.

Hx

still here . . . x

Ellie:

🖤

My phone buzzes again.

Jessica:

hope ur ok. thinking of u 2day.

Jx

It's the first time she's messaged me since that day on the river. Two weeks and two days since the day I told her to choose, since the day she made her choice. So how can she be thinking of me, when she won't even speak to me? How can she care, when she doesn't even call? I want to hate her, but the feeling takes up too much energy.

I sleepwalk through the day, and at lunchtime, decide to stick with Hayley. Literally. Even when she goes to the bathroom, I wait outside for her, like a needy, desperate child.

'Hi, Ellie.' And this time, when I look up, it is him. Jess's Ash.

'Hi.' I stare into the distance and pretend there's something interesting in my eyeline.

'What are you doing?' he asks.

'Standing.'

'Any particular reason?'

'I'm waiting for Hayley.'

'Outside the toilets?' he says, his eyes warm.

'We're, um, discussing something important.'

'I see,' he says. And there's that smile again, the heroic one, the one where it feels like he's fighting every urge not to laugh at me.

'Anyway . . .' I say, trying to move him along.

My phone buzzes again.

Dad:

Be home as early as you can. Mum wants to do the cake straight away.

I gulp down the lump in my throat.

'Are you OK?' Ash asks, and the heroic face, the one from before, is gone.

'I'm OK,' and just like that, my voice cracks. 'Sorry, I'm, er, bad day.'

'Do you want to talk about it?' he asks, watching me.

'It's my brother's birthday,' I say suddenly. 'He died a few years ago, so . . . it's hard.'

I wait for him to make some awkward remark, tell me he's sorry for my loss, or leave, but he doesn't, he just carries on looking at me.

'Are you doing anything, you know, to remember him today?'

'Cake. We always have cake. Chocolate. His favourite.'

'Chocolate? Clearly he was a sensible boy.'

I laugh, the sound unexpected, even to me.

'Amis was so many things, but never, ever sensible.' I smile.

He grazes my hand and looks sympathetic, which sort of makes the weirdness of the day feel less weird.

'Ellie, are you ready?' Hayley says, emerging from the toilets.

'Yep, yep, let's go,' I say, smiling at her, and then I look up at him, and let myself feel the comfort of his presence for just a second longer.

'Bye.' I wave at him.

Five minutes later, my phone vibrates in my pocket.

'Hay, I'll see you later,' I say, my hand curled around my phone.

'Are you sure?' she asks supportively.

'I just want to be alone for a bit.'

She squeezes my arm.

I pull my phone out of my pocket, expecting to see another message from Dad.

It's a link to a song on Spotify.

Ash:

'Street Spirit', Radiohead

And I can't help but press the link and listen to it straight away. And it's soaring, and beautiful, and heartbreaking, and just everything. Everything I feel in this moment. Everything I've felt since I woke up this morning.

I type a quick reply.

Ellie:

how did u kno?

And then I think: my turn.

Ellie:

'Pictures of You', the Cure

About five minutes later, he sends a reply.

Ash:

how did u kno?

And then seconds later:

Ash:

'Wish You Were Here', Pink Floyd

Now this one I know. And love. I type quickly. My fingers too slow to keep up with my brain.

so now I kno

Ash:

kno w@?

Ellie:

w@ ur listening to on those earphones of yours

Ash:

ru ok?

Ellie:

mostly. 2day I just feel a bit like this

'Pink Moon', Nick Drake

The reply comes more quickly this time. Like it's something he knows.

Ash:

sometimes I feel like that 2

And I can't help myself, because the simple poetry of it always moves me. That clean, folky guitar riff and his high, sweet voice. The words, reaching out through the music, telling me it's going to be OK. Even if it wasn't for him. Poor Nick Drake.

Ellie:

lk a pink moon is on its way

Ash:

lk it's all written, but we just don't kno it yet

Ellie:

maybe we do kno it

Ash:

maybe we do

And how many boys know the lyrics to 'Pink Moon'? How many boys even know who Nick Drake is? Round here – not many. Not any.

Is it weird to say I thought there was a club, and that I was the only member of it? The only one who couldn't use normal words to speak. Had to use music and songs and lyrics to feel. To know.

And I don't want the conversation to stop. If a WhatsApp chat can actually be called a conversation, which it probably can't be, not really. But it's maths and Mr Potts is not a man who will tolerate even the hint of a phone, the saliva foaming at the corners of his mouth as he eyes you warily, his hand reaching out to tap his palm and force you to hand it over. So I tuck it away. My own little secret. My own pink moon.

And then at the end of the day, when I emerge from school smiling and listening to 'Pink Moon' on repeat, I see them. Like they're in that Winona Ryder film, *Heathers*, the three of them leaning against a table in the playground, looking too cool, too beautiful to even be there. Jess is laughing, her head thrown back roaring. And he's looking at her. Watchful and amused. Connected. And I feel stupid and inane.

And then they look up and see me – and Jess waves. A sort of weird, half-hearted wave. Like she wants to talk to me, but she can't tear herself away from him. And he looks at me and smiles as a notification pops up on my phone.

Ash:

& it's a pink moon, hey it's a pink moon

And now I can't stop thinking about him. About how he feels the way I feel, when he hears Nick Drake – part soothed, part heartbroken. So I put my phone away in my bag and refuse to look at it again. My best friend's boyfriend knows who Nick Drake is. This is not something I should care about.

So, why do I keep listening to 'Pink Moon'?

16

Chocolate Cake

'Put the candles on the side, Ellie.'

I put the remaining candles down and stare at the cake, as Mum carefully pushes the rest into the hard chocolate topping. A chocolate sponge with chocolate chips and multicoloured sprinkles, Amis's favourite. So sugary, you feel diabetic just looking at it.

When he was at his worst, Mum made one every day. The only thing she could tempt him to eat. She'd make a fresh one every morning, so for a while, chocolate cake became my breakfast too. Even looking at it feels sad. None of us want to eat it. Not without him.

'Twelve candles,' Mum says, staring at the cake. There's no smiling at the memory of my naughty little brother. No stories about how much we loved him, or the hole he left inside of us when he was gone. Just this. Twelve candles.

Dad lights them quietly, his eyes stormy. Because Dad was angry then. So angry with the world. He never talks about it. We never talk about it.

We blow the candles out together. Wordlessly.

Then Mum walks away, her shoulders heaving.

I want to run after her. To fold myself into her, and cry. To say, I don't know why this hurts so much, why this feeling won't go away.

And I want Jessica. My best friend. The one who's held me every year for the last four years, on this exact same day. Who never met my brother, but knows, innately, just how I feel, just what I need. Her body protecting mine, her chin on top of my head, her voice repeating, 'It's OK to cry, it's OK to cry.'

Where is she now? Where's my best friend?

And I wonder whether I need one any more. I wonder whether I'm OK alone.

Then Dad hugs me. Tight and fierce and defiant.

'I love you,' he whispers ferociously.

And I think: I'm not alone.

17

Katja's Song

Another day, another drama-related meltdown. Hayley's new script seems to ignore everything we've been talking about, but there's something about it that feels so special. It's the story of Katja, a young immigrant girl from Sarajevo, who arrives in Britain, looking for her English family. She doesn't know who she is, doesn't feel accepted by anyone, until she realises that the one person who needs to accept her the most is herself.

She learns that who she is is a multiplicity of different patches, that there's beauty in all of these pieces, in not being entirely uniform. I love the story, and the way it leaves the audience to define what identity really means. Hayley is a brilliant writer, but to me, it still needs something more. Something *else*.

I leave lunch early and head towards the music room. Just twenty minutes left to clear my head before dodging spittle and back-to-back equations. I've been writing a song about Katja and I want to work it through, help me flesh out the character.

I'm just starting to play when I hear the footsteps behind me.

'Why did you stop?' Ash asks curiously. 'Your voice sounds beautiful.'

I can feel my face turning that unattractive shade of purple again. Like a party balloon on the verge of bursting.

I look back at him. 'I don't really like people listening to me.'

'Why not?'

I turn back to the piano, silent.

'I've been listening to your playlist,' he says to my back. 'And I see it now. How Gloria Gaynor fits perfectly next to the Smiths.'

'My playlists aren't public,' I murmur to the piano keys.

'Jess shared it with me. It's good. Sort of takes you on a journey.'

I don't reply.

'So, what are you hiding from down here?'

'I'm not hiding . . .' I lie.

The Lie.

The Lie.

And the Green-Eyeliner Eye.

'Is it that kid, James? It feels like he's permanently wherever you are.'

Only when I'm eating a cheese sandwich . . .

'No.' I smile, turning back round again. 'James and I aren't even friends. We're just in the same drama group. We're working through some exam stuff at lunchtimes.'

'Oh.' He smiles thoughtfully.

'I liked the songs you sent me the other day,' I blurt out suddenly, staring down at my hands.

'Nick Drake is amazing,' he says, smiling at me. And the way he's looking at me feels weirdly familiar, like we might be the only people left on the planet.

I smile back.

'My dad used to play his *Bryter Layter* album all the time. I think it was code for when he was feeling sad.' I blush, unsure of why I've shared this level of information.

'Do you listen to a lot of music with your dad?' he asks curiously.

'We used to . . .' I trail away, shifting uncomfortably. There are so many things we used to do.

He looks at me quietly, lost somewhere between my thoughts and his.

'Although, technically,' I say, sitting up imperiously, '*I* sent *you* Nick Drake . . .' I look up from my hands, and dare myself to meet his eyes as he laughs at me. And it doesn't feel horrible, being laughed at by him. 'So, what other kind of music do you like?' I ask, before I can stop myself.

'Everything, really, but I guess my taste is a bit vintage. Nirvana, Pearl Jam, Pixies. I'm listening to a lot of Beatles stuff at the moment too.' His eyes motion towards my bag, covered with my homage to the only boy band I will ever accept as legitimate.

'*Yellow Submarine?*' I say, half smiling. 'It's a great album.'

'I thought it was "too pretentious" for you?' he says mockingly.

'OK,' I admit, fully smiling now. 'I love *Yellow Submarine*. I just love the purity of their earlier stuff more. I love the sheer happy, electric pop of it.'

'I prefer a bit of grit myself,' he says, grinning. 'A bit of angst, and darkness, and woe is me.'

'Teenage angst?' I say, raising an eyebrow. 'How original.'

'Fine,' he says, smiling back. 'What then, other than your boyfriends,' he looks pointedly at the badges on my bag, 'would you call good music?'

'Whatever makes you feel something, I guess.' And it should feel awkward saying a line like that to anyone, but it doesn't. Not with him. 'There's so much music I love, so many kinds, but I suppose there are things like "my boyfriends",' I say, mock air-quoting him this time, 'that just really speak to me. I love Joni Mitchell, but I also love Taylor Swift and Olivia Rodrigo. I think Blackpink are really fun, but I also adore Stormzy and Nirvana and anything written by any Gallagher. Oh, and Motown. Yeah, I love Motown.'

'Well, that makes sense. I can definitely see a hint of Diana Ross about you.' And maybe it's the fact that he's compared me to Diana, dark-skinned, black-haired Diana, but I start to feel he's making a point.

'What's that supposed to mean?' I ask irritably.

'Nothing. It doesn't mean anything . . .' He looks at the grimace forming around my mouth in horror. 'I was just joking. Although, you know, she's a legend, so I thought it was a compliment.' I shake the conversation off me, the ease of it, and start to backtrack. To make it into something it isn't, uneasy and blunt. Because that's how it feels to be in my skin sometimes. Blunt-edged and jagged, like I'll never really fit in anywhere.

I turn away from him and stare at the piano again.

'Honestly,' he says to my back. 'I love Diana. I remember seeing a clip of her on this TV show once. She was singing "Chain Reaction", and she had this picture of herself sewn on the back of her jacket, but it had real hair, or like wool hair on it or something. She was spinning around in a circle, and her real hair and the fake hair on her jacket were streaming out behind her, and it was amazing. I've always remembered that.' I turn back to look at him, and he's smiling in that annoying way of his, the one that can't help but make you smile back.

'That does sound pretty amazing,' I admit begrudgingly. 'And slightly ridiculous. Which is very Diana. I love her too. She just seems like she's really delicate and really strong, all at the same time.'

Is this what flirting is? Am I flirting with Jessica's boyfriend? I don't think anyone's ever flirted with me before, other than when I had to partner with Jeffrey Dean in Year 7 country dancing and he gave me a wobbly smile and told me I smelled like marzipan. I'm still not entirely sure if that was flirting or not.

'So, you never told me what *you're* doing here,' I protest, wondering if I do smell of marzipan, or if he smells of marzipan, or what it would feel like to be close enough to tell. 'If I'm hiding – what's your excuse?'

'I'm looking for Jess,' he says abruptly.

I stare at him. All easiness gone.

'This is the last place you'd find her.'

'Why's that?' he asks uncomfortably.

'I don't know. It just feels like we're not really friends any more. I assumed you'd know that.'

'I didn't. I don't,' he says defensively.

And *this* is definitely Not Flirting.

'You should probably go and find her then,' I say tersely.

'I probably should,' he says quietly. And even the silence that follows feels manly and thoughtful, in a way no silent moment with any other boy in this school could be considered remotely manly or thoughtful.

'OK,' I say, turning back to the piano.

And I don't hear him leave so much as feel him go. Even though I want him gone, even though I wish he hadn't heard me sing, it's more than that – I wish he hadn't mentioned Jessica. Because I miss her. And I'm angry with him for taking her away from me, and angry she was so willing to be taken. But there's even more to it than that, and I know it. And for that, I am mostly angry with myself.

I place my fingers on the keys of the piano. To the one place the words come out right.

Tell me what I'm doing wrong
Cos I don't even know my song

And then the bell rings, and the song, like everything else, goes unfinished.

A Girl Called Ellie

My name is Ellie. Ellie Pillai. You won't be able to pronounce my name properly when you read it aloud, and you'll probably misspell it at least a dozen times. You'll assume I have an accent, when I don't. That my parents are strict or religious, but they're not. You'll be shocked to see my mother wearing straight-leg jeans and a baby-blue angora jumper, looking to all the world like a brown Brigitte Bardot. My name is Ellie. Ellie Pillai. Blink and you'll miss me.

19

The Lightning-Bolt Moment

Mrs Aachara has asked to see me after school today and I'm nervous. We've been working on the play every lunchtime, and I'm not sure what she could want to discuss. I think about it all day, turning the facts over and over in my mind: maybe she doesn't think I'm good enough; maybe she wants to throw me off the course; maybe she's going to phone my parents; maybe she's *already* phoned my parents.

Oh God.

I look down at my phone and see a message from Hayley, who appears to have read my mind.

Hayley:

ru panicking?

DON'T PANIC

breathe. remember she likes u.

Ellie:

does she?

Hayley:

well she doesn't seem to h8 you the way
mr grange did

Ellie:

TY. THAT IS HELPFUL

Hayley:

is it?

Ellie:

NO

I can feel my pulse quickening, my breath coming out in thick, heavy gulps. Is this a panic attack? Am I having a panic attack? Is this what it feels like to die? Can I see lights approaching? I think I can see lights . . .

I approach the drama studio and stand outside. My mother says that in times of anxiety, you should oxygenate the brain – slow and steady breathing, in through the nose; out through the mouth. That it will clear your mind and help the brain to work more efficiently. I close my eyes and assume an 'ommm' position, head to the sky, thumb and forefinger touching on both sides. But just as I'm beginning to feel something akin to calm, the door swings open in my face.

'Hey!' I shout sharply as the door narrowly avoids my head. 'Watch yourself!' As soon as I say the words, I can feel the heat rising in my stupid brown face. Because the person emerging is accompanied by a sixties girl group, resplendent in glorious gold spandex.

I need a minute, baby, I need a minute

Him again.

Him with his ever-present earphones.

Him of the long legs and green eyes and dark hair and strong arms and manly, thoughtful silences, him who ... oh GOD. The realisation comes crashing down over me like the wave that knocked me over on a beach last summer. The lightning-bolt moment.

I like him.

I really, really like *him*.

I'm sure I'm turning purple from the heat of my embarrassment, my breath more like a gasp, a final wheeze of life before I give up and cross to the other side. He looks at me, his face uneasy.

'Are you OK?' he questions, hand on my arm. 'What are you doing?'

'Yes,' I say, shaking his hand off me. 'Just bored of waiting for you to get out of my way.' I'm channelling my inner McQueen. Except a McQueen girl would never be mean to Ash. You can practically see them salivating every time they look at him.

He narrows his eyes and places his earphones back in. And I hate the look he gives me. I hate it. As he walks away, in the short distance

130

from the studio to the playground, a group of three girls is already surrounding him. Like they've been waiting in that spot all afternoon, in an effort to happen upon him at the exact right moment. I watch him remove his earphones and smile at one of them, while she waves a piece of artwork under his nose. The Instagram girls. The ones who leave the comments under all his posts, but have no idea what he's even posting about.

I don't have a chance to process any of this before I hear Mrs Aachara call out to me.

'Is that you, Ellie? Come in.' I try to adjust myself to this moment, and away from the lightning-bolt one. My best friend's boyfriend. Or is that ex best friend? Who knows. Whatever way you look at it, what chance would someone like me have with someone like him? My flirting technique seems to have been honed by watching too many nature documentaries. The human species don't seem to appreciate stroppy, high-handed females as much as the bee kingdom do.

'Ellie?' Mrs Aachara says gently. 'Ellie?'

'I'm here,' I say, swinging my focus back into the room. I look around and see a series of props; Year 8 are clearly doing *Romeo and Juliet* again, and a papier-mâché balcony I used myself a few years ago is sat out, looking slightly worse for wear in a corner.

'Ash is tidying these props up for me,' she says, her back towards me. 'He's a very talented artist, and I'm more than grateful for the help.' She bends over and starts picking things up, sorting them into piles for some unspecified later date, then dusts her hands on her denim boiler suit and turns towards me.

'Sit,' she says, gesturing towards the seats and making her way towards the kitchenette. 'Would you like some tea?'

'Yes – thanks. Black – and weak.'

'Me too,' she says, looking sideways at me as she fills up the kettle. 'I don't know anyone who takes their tea like that. My husband always said it was a waste of a brew. He was from Liverpool, but you could never tell unless it came to a cup of tea. Then he was as northern as they come.'

'So, what did you want to see me about, miss?' I ask, hovering awkwardly while the water comes to the boil, in possibly the longest minute of my life.

She gestures me to sit again.

'It's nothing to worry about,' she says, passing me the mug as I sit down. 'I just feel like we haven't had a chance to talk yet. You're quite reserved, you see, not in a bad way, but sometimes it's hard to see who you are, like you've perfected the art of invisibility.' She looks at me, as if willing me to meet her stare.

'Oh.'

'It's just that first day, Ellie, I saw something in you. A spark. And I wondered where that's gone. Where you've gone.'

'I don't know,' I say, reaching for the words. 'But I suppose I am. Invisible, I mean.'

'You aren't invisible,' she says firmly. 'Quite the opposite. I think you have presence, something special about you. Something different. I just mean that, sometimes, I think you make yourself small. You put yourself in a box, you withhold that presence. But I saw it,

132

that first day we met, when you made that comment about being brown. You didn't think about it, you just said it, and it was right. I can imagine, growing up in a place like this, that you haven't always felt you fitted in.' I look at her, and suddenly realise that to come here, to this far-flung corner of east England, from almost anywhere else, would be a shock to most people's systems, but to do so as an Indian teacher in an almost entirely white school must have been, at times, unbearably hard.

'There's something extraordinary about you, Ellie. And my job is to find it, to help you find it.'

'That's not really your job,' I say, before I can stop the words from escaping my mouth, the meanness coming naturally to me now.

'Well, technically,' she says smiling, 'it's not on my job description. But when I see talent, I have to nurture it. That *is* my job.' She looks at me and screws her face up thoughtfully. 'Are you happy with your play?'

'What do you think of it?' I ask, hoping for her answer to guide mine. What's the right thing to say, when one of your closest friends wrote it?

'I think it's smart, accomplished, full of potential, but at the moment it lacks heart. I think that's where you come in. I think you know a way to make it better, but something's holding you back.'

I wonder whether she can read minds, or whether this is some strange voodoo, whether I'm really here at all. How can I be special, how can I have presence? I've spent the last four years of my life trying to erase my presence from most spaces. No presence means no crap jokes about my monobrow that lead me to shave it down the middle, no presence means no one laughing at me when I bleach my moustache blonde, because it worked for Jessica, and I hadn't considered we were different skin colours. No presence means not noticing that every girl of desire on the TV or in magazines seems to be white. No presence means not minding that there's never any mirror for me, for my life. But lately I've found myself standing on crowded buses, wanting to scream, to shout, to sing out loud. I'm suddenly finding that I want to be heard.

'Tell me, tell me what you think of the piece you're working on. Be honest.'

'I agree with you . . . it needs something more . . . I mean, to me, it feels filmic, big. There are moments when I feel we could express more with music . . . A sort of soundtrack, something that allows the characters to convey more than just what they're saying.' She looks at me strangely.

'I don't mean a musical,' I backtrack. 'I don't want the characters to sing. But what if there was a soundtrack, something more to connect to, as the background to the play. An extra layer to the story.'

'Do you have anything you can show me?' she asks, leading me towards the piano at the side of the stage; a pristinely kept, black, glossy upright.

I walk towards it and sit down. I can feel my heart beating in increments of three – uneven and long, so hard it feels like it might burst out of my chest. Maybe this is the end. Maybe the mere suggestion of being *me*, of showing who *I* am, is going to end me in some ironic twist of fate. I feel like I'm having an out-of-body experience. Watching myself from above – the sixties girl group, now angels singing overhead; a man in a yellow mac beckoning me towards the light.

Mrs Aachara is looking at me. Right at me. And I can't look back. Can't allow myself to register that she's there. Watching me. The first person I've ever willingly let watch me sing. The seconds tick by into minutes, while I sit, my hands poised above the keys. I am no longer a person, but cement, unyielding and immobile. I can hear her breath, slow and soft beside me, as she turns away, her disappointment writ large.

And all of a sudden, I'm back on stage again. My blonde moustache shiny with sweat as Mum watches me, her eyes vacant.

Sweat: moisture exuded through the pores of the skin, typically in profuse quantities as a reaction to heat, physical exertion, fever or fear.

No. No. No. No. NO.

I force my fingers to reach for the notes.

I screw my eyes up and shut them tight. It's dark and comforting, because I don't need to see the notes to know how to play them. To feel them. And then I'm singing. Like I'm somewhere else. Like I'm someone else. And I don't let myself acknowledge that Mrs Aachara is there. That she's in the room at all. Because I'm not looking at her, so she isn't, not really.

I open my eyes and she's still facing away from me, scared to turn until I've finished.

Then she turns to look at me, her smile knowing.

'You see,' she says. 'I told you. Special.'

Then she pauses, before asking more slowly, 'Do you think you could do that with me facing towards you this time?'

'I don't know,' I say bewilderedly.

Because honestly, I really, really don't.

♡ Song 3 ♡

Intro, Verse, Chorus - Katja's Song

It's a slow and steady build-up. Gentle and urgent.

> *I'm not the girl you want*
> *I'm not the girl you need*
> *I'm not the girl that you expect me to be*

It's something like a ballad, but more soulful, a little bit sad. I guess you could call it introspective. When I hear it, I see butterflies, their wings luminous in the sunshine. I see a freedom I want, but am too afraid to reach out and find. It's a song about being wrong about who you are. About not being sure of who you are. I wrote it because I get it. Because Katja and I are two sides of the same foreign coin. Because we both spend far too long thinking about who we're not, instead of trying to work out who we want to be.

20

Brooding Skies,
Just Like in the Movies

Walking home from the bus stop, I skip a little, which is something I like to do sometimes. Gallop. A completely free running, like no one's looking at me race with myself. Like I'm playing toy soldiers on a make-believe horse. I feel like a kid. Strangely carefree. Even though all I've managed to accomplish today is to realise I have inappropriate feelings for my best friend's boyfriend, and then sing to the back of my favourite teacher's head. Because I couldn't manage her actual face. Every time she turned around, I just froze, so she let me sing to the back of her glossy black hair. Over and over, until somehow it almost felt normal. Like her curtain of hair was a legitimate audience, and I'll be fifty some day, singing to myself in a room full of glossy black wigs – but only the backs of them. And now my weirdness feels like it's reached new heights. Like I have scaled the walls of weirdness and am heading up the mountain towards the summit of weird, the very pinnacle of it. Because not being able to look someone in the face is an entirely new fear, even for me. But she was in the room. And I can't help but feel proud of myself for trying.

So I have a gallop. Because galloping is what I do when I feel joyful. I gallop like I'm the only person in the world, like it's a normal thing for a fifteen-year-old to do when her best friend isn't speaking to her and she's spent the late afternoon singing to the back of someone's head. I gallop past the fish and chip shop on the corner and the miniature supermarket that has designs on being an organic greengrocer, when the only organic produce it stocks is overpriced strawberries in summer and a handful of weird nut bars that are highly Instagrammable but mostly inedible.

Every house on my road is a cookie-cutter version of the next, a modern housing estate in a tiny English village, red-brown brick with just a hint of ivy allowed to grow artfully over the fronts, to give the impression of age, gravity. Like us, our house is playing a role, trying to fit in, dressing itself for the occasion with its wrought-iron gates and heavy wooden door – but it's unmistakably new, trying just a little too hard with its wooden sign, on a road of houses with names like Sikes House, The Magwitch, Weller's Place – Dickens references for dummies.

When I reach home, my galloping has to end. Which is unfortunate, but timely – because I'm pretty sure Mavis at The Magwitch is smirking her horrible toothless grin at me, twitching at her equally horrible net curtains, judging me for my childish galloping, something she'll no doubt be reporting to my parents as one of the many strange and unpleasant things that the 'young people of today' get up to, without proper adult supervision. But the woman is faster than lightning, despite her apparent need for a mobility scooter, and when I look up in an attempt to shame her for watching me, all I catch is a light flutter on her nasty lilac curtains.

Once inside, as usual, the house is empty. Mum started working full-time after Amis died, Mum-the-Therapist – a singular irony given she's the most uncommunicative person you'll ever meet. I don't blame her for throwing herself back into work; some days I get the impression that having her clients to look after was the only reason she got out of bed in the morning. I just wish sometimes that I'd been the reason, and not them.

But I know it was too hard to be here after everything happened. Too hard to hang up one coat instead of two. I'm used to the look I get when people find out what happened, but I don't think she'll ever get used to it. The way people tilt their heads and mist over, like we're something to feel sorry for, delicate things, broken and incapable. But we're not. Not any of us. We're just people with a little bit of sadness inside us. Like we all have sometimes. Which is OK. Because feeling sad sometimes is OK. In fact, it's perfectly normal, just as long as you know how to not feel sad, afterwards or forever.

More than anything, I just miss my brother. I miss him microwaving my Barbie and hiding the remote control in places you could never, even possibly, hope to find it – like the freezer, or the bottom of the Play-Doh drawer, or, on one particularly memorable occasion, inside an unused sanitary towel, sticky side down, at the very bottom of my dad's briefcase. My brother was a beautiful person. I never really

140

understood that until he was gone. But he made things better. He was one of those people who made things better, just by being around.

When I hear Dad arrive home, I'm playing the piano in the front room, trying to finesse the song I played earlier to the back of Mrs Aachara's head, trying to prepare myself for the conversation with Hayley and the rest of the group tomorrow. I don't do public performances. I have no idea how and by what means, in the space of just twelve hours, I'm going to confront and conquer my sudden fear of forward-looking faces.

When Dad walks into the living room, he's still wearing his white coat from the hospital where he works as a biomedical scientist. My dad is not an effusive soul, he is in fact, quite literally, a man of very few words. He doesn't seem to like many people, or at least that's the impression I think he likes to give. But he loves Mum and me ferociously and perfectly. And yes, sometimes I wish he'd be more open with me. That he wouldn't just play me records now and then and pretend it's enough to fill the space between us. But I know he's trying, I know he's there. The kind of dad who defends me from my mother's perpetual disappointment by saying that I'm perfect as I am. That I'll be who I want to be. That I look like a young Aishwarya Rai (who?), that I remind him of my mother (how?). The product of two extremely pushy parents, who were never satisfied he wasn't a 'proper' doctor, he will painstakingly point out he has three PhDs and no desire to be anything other than a scientist.

Mum's family on the other hand didn't believe in educating women. The youngest by eighteen years, she was a late pregnancy, an unhappy surprise; my grandparents' disappointment she wasn't another boy, almost palpable. I've only met her elder brothers once – at my grandma's funeral, when I was two. By then they'd been living in Australia for fifteen years, their children not much younger than my mum. I don't remember it, but I've been told I cried blue murder whenever anyone with an Antipodean accent came near me.

The thing is, I know my grandparents were hard on my mum. I know she had no freedom, that when her brothers moved away from home she was effectively locked up until she got married. I know she wants to be different from my grandma. To want more for me than her mother wanted for her. It's just sometimes it feels like it's too much. What she expects of me is too much.

'I heard you playing from the driveway, *sina pillai*. What a lovely thing to come home to,' Dad says, wiping his glasses on his coat pockets. He kisses me on the forehead. 'Dinner?' he asks. And we perform the ritual.

'Yes.'

'What?'

'Sushi?'

'When?'

'Now.'

'I'll order. Just call your mother.'

And that's another thing about my parents. They don't do cooking, Sri Lankan or otherwise.

I call my mother and get her voicemail, but within seconds she sends me a text.

Mum:

WITH CLIENT. EVERYTHING OK?

Why does she have to write all her messages in capital letters? As if she's permanently shouting, or in a panic.

Ellie:

w@ sushi do u want?

Mum:

SPICY TUNA ROLL AND THING WITH CRAB.

I convey the order to Dad, who's already on the phone to the restaurant. You can find almost every type of takeaway imaginable in this area, just not the people to match.

Now that Dad's home, I stop playing and listen to the sound of him buzzing around the kitchen; setting the table, pouring himself a glass of wine. We wait for the food in companionable silence, and that's when the rain that's been threatening to fall all day begins to do so; in torrents, thick and heavy. It's biblical rain, the kind in movies, where the heroes proclaim their love under brooding skies, shirts clinging, their hands running through their hair.

It's so filmic, so intense, that when the door begins to pound with the sound of a fist beating against it, I can almost believe it's Ash, come at last to proclaim his undying love for the small, angry brown girl who keeps humiliating herself whenever he appears in her vicinity. But when

Dad opens the door, it isn't Ash. It's Jessica. And I can't tell whether it's the raindrops or the tears coursing down her face that have turned her into the mess of a human being I see before me. But I reach out to her.

She's my best friend, and nothing will ever break that.

21

Green Light

She won't talk about it – whatever it is that's happened, she isn't talking. I mean she's never been much of a talker. Never been the best friend that confides her deepest hopes and fears to you under the cover of a duvet late at night, stuffing her face full of sweets. It's like she doesn't even have hopes and fears. Just aspirations she considers attainable if she's willing to work hard enough to deserve them. Like a grown-up. The proper sort. The high-achieving sort with things like pensions and savings, the sort who wash their yoghurt pots out before they put them in the recycling. My dad has always called her Mrs King. Because even as a child, she was always this rational, grown-up person. A mini adult from the age of eleven.

But I know it must be Ash – because what else can make you cry like a manly, thoughtful, green-eyed seventeen-year-old boy can? He's obviously done something. Hurt her, cheated. I don't know what it is, but I know it's bad. I've never seen her like this, never even seen her cry, not even when we found her living without heating or hot water last winter because her mum had gone away and forgotten to pay the bill.

She sits down to dinner with us, and when Mum asks what's wrong, I mutter 'boys', which seems to make her cry even harder.

We go up to bed and watch *Breakfast at Tiffany's*, even though Audrey isn't her favourite Hepburn. Then I let her fall asleep on my arm, until I can feel nothing but pins and needles coursing through my veins.

But when I wake in the morning, she's gone.

I sit up quickly and call out her name. Then I race on to the landing and call it again. I feel suddenly panicked, frantic. I rush downstairs to the kitchen and find Mum drinking coffee, her overpriced soy milk sat neatly in a tiny jug beside her cup.

'Have you seen Jess?' I ask, out of breath. She looks up at me, and it seems as though the gesture itself and the words she's speaking are coming out in slow motion.

'She left about half an hour ago. She said she wanted to go home and get changed.'

As always, my mother is immaculately turned out, in a pleated, mid-length, leopard-print skirt and white shirt, lipstick, heels. Her hair is pulled back, giving her face an angular look. She doesn't look like a mother at all, more like a formidable opponent. It must be distracting, I think, for her clients to concentrate on solving their problems with a woman like this presiding over proceedings. She looks at me carefully and speaks slowly, with the voice I know she reserves for her clients.

'Are you OK, Ellie?'

'I'm fine,' I say. But really, I'm not fine. Are Jess and I friends again, or are we not?

'You haven't been spending as much time with Jessica lately,' she says, deliberately looking down at her paper. 'I think it's good you've been a little more independent. You're a talented girl, Ellie. Perhaps it's time you came out of her shadow a bit.'

My mother calling me talented is enough to make me choke on my own tongue, but the full effect of it is lost in the comment about my lack of independence.

I turn away and try not to breathe. Not to take in what she's saying to me. Not to wonder whether that's why she didn't bother to be there for me when Amis died. Whether she thought I should be by myself. Learning to be independent.

I feel a surge of hatred, and fear, and loathing, and sadness, and I don't know where to put it. I can feel it spilling out of me; like a tap that's running and running, with no care for where the hard edges lie. Spilling over into the darkness, into nowhere.

'Ellie?' Mum calls out behind me uncertainly.

I don't turn.

'Where are you going?' Mum says, her voice thin and high. And even as she says it, I can feel her eyes boring into the back of my head, willing me to look at her. To make it all OK.

'School,' I say quietly. And I don't know how my voice can sound like this. Angry and dejected and sullen.

Jessica, Jessica, Jessica. Why is she so bothered about Jessica? What Jess is doing, where Jess is, what Jess needs. What about me? What about what I want, who I am, what I'm doing? And I'm not in Jess's shadow – she's just the one person I can rely on.

That I thought I could rely on.

I run upstairs and get changed, and walk purposefully out the door before I can see Mum again.

Then I start running.

I run and I run and I run. Like my PE teacher Miss Hartley has been telling me to run for the last four years, while, frankly inappropriately, slapping my bottom like I'm some kind of donkey in need of either a carrot or a stick. And suddenly running seems easy, and freeing. Like I'm no longer a donkey but a horse, or at the very least one of those dinky ponies that no one can take seriously, because they're just too small.

Either way, I'm halfway out of the village in what seems like seconds; the rain beginning to fall like a scene from a movie. At first slow and measured, and then stronger, and less controlled. Just like me. The dinky pony who thinks she's a horse.

My phone is ringing and ringing, vibrating urgently at the bottom of my bag – and I know who it is, and I know what she wants, but I don't care.

Right now, I just need to run.

When I reach the school gates, they've only just opened. It's an hour before registration and the playground is empty of its usual suspects. No bullies, no cool kids, no trying-to-go-unnoticed kids, no teachers with combovers or Thor-like abdominals.

I walk towards the music room, jumbled and broken, a bag of bones no longer fully connected. I walk towards the piano. To a

148

moment I can stop and make sense of how I'm feeling. It's still raining heavily, and as I walk through the corridor, my hair, my clothes, my bag, are all dripping tiny wet footprints down the hall, a trail of watery breadcrumbs.

When I reach the music room, I sit down with my best friend. My inanimate best friend, the one that talks to me, that doesn't run away. I pour everything I feel into the keys, and even when I hear the footsteps, I don't stop, don't care whether it's Miss Mason or Ash or anyone really, just know I need it, to keep playing. But it's all too much for me. My hands are slipping and sliding on the notes, wet and out of control. I stop suddenly, the sound discordant and unearthly.

'Why did you stop?' comes the voice from behind me. This time, I don't turn.

'What do you want from me?' My shoulders sag, like the pony I rode in on is sat on top of them. 'I'm just a joke to you, aren't I? Something weird for you to laugh at. Well, go ahead, go ahead and laugh.' At this, I turn to him. My eyes red and swollen, tears spilling down my cheeks, my voice full of emotion, choking on it. 'So, laugh it up, I'm pathetic, I know. I hide down here like a frightened little mouse. But I'm not. I'm not afraid any more, so laugh at me, I don't care, I don't care, I don't care.' As I say it, I can feel myself folding inwards, collapsing under the weight of my emotions, of years of running and hiding, without even knowing it.

'That's not what I think,' Ash says softly. 'You're not a joke. You are funny, but you're not a joke.' I look at him, unable to decipher the comment.

'Funny? Funny-looking, funny-falling-over, funny-no-one-ever-even-looks-at-me-to-notice-I'm-falling-over? Yes, you're right. I'm hilarious,' I snivel.

'No, not like that,' he says, looking slightly tortured. 'And why do you keep saying weird like it's a bad thing? I like weird. Weird is interesting. Weird is good. I'm weird. Everyone is, in their own way. And yes, I think you're funny, because you make me smile. You make me laugh. And honestly, that's something I haven't felt like doing in a really long time.'

'Why?' I ask forcefully. 'Why do I make you laugh? I still don't understand you. I still don't understand why you're here.'

'I lost someone, Ellie,' and he's calm, so much calmer than me. 'And . . . I didn't cope well with that. I kind of coped the opposite of well with that. I stopped laughing, I stopped doing anything really, that wasn't self-destructive. I was an idiot. I went off the rails. And I'm just trying, every day, to be better than that. And you, I don't know. You make me feel like I'm better than that. And I like it. I like who I am when I'm around you.'

I stare at him, my tears suddenly stilled.

'So, no,' he says. 'I don't think you're a joke. I don't come here to laugh at you. I come because . . . I like talking to you. And listening to you. And looking at you. Because, as it happens, I think you're beautiful.'

I've spent the entirety of his speech staring inanely at the floor, but the word 'beautiful' suddenly breaks me. I am so many things, but I am so, not, beautiful.

'No,' I say. 'I'm not.' And then he's walking towards me as I repeat myself, racked with sobs, broken, broken, broken. And before I know it, his arms are around me, and they feel strong and firm and safe. And my face is in his neck, and my tears are running down his shirt, and he's hugging me tight and telling me it's OK, that everything is going to be OK. And I let him, let this boy, who had my best friend on my doorstep in tears last night, hold me. Because without him, without his arms, I fear I may just fall apart, turn into water, shapeless. And when he lets go, and tips my face in his hands, and looks at me like no one's ever looked at me before, I let him kiss me. Because I want to, even though I know it's wrong, or maybe because I know it's wrong.

And the chorus from Lorde, 'Green Light' is pounding round and round in my head, a dark, intense disco beat and bright piano heart. Because I can hear it, those brand new sounds. The sound of him, and me, and us, and this moment, so real I can feel their notes right beneath my fingers.

I've had a few kisses in my fifteen years on this earth, but none of them has ever felt like this. Not the kisses with boys who refused to acknowledge me the next day, not the pity kisses from friends of Jessica's boyfriends, not even the holiday romance where I pretended to enjoy the sensation of his tongue darting in and out of my mouth like a wet, limp lizard, when all I could think about was at what point it was going to stop, because my lips were starting to chafe and I was going to be late for dinner. I know *how* to kiss. I understand the mechanics. But then, somehow, it's like I've never been kissed before, because this is the only way to be kissed.

Everything about it feels right. Like we're exactly where we're supposed to be. His earphones are pressing into me and I reach out my hands and place my fists around them, my thumbs stroking the wires above them. Because I don't want to wait any more. Not for a green light, not for anything.

But then I see her face in the rain, the intensity of her tears, just like me, just like mine this morning, and I feel sick, sick to my stomach. And there can't be a green light. Not for this. Not for him.

And with the greatest of effort, I break away from him and start walking. But he's following me, saying, 'Stop. Please stop walking. I've wanted to do that for a long time. I've wanted to kiss you for a long time.' He's trying to hold my hand, when all I can think about is how he used to hold hers.

I walk and I walk, until the walk is no longer a walk, but a run. A dinky little pony run, but a run nonetheless.

And all I can think is.

He kissed me.

22

Levels of Ugh

I've been walking around for hours now. Like the man on our road who walks up and down relentlessly reading out number plates. I feel lost, and strange. I stand outside the school gates, unsure of whether I can go back in. It's late. I'm late. I'm going to run again. Do another round of the city, like a pony doing show jumps.

It's only when I turn away that I hear her. Screaming my name over the sound of the rain.

'Ellie! Ellie!' I run towards her and she grabs hold of me, throwing her skinny arms around my shoulders, hunching me under her arm. 'Where have you been? Your mum's been calling every five minutes. We've been so worried about you. She said you were upset. What's going on, are you OK?'

'Where have *you* been, Jess?' I ask bewilderedly, and I didn't know my heart could hurt, but suddenly I feel it.

She looks so forlorn, so confused, that I can't even bring myself to be angry.

'I'm sorry,' she says. 'It just got so complicated. I don't know what to tell you, where to start.'

And even though it's nowhere near enough, I take it, and I say, 'It's lucky I like you, Jessica Leigh King.' And she laughs. The sound rich as honey; healing and contagious. And soon we're both laughing, hysterical, holding on to each other like we're about to collapse under the weight of the joke, rain flying off us like a pair of wet dogs. We laugh so much that my stomach starts to hurt. Like a period pain, deep and wringing. We laugh long and hard, like the sound of it will conjure the magic to erase everything. The way we laughed when James Godfrey started sending her pictures of his chest because he thought it was sexy, but all we could notice was the pinkness of his nipples, like tiny sugar mice. My best friend is back, and I am not losing her again, not for anything, not for anyone.

As we walk into the reception, the secretary looks at us like two errant toddlers. 'Stand there,' she instructs, waving us towards the welcome mats. I feel as though I've had a whole day, a whole life already, and it's only eleven o'clock.

'Ellie, your parents have been calling every five minutes since the phones went up. Call them now, please. Jessica, get to class. If you're too wet then you can change into your PE kit or borrow something from lost property.' That's when we stop laughing, and she's sad again. Sad because of Ash. And all I can think is, I should never have kissed him, never have listened to him when he told me I was beautiful, like some naive little girl that believes her dog went to the farm, when really it just died. The dog died.

We turn to each other.

'Meet you by the gates at lunchtime?' she asks.

'Yes,' I say, taking hold of her hand. Because this moment isn't about Ash. It's about me and my best friend. And nothing is going to break that. Not a boy, not my inability to drink coffee or appear cool. Nothing.

As she heads down the hallway, I walk towards the changing rooms. I know I should call Mum, but I can't.

I dial the hospital and wait to be put through to Dad.

'Ellie, thank God. Where have you been? Why did you run off like that? We've been worried sick. They said you never arrived at school.' He trails off, and I can hear his breathing, heavy and uneven.

'I'm OK, Dad. I'm sorry. I just needed some space.' He inhales deeply, and I can almost see him playing with the spiralling cord of those ancient landline phones, the kind they have in every department of the hospital.

'We need to talk about this properly. Tonight.' Followed by a gruff 'Call your mother.'

'Dad, I can't. I've already missed two lessons. Can you call her for me?'

He grunts, the sound of resignation deep in his voice.

I hang up the phone and realise I have drama now, and wish with all of my witchy powers I didn't. Because today is the day Mrs Aachara wants me to speak to the group about Katja's song. Then I realise I have no witchy powers. I just hear songs, and see girl groups, and imagine I'm being rejected by fishermen in yellow rain macs.

I change into my PE kit and borrow a jumper from lost property, then I walk towards the studio, the same stretch of hall I walked with

Ash earlier today. It feels surreal, because even now I can feel it. His lips against mine. The warmth of his hands on my face. The gentle way he brushed my fringe back to look at me.

And it's awful, so awful, because despite everything, despite the fact I despise him, hate him, loathe him for what he's done to Jessica, for what I've done to her, I can't help but want him. And the levels of ugh in this statement are almost too much to bear.

23

Blonde Moustache

When I arrive at drama, Hayley is deeply annoyed. In the way that only Hayley can be. Like a dragon on its best behaviour, smoke billowing out of its nose, ready to burn you to the ground at any given moment. It's Hayley before coffee – except this time, she's *had* coffee. Which is a bad sign. A very bad sign. Mrs Aachara has mentioned we've talked about the play, that I have some suggestions on how we can add more depth, and Hayley is fixated. Fixated on the word 'depth'.

The problem is, I don't know how to approach the subject of the song, how to explain quite what I meant when I wrote it.

'So, Ellie, Mrs Aachara mentioned you had some suggestions on how we can improve the play.' She holds on to the word 'improve', dragging it out behind her. 'From your little *chat* yesterday.' She turns towards me and hisses under her breath, 'I can't believe you complained to her about my script!'

'That's not what happened!' I hiss back desperately.

'Er, sorry, what are you two saying?' David asks, leaning in to hear our spittle-exchanging unpleasantries.

'We can't hear you,' James says irritably. 'And this is about all of us.'

'We were talking under our breath because we didn't *want* you to hear us,' Hayley says, glaring at him. 'Anyway,' she says, narrowing her eyes, 'go on, Ellie. Tell us how we can *improve* the play. I mean, you could have said this to any one of *us*, as opposed to Mrs Aachara . . . but go on.'

'I wouldn't say improve, Hayley,' I say, desperately. I can't lose another friend, I can't lose Hayley. 'Just change it up a bit, add . . .'

She cuts me dead mid-sentence. 'OK, not improve. Add *depth*.'

'Well, I've been writing . . .'

She cuts me off again. 'Oh, so you've been *writing*, have you? It would have been useful to share any *writing* thoughts earlier in the term. I mean we're halfway through now, Ellie, we can't just go messing around with the characters when we've all started learning the lines and designing the set and . . .' This time, Hayley is cut off – although, surprisingly, not by me.

'Maybe if you let her finish a sentence – or any one of us for that matter – we could see what she has to say, and move on from this. This is a *group* project, Hayley. All of our results depend on it. So if Ellie has something she wants to add, then she's entitled to contribute. And we can ALL decide TOGETHER whether we want to make any changes.'

I've never heard James Godfrey talk about anything other than himself for such a prolonged period of time, although technically, when he's talking about the group, he is in fact also referring to himself. I smile gratefully at him and wonder whether his nipples really do look like sugar mice, or whether Jessica and I were just particularly hysterical that day. But he isn't looking at me, he's staring at Hayley.

I can tell she's irritated, but she listens and takes a breath.

'Fine. What have you been writing?'

It's now or never. Incur the wrath of Hayley by talking about the song, or incur the wrath of Hayley by not talking about the song.

'So, I've been trying to get to the bottom of how Katja's feeling,' I say, sneaking a look at her. 'Why she behaves the way that she does. Why she pushes people away, why she feels so lost. I tried thinking about identity, what it really means to any of us, and the idea that we all believe, rightly or wrongly, that we should know who we are, and be secure in it.' I stop. Unsure of how to go on. 'So . . . I was at the piano, and I started writing those ideas into a song, and it got me thinking about having a soundtrack to the play, a way to add more . . .' and at this, I give up on looking at Hayley, whose demeanour can best be described as stonelike, and turn to James and say, 'depth . . .'

'OK,' he says encouragingly. 'So let's hear it.'

'Right now?' I ask, panicked.

'Yes, Ellie, now,' says Hayley impatiently. 'We've all been waiting for you to tell us your idea, and we can't move on without hearing it.' I'm sure if she was feeling a little less hatred for me, she'd see the look of terror on my face and be a tiny bit kinder.

'I can't do it here,' I plead. 'Not in front of everyone.'

'Oh, come on, Ellie!' says Hayley, unmoved. 'If you can't do it here, in front of all of us, then how are you going to do it in the exam?'

159

I've thought about this a lot over the last twelve hours, and I don't know the answer to it. I just know I want to try.

'Give it a rest, Hayley,' says James, looking at me with something resembling sympathy. 'She's obviously not feeling great. Why don't we just go to the music room and give her some privacy? Besides, if she's our secret weapon, we don't want to give the other side any ideas.'

'It's not a game of football, James,' says Hayley, deadpan. 'We're not in competition with the other groups.' But I can also see her face registering that maybe it is. Because she does want to be the best. 'But fine,' she says, crossing her arms. 'Let's go.'

'I'll let Mrs A know,' James says, sprinting away. I watch him talking to her, his hands waving animatedly at his sides. She turns to me and smiles, emitting a tiny, imperceptible wink. I consider vomiting.

We walk down the corridor to one of the smaller music rooms and file silently inside, nausea swelling in the pit of my stomach.

I sit down at the piano and close my eyes.

What would happen if I opened my mouth and projectile-vomited instead of singing? My sideburns feel sweaty, like every inch of my face is covered in moisture. Except my mouth. Which feels suddenly Saharan in its dryness.

Blonde moustache, blonde moustache, blonde moustache.

After about a minute, Hayley sighs heavily. My eyes fly open and I stare at the five of them. Andy gives me a smile, and David gives me a silent thumbs up, while Hayley stands unimpressed next to them.

'Can you just . . . turn around?' I ask, attempting not to dry heave.

'Oh, for the . . .' Hayley begins, but this time Lauren cuts her off.

'It's fine, Ellie,' she says kindly, turning around while the others throw irritated glances at each other. When they've turned away from me, I screw my eyes shut and try to remember it's my choice to be afraid. That I can choose not to be. That I can be *that* Ellie. The one who has a voice. And as quietly as I can, I start to sing the song I wrote for Katja.

> *I'm not the girl you want*
> *I'm not the girl you need*
> *I'm not the girl that you expect me to be*

There's something so soothing about the sound of the music that for a minute I forget that I'm Ellie Pillai, awkward, shy and betrayer of best friends, and as always, I'm lost, but somehow found.

When I stop, the silence overwhelms me. I open my eyes and look at them. Just like Mrs Aachara, they have their backs to me, too afraid to move.

'Is everyone OK?' I ask nervously.

'OK?' says Hayley, turning around to look at me in amazement. 'That was better than bloody OK, Ellie. Where have you been hiding THAT?' And as the rest of the group turn, they're grinning too – even James – almost deliriously, almost obscenely.

'Nice work, Pillai. See, I told you,' he says to Hayley. 'You really need to shut up sometimes, you know?'

24

Nice Legs, By the Way

When James Godfrey corners me in the hall after drama, it's hard to believe it was his encouragement that got me through the lesson.

'So, that was interesting back there,' he says, throwing his bag over his shoulder.

'Er, right. Yeah. Thanks for sticking up for me.'

'I wasn't sticking up for you, Ellie, I was sticking up for the rest of us. Because, believe it or not, we are allowed to have an opinion about this play.' For a minute normal service resumes, as I realise he was less encouraging me, more putting Hayley the Dragon in her place.

'You're really talented, you know,' he says genuinely. 'When I heard you on the bus that day, I mean, I knew you could sing . . . but that was really good, Ellie. You need to have more confidence in yourself, because out of everyone here, you're the one who's going to be someone.'

I stand there, staring at him. Incapable of a response.

'Nice legs, by the way,' he says, looking smug as he points at my tiny PE skirt. 'You might want to shave them the next time you decide to wear a skirt, though—' and just like that, the moment is gone.

'Shut up, James, she's hardly wearing it to impress you,' says Hayley, coming up behind us. 'Ellie is not a slave to the marketing of femininity or the ridiculously unfair standards of beauty imposed on women by society. She's an individual.' She comes between us and turns her back to him, closing him out of the circle. 'That was amazing, by the way. Sorry for being such an uber-bitch.'

'Whatever,' says James, beginning to walk away, but even as he's walking, I can see him looking at her.

'We need to get together after school,' Hayley says excitedly. 'Discuss the music, how we're going to use it. You were right, Ellie, this is going to elevate the whole thing. We need to work on your stage presence too. Or just getting you on stage and singing in front of people – otherwise none of this is going to work.' At this, James turns.

'Shouldn't the music be something we decide on together, as a group?' he asks.

'There's no time,' Hayley replies matter-of-factly. 'Half term is next week. Besides which, Ellie and I are the writers. How you guys interpret what we write is up to you, the direction, the characterisation, but we need to write it up, put the structure together first.'

'Where are you meeting?' he asks. 'I'll speak to the rest of the group and we can meet you there.'

'Let's meet back here,' I say before Hayley can explode. 'Three thirty. I'm sure Mrs Aachara won't mind if we use the studio.'

Hayley turns to me as he walks away, her eyes as wide as saucers.

'Really, Ellie? REALLY?' she hisses. 'That boy is so annoying! Why can't he just let us get on with it?'

'To be fair, if it wasn't for him, there wouldn't be any music to talk about.'

'Yes, well,' she says, shame-faced. 'Sorry about that. I just thought you'd complained to Mrs Aachara about my writing.'

'Is that what she said?' I ask uncomfortably.

'Well, no,' she admits. 'She just said you had an idea for the play and she thought it might give some extra depth to the characters.'

'Right . . .'

'I just thought if *you thought* the characters needed extra depth, and *she thought* the characters needed extra depth, that you both thought my writing wasn't any good.'

'Hay,' I say, squeezing her arm. 'That's a pretty big leap. You're a brilliant writer. I just had this idea about adding music – and I didn't really know how to say it.'

'Why didn't you just talk to me about it?' she asks kindly.

I stare at the Dragon. The sometimes scary, unforgiving Dragon. But I know it isn't that. I know Hayley would have listened. She's only scary when you hurt her. Only scary because she's *been* hurt.

'I don't know, Hay . . .' I trail off. 'I just feel like half the time I don't really trust my own opinion.'

'Well you need to trust your opinion, because that was really good, E. We just have to work on building up your confidence. I've never seen you that nervous before. I mean, I know you get *nervous*, but that was . . .' She leaves the sentence hanging, as if there's a word that could describe the phenomenon. Blonde Moustache Syndrome.

'It's just singing is all me,' I mutter. 'Acting is different. I'm playing a part, I'm not being me.'

'Well, that's the way to look at the play then, isn't it? You're not being Ellie Pillai, you're being Nermina, Katja's friend. You're singing as her.' I mull it over. The logic of it feels soothing.

'Look, Hay, I have to go meet Jess now. Can we talk about this a bit later?'

'Jessica?' she asks, surprised 'Is the Queen finally gracing you with her presence?'

'She had stuff going on,' I mutter defensively. And I know this isn't enough. Not for her and definitely not for me.

'Hmmmmmm,' she harrumphs. And I take it as the ultimate kindness that she doesn't labour the point. A sorry-I-was-an-uber-bitch-and-terrified-you-into-singing-to-our-drama-group-in-the-music-room-that-smells-of-damp-dirty-socks.

'Can we talk a bit later?' I say in my most wheedling tone.

'With your friend *James*,' she says, exasperated.

'Yes,' I reply. 'With *him*.'

'*Fine*,' she says through gritted teeth. And never has a word sounded more ominous.

I turn away from her and up the corridor, walking quickly, my eyes cast to the floor – looking up only to avoid large obstacles, irritable teachers or boys with green eyes: except I don't do a very good job.

'Owwwwww,' says Elina, as I walk head first into her chest.

Ugh. I had not factored in an encounter with the other twin. The Better Half.

'I'm so sorry,' I say, as I watch her rubbing her chin where my head ricocheted into it.

'It's fine,' she says, grimacing slightly. 'Where are you off to in such a hurry?'

And I wonder if they're the kind of twins that share everything. I wonder if he's told her about the kiss. I wonder if she thinks I am a horrible, terrible friend and that Jessica could do so much better. I wonder what she thinks of her brother, running around kissing random teenage Meryl Streeps in music rooms.

Shut up, Ellie.

Stop talking.

'So, where are you going?' she says again, slowly, like I'm hard of hearing.

'Oh . . . Jess and I are heading out for lunch.'

'Say hi for me,' she says brightly. But the brightness feels forced, because she knows that sides have been taken, lines have been drawn.

'I will . . . I'd better . . .' But suddenly he's there. The Lesser Half. Looking at me. Utilising his talent for appearing out of nowhere.

'Hi,' he says intensely.

Say something, Ellie.

Anything!

'I have to, um . . . go.'

I try not to look at him. I try not to remember his face when he told me he'd lost someone, or the fact he told me I was beautiful, hours after he broke my best friend's heart. Or the other thing. The kissing thing.

For a second, it feels like seasickness. My breathing feels heavy and there are spots appearing in my peripheral vision. Don't faint, Pillai, don't you dare faint like some kind of minor Austen character, wearing her ill-fitting corset too tight. I round the corner a little too fast, my mind full of Mr Darcy, and suddenly there's a door opening in my face, and the sensation of falling.

'What are you doing hiding behind doors, Pillai?' It's James Godfrey, less Darcy, more odious Mr Wickham. He pulls me up. 'Are you OK?'

'I'm fine,' I say, straightening up. For a second I cling to his hand, while he just looks down at me, part concerned, part worried I might crush his hand with my current Hulk-like grip. I try to steady myself – in through the nose, out through the mouth – just as Ash appears around the corner.

'We need to talk about this morning,' he states bluntly.

'What about this morning?' I mumble, gripping James's hand tighter. 'I mean, there's nothing to talk about, is there?' I try to subtly nod my head towards James, but fear subtlety may not be my strong suit, or that I resemble someone with nits trying to scratch their head with their shoulder. 'It's all, um, *fine*. So, you know, you should . . . carry on,' I say, miming a 'run along' motion with my free hand.

'Carry on?' he asks, his voice somewhere between amused and irritated.

'Well, no, not carry on *exactly*,' I say, heart racing. 'I just mean, you know . . . erm . . . OK . . . bye.'

Ash looks pointedly at James's and my hands, and I let go suddenly, doing everything I can not to run like I'm in the hundred-metre sprint – which to Miss Hartley's chagrin, would usually look like me walking anyway, but with my new-found pony speed, resembles something closer to a trot.

I tug at my skirt where it's risen up my thigh, and start walking as fast as I can. From the corner of my eye, I see James shake his head as he looks at Ash, 'I don't know what's wrong with that girl.'

I don't know either.

25

Paradise

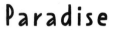

'Sorry. I ran into Ash and Elina,' I say breathlessly, as I run up to Jessica at the gates. 'Elina said to say hi.'

'Oh,' she says. Nothing more, nothing less.

'What happened, Jess? What did he do?' Because I want to know what he's done, so I can hate him some more.

'I don't want to talk about it,' she says quietly. 'Can we just not?'

I nod, even though I do want to talk about it. Even though, really, I need to understand.

'Look,' she says, taking my hand. 'Let's just say it didn't work out.'

'OK.' I nod again.

'It doesn't feel like it's OK,' she says, sighing.

'We haven't spoken in weeks, Jess. And I know you don't want to talk about it, but I'm just trying to understand what happened. Why you shut me out like that.'

She stares at the ground.

'I know we had an argument. I know I upset you. But you just dumped me, Jess. You wouldn't even speak to me.'

'I'm sorry,' she says quietly, reaching out and linking her arm through mine. 'I just lost my head for a while back there. But I missed you, E. I missed you so much.'

'You didn't need to miss me. You could have just talked to me.' I try to sound supportive as opposed to accusatory, but I can't help it. I still feel angry.

'I'm sorry. I just got carried away. You know what it's like when you first start going out with someone. You lose yourself in it—' And I think, no, I have no idea what that feels like. 'And you know what, Ellie, you made it clear you didn't want to be a part of it. That you didn't want to get to know anyone new.'

I shrug. Because honestly, we're both a little bit right, and we're both a little bit wrong.

'I didn't mean it, Jess. You know at least half the things that come out of my mouth are complete nonsense.'

'I'd say more like seventy-five per cent.' She smiles. 'Anyway, I'm sorry, E. I'm really, really sorry. You're such a good friend,' she says, clasping my hand. 'I know I don't deserve you.'

I want to scream I kissed him. I am not a good friend, Jessica. I am not.

'You've all been so good to me, I don't know what I would have done without your family.' And when she says family, what she actually means is my mother. She doesn't know what she would have done without my mother. And I still feel floored by that. The idea of Mum being there for her, when sometimes it feels like she can barely see me.

We walk quietly through the pretty part of the city centre, with its quaint shops and high-street fashion, and head into the industrial part of town, near the old railway line, the undeveloped part of the city, the place the estate agents call 'up and coming' and the rest of us walk through fast at night.

'All right, darlin'.' And suddenly a car is crawling alongside us, and a man in his forties pokes his head out the window and nods at Jessica. Usual behaviour, usual routine.

'Hi,' she says politely, trying to ignore him.

'You're beautiful – do you know that? Where are you going? Need a lift?'

'We're fine walking.'

His passenger, sat in the front seat of the car, leans over. 'Where's your mate from? Speak any English, does she?' Then, leaning back to his friend sniggering at the wheel, he mock-whispers, 'They're everywhere, that lot. Can't swing a cat without hitting one, or having one try and blow you up.'

'Shut up!' Jessica screams at him. 'How DARE you? How DARE you!' She swings towards the car and starts walking into the road towards them.

'All right, love!' says the driver, laughing. 'He's only joking. We love a curry as much as the next bloke, don't we, Dave?' Jessica is shaking with rage, and I'm doing everything I can to hold on to her, to stop her marching into the middle of the road and smashing their car with her fists. Because this is what Jessica does; what Jess has always done. Been my defender. My protector. The Lancelot to my Guinevere – which is ironic given she's the one that looks like a medieval queen.

171

But despite the severity of the situation, all I can think about is my stupid tiny skirt, my PE knickers on display every five seconds as another car drives past, creating a breeze.

'I look like a terrorist? That's the best you've got? It's hardly original, is it? You look like a geriatric baboon's backside. Now that's original,' I say, holding tight to Jessica, as she tries to extricate herself from my grip.

'A baboon's backside?' she says, looking at me, her eyebrows knitted. 'Oh my God. He does! All tight and pinched and pink!' And then we both start cackling. Manically, hysterically, falling over each other, doubled over with laughter. And as the cars behind start beeping their horns, with a couple of cursory swear words, Tweedle-dum and Tweedle-dumber are gone.

'Baboon's ... back ... side ...' Jessica says between guffaws.

'Tight ... and pinched ... and pink ...' I stammer between mouthfuls of laughter.

And even though I'm not shaking or sweating with fear, because for me their words are just an ordinary, everyday occurrence, in between the laughs, my heart feels a little heavier.

'Just another day in paradise,' I say sarcastically, as we both start calming down.

'Baboon's ... back ... side,' she says giggling.

And that's it. We're off again.

26

A Girl Called Ellie

My name is Ellie. Ellie Pillai. I'm small, with dark hair and dark eyes. Insignificant, inconsequential. You might see my colour before you see me. You might assume I'm clever, good at maths and science, but I'm not. I like music, and drama, and English. The woolly subjects my mother says will get me nowhere. My name is Ellie. Ellie Pillai. But who am I really?

27

Aaron Green Is a Boy
Who Is Mean

It's three thirty and the bell is ringing to mark the end of the day. I've spent the afternoon scribbling – *'Won't you love me?' she cried out to the man in the yellow mac* – all over my history essay, which is supposed to be about the Tudors, a time well before yellow macs were even a thing. I can't focus. Because this day alone has been more eventful than the entire four years that preceded it.

'So, what was going on with you and Jessica's boyfriend this morning?' James asks, as we stand outside the studio, waiting for Hayley.

'He's not her boyfriend.' Sugar Mice Nipples.

'Her friend with benefits then.'

'Shut up, James.'

'Well . . . what was going on with you and the boy Jessica spends most of her time with then?'

'Nothing. Are Andy, David and Lauren coming?'

'Not a discreet subject change, Pillai. David and Lauren said you could figure it out on your own – they seemed pretty nervous about whether you could do it for the exam, though.'

Blonde moustache. Blonde moustache. Blonde moustache.

'Personally, I think you'll be fine.'

I look at him and try not to be impressed at how confident he is, when I can't even guarantee that myself.

'You will, you know. Be fine. Confidence, Pillai. Stop underestimating yourself.'

Why is he being normal? Nice even.

'And Andy can't make it. He's got basketball practice.'

'So, why are *you* here then?' I ask, watching him closely. Because I'm starting to get the impression he enjoys these rows with Hayley.

'It's not for Hayley to decide what we do or don't do. We're all entitled to an opinion.'

'Are you talking about me?' Hayley asks innocently.

What is it with people appearing out of nowhere? Either I am completely unobservant or there really are witches in this school.

'I never said it was up to me to decide, I just said we don't have time to argue,' she says coolly.

'Let's get on with it then,' he says irritably.

We walk into the studio, and Mrs Aachara is stood with Ash, surveying the sad excuse for a balcony Year 8 are using for *Romeo and Juliet*. I turn away and try to pretend I can breathe. I wonder how covertly I can put my head between my legs and breathe into a paper bag.

'Hi, Ellie. Hayley. James,' she says nodding. 'Do you need to talk to me?'

'We wanted to use the studio to talk about the play,' Hayley says, all confidence in the face of all things.

'As long as you don't mind Ash and me painting, that's fine,' says Mrs Aachara, looking distractedly at the pile of papier-mâché.

I try to focus on the conversation with Hayley and James, but all they seem to do is bicker. Hayley thinks we should focus on one song, the one I played earlier, and create vignettes and varying refrains of it throughout the play; something we keep coming back to, that ties it all together. James thinks we should make it into a musical, that I should be writing songs for all of the characters, but that was never my intention. The music was never supposed to be a focus, just a soundtrack, something in the background.

'Not everyone can sing, James,' says Hayley. 'Just because we're drama students, doesn't mean we can actually sing. Ellie can sing, but we're all going to sound pretty crap next to her, aren't we? So why are you so determined to push something that isn't going to work? Not in any possible way.'

I'm bored of this conversation now, bored of pretending I care.

'James,' I say. 'It's a great idea, honestly.' Hayley shoots me a look that is most definitely murderous in intent. 'But we just don't have time to create anything more complex. We can be thematic with the song, make it feel different in different refrains, but it's going to be hard enough to do that by itself, without the need for adding anything more. I think the rest of the group would agree, it's just too ambitious.'

He sighs, annoyed he's being cornered.

'I'm going to the toilet,' says Hayley, clearly as bored of the conversation as I am, and no longer hiding it well.

'James,' I say gently, as soon as she's out of earshot. 'You know she's right.'

'Whatever. I just hate that she has to be right about *everything*. She's so . . . self-righteous, such a know-it-all,' he says dejectedly.

Pot calling kettle, come in, kettle . . .

I watch him carefully.

'You like her, don't you?'

'She's infuriating,' he retorts.

'I mean, you *like* her, don't you?' He looks annoyed.

'I don't know. I mean, she's just different, isn't she? There isn't anyone quite like her.'

'There isn't,' I say, thinking how nice it is that being different seems somehow in favour with him, a good thing. I'm warming to James now I'm getting to know him. Starting to see that maybe I'm the one that's been wrong all this time, assuming, judging, thinking everyone fitted into nice, neat little boxes.

There's a sudden peal of laughter from the corner of the room, and I look up to see Ash and Mrs Aachara, his hand on her arm, her head thrown back, the most glorious cackle issuing from her mouth. There's an intimacy to their conversation I'm starting to find uncomfortable – and then I remember he was here before, volunteering to help out with the prop cupboard, his kindness taking on another, more sinister agenda.

I can feel the acid rising in my stomach – because I thought *my* moral compass was off, but he's flirting with a teacher, so he wins. His moral compass is pointed in entirely the wrong direction.

'Are you OK?' Hayley asks, throwing herself down next to me. 'You look really pale.'

'I'm fine.' But I'm not. I am decidedly un-fine.

'Everything OK?' Mrs Aachara asks, turning to us. 'Does anyone need a lift home?'

'NO!' I shout. Except there's no need to shout. Because there are five of us, and we're stood approximately a metre apart in a largely silent room.

Ash is staring at me, and all I want to do is scream, 'YOUR COMPASS IS BROKEN,' while the chorus to 'Green Light' plays on repeat in my head.

'I think it's time all of us went home,' Mrs Aachara murmurs, clutching at her forehead. 'These paint fumes are going to my head.'

Hayley turns to me, as I watch Ash put his earphones in and disappear down the corridor.

'Mum's working late, E, so I can get a lift if I'm quick. You sure you're OK?'

'I'm fine. See you tomorrow, Hay.'

'About earlier . . .' James whispers as she walks away. 'You know, about Hayley . . . Don't mention it to her, OK?'

I nod.

'It's not a secret or anything. I just want to ask her out in my own time. When she's being less annoying.'

And while I'm pleased he feels comfortable enough to share

this with me, I'm not entirely sure he's going to get the answer he wants from her.

I leave Mrs Aachara putting the last of the paint away, and walk to the bathroom to wash my face. In this light, it's like I've stolen my mother's face. I stand for a while and stare at myself: Narcissus in reverse.

Then I walk silently into the playground. No soundtrack, just my thoughts, tumbling and knotty. I can see Mrs Aachara's little red car, the last one still parked at the school, right in the corner by the basketball courts.

And inside I see her. Her tiny, birdlike frame, lit up against the darkness, her head turned to the side. Resting against Ash's shoulder.

Ash's shoulder.

As I sit on the bus, I hope against all hope that I was hallucinating. That the paint fumes really did go to our heads, and somewhere James is seeing ponies, and Hayley is part of a sixties girl group. How could Mrs Aachara do that? She's a teacher. He's seventeen. And he kissed me. And Jessica. And probably Hayley and Miss Hartley, and Billy and Addy McQueen too. In fact, is there anyone, in the entire universe, that Ash Anderson hasn't kissed? And what am I going to *do* about what I saw? Who do I tell?

This is what happens when your moral compass is broken.

I can feel a song forming. Somewhere so deep down, only I can see it. Because when your heart breaks, the notes stick it back together again, like so much paper and glue.

And I remember Aaron Green – the Year 12 version of Jessica – who told me I was pretty, and who I spent two hours kissing at his brother's party, and then the next day, he pretended he didn't even know my name. So, I wrote 'Aaron Green Is a Boy Who Is Mean' – and I love that song. Even though no one will ever hear it, because apparently I can only sing to the back of people's heads, in rooms with fewer than six people in, and Aaron Green will never admit he has met me, or even knows me – despite spending three years going to the same piano teacher as me (and yes, he was one of the 'special' pupils she continued to teach after she *retired*).

Ugh.

And suddenly the words are writing themselves in my head. And as much as I hate him right now – Ash, not Aaron Green (although on second thoughts, maybe I hate him too) – I have to say, this one feels like something special.

♡ Song 4 ♡

Intro, Verse, Chorus, Middle 8 – No Fairy Tale

It's got the energy of a pop song, with the heart of a ballad. A song about how we disappear and reappear again, how we can make ourselves as big or as small as we choose to.

Did you ever feel so small
You wonder if you're really there at all?

But as much as I hope someone is going to save me, I know the only person who really can – is me. So I don't want to wait around, hoping that feeling goes away. That feeling of not belonging to anyone, or anything, of being something 'other' that doesn't really count. I have to stand up, and fall down, and get things wrong, over and over again, until getting things wrong becomes learning how to get things right.

Wake up with your sword in hand
Cos you're the hero of this land

28

Mum

I can't avoid Mum forever, but, portentously, she's gone to bed by the time I arrive home in the early evening. Dad is saying little, but resembles a thundercloud as he walks around the kitchen, darkly muttering under his breath. I can't make out much of what he's trying to say, but I know it isn't good. He's pacing, never a good sign, and his Sri Lankan accent, which seems to get stronger whenever he's annoyed or about to tell me off, is almost merging into Tamil, an entirely different language.

'You need to talk to her, Ellie. I haven't seen her like this in a long time. Not since . . . well, not for a long time. I don't know what's going on between you two, but she's not herself, she's not coping. Do you remember what it was like before, what she was like before?'

But how could I forget? The crying jags, the days of silence followed by the flurries of activity, moments of intensity so bright they can still burn me.

'This needs to stop, Ellie. You have to talk to her. You need to talk to her,' he finishes, looking at me closely.

'I miss him too, Dad.' I don't know why I say it. Maybe because it's underneath the surface of everything, always so close.

'I know,' he says slowly. And he's holding it all back, holding it all in. 'Me too.' He hugs me tightly, murmuring into my hair. 'She loves you so much, Ellie. Maybe she doesn't always know how to show it the way you want her to, but the world your mother grew up in, it wasn't like this world. Your grandparents, they were difficult people, Ellie. They didn't mean to be unkind, but they had no interest in your mother.'

'What do you mean?' I ask quietly.

'Not all parents want their children, Ellie.'

'So, they didn't love her?' I whisper.

'It's complicated, *sina pillai*. I'm sure they loved her in their own way, but not in the way we think about love. And I know sometimes you think she doesn't love you,' he continues, 'or that I don't love you, because we don't always know how to say the right things. But in our world, you don't cry over things. You get up and you move on with life, and it isn't always the best way, but it's the way we were taught. Maybe we didn't show you enough that we love you, that we need you – but you're our everything, Ellie. Your mother, just, well, she's a person of routine, and structure, that's how she shows love.'

And I know all of this. I do know. I do know Mum is Mum, and that she loves me. But I never feel like I'm enough for her. I never feel like I'm quite enough for myself.

'I'll talk to her, Dad. I promise.' I hug him and feel a tear working its way through my hair. A tear from my stoic, kind Dad. And I go to bed, wishing that life was simpler, that wondering if anyone was going to ask me to the winter dance was still my biggest concern in life. And Ash and Jessica, and all the drama at school feels so small now. Because it is so small. Because home, and family, and real life, and *me*, is what really matters. Being enough for *me*.

And all I can think, as I drift off to sleep, is MUST TRY HARDER. Because life is short, and I know that better than anyone.

There is no time to waste.

The next morning, the house is quiet as I walk down the stairs ready for school. It's the last day before half term, and all I want is for this day to be over.

When I walk into the kitchen, it's empty, no sign of either of my parents. Dad's coat is missing from its usual spot on the bannister, but Mum's leather jacket is hung up under the stairs.

I walk up the stairs quietly, and desperately will for her to be out, but their bedroom door is ajar, the room dark and dank, the hint of a shape beneath the covers. For some reason, I walk straight in. I ignore the shape and walk directly to the window, yanking the blinds open, light flooding the room.

I watch as the shape begins to writhe, to register the daylight, for the discomfort to set in. And despite my assurances to my father that I'll be kind, that I'll talk to her, that I'll try to help, I find myself harsh, brash, brutal.

'Get up. I need a lift to school. Mum. Mum!'

'What is it, what do you need?' comes the slow, sleepy voice from under the covers.

'I need a lift to school. Get up!'

'OK, OK!' the voice replies, and the edges of it, which seemed blurred and indistinct, seem suddenly to sharpen and come into focus. 'What time is it?' she asks sleepily.

'It's 8.05, so you need to get up. Now.'

She pushes the duvet back violently.

'It's late,' she says, rubbing her eyes and pushing herself to the edge of the bed. 'I need to get to work. Can't you take the bus?'

'Dad phoned in sick for you,' I plead knowing my father has done so, knowing he's left her to sleep and rest and think. But I guess I'm not so unlike my mother after all. Life goes on. Structure and routine is how she shows her love, and so perhaps structure and routine is just what she needs, to be shown love.

'It's time to get up, Mum,' I say more gently this time. 'I need you.'

She turns to look at me, her hands clawing at the side of the mattress.

'I'm here,' she says, her hands loosening their grip on the bed. 'I'm here.' And this time, one of those hands is letting go, and taking mine firmly in its grip.

'I'm here, Ellie.'

And for the first time in a long time, I believe her.

29

When East Meets East

We're in the car on the way to school. Little has been said, but something seems to have shifted. Despite her fragile state, Mum has managed, in just twenty minutes, to pull herself together. She's wearing delicate black harem trousers, off-white brogues, a white shirt and her oxblood silk bomber, looking every inch the style icon, with her hair pulled back and a lipstick to match her jacket.

At the wheel, she's back in charge. Every so often, she takes her hand off the gear stick and places it on my leg. It's a tiny gesture, but for us, it's huge.

'So,' she says, 'how are things going at school?' It's such a simple, innocuous question, but the answer feels so complicated, I don't even know where to start.

'Fine,' I say, shrugging. She gives me her very best side eye. The one that asks more, without asking more.

'Well,' I volunteer, 'Jess had this new boyfriend.'

'Had?' she queries, eyes on the road.

'That day she came over, when she was upset – they'd broken up.

I'm not sure what happened. But anyway, when they were going out, she started ignoring me. And it was horrible. Because I thought she was my best friend, and best friends don't do that, do they?'

'You know . . .' she says, and I wait for her to tell me what I should have done differently, 'sometimes, your best friend needs to be you.'

'Meaning?' I ask tetchily.

'It means, I know Jessica is important to you – but you need to trust your own instincts, Ellie. Be your own person.'

I sit silently, trying to understand how to piece that statement together without getting annoyed.

'I just worry you compare yourself to other people too much. You don't see how special you are. How *you* you are. We all need good friends, even best ones, but we need to be a friend to ourselves too, and realise we're enough on our own.'

I nod, trying to take it all in.

'Is there anything else you want to talk about?' she asks in her Therapy Voice.

'You know I told you about her boyfriend?' I stammer.

'Yesssssss,' she says, side-eyeing me again.

'Something . . . happened between us.'

She swerves suddenly.

'Not when they were going out,' I say pointedly. 'I would never do that.'

'What happened?' she asks, panicked. 'Did you use protection, Ellie? Because you should never, never do anything, without protection. Have you seen a GP? I'm happy to take you to see Dr

188

Martin . . . But I still think you're too young, and I hope you didn't feel pressured . . .'

'Mum, no! Stop talking, please. It was just a kiss. Ugh. Gross.'

She exhales loudly, like every breath she's taken in for the past fifteen years has suddenly and involuntarily been expelled.

'Sex isn't gross, Ellie. Not with someone you love.'

I. Want. To. Die. Because I know sex isn't gross. Well, technically I don't. But talking about it with my mother definitely is.

'Oh God, please, Mum. Never say sex again.'

She rolls her eyes.

'So, you like him?'

'He's Jessica's ex-boyfriend and I'm pretty sure she still has feelings for him, so, no . . .'

'That doesn't really answer my question,' she says sneakily. 'You know, I don't think I've ever heard you talking about a boy before, Ellie. It's nice. Why shouldn't you have some romance in your life?'

'Yuck. Mum, please! You make it sound so . . .'

'Nice?'

'Embarrassing.'

'Well, it isn't. It isn't embarrassing to like someone. It's a very healthy, very normal emotion.'

'Right, thanks.'

'And how's school going? Did you speak to Mr Gorley about Dad and me coming in to see him?'

I huff quietly, hoping if I refuse to reply, she'll forget she said anything.

It works.

But when we arrive at the gates, the universe has other ideas. Mrs Aachara, stood by the reception doors, suddenly locks eyes with me and begins a swift, determined walk across the playground. I slide frantically down in my seat, hoping there's someone behind us. Someone more interesting she's coming to talk to, like Aaron Green the day after his brother's party. I still despise Aaron Green.

'Mrs Pillai?' she says, reaching the car slightly out of breath and leaning into the window of Mum's vintage Mini Cooper (because my mother is a hipster, and yes, the irony of my lack of hipness has not gone unnoticed by either me, or anyone with eyes who has ever met us).

I slump in the passenger seat.

'I'm Mrs Aachara.'

This. Is. Not. Happening.

'Mrs Aachara is new to the school,' I manage awkwardly.

'I'm replacing Mr Grange,' she says, as if that explains everything. 'It was just for a term, but I heard this morning he's going to take a sabbatical for the rest of the year. Let his skin heal up.'

'Right,' says Mum, looking appalled.

'I heard he grew scales,' I say, jumping in again.

'I think that was an exaggeration, Ellie,' she says, and then, to Mum, 'Playground talk. Although he has been very unwell with it. Stress-related apparently – hence the sabbatical. Between you and me, I think he's looking at other career opportunities.'

'I'm sorry,' Mum says, looking at her. 'Who are you again?'

'Well, she's not the careers counsellor,' I say hysterically. 'The last time I saw the careers counsellor, they said I should be a fish farmer! Maybe Mr Grange should be a fish farmer. Fish are very relaxing.'

Fish therapy? The man in the yellow mac with a fish? Fish as a way to increase dramatic tension? What else can I talk about? What else is there to say about fish?

Mrs Aachara and Mum stare at me.

'Oh, look at the time ... you're going to be late, miss!' I exaggeratedly mime checking my non-existent wrist watch.

'Oh,' she says, checking the real thing. 'You're right. It was lovely to meet you, Mrs Pillai. I look forward to speaking with you more another time. You'd better run too, Ellie.'

'Pleasure,' says Mum, her voice registering the exact opposite of the sentiment.

As she walks away, Mum turns to face me.

'What a strange woman. Why on earth would she think I would care that Mr Grange has a skin condition?'

'No idea. Very, erm, odd,' I say, starting to sweat.

Sweat: to perspire, especially freely or profusely.

Mum stares at me.

'She's really weird,' I say for additional effect. 'Everyone says so.' And even though I really don't like Mrs Aachara very much in this moment, I still feel disloyal for saying anything other than the actual truth. Which is, she might think it's appropriate to put her head on the shoulder of a Year 13 boy, in her car, in the dead of night (OK, 6 p.m.), but she's the best teacher I've ever had. That any of us has ever had.

But I can't let Mum know the truth. We've been trying so hard to get along. I have no idea how she'd react if she knew about the Lie. My hunch is: not well. Not very well at all.

'You know, I got an email from St Hilda's yesterday. One of the girls is moving. They have a place available next term. What do you think? No more weird teachers . . .' she says, half laughing. But her eyes – her eyes look serious.

'I don't want to move schools, Mum.'

She looks at me, her mouth set in a line, struggling not to tell me all the reasons St Hilda's School for Girls Who Must Be Watched is better than Bridgewood.

'Well, I hope she's better than Mr Grange,' she jokes. 'That terrible play in Year 9 . . .' Translation: I was a disaster in Mr Grange's terrible play in Year 9. 'Not that it matters to you any more,' she says, ruffling my hair.

Dear God, High School God I mean. That benevolent being that you are. That stops me from having my clothes stolen on the odd occasion I'm forced to go swimming. Can you help me out a bit here?

'You'd better go, Ellie. I need to get to work and you're going to be late.'

Thank you, High School God. And for a second, my brain starts playing *Grease*, 'Beauty School Drop-out'. And I imagine I'm Frenchie, cavorting with some angelic being dressed in a yellow rain mac, telling me I'm not going to pass my exams.

Great. Thanks, angelic being. Good to know even you think there'll be no graduation day for me.

'I'm glad I could drive you in today, Ellie. It was nice. Perhaps we could do it more often. I don't always need to be at work so early.'

'I'd like that,' I say, smiling at her. And at the same time as feeling happy that she's finally trying to see me, I hate myself for lying to her. And the idea of what's going to come next. All this good work coming undone when she finds out not only did I lie about my GCSE options, but I might not even get a passable grade.

Dear gods (any of them).

Please send help.

30

The Inappropriate
Shoulder Moment

All morning, I've been trying to work out how I'm going to face Mrs Aachara again. I hope that maths will never end, which is a feeling I've had exactly never in my life before. I drag myself out of my seat and even consider asking Mr Potts some questions in order to slow my departure, then watch as he sprays an unsuspecting Jeffrey Dean with saliva while explaining the law of indices, and decide this is not the best plan.

I walk, or possibly shuffle, as slowly as possible to the studio, and stand at the back of the line, not thinking about the Inappropriate Shoulder Moment, apart from thinking about it almost continuously.

'Ellie – over here!' says Hayley, waving at me from across the room.

And this is the moment my invisibility would once have been useful. But no, I have to choose today, now, to start being seen. To start singing in front of (well, behind of) people, so they notice/care where I am in a lesson.

'Ellie, James and I had a great session after school yesterday,' Hayley is saying bossily as I drift over, attempting to avoid Mrs Aachara. 'We've decided that Ellie's going to rewrite the song during half term, so she can start breaking it down into different refrains for different characters throughout the play. It's going to be called "Katja's Song".'

Hayley is of course playing Katja, while I'm a friend from Sarajevo, who handily has very little stage time, so can focus on creating the music offstage. The idea is that the song, while being about Katja, could also be about any character in the play.

'Are you going to be OK doing that, Ellie?' asks Andy. 'Because if we're going to add anything in, we just want to make sure you feel . . . totally comfortable with it . . .'

'She'll be fine,' says James without so much as a look in my direction.

And this time, not only do I want to believe him, but I do. Because I need to be. I have to be.

'In the end, we just felt it would be too complex, too ambitious to try and create more songs, and it makes sense to keep it as a background refrain, something designed to help it all hang together,' James continues. Hayley and I look at each other incredulously.

With agreement from the group, we move on to look at the scene where Katja meets her brother Arthur for the first time. Arthur has just found out his father had an affair while working for an NGO in Sarajevo, and Katja is his half-sister. James is playing Arthur with the perfect mix of disbelief, confusion and joy. Angry at his father's lies, worried for his mother's mental health, but curious about this new person, this sister that means he's no longer alone in the world. But Katja, feeling rejected, is angry, lost, ready to run.

At just this moment, Mrs Aachara joins the group and watches as the scene plays out. Even I have to admit that James can act. Like Hollywood-level, Oscar-some-day act. For all his posturing, all his swagger, he can truly inhabit someone else's words.

When the scene ends, we all clap, impressed. 'Great work!' says Mrs Aachara. 'Hayley, the writing has really sharpened up since we spoke yesterday, and James, that was a well-rounded, relatable performance. Well done.' He beams.

I blank my mind and try not to catch Mrs Aachara's eye, but it's almost as though she senses my discomfort, my eyes to the ground, avoiding her.

'How are you doing with integrating your song, Ellie? I had some ideas about where to add the initial refrain. Do you want to talk about it now, or are you still in the middle of workshopping?' She looks so earnest, so genuine, that I can't help but feel my heart push out to her.

'We're fine – I think we have it all figured out.' I'm curt to the point of rudeness.

'No, we don't, Ellie, nowhere near,' says Hayley, looking at me like I've been replaced by a girl with a giant panda head. She's side-eyeing me, like Mum's been giving her lessons on the best ways to unnerve me.

'I don't think we need a teacher to tell us how to do it, Hayley. I think we need to be original, work it out for ourselves.'

'Don't see me as a teacher,' Mrs Aachara says gently. 'Think of me as a director, a fellow artist.'

'But you're not,' I say bluntly. 'You're a substitute teacher.'

'Ellie!' hisses Hayley, and all I can see is James, his brows arched into his hairline, a grim, disappointed look on his face.

'That's OK,' says Mrs Aachara, smiling thinly. 'I know this is a stressful time of year. Exams, half term. It's probably best you get on with it anyway. You know where I am if you need me.'

'Ellie,' Hayley hisses again. 'Toilets. Now!' She marches me towards the girls' bathroom with all the fervour of a soldier marching a traitor to the firing line, and pushes me roughly inside.

'What's going on with you? I know stuff with Jessica has been difficult, but I cannot understand what the hell is wrong with you today. You've been in a foul mood ever since you walked in. The way you spoke to Mrs A just now was rude and embarrassing. After everything she's done for us.'

'She hasn't done anything, Hayley. She's a teacher. She's doing her job.'

'She's given every group two extra hours every week, E. That's her own time.'

'Well, maybe she likes spending time with students a bit too much.'

'What are you getting at, Ellie?' she says, frustrated.

I turn away from her, my shoulders low.

'Oh, E, what is going on with you?' she asks more gently, enveloping me into our tall girl, small girl embrace.

'I don't know, Hay.' I give into the feeling of comfort, of being held.

'I'm just an idiot.' I want to tell her so much that the words are lodged in my throat, a primal scream in need of release – bring on the man in the yellow mac.

'You're not an idiot. Come on. There's something you're not telling me. Talk.'

Say it.

Just say it!

'I think Mrs Aachara is having an affair with one of the students,' I announce. 'I've seen some things that have made me suspicious. Some things that just don't feel right.'

'Ellie, that's huge,' Hayley says, looking shocked. 'Are you sure? What is it that you've seen?'

'All these strange, flirty little moments – and then, last night, I saw them together in her car. And they were touching.'

'Touching?' she says, horrified.

'Well, her head was on his shoulder.'

'That's less exciting . . .'

'Hayley! It's still inappropriate.'

'So, who is it then?'

I exhale deeply and swallow down the razor blades in my throat.

'His name is Ash, he's new this year – he's in Year 13.'

At this, her face changes, relief breaking out in tiny stitch-like lines.

'As in Ash and Elina? The twins?' She's looking at me curiously, almost through me, the corners of her mouth twitching upwards.

'Yes,' I say, feeling unexpectedly stupid. Why is she smiling, why is this suddenly a joke?

'Ellie. He's her son. They're her kids.' And instantly, it's like I can't breathe.

'They can't be. I mean, they can't be. They don't have the same surname. And they're not Indian, are they? ARE they? I don't understand. How do you know that, what do you mean?' The words are tumbling out now, falling over each other, desperate to get out and justify my huge, ridiculous, overblown statement.

'Ellie, they're mixed race. Their dad was white, from Manchester or Liverpool I think, but they all lived in London. Mrs A kept her name for work, but they have their dad's surname. Mum says it was really sad, he died really suddenly, after a short illness, about a year ago. This is her first job since it happened. She was head of drama at some private school in London – but she wanted to get out of the city. Somewhere quieter. She has friends here, that's why they came. Mum said we're really lucky to have her – she works with the National Youth Theatre. Anyway, Ash and Elina are always in the staff room in the mornings – all the teachers get in early to prep, so I've kind of got to know them. They're nice.' At this she stops and looks at me, finally registering the expression on my face. 'Ellie, why on earth would you think Mrs Aachara would do that?'

Oh GOD. What have I been thinking? What have I been *saying*? I have completely, utterly and totally lost control of my senses.

'I don't know . . .' I'm considering having a panic attack, or fainting. I don't know which yet. But surely I should have some kind of reaction to this. Something melodramatic, in line with the soap opera I've evidently just written in my head.

'I just kept seeing them together, and he always seemed so . . . overfamiliar.' It sounds so stupid now. I can even see it. The family resemblance. The intonation in their voices, the perpetual year-round tan. I clutch my head in my hands and sink to the floor.

'Come on, E, it's not that bad. It's not as if they walk around with their personal information printed on their jackets. It's an easy mistake to make. Don't beat yourself up.'

I can't believe how rude I've been to Mrs Aachara. How ungrateful. Over a Completely Appropriate Shoulder Moment with Her Very Own Son.

Her son.

Note to self. Do not watch soap operas. Or scripted reality TV.

31

The Best (at Getting Things Wrong)

At the end of class I approach Mrs Aachara tentatively.

'Excuse me, miss. I was hoping I could talk to you for a minute.'

'Of course, Ellie. Is everything all right? You don't seem quite yourself today.' Understatement.

Huge.

'I'm really sorry, miss. I was incredibly rude to you just now. You've been nothing but kind to me, and you don't deserve to be spoken to like that.' I sneak a look at her and hope against hope she can sense my sincerity.

'Do you want to sit down, Ellie?' she asks kindly.

'I don't want to get in the way of your lunch, I just wanted to apologise. And to say . . .' and at this, I take a deep breath, 'you've really inspired me. You're an amazing teacher. You've taught me, and all of us, so much . . . but especially me. Having someone like you, so confident, so talented, it makes me believe that things are possible. For me, I mean. So, thank you.'

She smiles.

'It's nice to know I'm making a difference,' she says softly. 'It's been a difficult week. I think I needed to hear that.'

'Is everything OK, miss?' And I'm suddenly aware that last night, backlit in her tiny red car, she looked tinier, and sadder, than ever.

'I probably shouldn't be talking about this with a student, but I like you, Ellie. I'm sure we'll be great friends one day.' She smiles again, and tucks a lock of wavy hair behind her ear. 'My husband died a year ago, and it's just been one of those weeks. I'm still trying to adjust to my life without him, and sometimes it feels like I'm never going to get there.' Her voice rises, and the tears I know she's fighting, the ones that are trying so hard to choke her, seem almost to get the better of her, until she shakes them off, a veritable Taylor Swift. '*But*,' she says rallying, 'I'll be fine. And having someone say something lovely to you always helps.' At this, she beams, her smile beatific, bestowed upon me like a crown.

'Can I do anything to help?'

'Well, actually,' she says, all crafty delight, 'I was hoping we could arrange some time over the half term for you to come in and talk to me about "Katja's Song", and how it's going to work with the play. I have some tips, which despite,' and with this, her eyes sparkle, 'being a mere substitute teacher, I think may really help. Also, if you aren't studying for the whole holiday, I'd love to get a couple of hours of your time to help sort out the props cupboard.'

'When do you need me?'

'Thursday ideally, about midday.'

'I'll see you then.' And with that, it's lunchtime, and the rest of the day passes in a blur.

End of school.

Friday.

Half-term holidays.

All in that order, all waiting for me.

32

Soundtracks

When I walk through the corridor on my way out of school, I feel on top of the world. I don't know why. It's not like anything's changed. Nothing fundamental, nothing important. But then, somehow, it's like everything's changed. Everything important, everything fundamental. Like the structure of water, and the speed of sound, and the vibration of light is different now – and I don't know why.

I walk slowly, taking my time to march to the beat of my own soundtrack. I've stayed late to pick up some books, and the school is empty and unnaturally quiet. I like it like this, even though I also fear it. Its unknowingness. All I can hear is the sound of my own footsteps clacking against the tiles, familiar and comforting.

But then I hear it, the reedy, distant echo of something far away, but also nearer than it should be. I stop for a moment, aware of the intrusion of the sound, nervous of its origin. I look around. What once seemed quiet and everyday now feels sinister and dark, the prospect of danger lurking in every doorway. My eyes dart around me in a paranoid frenzy. I've seen enough horror movies to know that this is the moment of truth. The moment that the clown, his knife dripping in blood, emerges behind me and stabs me to death, his eyes dark, his laughter hysterical as his red wig bobs up and down with the thrust of his knife.

I'm wearing the worst underwear to be murdered in. Oversized black pants that look like they were built for my granny. Surely I am not the type to get murdered in an empty school corridor, my unflattering underwear left on display as a final adieu to high school life. Surely that sort of thing only happens to good-looking, blonde cheerleader types. Surely one of the only upsides to high school invisibility is not being visible enough to become the target of a clown serial killer.

I attempt deep breathing. I am calm. I am centred. I have nothing to fear except fear itself, and a random, one-off clown serial killer attack in England's smallest, sleepiest city. Just as I'm beginning to feel the urge to run, my eyes follow my ears to the sound – and in one of the classrooms, just off the main corridor, I see Ash, sitting on a desk, his feet balanced on a chair beneath him. His shoulders are hunched, his face turned away from the light, his earphones pumping out the reedy echo which moments before I had mistaken for evidence of a clown assassin.

I don't want to go to him, but I can't help myself. He looks so sad, so misplaced. And I realise he lost his dad a year ago. And I remember the hole. The one that loss leaves. The one that can never be filled, never even be papered over, but will always be there, gaping and open, exposed to the world.

I walk over to him and place my hand on his shoulder. He looks up at me, startled, and says nothing. Offers no words of explanation or apology, just looks at me, into me. A silent exchange. He takes one earphone out and offers it to me, moving over to make space for me on the desk. I sit down and place it in my ear: and the sound of Nirvana, 'Something in the Way' sears a hole in my heart. It's that low, quiet guitar, raw on the strings, like a heart disintegrating.

He reaches over and takes my hand in his, and we just sit there, silently. At the end of the song, I take the earphone out and hand it back to him, gently withdrawing my hand from his. He doesn't even look at me, just replaces the earphone and continues staring ahead. I want to walk away, but the change in elements is pulling me back. So I let it. I turn and walk back to him, and kiss him softly on the cheek. And all I want is to tell him it's going to be OK, to stay next to him until the feeling passes. But I can't. So I walk away from him, feeling his eyes fixed on the back of my head, waiting for me to look back.

But I don't.

Even though I wish. I wish that I could.

33

Two Angry Tamils

'ELEANOR EVE PILLAI. GET IN HERE, RIGHT THIS INSTANT.'

The sound of Dad's voice comes booming down the hall at me, the moment I step in the house. This is so, not, a good look.

'Hi . . .' I say quietly, as I enter the front room. Mum's sat on the sofa while Dad paces up and down in front of her.

'Where have you been?' he demands.

'At the library, taking out some books . . .' I respond weakly.

'And why should we believe that?' he says, his eyes flashing.

'Because it's true,' I reply, my voice rising.

He starts laughing, and it sounds frenetic, like he's the villain in some Marvel superhero movie.

'I'm just so disappointed, Ellie. I can't believe this. I can't believe you would lie to us like this.' He's looking at me like he's about to start crying, and my heart is literally in my mouth.

It's happening. This is officially happening.

'I called the school, Ellie,' Mum says quietly. 'I spoke to Mr Gorley. To try and get that parent–teacher meeting in? He told me not to worry about your drama mock. He said Mrs Aachara said you were showing promise, that she thought you were going to do much, much better than the 2 you got at the end of last year. I thought I must have heard him wrong. I thought he'd made a mistake. But that woman. That woman from this morning. She's your teacher, isn't she? You're taking drama, and you've been lying about it, all this time.'

The pitch of her voice has been rising with every word, the quiet anger now closer to a scream.

'I . . .' I stutter.

'You lied to us, Ellie. If you can lie about this, what else are you hiding?' she says hysterically.

'Mum, you don't understand, I . . .'

'I understand,' she says, her eyes flashing. 'Sit down.'

I sit on the sofa opposite the two of them, and watch them, like the jury in *Twelve Angry Men*, except it's Two Angry Tamils, and I am nowhere near as persuasive as Henry Ford. And then I start hearing the music, with its heavy crescendo, and it's like the old cinema ad is playing. People screaming about lives being at stake while jurors argue about possibilities and impossibilities. I want to tell them they don't understand. That none of those points mean anything.

I'm going down.

'A 2, Ellie. A 2?' Mum shrieks. 'How's that going to look on your CV? What opportunities do you think failing drama is going to give you in life? This would never have happened at St Hilda's. Never. The teachers would have kept us far more informed.'

'Maybe you're the one that needs to be more informed,' I mutter angrily.

'What did you say?' Dad thunders.

I look straight at him, unable to hide the fury in my voice.

'Maybe if you showed the *slightest* interest in anything I actually care about.'

'Subjects you're going to fail, you mean.' Mum glares at me.

And something about the word 'fail' tips the fear I've been feeling into something else. Something powerful.

'I am not,' I seethe, 'going to fail at this.'

'Well, your mock grade says otherwise, Ellie. I told you, don't waste your time on things you're just not good at,' Mum says cuttingly.

'Are we in the same room?' I shout. 'Did you not just tell me that Mrs Aachara said I was going to do MUCH BETTER than my mock? Did you hear that, or did you not?' I hiss.

'Well . . .' Dad says unsurely. 'Is that what Mr Gorley said, Nimi?'

'That's not the point,' Mum shouts. 'You lied to us. For a year and a half, you've lied to us. I'm calling St Hilda's in the morning, Ellie. It's time we took control of this.'

'Control? All you do is control me! Because you don't want to hear the truth,' I scream. 'You never do. So I just tell you what you want to hear, because I'm not allowed to have an opinion, am I? I'm not allowed to do something I care about, am I? I'm not allowed to disagree with you, am I?' I'm panting now, my voice coming out in thick, heavy gulps.

'So, I wanted to do drama. You were never going to let me do it.

And I've worked really hard at it. I've worked really hard to get better. And Mrs Aachara says I have. She says I'm special. She says I have talent. And you know what, Mum, maybe I do. Maybe you just don't believe that's possible. Maybe you just don't believe in me. But I have to believe in myself. Isn't that what you told me this morning? That I need to trust my instincts? Or is that just when they're the same as yours? When they're what you want?'

Mum's looking at me, shocked and angry, and sad, and I don't know. Something else.

'Ellie, if you wanted to do it so much, you should have talked to us,' Dad says more calmly. 'You shouldn't have lied. Can't you see that?'

'And can't you see that I didn't have a choice? Talk to you? Are you joking? Mum didn't talk to me for a year after Amis died. Nobody talked to me. No one ever talks to me about anything. You just talk AT me. Tell me what to do, how to feel, who to be.'

'Ellie, that's not fair,' Mum says, her eyes filling with tears. 'After Amis, I . . . I couldn't . . .'

'You couldn't what? Hug me? Tell me you love me? TALK to me? You can talk to Jessica, though, can't you? You can be there for Jessica, can't you? She's always telling me how great you are, and how lucky I am to have you – but you don't talk to me, do you? You're not there for me, are you? I guess you think I just need to be more "independent". Isn't that what you said? Well, I made an independent decision, and you might not like it, but it was MINE.'

'Ellie,' says Dad, trying to sit next to me. 'That's not . . .' and he's looking at Mum unsurely. 'We're just trying to help you. We have to think about your future.'

'I don't want to think about my future. I want to be fifteen.'

He tries to put his arm around me, but I push him away.

Then I stand up and run to the door. I make my way on to the street and start running.

The dinky pony is back, and this time she definitely feels like a horse.

♡ Song 5 ♡

Intro, Verse, Chorus, Middle 8 – Young

It feels like I've been writing this forever. The chords coming together, piecemeal and stilted, until suddenly it just appears, all staccato anger and pleading, soulful apology.

> *You tell me that I'm young*
> *Too young to know my own mind*

And it's everything I feel. Everything I want to say, in one searing, joyful moment. And this is how songs write themselves. Making sense of nothing. Making screams into harmonies and horn sections.

> *I'm too young to play these games*
> *But I'm not too young to run away*

And suddenly I feel free. Even it's only for four minutes and nineteen seconds.

Run, run, you can fly
And leave this world behind

34

Parklife

Friday night on the east coast of England. I'd like to say it's all glamour, and there are a fair few girls in outrageously tiny skirts and ridiculously high heels, tottering around with bottles of white wine – but LA this is not. The weather, for starters, is a hotch-potch of rain and mist, dark dampness and countryside air, despite the apparent city; and a park near the city centre, not far from the cathedral, becomes the centre of the world, for one night only. This is the place where those of us unable to get into clubs or bars yet gather to hang out, make out, pretend we're hip, part of the conversation. This is our metropolis.

And this is where I run, still in my school clothes, my phone vibrating frenetically in my pocket. Because this is where Jessica is, with all her other friends, the skinny, beautiful Instagram crowd, and I need to talk to her.

When I arrive, there's music playing off a tiny speaker connected to someone's phone, and there are people dancing and drinking, boys doing tricks on skateboards and girls taking photos of each other, filtering pictures ready to upload. This isn't somewhere I usually go, and something about it makes me feel more lost than ever.

'Hi, Ellie.' And when I look up, I see Ash standing there, and something about that makes me feel a little less lost.

'Hi,' I gulp.

'Is everything OK?' he asks, watching me closely.

'Not really.'

'Is this about what happened yesterday?'

'No,' I say bluntly. 'I just need to talk to Jessica.'

'She's here somewhere,' he says, looking around.

And all I want is for everything to stop. For Jess to tell me it's OK, for anyone to tell me it's OK. Or just to forget. He looks at me, his eyes filled with concern.

'Elina!' he shouts at his sister, who it appears is the impromptu DJ in charge of the pavilion speakers. 'Have you seen Jessica?'

She shrugs.

'I have to find her,' I say, walking away. He grabs my arm.

'You're upset,' he states.

'I need to find Jess.'

'Can I do anything?' And he won't let go of me.

I shake my head.

'I just want to forget this day.' I watch as one of the boys behind him swigs from a can of cider.

'Do you have anything to drink?' I ask him quickly. And I don't know what I'm saying – I just know I want to have a good time. I want to be like all these normal people, out on a Friday night, having a drink at the park, not having to lie to their parents for over a year, just because they want to take a subject they actually care about.

'What's wrong?' And for some reason, I want to tell him.

'I had an argument with my parents. I lied about something. It's stupid. They just never trust me to make my own decisions.'

And right on cue, my phone starts vibrating again, as though Mum has a sixth sense I'm talking about her.

'They want to send me away.'

'Away where?'

'To some stupid school where they can control every single thing I say and do and feel. And I have to wear a smock dress, and a hat. My head's too small for hats.'

He smiles.

'So, tell them you don't want to go.'

'Try telling my parents anything.' He opens his mouth to reply, and I cut in. 'Do you have anything to drink, or not?'

'No,' he says, looking away. 'I don't really do that. And neither should you. Not when you're upset.'

'Great,' I reply irately. 'Another person telling me what to do.'

'I'm not telling you what to do. It's just never a good idea to drink when you're upset.'

'You know what – my mum just told me I'm terrible at the one thing I actually care about. And I just want to forget that. I want to pretend I'm not a huge disappointment to her.'

'Then you should go home and talk to her.'

'I told you, my family don't do talking.'

'Listen, Ellie,' he says quietly. 'I used to drink to try and forget things too. Trust me, it doesn't work. You should go home and talk to your parents.'

'Thanks for the advice,' I say curtly. 'But I think I've been patronised by enough people today.'

'I'm not trying to patronise you . . .' he says, frustrated.

'Ellie!' I turn to see Hayley running towards me. 'You're here. You're never here!'

'I am,' I say, plastering on a fake smile.

'Come,' she says, pulling me away. And when I start walking, I can feel his hand, still tugging at my sleeve. I look up at him and repeat the words I have spent a lifetime saying.

'I'm fine,' I state.

He lets go of me and Hayley marches me over to where the drama kids are passing a hip flask around. I have no idea what's inside, but it's warm and fiery and hits the back of my throat like a steam train. We're all laughing, all talking and shouting anecdotes at each other, shifting aimlessly from side to side in an effort to keep from freezing, and all the time I'm looking around for Jessica.

And I don't care that Ash is looking at me disapprovingly. Because I'm having a good time. I, Ellie Pillai, am at the park on a Friday night, and I'm having a good time. And for some reason, people want to talk to me. Maybe because I'm talking to them. Maybe because whatever's in this flask is a little bit magic. And it's reminding me that I'm funny and nice, and good company, and actually it's OK to show that to people. To let people see me.

And when I catch his eye, I smile at him, and he half-smiles back. Because I am perfectly in control of how I'm feeling.

Just as I'm about to start telling the group about the time Mr Grange almost fell over his chair when my mother walked into a Parents' Evening wearing a mini dress, I see James Godfrey, currently installed in the cool kid crowd, begin to break from his group and walk over. It's weird, unnatural, like seeing a dog walk on its hind legs.

'Hey, Ellie,' he says, pushing his way into the circle and standing next to me.

'James,' I say back, slightly tipsy. Hayley looks over, registers James's presence and rolls her eyes accordingly.

'Having a good time?' he asks, looking at Hayley in what I imagine he considers a subtle manner. 'I've never seen you here.' The group he's left are looking over, nudging each other and laughing, and I start to wonder whether I'm the subject of a joke – but the alcohol is taking the edge off my discomfort, and I'm defiant, direct.

'Yeah, I'm good, James. What are you doing? Why are you talking to me?'

'What do you mean, "Why am I talking to you?" We're in lessons together every day, Ellie. Why wouldn't I talk to you?' Suddenly my defiance feels out of place, stupid.

'I don't know, I just mean, I just thought, you know, people like you don't really talk to people like me outside of school.'

He looks at me like I'm a bug under a microscope, one he's considering squashing when he's finished his observations.

'I don't really buy into that kind of thing, Ellie. I would have thought you'd know that about me by now.' And maybe I do know that about him by now. Maybe I just can't admit it. Because admitting it would mean I'd been wrong about everything. That I'd been afraid of nothing.

'Um, I'm not sure if you remember the chest pics you sent Jessica . . . I wouldn't exactly judge you the most enlightened person on the planet after that.'

He laughs and looks embarrassed.

'OK, fair enough. But that was three years ago. We all do stupid things. I mean, I don't even like Jessica any more – she's totally stuck up.' Which annoys me. Because it's a popular misconception that Jess is arrogant or thinks she's better than other people. She's the opposite of that. She's a beautiful, smart, tough girl, who's actually deeply insecure, who's had a hard time of it, whatever anyone thinks.

'You know you're talking about my best friend, you *arse*.'

'All right, all right! What's with that anyway? You're just so . . . different. I've never understood that.'

'But we're not. Not really.' And I don't know whether it's the alcohol coursing through my veins, but it's the first time I've ever realised that.

'OK, OK, whatever. Anyway, I'm not the popular, idiot footballer stereotype you have me down for . . . I'm deep.' We look at each other and burst out laughing. Because he's funny, and nice, and sometimes people surprise you, in the best possible way.

And then I finally spot Jessica, just as James is midway through telling me he wore a badge with her name on it for the entirety of Year 8. Ash is passing her a note and she's looking down at it, her hand clasped loosely round it. And she's upset. Their body language so personal, yet so removed from one another, so hostile. Like lovers, like fallen lovers.

And I love her and hate her in equal measure, because I can see her watching me, signalling that she'll be over in just a minute, her hand tightening around the note, with every second he's talking to her.

And this time, there is no song in my head, it's out loud. Playing right off the tiny wireless speakers Elina's set up in the pavilion. The irresistible beat of Robyn, 'Dancing on My Own'. And I think, yes, that's it. And as I look around, we're all in some kind of music video. Arms going up and down to the beat of the song, like robots. The cool girls, sashaying like Beyoncé, the cool boys drinking rhythmically, like they're matching the beat, the drama kids singing back up – and me, spinning in circles.

This is all just a bit of fun, I think. And I need to have fun. So much more fun.

That's when I ask for the hip flask again, and this time I don't just take a sip, I take a nice, long, well-rounded gulp.

Because I'll never be the girl he's taking home.

35

Drunk in Love

I'm not really sure what happens next, it all starts getting a bit blurry after the badge story. I'm just suddenly aware that James is possibly the funniest person I've ever met, and everything he says is, like, the funniest thing I've ever heard. I'm not cold any more, there's a fire inside me, a warmth, maybe even a blaze. I feel confident, invincible, ready for anything. I am the life and soul of this party, a mover and shaker. And suddenly I'm standing among all of James's friends, and I've crossed circles, and I'm one of those people, the ones who cross over, who all of a sudden cool. Everyone's laughing at me, at some story I'm telling about how Mr Grange is a complete perv, about how he used to open the windows in the studio in the deepest winter, to try and get the girls' nipples to harden so he could see them through their jumpers. I'm doing an impression of the nipples, with my hands stuck up my jumper, and Hayley is looking at me, and I know it isn't a good look, but I'm just going to ignore it, because nipples are just, so, funny. And like, why are boys so obsessed with them – when their mothers, and grandmothers, and aunts, and sisters have them too?

Mothers. Mothers. Mothers. I don't want to think about mothers. Or hats. Or smock dresses. Or nipples. Or feeling sad and like I'm just a disappointment, to everyone, everywhere, all the time. But maybe that's my gift. My ability to make everyone feel disappointed, regardless of their age, class, race and socio-economic background. I am an Everyman of disappointment.

Like Jessica. Like how disappointed and angry and sad and weird she was when I saw that note Ash gave her, that she tried to hide from me, like she hides everything from me, because she is a hiderer, which is a person who hides things, because they like to hide. And I told her. I said, STOP LYING. And STOP HIDING. And STOP BEING A KILLJOY, because I am not going home with you, and YOUR STUPID LOVE NOTE.

Not sure if I said the love note bit . . . did stand on it, when she dropped it, though.

And James's friends have a hip flask, but theirs tastes different. Coarse and strong. And they have beer, and something called Cointreau too. It tastes like oranges and happiness, and sadness, and you know, oranges. Which are a fruit. And one of them, whose name is Adam something or other in Year 12, one of stupid Aaron Green's friends, one of those footballing, athletic types with strong forearms and a six pack, is leaning into me, telling me I'm sexy (sexy!), that he can't believe he hasn't noticed me before, that I've got great legs and pretty eyes and nice hair, and I'm not sure what I say to this, but I think it involves hysterical, frenzied laughter. He puts his arm around me, and his hand is suddenly in the pocket of my trousers, pulling me closer – which I might think is quite romantic, other than that I'm starting to feel a bit sick, a bit dizzy, a bit like there's two of him, and I'm not sure if I like either.

He walks me away from the crowd and backs me into a tree, leaning into me, his breath high and soft on my face. And then he's kissing me, his hand slowly creeping between the buttons of my shirt. And I can hear voices, pressing, urgent, shouting my name. And I want to shout back, but I can't. Because my brain is no longer connected to the moving parts of my body.

And even as he's kissing me, I'm thinking it doesn't feel right, and I'm not really sure I like it. His tongue feels too big for my mouth, and Lorde, 'Green Light' isn't playing, and there is no magic, just acid, rising from the depths of my stomach like a long-lost monster, woken from sleep.

And the monster is coming, and it's bad, and it's levels of ugh-ness never before experienced.

And then Adam is gone – and I can hear James shouting, and maybe Ash too, is that Ash? Then there's pushing, and some sort of fight, somewhere, somewhere in the distance. I feel like I'm about to fall, but then there's Hayley, holding me up in our tall girl, small girl embrace, and I'm safe. And she's holding me up under one arm, and James is under the other, and I hear him say, 'It's OK, I've got her.' And then he's gone, the Ash figure, all tall and beautiful and golden. Why is he so golden? And then comes the sick, and oh my God, the sick. So. Much. Sick.

II

Going Up

36

The Hangover

When I wake up, there's a possibility my head may have completely exploded. I can't move. My brain is a throbbing, hot, horrible mess, and the night before a blur. A black pit of nothingness. My mouth fills with saliva as I run to the toilet and throw up whatever's left in my stomach, though it's hard to believe there is anything, given the streams of vomit projecting through my mouth and nose the night before, the only thing I can clearly remember.

It's the pool of blackness that disturbs me most. Even more than the throbbing headache that is threatening to crack my skull open like an egg. The moments between seeing Ash give Jess the note and having Hayley haul me up the stairs to my bedroom, while my mother (oh GOD, my MOTHER) stood shivering in the doorway, are gone, swallowed whole in the abyss of my mind.

But as much as I wish I could, I can't forget the argument that came before it. The shouting, and the park, and Ash, and drinking until I could no longer stand.

I consider calling Hayley, but getting off my bed to find my phone is proving trickier than expected. The world is spinning, like a merry-go-round that refuses to stop. I close my eyes and wait for the dull throbbing to ebb away, but instead I hear a knock, quiet but urgent on my bedroom door, and Mum whispering my name.

'Ellie? Are you awake?'

I attempt to raise my head from the pillow to look at her. A shaft of light has followed her in, and is shining directly on the centre of my face, burning a hole in my head like a shotgun.

'Yes,' I moan.

'What on earth happened last night?'

'I don't remember . . .'

'Why didn't you pick up your phone?'

'I didn't want to talk to you.' I look at her, the nausea overwhelming.

'Well, yes,' she says, clipped, 'but you should have let us know you were OK. Your dad and I were worried sick.'

'I'm sorry,' I say, sighing and turning away. I may as well get used to saying those words, because I am going to be repeating them a lot over the next few months/years/lifetime. Probably on the phone, from St Hilda's.

And when I think about that, I feel even sicker.

'It's OK,' she says, exhaling. And the 'OK' bit makes me turn so quickly, I almost vomit again.

She sits down next to me on the bed and strokes the hair off my sweaty forehead, staring at me until I feel she might be a shaft of light too.

'Do you want some water?' she asks, concerned.

I nod.

She holds the glass to my lips while I lap at it.

'I'm sorry too,' she says, placing the glass back at my bedside.

I stare at her, unsure of whether or not I'm still drunk.

'What you said last night . . .' She trails away, her voice catching. 'About me not listening to you, it's true. I didn't know you cared that much about drama. And I . . . I should have.'

I turn away.

'Ellie,' she says, turning my face back towards hers gently. 'Did I ever tell you about the day I got my A level results?'

Here we go again. Mum and her perfect A level results, Mum and her perfect everything.

'I got the highest results in my year,' she says proudly.

Bingo.

'But I still couldn't convince my parents to let me go to university,' and her voice is quieter now. Weary, and sad. 'That I had the potential to be something more than they thought I should be. They wouldn't listen. They never *listened*. And I, I promised myself, I would never do that to you, or to . . .'

She looks at me closely, the two of us too fearful to move.

'I was never good enough for them. I could never impress them. It didn't matter how hard I tried. I was an inconvenience. I barely remember my brothers being at home before they left. All I wanted . . . was to make something more than that. A real family. All I wanted was to do it all differently.'

She holds her head in her hands for a second, while I tussle with the urge to vomit. Hard.

'I'm not good at talking about things like this,' she says desperately.

'You're a therapist,' I slur quietly.

She gives me a look.

'I'm still angry with you, Ellie.'

And this is what comes of thinking you're funny and Pushing It, when you're already on Very Thin Ice.

'You lied to me, to Dad and me . . . I still can't believe you did that. I still can't believe *how long* . . .' she starts ranting.

'Can we go back to the bit where you're sorry for not listening?' I ask weakly.

She sighs.

'Look, Ellie, if you want to be treated more like an adult, then you have to start acting like one. That means not running off at the first sign of an argument, or drinking until you're incapable of standing. We have to talk about things. You have to talk to me.'

'I'm sorry.' And I can feel the lump in my throat starting to throb. Because my brain is a broken egg, full of broken thoughts and fears and confusion. And vomit. There is definitely vomit in there somewhere.

'I just feel like I always disappoint you, Mum. Like I'm never enough for you. But I'm never going to be Jessica. I'm never going to be the best at maths or science or geography, or maybe even the best at anything—'

She grabs me by my shoulders.

230

'You are the best at being you, Eleanor,' and there are tears in her eyes. Real tears. Tears for me, and how I'm feeling. Because she's in the room with me this time, not distant and distracted. She's here.

'And that will always be enough for me. You will always make me proud, and you always have. I'm sorry,' she says, her voice shaking. 'I'm just like them, I tried so hard, but I'm just like them . . .' She turns away.

'No,' I say, sitting up. And the blood is rushing to my head, like I'm about to pass out, or worse, vomit again. I grab her hand. 'You're not, Mum.'

She wipes the tears from my snot-smeared face.

'I am. But I'm going to be better,' she whispers. 'Let's make a deal.' She leans in towards me. 'I won't tell Dad about the drinking – if you PROMISE ME, and I mean it, Ellie, PROMISE ME, this will never happen again. I don't think telling him you got carried home by some good-looking boy is likely to help matters much.'

Good-looking boy?

'Really?' I mutter. This must be a hangover hallucination, because there is no way my mother is being this understanding about her alcoholic daughter.

'Yes,' she says, hugging me, and Mum doesn't really do hugging. 'You're a good girl, Ellie, and I trust you. I believe in you.' This time, there's no hiding the emotion in her voice. 'I hope you know that.'

'What about drama?' I whisper.

She pulls back a little, and it's hard not to read the look on her face as angry and frustrated.

'I'm not going to lie to you, Ellie. Dad and I have talked about it,

231

and we can't pretend we think it's a good idea. I mean, what on earth are you going to do with a drama GCSE? What's it going to look like on your CV? But if you really, really want to do it, then we want you to try. I just don't understand it. You're not a . . . show-off, Ellie. You're not one of those girls that wants to be looked at. You've never shown any interest in reality TV or anything.'

I decide not to mention my obsession with *The Real Housewives*, as I don't think it's likely to help my cause.

'You just don't seem that . . . confident,' she says carefully, 'when it comes to putting yourself out there for things like that.'

'I'm learning to be confident, Mum. It's helping me with that.' And I try not to resent her; to understand why she would think that. I just know that I'm changing. That I can change.

'OK,' she says, unsure. 'But we still want to meet with Mr Gorley. And Mrs Aachara. And no more lies, Ellie. My heart can't take it, OK? I don't want to lose you. I can't lose you. I know I'm not the best mum in the world, but I do love you, all right?' she says, tears in her eyes. 'I'm not a monster. You can talk to me. I want you to be able to talk to me.'

I can feel my head beginning to spin, and I don't want her to think that vomit is my official response to this conversation.

'Please don't run off like that again, Ellie. I don't know what I'd do if something happened to you. I couldn't . . . I wouldn't . . . I couldn't cope if I lost you. Like I lost Amis.'

'Mum, Amis died of leukaemia. It wasn't your fault. You couldn't have done anything.' And I don't even know what makes me say it.

Why it even occurs to me that she might blame herself. But the next minute, my mum is crying softly on my bed, and I hold her, tight.

'I love you, Mum.'

She cries some more.

'I'm sorry,' I mumble, 'but I feel really sick. I think I'm going to throw up again.' I can feel her back shaking, and I wonder whether she's going to start wailing.

'Ellie,' she croons. 'Ellieeee . . .'

I take a deep breath. Forcing the sensation of nausea to subside.

'Are you OK, Mum?' I ask lightly.

She lifts herself off my shoulder, and I can see that she isn't wailing, she's howling. With laughter.

'Poor girl. I mean, you deserve it, but all I can smell in this room is sick: It's horrible.'

'Thanks,' I sigh.

'Seriously, Ellie, I'm still upset with you,' she says between laughs, 'but we need to sort this room out. Can I open a window?'

'Yes, but leave the curtains closed,' I sigh dramatically.

'You haven't forgotten Granny and Aunty Kitty are on their way, have you?'

Oh God. Now I am guaranteed to be sick again.

'Right, let's get all this stuff in the wash while your father's at the airport and then you can go back to bed. I can buy you a couple of hours of feeling unwell with a stomach bug, but you'll have to get up for dinner. And tomorrow the uncles are driving up from London, so you'll have to be better by then.'

She looks grim at the thought of all this, and I suddenly realise she dreads these visits as much as I do – the arrival of the lesser-spotted, but deadly, Sri Lankan mother-in-law.

These family visits are painful on so many levels, partly because they get taken over by Tamil, which I don't actually speak or really understand, and partly because it's just days of being criticised in code – 'you look well' = you look terrible, 'that's an interesting haircut' = your haircut is terrible, 'how are you doing in your studies?' = my daughter/son is doing better, or I've heard you're doing terribly, but I thought I'd make you say it out loud as a lesson to yourself. I face my pillow and try to refrain from being sick again, and this time it isn't just the alcohol.

Mum gathers up my clothes and looks at me grimly. 'Sleep!' she instructs me. We exchange a look – one ally to another. If we stick together, we can get through this. And with that, I'm gone, a line of drool spilling gently down the side of my chin and on to my pillow.

37

You Kept Talking About Nipples

When I wake up, I turn to look at my bedroom clock. It's almost 5 p.m. and I've been asleep for most of the day. I can hear voices downstairs, an accent, and the smell of mothballs that seems to accompany my grandmother wherever she goes, is pervasive; sour and homely.

I love my grandmother, but she is not a woman who is always easy to love. Brusque and unforgiving, she plays her children off against one another, watching as they fight it out for her approval – *Game of Thrones*, before *Game of Thrones* even existed. But there's something about her as a woman, as the matriarch of her family, the leader who pushed everything through when her husband died, leaving her with less than nothing, that is impressively strong and, in her way, loving.

I reach over to my phone, which Mum has put to charge by my bedside, finally within reach, and see seventeen missed calls from

Hayley. I tentatively press the 'call back' button and hope for an answering machine.

'Thank God,' she says dramatically. 'I thought you were dead.'

'Really?' I ask tentatively. 'Was I that bad?'

'You were better when I left you last night, but not hearing anything from you all day really worried me. Are you OK? Did your mum freak out?' She takes a breath. 'Honestly, don't worry about it, we all do stupid things sometimes.'

Instant panic sets in.

'What stupid things? What did I do?'

She hesitates, and I wonder whether I danced naked on the pavilion, my pants on my head.

'First of all, you were just really chatty and fun, the way you are with me all the time, but you know – with everyone. But then you went over to speak to some of the boys, and that's when it all went a bit wrong.' That pause again, the one that seems to suggest something horrific is coming.

'OK,' I say, because I remember that vaguely. 'James's friends.'

'No, Ellie, they weren't James's friends, they were just some guys he plays football with. Anyway, he told you not to go over there. You were already wasted, but you wanted another drink.' This is starting to feel worryingly familiar.

'You kept talking about nipples.' Oh no . . . 'And hats. I tried to get you away from them – but you basically told me I was boring and a killjoy and to go away. Which I did.'

'I'm so sorry,' I cringe.

'It's OK. Let's just say you weren't exactly yourself. Anyway, Jessica tried to get you to go home with her too, but you wouldn't. You told her she was boring and a killjoy and to go away, which she did.'

'Oh God . . .'

'Then James had a go at getting you to leave. You told him he had a Lego haircut on a Ken doll head. That bit was quite funny. Particularly given you threw up on his shoes half an hour later.'

'Surely this can't get any worse?' I groan.

'It can, yes,' says Hayley, almost sounding like she's enjoying herself. 'Although, actually,' and at this, her voice takes on a more serious tone, 'it could have been a lot worse, E.'

That's when I remember Adam. Lovely, friendly Adam, or so I had thought.

'That guy Adam was all over you. I mean, honestly, he was practically groping you. That's when James and I decided you should go home, whether you wanted to or not – but by the time we turned around to get you, you were gone.'

I have a sudden memory of the pavilion, its flashing lights fading into the background as we walked away, his hand in my pocket.

'At that point, we started to panic, because we didn't know where he'd taken you – or if he was even with you at all. So, James, Ash and I started looking for you. You hadn't gone far, hardly surprising given you could barely walk.'

And I remember that too. Not knowing where I was, but knowing instinctively that I didn't want to be there. His hands roaming my arms, and under my shirt. His tongue too big for my mouth.

'Was I being . . . sick?' I ask, wincing. Because I remember being found now. The feeling of relief. Of being somewhere safe.

But PLEASE GOD. Please don't let Ash have seen me being sick.

'Technically, yes.'

'What do you mean?' I say nervously.

'Let's just say Adam got what he deserved.'

'Meaning?'

'Meaning you were sick on him, Ellie, or should I say, *in* him. You were sick in his mouth. We heard him sort of whimpering, that's how we knew where you were.'

'Oh no . . .' I gasp.

'Oh yes. You did not look in any fit state to be kissing anyone – and he knew that. He got what was coming to him. Seriously. That, and Ash almost punching him.'

'Ash almost punched him?'

'I almost punched him. Idiot. Anyway, James and I took you home after that.'

'James?'

The good-looking boy . . .

'Yes. James.'

And the nausea of my mother thinking James Godfrey is attractive is almost worse than the belief, somewhere in my heart, that it might have been Ash who took me home.

Oxygenate the brain, Ellie. In through the nose, out through the mouth.

Because the vomiting seems like nothing now, a small price to pay

238

for the drama I've caused. But then I think about Granny and Aunty Kitty downstairs, and the smell of my breath right now, and my hairy legs and inability to take a shower without passing out – and maybe my karmic retribution is coming.

'What about Jessica?' I ask meekly. 'What happened to Jessica?'

'Actually,' says Hayley thoughtfully, 'I don't know. She and Ash had a fight. They were both in a terrible mood – she left after she spoke to you.'

I mull this over, as much as it is possible to mull something over when your brain is ostensibly mush. But I have to stop focusing on other people – because they're not what matters. I matter. Being the best person that I can be matters. And I'm pretty sure that the best version of me doesn't go MIA on a night out and vomit on people's tongues/shoes, in an episode I will now refer to as Sickgate.

Like my PE report says pretty much every year – Could Do Better.

38

A Girl Called Ellie

My name is Ellie. Ellie Pillai. I'm fifteen years old, and until him, no one other than my dad has ever told me I'm beautiful. The place where I live doesn't have many people who look like me, but I've always tried to fit in, to be just like everybody else. But sometimes, it seems like the more I try to fit in, the more I stick out. I don't belong here, do I? But then, where do I belong?

39

Jaws

I've just about managed to shower and change myself into something clean. And I do feel clean. Scrubbed, wiped clear. The water washing away the remnants of my sins, hot and foamy.

But finding something to wear that will satisfy Granny is a mission. Nothing too short, tight, modern or masculine (jeans, apparently, are masculine – as are any kind of trouser not primary-coloured or bejewelled). In fact, the only things Granny would really be happy to see me in are a sari, a salwar kameez, a skirt suit (below the knee, preferably with eighties-style shoulder pads) or some kind of bridal attire, although even then the happiness would be limited to the fact you were getting married, as opposed to approval of the actual garment itself. My mother's and my style is a complete mystery to her – or as she once put it to Mum, 'Why you wearing the leopard print? So unflattering on your skin tone.' And to me, 'Why you wearing flat shoe, when you so short?'

In the end, I've plumped for a mid-length dark green silk dress with long sleeves – a Victorian-looking affair which my mother bought for me last Christmas. The sleeve has a slight puff to it, and the top is high-necked with darts in it, fitted to the waist and almost gothic in appearance. I've always quite liked it, but never found the confidence or an occasion to wear it. Well, today. Today is that day.

I head down the stairs, towards the light and the noise, and walk into the living room to see Granny giving Mum a lecture on how to walk. Whenever I see Granny, or even just before I see Granny, the theme song to *Jaws* starts playing in my head; like something dangerous is lurking nearby, and is just about to attack. Because you won't see it, until the very last minute. Until it's too late to stop it. Because Granny is slick. The Great White Shark of biting remarks.

'You must hold yourself up *straight*. What is this fashion with all these young people who walk like apes, their arms dragging on the ground? Lift your shoulders, walk with pride. You're a Sri Lankan!' She's holding court, and everyone around her is in awe, or terrified lest they be the next subject of her attention.

'Hello, Granny.'

Dur, dur . . . dur, dur . . . dur, dur . . . da-na-na-na, da-na-na-na . . .

'Ah, ah, Ellie! Come over here and let me look at you. Your mother says you are ill. What is she feeding you?' Granny's Sri Lankan accent is strong, albeit with a slight American twang now she lives there with Aunty Kitty. Her English is good, but she's a classic head wobbler, forever moving her head from side to side, like one of those bobble-headed toys people keep on the dashboard of their cars.

'You are looking thin. Is good.'

'Ellie's always been beautiful,' says Dad, coming to my rescue.

'Yes, but before she had the – what do you call it?' She turns to Aunty Kitty for guidance.

'Puppy fat,' Aunty Kitty offers helpfully.

'Yes, that. The puppy fat. Now she is nicer. Thinner.' I try not to be offended and become suddenly very aware of my mother's breathing, in through the nose, out through the mouth – she is clearly oxygenating her brain in a time of high stress, or else she's about to start whistling like a kettle.

'We don't really like to talk about things like that, *Amma*,' says Dad, looking at Mum's face in horror. 'We just want Ellie to be healthy and happy, those things don't really matter.'

'Of course they matter,' snaps Granny. 'You want her to meet nice man? Or end up alone like your sister here? Yes, yes, she has good job, lots of money, nice house, but she has no husband, no children! Who will look after her when she is old?' Aunty Kitty is studiously looking at the floor, trying to pretend the conversation isn't about her. I suspect she's heard it a million times before, so blocking it out is no longer a challenge for her.

Aunty Kitty works for a large American law firm, and the uncles all like to gossip about how much they think she earns. We know it's a lot. She's always wearing those shoes with the red soles, the ones whose price tag almost gave my dad a heart attack when my mother asked for a pair last Christmas. But despite Granny's insistence and many introductions, Aunty Kitty refuses to get married, and the various suitors dragged out for her over the years have always been met with an icy reception. She's in love with her job, and her job seems to love her back. Every year she has a new job title, a new promotion, and for the last few years she's been based in New York, which, next to London, looks to me like the most exciting place in the world. When she's not with Granny, she can be really nice, but Mum says a lifetime of 'that woman' has rubbed off on her.

Despite her success, I don't really get the sense she's happy. Granny was insistent on going with her to the US. Aunty Kitty has always struck me as a very strong woman, but she is also aware of her obligations – that as the unmarried child and only daughter, her mother is her responsibility, by which logic I'll probably be living with Mum forever.

'That's a nice dress, Ellie,' Aunty Kitty says, looking at me approvingly. 'I brought you some things from New York – we can get them after dinner.' And that, right there, is the best thing about these trips, even if competition for 'best things' is pretty much non-existent. Aunty Kitty has amazing taste, lots of money and no kids – so she is forever sending us things. I suspect my dad is her favourite brother, as I suspect he is also his mother's favourite child.

'Thank you, Aunty,' I say, all respectful, nice Sri Lankan girl, I'll roll the niece-of-shame out tomorrow, when I can find the strength, 'I'd like that.' And maybe it's because I'm too hungover to care, but I don't let Granny's digs get to me tonight. I eat my dinner, and don't worry if I'm thin or fat; just knowing that I'm loved, so loved, and maybe, just maybe, that was always enough.

40

The Pillais

The morning comes, just as promised, and the hangover which was killing me by the time I went to bed is gone like a puff of smoke, as though a genie wished it away. Mum is seriously unimpressed by this fact, repeatedly telling me that hangovers get worse as you get older, and not to get used to a mere twenty-four hours of vomit-inducing nightmare. She really needn't worry. I don't ever want to feel sick coming out of my nose again. There is no world in which any feeling or event is worth that burn.

I turn to my side and see the gifts Aunty Kitty brought me from New York. Foundation and powder in a colour that actually resembles my skin tone, a brush set and a beautiful eye palette. Best of all is the jacket – which I still can't quite believe I own. Oversized brown leather and shearling, it makes me feel like Ali MacGraw in *Love Story* – minus the terminal illness and in-laws who think I'm not good enough. I try not to overthink the comments that came with the giving of these gifts (mostly from Granny) – that perhaps I should make more of myself.

Today, the Pillais arrive to celebrate Granny's seventy-fifth birthday. And when I say *celebrate*, what I actually mean is *compete* for her attention and, very occasional, approval. The kitchen is a low hum of activity as Mum and Dad prepare food, the non-chefs doing their best to prepare a Sri Lankan feast. I let myself enjoy the noise. Even Granny's instructions, barked at my parents and aunt with Gordon Ramsay efficiency. Much of the food will come with the uncles, who will be bringing dishes and stringhoppers from London, but Mum has made caramel pudding and Dad has attempted milk toffee. I'm pretty sure it's supposed to be solid, as opposed to mousselike, but when I mention this, he tells me not to push it, in a voice so menacing I know, for once, it must be Mum defending me from Dad's wrath and not the other way around.

When I hear the cars on the driveway, I feel a momentary jolt of reality. My family are about to descend, like a swarm of locusts intent on destruction, and I can feel my neighbours' disapproval before I even see it. Too many of us in this little village, too many non-white faces, too many accents, too many unknown fragrances and colours. And the noise, the noise of three extra cars with six extra adults and eight extra kids – a scary amount of different for this little outpost of east England. And it's not that they hate us, in fact we could even, on occasion, call them friends: but there's something about the change in atmosphere when they feel they're close to outnumbered, when suddenly we are less of a minority.

'*Annan!*' This is my Big Uncle, my dad's younger brother, arriving, with Aunty Delia and his three children, Joseph, Peter and Esther. Peter is twelve, the same age Amis would have been, sweet and clever, while Esther is six and quiet as a mouse. Joseph, their elder brother, is fifteen, and the worst kind of bully.

'*Annan!*' This is my dad's youngest brother, or Little Uncle, arriving. His wife is Christine, and his children are Hope and Grace. The product of a devout Catholic marriage, their names hide much of their personal blemishes – i.e. Hope is vain, and Grace is mean, and occasionally the roles reverse. Hope is sixteen, and annoyingly beautiful – as in beautiful, but mostly annoying. Grace is eleven, but showing worrying Hope-type tendencies for the future, both in the looks and attitude department.

'*Annan!*' This last one is Middle Uncle, who, as the name suggests, sits in the middle of the three brothers, with his wife, Helen, and their children: Andrew, fourteen, Daniel, twelve, and Ethan, nine. Andrew is one of my favourite people. We don't see each other very often, but when we do, there's a silent acknowledgement that when it comes to Hope the Mean and Joseph the Bully, we will always have each other's backs. Like when Hope told me I shouldn't wear yellow because it made me look dark, and Andrew told her there was nothing wrong with being dark, and that Hope was brown and should stop being in denial about it.

The Pillais all live in London, and for that reason I have never fully understood why we don't. They see each other every week, attending the same Catholic church service on a Sunday, and celebrating all of their birthdays and major holidays together during the year. We travel to see them, and they to us – but it isn't quite the same as being part of their day-to-day world. Not that I mind. I don't fit into their world, any more than I do mine.

There's always the sense with my cousins that I'm the country mouse, the unworldly one, the one who doesn't fully understand or appreciate my heritage; a coconut, as they sometimes call me – brown on the outside, white on the inside – because I don't speak Tamil, or eat enough Sri Lankan food, or have Sri Lankan friends, or even that many friends who aren't white. Because there are only six people in my entire year who aren't white, and frankly we try not to club together too much, to stand out.

Dad leads them all into the house, and the women instantly congregate in the kitchen; it's like the 1950s in there, minus the aprons and circle skirts. They're unpacking food from cool boxes, putting the hob on, throwing together dahl and rice and seasoning Mum's meat curries like three brown Nigellas, licking fingers and tasting dishes and demanding spoons and plates. Aunty Helen strokes Mum's arm, an unspoken camaraderie signifying the terror of hosting Granny, before pulling me into a bearlike embrace.

'Ah, so beautiful now, Ellie! How is your revision going? Andrew doesn't even know his times tables yet!' she says, cackling. I love the way she laughs at her boys. The way they look at her with equal parts embarrassment and adoration. It looks so fun, so easy, to be part of their family. And then she releases me and is off, bustling around the kitchen, squeezing everyone and keeping things on track.

'So . . . Hope has a boyfriend now,' Aunty Christine whispers to the women conspiratorially, as she chops the roti for the kottu. There is a collective sucking of breath through teeth. This, I think, will always be the visceral sound of gossip to me.

'No! Is he Sri Lankan?' asks Aunty Delia under her breath.

'No, but he's Indian. Nineteen, studying to be dentist.'

'Ah, ah. You like him?' probes Aunty Helen.

'Nice boy, nice family. What's not to like?' says Aunty Christine.

'But – so young!' exclaims Aunty Delia, scandalised.

'Yes, but she is going out with her friends, I can't control these boys always looking at her, better she has nice boyfriend. Nice Indian boy with good prospects.'

'True, true,' says Aunty Delia, 'but if you're ever worried about her, you know I can always send Joseph to check up. He can keep the boys away.' The aunties all exchange a look – wimpy Joseph would have a better chance of keeping the girls away than the boys.

'Yes, yes, thank you, thank you,' says Aunty Christine, her eyes fixed on the chopping board.

'They're growing up fast,' Mum interjects. 'All of them. It feels like yesterday Hope was just a baby.'

'Such a beautiful baby,' says Aunty Helen. 'And Ellie too! Fifteen! How time flies. I had twenty-four-inch waist then. And skin like silk!' They float off into a reverie then, talking of a time when they were young, when life felt different, when everything seemed possible. It's hard to imagine a time when they were girls and not mothers. Except for Mum. She feels frozen in time somehow. A child in an adult's body, just playing at motherhood.

I listen at the door for as long as I can, then drift next door to where Granny is in full command of her fans.

Dur, dur . . . dur, dur . . . dur, dur . . . da-na-na-na, da-na-na-na . . . The *Jaws* theme starts playing in my head, just as I see her coming into full view from the safety of the doorway.

'*Amma*, sit down.' '*Amma*, are you comfortable?' '*Amma*, you must rest.' She's sat next to my dad, with Aunty Kitty to her right, despatching advice and opinions like rain upon unwilling flowers.

'And Peter's tuition? How is this?' she's asking Big Uncle.

'*Amma*, he is doing very well, showing much promise.'

'And Grace, how are her piano lessons?' she asks Little Uncle.

'I'm not sure she's going to be a concert pianist,' he jokes, 'but she's enjoying them.'

'To be good, you must practise. Is she practising?'

'Yes, *Amma*, but she's only eleven. I want her to have fun, enjoy it.' She looks at him as if not quite sure how to respond.

'It is not about fun, it's about being best,' she says haughtily. 'I fight for everything I have. Everything. Why you all so concerned about fun? Fun does not pay for house, or find husband. Fun is for later. When you are married. Or maybe not after you are married. Marriage is not fun either.' She laughs quietly at her own joke.

'And what of Ellie? What will she do next year?'

'She's doing well, *Amma*. On track for good grades in English and maths, maybe history too if she puts in a bit more effort. And she's taking drama now as well.' He tacks the sentence on the end, as if he's trying out the feel of it in his mouth; by the look of him, it appears to feel unpleasant.

Dad hasn't stopped being angry with me since the fight. Since he found out I lied about drama and came home later than he cares to know about, with someone he cares even less to know about. But Mum (Mum!) seems to have calmed him down. And I don't know how or what she's said to him, but his seething is currently only low-level, for which I am legitimately grateful.

'Drama?' says Granny, horrified, and Dad isn't exactly un-horrified either. 'What is this drama? A girl like Ellie must be smart.' I try not to think about what she means by 'a girl like Ellie' and ignore the *Jaws* theme, reaching its final crescendo as the shark finally attacks, dragging his unsuspecting victim underwater, leaving only a pool of blood and a fisherman's hat behind. It's probably the man in the yellow mac.

Which is the moment I decide that facing my cousins is probably preferable to hearing Granny's opinion on my life choices. I walk up the stairs, following the sound of Joseph's haughty, annoying voice, bossing Peter about what music he can play.

'What is this thing?' he asks accusingly, as I step inside.

'It's a record player,' I sigh.

'But – why?' he asks.

'Because vinyl. No other reason required.'

'Whatever, weirdo,' he says dismissively. 'You're so OLD.'

I don't reply.

'Yeah, fifteen is ancient, Jo,' says Andrew, rolling his eyes at me.

'That's not what I meant,' he says, ruffled.

'Were you being sarcastic?' I respond. 'You need to work on your intonation.'

'Definitely,' says Andrew. 'It was coming off more . . . stupid than sarcastic.'

'This looks so good on me,' says Hope, ignoring us as she parades around in my new leather jacket. 'It's such a waste on you. Oversize coats always make short people look frumpy.'

Nice.

'Ellie's not frumpy,' says Peter loyally. Joseph shoots him a look, designed to say 'You will pay for that later.'

'I never said she was frumpy,' says Hope. 'I said she was short.'

Not better.

'So, have you got a boyfriend yet, Ellie?' she asks, still preening.

'Doubtful,' says Joseph, sniggering.

'Do you have a girlfriend?' I ask curtly.

'Well, Vimal, that's *my* boyfriend, took me to the OXO Tower – that's in London, Ellie. It was so romantic.'

Ugh.

'I met him at Starbucks. He asked for my number and when he got his latte, I wrote it on his coffee cup.' I am aware of all this, having seen the self-same cup posted on Instagram to mark their three-month anniversary. This will probably be the opening gambit in the groom's wedding speech. Pass me the sick bucket. 'His parents met Mum and Dad last week.'

'Seems a bit soon,' I say, unconvinced.

'You've never had a boyfriend, so it's hard for you to understand,' she says condescendingly.

There follows a pause, in which I consider throwing myself at her, *Fight Club* style.

'Can we watch TV, Ellie?' Daniel asks, quiet as always in a corner.

'Sure. The remote's by my bed.' And after that we watch *The Princess Bride* in comfortable silence, while I notice an uncanny resemblance between my cousin Joseph and the evil Prince Humperdinck. And I realise I quite like my cousins, even the mostly annoying ones, because for better or worse, they're my blood, and we understand each other – and one day, when we are fully grown up, we may even be friends. And sometimes, I know, I just run away from things – and me, I'm the only one that can fix that.

Note to self. Fix that. You are neither a pony nor a horse.

41

Sunday Night Dinner, Tamil Style

When dinnertime arrives, we descend on the food like animals, as though we've been starved for days. These Sri Lankan feasts are for special occasions only – birthdays, weddings, anniversaries, funerals. Something about them, their smell, the colours, the way the food is arranged on the plates, makes my mouth water just to think about.

'To *Amma*,' says Dad, raising his glass of arrack. The men follow suit, while the women sip their wine, and we all toast Granny, while she sits queenlike on her throne, the good chair my mother doesn't let anyone sit on, a designer piece that cost almost a month's salary and which Granny has already complained is uncomfortable.

'To *Amma*,' says Big Uncle, eyeing Dad suspiciously, because even at this stage of the evening the competition is fierce. The older cousins – Hope, Joseph and I – have been allowed a glass of wine with our dinner, but the smell is making my head spin, the memory of Sickgate causing the vomit to fire up my throat like a starting gun. I put the glass back down and sip at my water, trying to ignore Mum's smug demeanour whenever she sees me deep breathing.

'I must speak,' says Granny seriously, cutting through our relaxed chatter.

Dur, dur . . . dur, dur . . . dur, dur . . . da-na-na-na, da-na-na-na . . .

'I have been thinking. About you all.' A statesmanlike pause. 'I am getting older. The children too are getting older, and I would like to help them. Kitty and I have been talking. Now I live in US, my house here sits empty, and I do not wish to wait until I am dead to sell it.' We all look at each other, not quite sure what this means.

'So, I am going to sell it. The money will be divided between the children – and none of you,' she says, gesturing at the gathered aunts and uncles theatrically, 'will get a thing.' We look at each other, not truly able to comprehend what this means, just that we are going to be given some money, and that undoubtedly there will be conditions.

'Kitty will set up trusts for each of you,' she says, looking at us carefully – even the little ones who have no idea what any of this means. 'When you are eighteen, you will have money. It must go towards university education first – what is left, is up to you.' The aunts and uncles look at each other, bewildered and relieved.

'There is one final thing, then I do not wish to talk of this again.' This time, the pause doesn't feel deliberate. 'I will not,' and at this her voice trembles, 'forget my Amis. My beautiful boy, he too should be here, he too should have future. But God,' she says, clasping her hands together, as if in prayer, 'he know best.' It's the first and only time I've seen my grandmother appear vulnerable. Even after my brother's death, even at his funeral, she was a stone, a rock refusing to move, a constant for my father, a woman who fed my mother soup for a month while she refused to get out of bed. 'He too will have his share. But it will go to Ellie. His sister. She has been through a lot, and she deserves it. It is for him, and he would want it to go to her.'

The lump in my throat is throbbing, my eyes hot. And the Pillais look at me, with no fight in their eyes, simply acceptance that this is the way it should be. Granny continues. 'I am finished. You may eat. Peter, your jaw is becoming very square, is not good. You need to put on weight. Delia, what are you feeding him?'

And this is the moment I look up to find my parents. Dad is on the sofa, chatting contentedly with Little Uncle and teasing Grace about her plaits, but Mum, Mum is nowhere to be seen. I stand up, winding my way around bodies until I find her in the kitchen, her head bent low over the island, her elbows barely supporting her frame as she weeps quietly. I put my arms around her and we just stand there, Mum and me – two allies in the war against disapproving Granny, who have suddenly realised that we're all on the same side – that we were always on the same side.

42

Signed, Sealed, Delivered

After a hideous night's sleep, where I've been relegated to the living-room floor with the majority of the kids, while Aunty Kitty has had to suffer the indignity of sharing a bed with her own mother – the cousins, aunts and uncles, plus Granny, have all gathered their things, ready to head back to London.

We finish our rounds of hugs and kisses, cheeks scratching cheeks as we bid one another goodbye, but as I reach Granny, I lay my arms tight around her neck, suddenly realising how much I'm going to miss her, the sense that whatever's coming, she can face it, that with her I'll always be safe. However old she is, however fragile, this woman is a tigress, and I love her for it. Love her ferocity, even if sometimes it can cut deep.

'Goodbye, my Ellie. You will visit me soon?'

'I love you, Granny.'

'Yes, yes, love is very good.' She's not a woman who ever can seem to say 'I love you', but it's written there, in everything she does. Even in the moments when it feels hard and harsh and unkind, there's love in there, buried beneath barbed wire. 'I will miss you, Ellie. You are good girl. Work hard and be good for your mother. She is very tired. I see in her eyes.' I look over at Mum, who does look exhausted, beaten. Has she always looked like this? The artfully applied make-up seems to hide so much.

'I will. I'll miss you.' My heart feels heavy, it swallows my words. She kisses my cheek.

'I am always here, *en anbe*, if you need me.' She croons the words *my darling* in her strange Sri Lankan/English/American accent and I can taste it on my tongue, the feel of her regrets. Having all of her family together, like this, is not something that happens often. And she's touched by it, sorry it's over.

As we wave them away down the driveway, our neighbour Mike, who is always suspiciously outside his house whenever we are, says, 'Family visit, eh? Don't know how you fitted the lot of them in there.' Dad smiles, but I can tell he has little time for niceties, now niceties are no longer required.

'We Sri Lankans don't do hotels, not when there are relatives to stay with,' Mum says, smiling. And I want to say, the word 'relatives' should be considered in its loosest possible sense. Like the time we stayed on some random aunty's floor in Florida (a cousin twice removed, whom my dad had met once, on his wedding day). Sri Lankans don't do hotels, where there are any other Sri Lankans in the vicinity. Mike seems confused by the concept, but nods his head and smiles.

It's only then that my brain allows me to think back to Friday.

To the mess with Jessica. The jealous, drinking myself into oblivion, horrible, worst possible version of me, mess with Jessica.

'Mum,' I say slowly. 'Can you give me a lift to Jess's?'

'OK,' she says, eyeing me. 'Give me five minutes?'

I wait for her in the front garden, even though it's cold, even though there's a slight drizzle in the air and my hair is beginning to resemble that of an Asian clown serial killer. Because if I go inside, I might just lose my nerve and watch *Friends*, the model for all good friendships instead.

Mum arrives back downstairs, immaculate in a sand-coloured trench coat, ankle-skimming black jeans and a grey polo neck, the non-Granny-approved outfit she'll have been itching to wear for days. The car is freezing when we get in, and we sit in companionable silence, the radiator slowly thawing us out.

'So, what are your plans for half term?'

'Revision mostly, but I also have to go into school on Thursday – I've got some work to do on . . .' I pause, unsure of whether to go on.

'On what?' she probes.

'The music I'm writing. For drama.' I look sideways at her, and hope the last few days haven't been a hallucination. The mention of drama definitely blindsides her more than she wants to let on. In the space of a second, she looks confused and contrite, and maybe even a little bit angry; but somehow, she hides it.

'Music?' she enquires, feigning composure – and I have to be grateful for that. The pretence. 'Why would you have music to work on for drama?'

'I've written a soundtrack for our play . . . It's a lot of work, but I feel really excited about it.'

She's quiet for a moment, digesting the statement.

'Sounds exciting. Maybe you can play it to me some time.'

'OK,' I say quietly.

And it feels like the best I could have hoped for.

We're both smiling, lit up, because Mum's listening to me, and I'm listening to her, and there is nothing better than this feeling – other than the feel of piano keys beneath my fingers, or listening to Lorde, 'Green Light' on repeat.

I turn the dial on the radio and tune into one of those channels that Hayley says only old people listen to. She keeps telling me I have an old soul, but surely that would at least make me a little wise, not someone in need of driving to her best friend's house to apologise for her drunken buffoonery. Which, I know, is a totally old person word, but seems to fit this situation perfectly.

But I've come to love the radio. The fact you don't get to choose. That sometimes you hear the beauty in something you would never have willingly listened to. Then, out of nowhere, the twang of guitars and euphoric screeching fills our car. I can see Mum next to me, starting to shimmy a bit behind the wheel, the two of us nodding our heads in appreciation at Stevie Wonder, 'Signed, Sealed, Delivered', dancing in our seats, rocking from side to side, mouthing the words under our breath.

She turns the volume up and I put my feet on the dashboard, while the chorus hits us with its irresistibly happy, potent sound.

Like it's trying to tell us something. Like Stevie Wonder is personally telling us that it's all there for the taking, if we just want it enough. And we're full-scale singing now, warbling along like Stevie's backing singers, adding in all of the high notes, waving our hands in the air like Thelma and Louise, about to throw ourselves off a cliff. And for just a moment, on this dull, grey day, the sun appears from behind a cloud, and I grin at her, and she grins at me, and it's one of those perfect moments; a snapshot in time. Me and Mum, bathed in sunlight, Stevie in the background.

We're still smiling, still lightheaded from the music, when we pull up outside Jessica's house. But as soon as we arrive, my mood shifts. I don't come to Jess's house often, but something about it feels wrong. There's rubbish strewn all over the driveway, and what looks like weeks of recycling piled up by the door. I jump out of the car and inspect the bags, which are full of what looks like broken glass. I knock urgently while Mum follows me to the door silently.

When Jess finally appears, she's dressed in biker boots, skinny jeans and a Thrasher T-shirt, her face unreadable.

'Hi,' I say, gesturing to the chaos around me. 'Bin men on strike?' She looks edgy and perturbed. 'Can I come in?' I ask gently.

'I haven't had a chance to clean up. What do you want, Ellie?'

'I came to say sorry about Friday. I was drunk, in case you hadn't noticed . . .' and at this, I think I see a smile. 'I was a mess, and I'm sorry for how I spoke to you.' She eyes me cautiously, carefully, her doctor's brain calculating the risk to her heart.

'Hi, Jessica,' Mum says from behind me. 'Can we come in?'

'Mum and I haven't had a chance to tidy up, we've been so busy lately. It's probably better you don't,' she says firmly. Mum looks at her, and it seems through her, and speaks slowly, cautiously.

'Is your mum in, Jess? I'd love to talk to her.'

'No. She's at work.' Her arms are crossed over, forming a barrier between us.

'I'd really like to come in, please, Jessica,' Mum says more firmly. 'We'll only be a minute.' For a second, Jess's body collapses a little, and she finally steps aside, gesturing us to come in. As the door closes behind her, I can see the house isn't a mess at all. In fact, it's pristine, but something about it is off, not quite right. And that's when I notice that all the photographs are missing from the walls, and the place has an emptiness to it, like a house half asleep. The kitchen is empty, bar one bowl and plate drying neatly on the rack.

'Where's your mum, Jessica?' Mum asks again.

This time, Jess doesn't even try to pretend. She looks at us with a hard stare, a dead stare. 'She's gone. We had a fight. She left.'

'When?' says Mum.

'I don't know exactly. About ten days ago.'

'Is she off her medication, Jess, do you know?' Mum asks, and the intimacy of the question catches me off guard, because I had no idea her mum was even on medication.

'She's been taking her meds fine, we just had an argument and she left. I thought she'd be back – you know what she's like. She gets angry sometimes, forgetful, but this is the first time she's been gone this long.'

262

'Have you phoned the police?' Mum questions.

'Not yet. I thought she'd come back.'

'What have you been living on, Jessica?' Mum asks gently. 'Did she leave you any money?'

'We had some food in the cupboards and I have some birthday money, so I've been eating a lot of rice and pasta. Turns out you really can live on a shoestring,' she says, laughing bitterly. 'I should write a cookbook.' I put my hand out and wrap it around hers.

'Are you OK?' And that's when the floodgates open, the tears spilling down like rain at a touch of human warmth, the release of so many years of being let down, of being forgotten by the one person you're supposed to be able to rely on. I want to find something funny to say, something to make her laugh. But there's nothing. No words, no jokes that can take that look from her face.

'No, I'm not OK. I don't know what I am, but I'm not OK.' Mum pulls her into an embrace, and even though she's smaller than her, it's a powerful embrace, a woman taking charge.

'It's going to be OK,' she says, squeezing her hand. 'Ellie, help Jessica pack some things. She's coming to stay with us while we work this out.' And Jess and I succumb to it, to being told what to do, to being saved by this tiny little powerhouse of a woman I call my mother. And I feel so sad, but so proud at the same time. It took me a while to see it, but she's really rather extraordinary. We pack silently, and walk out of the house, hand in hand.

'I'll sit in the back with you.' We squeeze into the back of the car, and I can't help but notice Ash's note, hidden beneath the pencil case

263

in her bag. She smiles uneasily at me as I gently push her head on to my shoulder.

'Geriatric baboon's backside?' I offer quietly.

'What was that, Ellie?' Mum asks from the front of the car, while Jessica giggles quietly into my jumper.

'Nothing, Mum,' I respond. I stroke Jess's hair and turn to her. 'It's going to be OK,' I say gently. 'You're not alone.'

And she isn't.

43

A New Beginning, Sort of

When we get home, Mum sets Jessica up in the spare room. She calls the police and reports her mother missing, but is informed hours later that she's only ten miles away, staying with her boyfriend at a house his brother owns. Turns out Jess's mum is sick. She has bipolar disorder, and often refuses to take her medication, which can make her mood swings extreme. And suddenly their purple house and forgetting to pay the bills isn't quite the free-spiritedness I'd thought it was; not glamorous or funny, but scary and unpredictable. And my friend Jessica, the mini grown-up at the age of eleven, makes sense too, just like Mum's interest in her, always checking to see where she is and what she's doing and how she's coping; the manicure, just the two of them.

All that time I spent wondering why Mum wasn't asking me how I was doing, why it wasn't me she was interested in. It's not that she didn't care. Not that she chose Jessica. She was just trying her best. Not always getting it right, but trying so hard to be there for both of us, in ways I could never really imagine. And it's like we've been hiding from each other in plain sight – just like Jess has been hiding all of this in plain sight. And I should have seen it. Jessica King is a carer. She's been a carer to someone with a mental health problem, and I never even knew it.

When Mum finally rings Jess's dad, we hide at the top of the stairs, Jess gripping my hand.

'He'll take me away from her,' she whispers frantically.

'She did that to herself, Jess.'

'You don't understand,' she says, turning away from me.

'*Talk* to me then.'

'Jessica,' Mum shouts up the stairs. 'Can you come down here, please?'

And I watch her walk down the stairs, her heart in her hands.

'Dad?' she whispers into the receiver. And I don't know what he says in response, I just know she's suddenly crying.

They'd all known Jess's mum was struggling, but Jess had been so adamant about staying with her, taking care of her, telling everyone that everything was fine; making the lie seem so plausible that nobody knew how erratic her behaviour had become. And all those nice, neat little boxes I like to put everyone in seem stupid and naive and thoughtless now, because we are all of us fighting something.

When she finishes the call, she comes back to sit with me on our creaky top stair.

'Promise me you won't keep anything from me again?' I ask, as she puts her head on my shoulder.

'It wasn't like that, Ellie. I didn't mean for it to be like that.'

'I know,' I say, squeezing her hand. 'I just want you to know you can trust me, that you can talk to me.'

'I know,' she says, returning the squeeze. 'Dad's picking me up tomorrow. I'm going to stay with him and Barbara for a bit. You can come and babysit Alfie with me.'

'I'd like that,' I say, smiling at her. 'We can order pizza on your dad's credit card again.' She grins, both of us remembering when he left his credit card details on their Sky account and we spent the evening buying films, but only watching the first five minutes to see if we could guess the ending. One of those films was about a clown serial killer. Clearly it had an impact.

'There's something I need to tell you, Jess.' She looks at me, her head tilted softly to one side. 'On Friday, the reason I got so drunk . . . I'd had an argument with Mum and Dad. A bad one. They found out I was taking drama.'

'Found out?' she asks, scrunching her eyebrows together.

'They thought I was doing computer science . . .'

'Why?' the eyebrows ask.

'Because that's what I told them.'

She sucks her breath in quickly.

'Computer science?' she says, sitting up. 'You? You hate algorithms. You can't even spell algorithm.'

'Thanks . . .'

'Sorry, I just mean, I'm surprised they'd think you'd want to take it.'

I imagine Mick Jagger serenading me with the Rolling Stones, 'You Can't Always Get What You Want'.

'It doesn't matter what I *wanted* to take, Jess. Dad thought it would be useful for me to learn how to write code. I asked about drama, and they said no. I didn't know what else to do. I wanted it so badly.'

'I can't believe it . . . It's so unlike you, Ellie.'

And I want to say, no, it isn't unlike me at all. I lie all the time. About how I'm feeling, and what I *want*, and why I don't go to the park on a Friday. Not because Mum and Dad won't let me, but because I'm scared. Because I don't fit in. Because sometimes people say stupid things, like the time someone asked if I had a temple in my house, or if I'd ever eaten pizza.

'So, what's happening now they've found out?' she asks, staring at me.

'Dad's still furious, Mum's been better. They're not happy, but they've agreed to let me finish it. They're listening to me, which, you know, is a start.'

'Oh E, I wish you could have told me. Maybe I could have helped.' She looks away momentarily. 'Not that I'm one to talk about lying,' she finishes glumly.

'It's not the same, Jess. I wasn't brave enough to be honest. You – you've been too brave.'

'Everything's such a mess.'

'Your mum? And Ash?' I say sympathetically.

'Mum's been bad for a while,' she says, running her hands up and down her thighs anxiously. 'I guess I didn't want to face up to it. I knew Dad would freak, and I just thought she'd get better. She has before.'

'Before?' I ask gently.

'She gets like this sometimes,' she says quietly. 'Angry about stuff. Upset. And then, I don't know, it sort of passes. She changes her medication, or she goes back on it, or she starts seeing someone . . .' She trails away.

'You've never really talked about it before,' I say quietly. 'I always thought your mum was just this dramatic, wild, creative soul. I never knew any of this was happening, and I'm sorry. I can't believe I didn't realise.'

'But she is, Ellie. She's all of those things. She's just other stuff too, and it's complicated, and that's why I want everything else in my life to be not complicated. I try not to think about it. I definitely don't want to talk about it.'

And I feel awful, knowing that all this time she's been going through this without me. Without her best friend to hold her and tell her it's OK to cry. To feed her chocolate cake and make her laugh.

'I like complicated,' I say, smiling and turning to hug her. 'In fact, I love complicated. I thrive on complicated. So you can talk to me about anything, any time, always.'

'And the Ash thing,' she says, looking down at her hands, 'that doesn't really matter. It's not important. He's a good person, Ellie. Sometimes things just don't work out the way you want them to. I don't want you to hate him.'

'Why are we even talking about him?' I say, thinking of the note hidden in her bag. 'He hurt you. The end.'

'No, E. It's not the end. It's more complex than that, and honestly,

269

I don't want everyone to think he's a bad person, or that any of this is his fault. I've had a lot of stuff going on.'

'OK,' I say, stroking her hand. Because she seems vehement about it, and I want her to stop worrying about anything other than her, and if she's OK. 'But let's focus on you, not Ash Anderson.'

'OK,' she says, smiling.

'Let's make a pact. No more lies. Would Tony Curtis lie to Marilyn Monroe?'

'Actually, that's pretty much the entire premise of *Some Like It Hot* . . .'

'Details, details. Besides, lying clearly doesn't agree with me. I must have vomited at least a thousand times on Friday.'

'I don't think that was the lying, Pillai . . .'

'It was probably the fifty per cent proof rum, and the beer, and the vodka . . .' I trail off, nauseous at the thought.

'Where did you get all that from?'

I shrug my shoulders.

'I don't know. Just some boys.'

She looks at me deeply and takes my hand.

'Don't do it again. Alcohol is very ageing,' she scolds jokingly. 'But seriously,' she says, affecting her doctor's voice, 'if it makes you walk into a road when there's a car coming, or fall into a river, or go off with some boy you barely know, then it can age you until you're practically dead.'

'I know . . .' I mutter. 'I'm such a . . .'

'You're . . . *complicated*,' she smiles.

That night, she falls asleep holding my hand, and the next day she's gone, picked up at 9 a.m. by her dad, on her way to a new life, a safer life. And I feel so happy for her, but so sad at the same time, at what she's been through to get here. It makes me see that despite everything, despite all of those feelings of abandonment, I was never truly abandoned, never truly forgotten – only a little pushed to the side, sheltered from the nuclear fallout of my parents' emotions.

I sit down at the piano and play 'Katja's Song', and this time the person listening at the door isn't Ash, but my mother, and even though she doesn't make my heart race in quite the same way, I'm glad she's there anyway.

44

You Can't Hurry Love

The rest of half term passes in a blur, and when Thursday arrives, I stand outside the school gates ready to atone for my idiocy. Something about its emptiness feels almost ghostly, the ideal place for a clown assassin to hide between killings. I've worn better underwear, just in case.

I'm listening to music today. Real music. Not the kind that plays in my head, but the real kind. The Motown music Mum loves so much, my headphones pumping out soul: tambourines and bass lines and gospel-influenced harmonies.

I feel hopeful today. Like I can see somewhere I want to get to, someone I want to be. I've been working on 'Katja's Song', peeling back the layers, realising I have a voice. I talk to Jess every day, and she's settling in at her dad's, learning to relax, learning to be a kid again. I'm thinking about her, and Mum, and how proud I am of myself for trying. For writing a song, and playing it to people. For making things better with Jess. I'm humming along to the Supremes, 'You Can't Hurry Love', my headphones enveloping my head, my eighties-style aviator reading glasses, my one hint of coolness, nodding up and down on the bridge of my nose as I close my eyes and shimmy to the beat.

I am a horrible dancer. Fact. But this song, this song always makes me dance, with its low, intense bass and those bright harmonic horns. Diana's voice; milky and needy and everything that's right with music. Everything that makes Motown so moving and happy and heartbreakingly brilliant.

I'm mouthing the words to myself, pretending I'm her, sixties girl group arm movements and all, so lost in the music I don't see him coming until I'm crashing head first into his chest. My earphones fall to the floor, the Supremes blaring loudly into the empty corridor about love not coming easy.

You can say that again.

'I'm so sorry,' I say, looking up at him, shame flooding me at the memory of Friday. 'Sorry,' I say again, trying to tidy myself up.

'You already said that,' Ash says, looking at me closely.

'I'm here to tidy up the props cupboard. I mean, I'm here to see your mum.' I try to feign composure, but fail horribly. 'I mean, she knows I'm coming, she *asked* me to be here. I'm not stalking her or anything. In fact, she asked me to be here, at this exact time. Which is why, you know . . . I'm here,' I ramble, my face crimson, the heat working its way up my neck and into my brain, which is preparing itself for spontaneous combustion, should this moment get any more awkward.

'So, how are you?' he asks.

'What do you mean?' I fumble, trying to banish the sixties girl group, who seem to have made their way out of my headphones and into the school corridor. They're wearing yellow rain macs over their sequinned dresses, twirling open umbrellas like Debbie Reynolds dancing with Gene Kelly in *Singin' in the Rain*. Maybe Gene's the man in the yellow mac.

He stares at me as my brain tumbles from subject to subject, attempting to stop somewhere normal.

'After last Friday. Are you feeling better?'

'Oh, Friday, right,' I reply. And there is no way of ignoring my behaviour on Friday, however much I try. 'I'm so embarrassed,' I breathe. 'I hear you helped find me. I'm sorry you saw me like that. I mean, I'm sorry people had to look for me at all.'

'You say sorry a lot, don't you?' he grins.

'Yeah, it's pretty much my fallback phrase, given I'm always doing something stupid.'

'Not being able to find you was definitely not your fault. He should never have touched you.' He balls his fists up angrily.

But I don't know what to say to that – because I was the one drinking, I was the one talking about nipples and putting my hand up my jumper. I was the one who liked it when he said I had nice hair and nice legs and kept ogling his forearms like some kind of forearm pervert. So maybe it was my fault?

'Although you definitely got your own back,' he says smiling.

Why, High School God? Why did he have to see me throwing up in someone's mouth?

'I'm an idiot. I should never have drunk that much. I don't really

274

drink, so I haven't got much of a tolerance for it. In fact, the last time I had that much to drink I wet myself on a slide.'

He looks at me, horrified.

'Oh, I was only four,' I say, trying to pull the conversation back, but realising this sounds even worse. 'My mum gave me vodka instead of cough syrup by mistake – she was tired from my brother being up all night, and she got confused with the bottles. I was drunk at preschool and kept falling over and wetting myself.' Oh my God, why am I talking, WHY AM I STILL TALKING?

He looks at me, his brow furrowed. 'I see. So you've basically been drinking since you were a toddler? Hardcore.'

'Seriously, though,' I say, shifting from side to side, 'I should have listened when you told me not to. I just wanted to forget everything for a while.'

He doesn't reply.

'Mission accomplished!' I say, with forced jollity into the silence that follows. He frowns.

'Ellie!' I turn to see Mrs Aachara heading up the hallway towards us. 'I see you've found Ash. I roped him into helping too.' He looks embarrassed, the way we all do when faced with our parents sometimes, trying to look like we're still cool, still independent.

'Can I leave you to it?' she asks, walking straight past. 'I need you to work out what can be saved. Be ruthless. I've got no budget, but I'm sure we can make do with fewer props that are better. I've got some things to prep for next week. Then, Ellie, you and I can have a chat, go down to the music room. OK?'

275

'OK,' I say, unsettled.

'Come on,' he says, turning to me. 'I'll even put Diana Ross on for you if you're nice.'

We hit the cupboard hard, taking everything out and discussing what looks tired, what can be improved, what needs to go to recycling, and what Ash describes as an abomination of papier-mâché and broken artistic dreams.

He's funny, and lovely, and so easy to talk to. And now I know Jess doesn't hate him, I can even let myself enjoy his company. He tells me about London, about moving, about his mum and how happy he is that she's back at work. About his art project, and how she's the girl with kaleidoscope eyes, because she's lit up inside again – and how hard it's going to be to leave her for university next year. And I find myself confiding in him, telling him about my mum, my brother, our loss, the feelings that sometimes overwhelm me with their sadness and joy.

'I can't imagine what it was like to lose your brother. You're amazing, Ellie, to survive it, to be able to talk about it, to move forward.'

'I don't know if I have moved on, not really. I'm not sure any of us has – but we're trying.'

'Well, I still think you're pretty amazing, Diana.'

'Diana?'

'Ross. Really delicate and really strong at the same time.'

He remembered. And suddenly, my heart feels supersonic.

'What about you?' I whisper. 'It must be strange having a twin, someone you can share so much with. You seem so alike.'

'Elina's amazing,' he says, looking away. 'In fact, that's what I was trying to tell you the other night.'

'About Elina?'

He clears his throat. 'Sort of. When my dad died. I . . . I went off the rails a bit. I started drinking. Missing school. Sometimes I'd wake up in places with no idea of how I got there. I didn't care about anyone, just me, and how I felt, what I was going through.' He looks at the ground, his eyes distant.

'I got kicked out of school, Ellie. And not long after that, I ended up in hospital getting my stomach pumped. I became this person I didn't recognise. Someone my dad would have hated. Because I wanted to block things out, and not think about them. And it doesn't work. It never works. Elina made me realise that. I was drinking myself into a stupor – trying to pretend I was OK – and I had to stop pretending, and not be OK, and that's where I am now. Learning to clear up after myself.'

I graze his hand.

'I haven't had a drink in almost a year now,' he says, looking down at my hand. 'I wasn't trying to patronise you the other night, I was just trying to be your Elina. I don't want you to make the same mistakes I did.'

'I should have taken your advice.' I smile. 'Hangovers are hell.' I pick up his hand and hold it, because it feels like the right thing to do. But then he stares at me, so I let go and pretend to be unnaturally interested in the fate of some creepy-looking doll heads.

And we carry on like for this for a while, just talking and listening to different songs on our phones, educating each other on the things we like, the conversation easy. As we reach the end of our task, we head towards the final props to be sorted, a miscellaneous mishmash of random, unloved articles. We're suddenly close, inches apart, the space between us electric: and I could swear, for just a moment, I hear his heart beating, loud and out of step.

But then I think about his note, quietly tucked away under Jess's pencil case.

'Does this mean we're friends now?' I ask, sitting back on my heels.

'Sure,' he says, looking down. 'Friends.'

And just then, Mrs Aachara pokes her head through the door, saying we've done an incredible job. And that afternoon, I sing to Mrs Aachara's face. Not looking at her, but at least when she's facing in the right direction. Because for the first time ever, I want someone to see me.

And then I go home, and life carries on, even though the world has just turned, and only we know it.

♡ Song 6 ♡

Intro, Verse, Chorus - Earphones

There's a moment when I put my earphones in and the music takes over everything. It takes me places, makes me someone else.

And when I talk to him, that's how it feels. Except the someone else is just me. The me I could be, if I would just let myself try.

When you hear that sound, it turns it all around

And this song is anthemic but gentle, insistent but uncomplicated, the way it feels when I'm with him, in notes and keys and words.

It's playing whenever I look at myself, whenever there's a pause; filling the space between my words and my thoughts, my head and my heart; whenever I think of him.

45

Hello, Goodbye

When Monday rolls around, Ash and I have been talking every day. And suddenly I understand what Jessica meant: how easy it is to get lost in new relationships, because there's no one else I want to talk to, no one else I'd rather see. And I know that's weird, and not really right, when the person making you feel that way is your best-friend's-very-recent-ex-boyfriend, but it's like the Beatles, 'There's a Place' – that line that talks about the things someone says, and does, that you just can't stop thinking about. Because everything he says goes round my head, more times than I know is strictly necessary.

We talk about films, music, books – the way we grew up, how awful it is that his mother's family don't visit them, how they hated his dad and thought his mum should never have married him. And it's like I'm finally talking to someone who understands me. Someone who knows what it is to not fit in anywhere, not even the places you think you should. He's never felt white, but never felt brown either, never felt like anything other than Other. But he looks like him. Like the most beautiful, confident boy in any room. How is that possible?

So I walk into school thinking about him. Which is bad, I remind myself, as I scan the cool girls' wall for Jessica, because he's my best-friend's-very-recent-ex-boyfriend, who will probably just Aaron Green me, in the harsh and unfavourable light of this high school corridor.

But Jess isn't at the cool girls' wall, although there's a space for her, right between the McQueen sisters. I walk past her form room, and she's there. Sat on the ground, peering at her phone.

'Jess,' I say, looking down at her. 'Is this the new cool place to hang out? Am I going to find Billy and Addy and the rest of the lemmings here tomorrow?'

'Very funny,' she says, standing up.

'Everything OK?' I ask, glancing at her phone.

'Fine,' she says, sliding it into her pocket. 'Barb's picking me up after school. No more bus for me.'

'It's not the same without you.'

'I'll be back soon enough,' she says, and I think, I hope not. I hope she never gets the bus again if it means going back to that purple house.

'Lunch today?' she asks brightly.

'Definitely. So, how are you?'

'Fine. Good. I mean, Alfie is pretty much a twenty-four-hour party person, but other than that,' she says, smiling.

'Good thing he's so cute. He can get away with murder, that kid.'

'I know. Although Barb might actually kill him. She's so exhausted.

She's back at work full-time, and Dad isn't being as helpful as he should be. I'm going to offer to babysit a couple of nights a week.'

'You don't have to look after everyone, Jess.'

'I know that,' she snaps irritably.

'Sorry,' I say, taking her hand. 'I just want you to think about yourself for once.'

'I know,' she says, grimacing. 'I don't mean to snap. It just feels weird. Being back at school, not knowing what's happening with Mum.'

And then I spot Ash and Elina at the end of the hall. We both do. Jess shifts uncomfortably and looks a little like she might throw up.

'Hi,' Ash says, walking towards us, as Elina turns into the sixth-form corridor. 'How was your half term, Jess?'

'Fine.' Awkward. Silence. Because Jess's half term was many things, but none of them particularly fine.

'All right, Ellie?' and Adam of the Forearms is walking past me, smiling, or possibly something-else-ing at me, while his friend elbows him and grins.

Ash glares at him and moves closer to me, his fists clenched at his sides.

'Is that . . . ?' Jess asks under her breath, because I'd forgotten she'd gone home by the time Forearms and I disappeared.

I nod.

She turns towards Adam, her body language emitting a sound only I can hear. A sound that says: You Will Die If You Come Anywhere Near Her.

Forearms continues on his way, while his friend laughs at something he's just whispered under his breath. I can feel my face getting hotter. The urge to run feels overwhelming.

'Did you listen to that song I sent you?' Ash asks gently, his fingers brushing against my hand. And for a second, I forget about Forearms, because all I can think about is Ash, and His Hand, Near My Hand. Then I look at Jess. Her eyebrows are so high they're practically lost in her hairline.

'Um, yeah,' I stutter awkwardly. 'I liked it. Although, you know. HATE the name.'

'Why?'

'Because it's terrible. Rolling Blackouts Coastal Fever? Anything with fever in the name is just wrong.'

'Actually, "Fever" by Peggy Lee is one of your favourite songs,' Jess says, looking at me. And the expression on her face says something along the lines of: WTF is going on here?

'Ha!' I say, slightly manically. 'You're right. I actually love all things fever. "Jungle Fever", "Catch It like a Fever", "Summer Fever" . . . All the fevers, ha!'

'So, what was this song?' she asks, ignoring my rambling and returning to Ash.

'Rolling Blackouts Coastal Fever, "Talking Straight".'

And her face is like thunder.

'What's that supposed to mean?' she spits.

'Nothing, I just thought Ellie would like it . . .' he says, glaring back at her.

What. Is. Happening?

'So, anyway. See you at lunch, Jess,' I say, pulling him away.

'Bye,' she hisses, turning into her classroom.

'So, how was your weekend?' he asks.

'Er – what was that?' I demand.

'What was what?' he asks innocently.

'THAT. With Jess.'

'Nothing,' he says sullenly.

'Are you using me to get to her?' I demand. 'Because I'm better than that, and I will not be Aaron Greened.'

'What? What does that even mean? And NO,' he responds firmly. 'I sent you that song because I thought you'd like the band. I don't know what her problem is.'

'What happened between you two?'

Silence.

'So,' he says, changing the subject. 'I know you're meeting Jessica for lunch, but what about coming out with me instead? There's this great new artist at the Shelley, and Elina can give us a tour.'

'I can't,' I say apologetically. 'Jess is having a hard time. She needs me.'

He rolls his eyes and I consider punching him.

'Don't do that,' I say sharply. 'You don't know what she's going through.'

'Not sure what nail polish to wear this week?'

And this tips me from mild irritation to full-scale fury.

'She's my best friend, and she needs me. And I'm not going to shove it in her face that you and I are friends now.'

'OK, OK, I'm sorry,' he says, holding his hands up in defeat. 'I like how loyal you are. It's a good thing. Annoying as hell for everyone else, but good for the people you're loyal to.'

I try to smile, but all I can think about is her face when she saw us together, like maybe me being friends with him isn't OK with her.

'Bye,' I say, brushing his arm.

He salutes.

Please let it be OK with her.

Buzz.

Ash:

'Hello, Goodbye', the Beatles

I press the link, smiling. Then type a reply.

Ellie:

hello, hello

Ash:

i don't kno why u say goodbye, i say hello 🩶

46

Broken Glass

In our form room, Hayley is waiting for me. I slide into the desk next to her and smile in what I hope is a winning way.

'What are you smirking about?' she asks inspecting my face.

'What are you talking about?' I reply, feigning annoyance.

'Ellie. The last time I saw you, you were throwing up in people's mouths – and on pretty much everything else in your immediate vicinity. And the last time I spoke to you, you were dying of shame. So why is it that today, when you should by rights be doing the walk of shame, you are sitting here next to me, smirking?'

And I do not need reminding of my behaviour on Friday. Of the feeling I get when I think about Forearms or the stupid smirk on his stupid face, or his friend's laugh, or the fact that it feels like everyone is looking at me today because they saw me screaming about nipples and throwing up on myself. But then there's *i don't kno why u say goodbye, i say hello* 🖤 – and somehow that makes it all feel better. Even if it's not a red heart, even if it's just blue, for friendship, or whatever blue hearts mean.

'Hayley, can we not talk about Friday,' I say quietly.

'Fine,' she says contritely, as if suddenly able to read my mind. 'But still. You seem different. You seem . . .' She narrows her eyes, cut off by the arrival of Mr Gorley.

And despite Forearms and the associated vomiting, it may be possible I am smirking a bit. Possible I may even be walking around with my underwear on the outside, my Calvin Klein pink bralette and blue cotton shorts, shocking everyone with their colourful display and awkward sizing.

Things are changing. My parents know about drama, and even though it isn't quite OK yet, I'm not in a smock dress singing hymns to a nun, so it's OK-*ish*. Mum and I are turning into *Mum and I*. Ash and I are . . . some kind of blue heart friendship emoji. Jess is OK. I've sung to Mrs Aachara's face (with my eyes shut, but still). The more I try, the more people respond to me. The more people respond to me, the more I want to try. It's like *that* Ellie, the one I was hoping for all those years ago, has finally shown up.

And then comes the daydream. The one with Annie Lennox, 'Walking on Broken Glass' playing, as Ash and Jessica and I all sit together on the green, talking about music and books and my unhealthy obsession with *The Real Housewives of Cheshire*, the sun shining above us in a big blue sky. And we're friends. All of us. No awkwardness at all. Or maybe Ash and I are more than friends, and Jess is OK with that.

Is a big blue sky what it feels like to fall in love?

'Ellie . . . Ellie!' Ugh. Mr Gorley. 'Are you *with* us, Miss Pillai?'

'Sorry, sir.'

'Right,' he huffs, 'you lot and your daydreaming. Dream now, children, because trust me, life is not the dream you're all hoping it will be. In fact, one day you'll wake up to discover you've shrunk two inches, your children despise you and your wife's idea of an interesting conversation is to discuss your flaws and inability to use a garden rake adequately with everyone she knows. Or is that just me? Anyway, off you go, my pretties. Fly, fly,' he says, waving his arms theatrically towards the door. 'Can I say "my pretties" any more, or is that discrimination? Just remember I applied it indiscriminately,' he says to our retreating backs.

'See you in drama,' Hayley says, eyeing me suspiciously.

'OK,' I say, looking back at her. Then I look at my phone and read his messages again.

'Stop . . . smirking!' Hayley shouts down the corridor at me.

'I'm not!' I shout back.

But this time, I know, I probably am.

47

Parklife Part II

By the time I meet Jessica for lunch, I've had the same daydream at least twelve times. I've completely failed to pay any attention in history, and now appear to be missing entire decades from my revision (i.e. 1042–1066 – but seriously, Edward the Confessor? Surely the dullest monarch ever. Like, he confessed – what else is there to know?).

As always, our walk is soundtracked in my head, Phil Daniels extolling the virtues of feeding the pigeons, as the two of us walk quietly out of the school gates and into the world.

'I've got Blur, "Parklife" playing in my head,' I murmur, as we walk into the park.

'Good song that.'

'Yeah.'

Awkward silence.

'So, what's going on with you and Ash?' she asks as we sit down at our usual bench.

'Nothing. We ran into each other over the holidays and we got talking about music. We've got some stuff in common, that's all.'

And that's it. That's all this is. Two people who like to disappear inside their earphones. Who understand each other. Blue heart emoji understand each other. Not red heart. Not like him and Jess.

'OK,' she says, not looking at me.

'It doesn't seem OK. Do you mind me being friends with him? You know, after everything.'

'It's fine. Like I said. He's not a bad person.' She studiously avoids eye contact.

'It's not exactly a ringing endorsement, Jessica.'

'You don't need my permission to be friends with him, Ellie. Like I said, he's fine. I just don't really understand what you've got in common.'

'Lots of things,' I reply awkwardly. 'But that's not really the point. I want to know if it bothers you.'

And then I wonder what I'm going to do, if it does.

'As long as I hear your playlists first, then it's fine,' she says, smiling. 'And,' she says more seriously, 'I don't want you two discussing me.'

'I'd never do that,' I say, relieved. 'How are things with your mum?'

She takes a deep breath and stares at the ground.

'I don't know, Dad won't let me talk to her. She has to have some kind of assessment first.'

'Makes sense,' I say gently.

'But no one understands her like I do,' she says, slightly panicked. 'She would have come back, Ellie. I know she would. That's why I didn't say anything. I didn't want this to happen.'

'Jess, you can't keep making excuses for her. She needs help.

And this is the most important year of our academic lives –' she grins at me, because she has said this exact line to me about five hundred times – 'so you need to be able to focus. I mean, what if you got a 7 in something?'

She hits my arm.

'You make me sound so . . .'

'Overachieving?'

'Ellie . . .'

'Jessica . . .' I singsong.

'What did you mean when you said you and Ash had stuff in common?'

'Well, he knows Kate Bush is a singer and not a porn star, so, you know, he's in a minority,' I joke.

She looks at me, unamused.

'I guess there's just things I can talk to him about, like . . . the fact we both come from Asian families, the feeling of being different, of not always fitting in. Losing someone. Stuff like that.'

She looks down at her shoes.

'You can talk to me about stuff like that too, you know. I know you think I don't understand, but I do. I know what it feels like to not fit in. To not fit the box everyone else thinks you should be in.' She sighs heavily. 'I just feel like I'm letting everyone down, E.'

'You're not letting anyone down, Jess,' I say, stroking her hand. 'You're not responsible for what everyone else thinks of you. You're just you. Nothing more, nothing less. What other people think of you isn't your concern. Just what *you* think. You know?'

She smiles beatifically, in the way only she can. 'When did you get so wise, Pillai?'

'I've been working on it for years.' I smile. Because that particular truth is something I'm only just coming to terms with myself.

'Sometimes, I get so tired of being me. Of being the me that everyone thinks I am.' And just like that, I get it. How exhausting it is being Jessica Leigh King. The most beautiful girl at school. The smart kid, the good kid, the perfect kid. When life isn't perfect. Not hers. Not anyone's.

And I think of Stormzy, 'Crown' – his powerful voice, melancholy and beautiful. Of how hard it is to be the person everyone looks up to, that they expect so much of.

'Well,' I say, trying to lighten her mood, 'I'm tired of you too. I mean, I love Cardi B as much as the next person, but you really have to mix it up a little.'

'Excuse me, oh Music God. You are such a cliché. You weren't even born when half the stuff you listen to was made.'

'All the best things happened before we were born,' I lecture. 'The Beatles, the Rolling Stones, the Beach Boys, Creedence Clearwater Revival, Marvin Gaye, the Cure, Joy Division . . .'

'How long is this going to continue?' she asks pertly. I throw my sandwich at her.

'Ellie,' she says hesitantly. 'There's something else I want to talk to you about.'

'Yes?' I say expectantly.

'Feeling better?' I turn at the sound of the voice. James Godfrey. He of Tampongate, and the more recent, politically charged Sickgate.

'Hi, James,' I say flatly. 'Sorry about the other night.'

'It's OK,' he says, slightly grimacing. 'It's good to see you upright, without anything dribbling from your mouth, though.' I feel Jessica tense next to me.

'I'm so embarrassed,' I breathe. 'I owe you new shoes, don't I . . . ?'

'And a new jacket, new trousers, a new bag . . .' he says, grinning. 'Listen, don't worry about it. I'm just glad you're OK.'

'Oh, er, right, thanks.' And he is once again proving he is not the colossal jackass I once took him for.

'Listen,' he says, suddenly conspiratorial. 'Do you think I could talk to you about something?'

'Sure,' I say casually. 'Go ahead.'

He looks at Jessica nervously. 'In private. You know, when you have a minute . . .'

'Hi, James,' Jess says casually.

'Jessica,' he says, nodding at her seriously, a boy whose crush was once so intense he wore her name written on the back of a badge for a year.

'Don't mind me,' she continues. 'I need to get back to school anyway. Library day . . .' she says, brandishing a book that seems to have appeared out of nowhere. And with that she stands up and starts walking away.

'Jessica!' I shout at her back. 'I thought you wanted to talk?'

'It can wait,' she shouts back over her shoulder. 'Bye, James,' she says, waving. And he just watches her. Almost against his will. Because when Jessica King moves, people watch. And I watch her too, watch her and wonder when she will ever trust me enough to be honest.

'What's up?' I say, turning towards him, slightly irritated. She was talking to me, she was ready to tell me something.

He looks sheepish.

'Come on,' I sigh. 'Spit it out.'

'It's about last Friday.'

'Yes,' I say impatiently. 'Friday.'

'You know, the night you were sick . . .' he continues slowly.

'Yes, I remember . . . Well, I don't, but carry on.' I look at him, and he appears to be busy inspecting his shoes, possibly for vomit stains. 'Come on, James,' I urge. 'What is it? Did I tell you about Wilbur?'

'Who's Wilbur?'

'No one.' Wilbur is the imaginary friend I had until I was eleven. Because yes, I'm the girl who had an imaginary friend, *at eleven*.

'No, no, nothing like that. It's not about you, although you did sort of make it happen.' Now we appear to be getting somewhere. I've done something stupid. Obviously. Not Wilbur-related, but not good nonetheless.

'Made what happen? Come on, James, I'd like to be alive by the time you finally finish this story.'

'Do you really not remember?' he asks, looking at me suspiciously.

'No, I don't remember. What did I do, not do or make you do?' I ask, slightly fearful of his reply.

'In the car on the way to your house . . .' He looks at me as if this should jog my memory, then starts to embellish with his hands, rolling them back and forth, 'you told Hayley I was a nice guy, that she could do a lot worse . . . then you made me kiss her.'

'What do you mean, I made you kiss her?' I ask, appalled.

'You started chanting "kiss, kiss, kiss" in the back of the Uber, and sort of pushed us together.' The vague memory of this is stealing, half formed, into my mind. I'm sat by the back window, feeling nauseous, when I bump into Hayley as I lean over to vomit down my sleeve.

'Oh . . .' I say. 'Sorry.'

'Don't be sorry. We did kiss, sort of accidentally, but then you know, properly. It was nice.'

'Sounds romantic . . .' I say, trailing off.

He doesn't reply.

'Well, you know I like her.' I do know this, but I also know that Hayley, despite having given me a detailed description of the entire evening, has failed to mention this to me. 'What do you think I should do?' he asks.

'Have you talked to her about it?'

'No. We took you home, then I walked her home, and that was it.'

'Right . . .'

'That's not a good sign, is it?' he says dejectedly.

'Well, you know . . .' I say, trying to think of something positive, 'we were all a bit drunk. Maybe she's forgotten?'

'I think she's avoiding me,' he says forlornly, and I have to admit I actually feel a bit sorry for him then.

'I'm sure you're just being paranoid, James. Hayley really isn't like that.'

'She totally brushed me off this morning.' This actually does sound a lot like Hayley.

'Oh . . . Did nothing else happen, nothing at all?' I'm hoping for his sake that she didn't punch him, or demand he 'unhand her' in mock Shakespearean language.

'Well, I walked her home.'

'That must have taken forever . . .'

'It did, but we talked, and the time just passed.' This doesn't seem possible. The idea of the two of them spending any time together, not arguing, seems absurd.

'You . . . talked?'

'Yes . . . and we held hands.'

'You HELD HANDS? Why didn't you mention that at the start?' I ask in a disbelieving voice – because this, of course, changes everything.

'Yes,' he says impatiently, 'but we didn't kiss again.' I roll my eyes again at the statement. Despite having a girlfriend almost consistently for as long as I've known him, James Godfrey clearly knows nothing about girls.

'James, not kissing doesn't make it any less . . . intimate. Holding hands means something, it's more than kissing, it's, I don't know, it's just really personal.'

'Oh,' he says, brightening a little. 'Well, we did. We held hands all the way back to her house. But I haven't heard from her since, and she isn't talking to me today,' he finishes, looking slightly less optimistic.

'I'll talk to her, find out what's going on.'

'OK,' he says, looking relieved at the offer. 'Thanks.'

'So that's it, then?' I ask.

'That's it.'

'Good. Let's head back to school.'

'Sure,' he says, standing up and dusting himself off. 'So what's going on with you and that Ash guy?'

'Nothing,' I say, surprised to hear him mention Ash. 'Why do you ask?'

'He seemed pretty worried about you the other night. I practically had to offer him a kidney to prove I was responsible enough to get you home.'

And I'm part cringing, part singing 'Hello, Goodbye'.

'But Hayley wasn't letting him take you anywhere without her, so . . .' he trails away.

'Hayley,' I grin. 'Scary.'

'Yeah,' he smiles. 'I thought he was going to kill Adam. Not that he didn't deserve it.'

He looks angry then, his foot kicking at the pavement as we walk.

'It's my fault. I should never have introduced you to him,' he says grimly.

'I'm pretty sure I was the one pouring alcohol down my own throat, James. I'm just as much to blame.'

'For what?' he says, turning to me, surprised.

'Everything,' I say, staring at the ground.

'No, Ellie, you're not. What Adam did – taking you away from everyone like that. When you were in that state. It was . . .'

'Can we not talk about this?'

'Fine,' he says, kicking at the pavement. 'I should have let your boyfriend punch him though.'

'He's not my boyfriend,' I say curtly.

'Well, he wants to be your boyfriend.'

'He doesn't.'

And I don't tell him about Jessica and Ash this morning, or the air between them, thick with feeling.

'O-K,' he singsongs, his eyes on the road.

When we arrive at the school gates, he leans down to hug me.

'Thanks,' he says. It surprises me, but it feels nice, friendly, honest, because I think we are friends now. As he walks away, he turns around just once.

'By the way – your *mum*,' and he makes a gesture like fire. And clearly, this is the kind of friend James Godfrey is going to be.

I roll my eyes.

And I'm so wrapped up thinking about why Hayley would fail to mention she kissed him, I don't even notice Ash as I walk past him on the basketball court.

'Nice lunch?' he shouts at me, over the sound of dribbling balls. I look up.

'Hi,' I shout back, smiling.

'Where's Jessica?' he shouts, not smiling. I shake my head, not sure what he's getting at. He throws the ball to one of his friends, and walks off court.

'I just saw you with James. You said you were going out with Jessica.'

I shake my head in confusion. 'I did, but then she had to go. I just ran into him in the park.'

'Why are you always with that guy?' he asks, shrugging his shoulders in irritation.

'I'm not always with him,' I say, annoyed. 'And he's my friend.'

'Like me?'

'Yes,' I say, faltering, 'like you.'

'OK,' he says, turning around.

'What's wrong with that?' I say, running behind him.

'Nothing,' he says flatly. 'See you later, Ellie.'

And with that, he's gone. And there are no sweet messages or songs from bands with terrible names. Just silence.

Just. Silence.

48

The Test Run

Today Mrs Aachara is taking us through a dummy run of the exam. We're all so nervous at the thought of external examiners that we keep messing up our lines, missing our cues, dropping our props and generally behaving like the total amateurs we are.

'Guys, let's stop for a minute.' She looks frustrated. And concerned. We stop mid-scene and retreat to the audience area by the piano.

'Hayley,' says Mrs Aachara. 'You need to slow down. The pace feels frantic. James,' she says kindly, 'good job, but you need to engage more with Katja; you aren't even looking at each other, you're losing the intensity. Before half term it felt like the dynamic between you was better. Get back to that.'

If only. Over the past week, any civility between these two seems to have completely disappeared, resulting in what appears to be all-out warfare. I've tried to talk to Hayley, but she shuns any conversation around James or anything that might or might not have happened on the night of Sickgate, while James appears to spend most of his time trying to provoke her by sullenly ignoring anything she has to say.

'Let's try again,' Mrs Aachara says patiently. 'Start from Act 2, Scene 1 – Ellie, can we include the music this time, it might help set the tone.' I try not to panic, because I haven't managed to play in front of them all yet.

I sit at the piano and attempt to oxygenate my brain. Then I look at the group, and try to remember I've changed. That I'm earning my confidence. I think about all the people I know who are struggling with their identity, whether it's Granny or Aunty Kitty or Jessica, or me or Mum. I channel my feelings into Nermina, the friend left behind in Sarajevo, who misses Katja. Who pines for her best friend, while trying to work out who she is without her, just her, on her own.

My fingers press gently on the keys, and before I know it, my mouth is open, singing. And I can see the effect it's having on the play, as Arthur and Katja circle each other on stage. That it's slowed the pace, and lent them some rhythm to perform to.

As the scene ends, Mrs Aachara claps her hands. 'Better!' she says, relieved. 'Much better. Ellie – the music made a real difference,' she says, grinning from ear to ear, and me, I'm grinning too.

As we drift towards the kitchenette, James grabs hold of my arm.

'I knew you could do it,' he whispers.

'Thanks,' I whisper back, strangely proud of myself. Three minutes and forty-two seconds. Eyes mostly shut, but more than six people in the room. All facing forward.

'Careful!' Hayley yelps, as Andy stands on her foot in the

cramped kitchenette. And I watch as James watches Hayley, and Hayley watches James, and Lauren regales us with cat stories, which we're all terrible at pretending we're remotely interested in, but James always listens, and nods and smiles in all the right places, like good people do, like Ash would do, if I talked to him about cats.

At the end of the lesson, I drag behind a little, waiting for a moment alone at the piano. Some lyrics are coming to me, the way they do sometimes, with a steady beat, a running beat alongside them. It's half ballad, half wistful pop; a little bit of me, in notes, and keys and words.

These lights tell me to go slow
But these lights will not guide me home

And suddenly, as if out of nowhere, Ash is sat next to me. As if he's always been there. Just close enough to touch.

'I'm sorry,' he says.

'Friends?' I offer, my hands still hovering over the keys.

'Friends,' he says, smiling.

And my heart. My heart feels heavy and lazy and full, with the feel of him next to me.

You know these lights can go
If you stop and tell them so

I put my head on his shoulder, and wonder whether this is what friendship is supposed to feel like. Like the steady beat of a song that's only half written. And even though I don't need him there, I like him exactly where he is. Just close enough to touch.

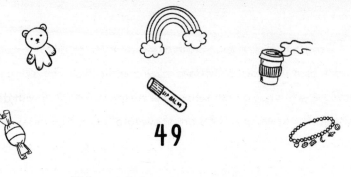

49

The Masterplan

I've decided enough is enough. It seems blindingly obvious that Hayley and James like each other – and being the good friend I am, it's my duty to step in and save them (and our GCSE grade) from themselves. I may not have much experience in the romance department, but I have an encyclopaedic knowledge of films, songs and books that do. And thus, I know. All those looks are pure Lady Gaga/Bradley Cooper, 'Shallow'.

Ash says I'm being nosy and interfering but he's also helped me come up with the Masterplan, so clearly he's come to accept my expertise in this area, even if it's more academic than practical.

'I thought James liked *you*,' he says for the hundredth time this evening.

'No, I'm just the friend of the friend that everyone wants to go out with. That's my role in life.'

'You are annoyingly oblivious sometimes,' he says, sighing. I decide to ignore his tone. It seems blindingly obvious, after the other day, that there's still something between him and Jess too, but I'm not masterplanning them, because I'm not sure how I'd cope if it worked.

I can hear Dad pacing around outside my door, as Mum quietly tries to coax him back downstairs. How does he know I'm talking to a boy? He either has a sixth sense (see: creepy-looking dad with dead eyes saying 'I see boys, who are showing a marginal interest in my daughter', as opposed to 'I see dead people') or I gave it away by the attractive shade of purple I turned when Ash called me over dinner.

'So, we're doing this at the park then?' he asks.

'Yes. Friday. You take James, I'll take Hayley.'

'Why am I helping you with this again?' he asks quizzically.

'Because you want to see Bradley Cooper and Lady Gaga express their undying love for one another?' I say hopefully. He ignores me.

'Should I pick you up?'

'I'm going with Jessica,' I say quickly. The last thing I need is my parents meeting Ash and telling him I used to lick chalk when I was a baby (this is true, apparently, I loved it). Not to mention it's entirely possible my dad will force him to take an IQ test, closely followed by a lie detector test, closely followed by reporting him to the relevant authorities as an evil monster intent on destroying his daughter's life and opportunities. Then my mother will tell him he's handsome and I'll have to consider drowning myself.

'Right . . .' he says.

'I don't mean it like that. It's just, my parents are a bit . . .'

'Strict . . . annoying . . . weird . . . robots . . . ?' he jokes.

'Not quite. But I promised I'd go with Jess, so it doesn't really matter.'

He's silent, so I attempt to Explain Myself.

'My dad is stood outside my door at the mere *thought* of me talking to a boy.'

'A boy, or a boy like me?'

'Someone with an encyclopaedic knowledge of Britpop?'

'I don't want him to think I'm a bad influence,' he says quietly.

'He wouldn't think that,' I say gently, 'because you're not. You're lovely.'

'Lovely?' he laughs. 'I've never been called *lovely* before.'

Not to your face . . .

'Anyway,' I say, ignoring his tone. 'My dad will love you. Just, you know, when I'm fifty, and he's come to terms with the fact I'm allowed to have friends of the opposite sex.'

Silence again. Followed by:

'OK. So, six thirty. Friday. Meet there.'

'Roger that.'

'I'm going to pretend you didn't say that.'

'Roger,' I say again officiously.

'You are so . . .'

'What, what am I?' I ask mockingly.

'If I say hilarious, are you going to cry again?'

'Shut up. See you tomorrow.'

'Roger,' he responds.

And when I put the phone down, I'm grinning like the numerous pictures of Lauren's cat. It's been two hours of arguments about the Beach Boys, *Pet Sounds* vs the Beatles, *Sgt Pepper*, him telling me about London, and art school, and next year – and me telling him about drama and the soundtrack, and how I played my song with my eyes shut, but somehow I need to open them.

And he's funny and clever and brilliant company, and my friend, who is moving away soon. And I know how friendship works, how to be a good friend – but no idea how to be anything more. How to be a Lady Gaga to a Bradley Cooper, when they're singing to each other like they're the only people that exist. Hayley and James can do that. And they'll be brilliant at it. And getting them together will have to be enough. Watching them together will have to be enough. Because someone, somewhere, deserves to be Lady Gaga. And if it isn't going to be me, it may as well be Mia from *Pulp Fiction*.

Buzz.

Ash:

'The Masterplan', Oasis

I lie on my bed and listen to the Gallaghers, all angry, downcast guitars and hopeful chorus telling me to cast my words upon the waves, when like me, my words can't swim, and will probably just drown.

But I ask you, Noel, if we're all part of a Masterplan, then who gets to decide? Who decides whether Hayley and James are meant to be together? Or whether Ellie Pillai gets a happy ending? And what her happy ending even looks like? Whether I get to dance like no one's watching, or I'm stood in a corner, wondering how I got invited in the first place. How much do I actually control of anything? Like Amis. Amis being gone. Who made that decision? Who took him away from us?

And it's all a bit much, to think that Noel Gallagher is the oracle I've been missing in my life. Although it's possible he might be. So I decide my masterplanning is over, and head downstairs to attempt a sensible conversation with Dad. Which, I'm guessing, is going to prove difficult.

50

Don't Think Twice, It'll Be All Right

When I get downstairs, I'm relieved to find Dad isn't there.

Mum's drinking a glass of red wine, sighing deeply, like it's the best thing that's ever happened to her.

'Long day?' I ask.

'Something like that,' she replies. 'More importantly, how are you? How's *drama*?' I sense her testing the word out in her mouth.

'Fine. I mean the exam's coming up, and we're definitely all getting nervous, but we had a breakthrough today, so that was good.'

She gives me a fleeting look, almost painful. I know how hard it is for her to be supportive when she thinks I'm failing, but at least she's trying.

'Tell me,' she says after a beat, patting the seat next to her.

'Well, Hayley and James have been fighting,' I say, sitting down.

'Why should that matter?' she asks, looking on the verge of a lecture. 'It shouldn't affect your grade, should it?'

'It's an ensemble piece – we're supposed to work together, Mum.'

'Well, I suppose that's good really. That you can pull each other's grades up.'

'Because if it was just me,' I stutter, 'I couldn't pull my own grade up, could I?'

I turn away from her, tears stinging my eyes.

'Ellie,' she says, putting her hand on my arm. 'That's not what I meant at all. I'm just trying to understand how it works. Can we start again?'

Silence.

'Please, *en anbe*.'

I turn back towards her. Try harder, Ellie.

'Well, today was better,' I continue stiltedly. 'We included the music I wrote, and it sort of tethered it, made it come together.'

'That's good,' she says brightly. 'So, you're pulling up *their* grades.'

I smile at her change of tack, and she smiles back.

'Hayley and James,' she asks in a suddenly hushed tone – 'are those the two who brought you home the other night? Are they a couple?'

'Not *yet*,' I say cryptically.

'And what about you?' she continues. 'What's going on with Jess and Ash?' Ugh. I'd forgotten I'd told her about that.

'Ash and I are friends, and Jess is fine with that.'

'Friends . . .' she says, sneaking a look at me over her wine glass.

'Yes, Mum, friends!'

'OK!' she says, waving her hands in submission.

After a minute or two, she takes hold of my hand.

310

'Ellie, can I talk to you about something?'

Oh God, not St Hilda's again.

'I know we haven't really talked about what you said to me a few weeks ago, but I think we should.' She swallows another sip of wine. 'I'm sorry if you felt I wasn't there for you when your brother died. I think you're probably right, that I wasn't quite here. But it was so hard, Ellie, I honestly don't think I'll ever get over it. It's no excuse, because I know you were just a baby too, and I wanted to be there for you – but I'm only human, and I just didn't have it in me; I wasn't good enough.' She looks at my hand, held loosely inside hers, like it's the most fascinating thing in the world. 'But you always seemed so strong, so capable, even though you were so little. And you've always been so close to your dad, I thought he had it covered, I thought you didn't want me. I thought you didn't need me . . . If I forgot you, if I didn't give you what you needed, then I'm sorry. I know it'll never be enough. But I am.'

'Mum,' I say gently. 'I know you love me.'

'I do,' she says back, her hand suddenly firm, 'and I'm going to be better at this listening thing, I promise.'

'I know,' I say quietly. And I do.

'My two favourite girls,' Dad says, walking into the kitchen. And relief floods me, that he appears to have forgotten the phone call, and, at least momentarily, The Lie.

He quietly pours himself a glass of wine and sits down opposite us. He takes a sip, his eyes half shut, then spits it out dramatically.

'That's awful! What on earth *is* that?' he asks Mum, his eyes flashing.

'It's non-alcoholic wine.' She smiles calmly.

'But – why?' Dad stutters.

'There's something I need to talk to you both about,' she says, steely. 'You know when I wasn't feeling well a few weeks back, I had that stomach bug and I couldn't keep anything down?'

My heart accelerates.

'Well, it wasn't a stomach bug . . .' she trails off.

And all I can think about is hospitals and crisp white sheets and tears and not knowing.

'I'm pregnant . . .'

Suddenly Dad's crying, his hand shaking around his glass, and me, I'm, I don't know what I am.

'Are you OK?' Mum whispers.

'Yes,' he says, swallowing lightly. 'You should have told me sooner. But yes, I'm OK. Of course I'm OK. We're having a baby. You're having a baby!'

'Ellie?' Mum whispers. She's looking at me so closely, I'm sure she can see right inside of me.

'It's great, Mum,' I whisper hoarsely. 'So great.'

But that's not how I feel. I don't know what I feel, but I know it isn't that.

'Really?' she says, looking at us both and smiling. 'I've been so worried about telling you. I'm twelve weeks. I wanted to be sure before I said anything.'

And I think: I already have a brother.

Dad wipes his eyes and smiles at us.

'I'm so glad we're all together like this,' Mum says, holding his hand. 'Do you remember when we used to listen to Dad's records on a Sunday night?'

'After our old-movie marathon?' I smile quietly.

'Less of the old,' Dad says, harrumphing. 'They're classic, not old.'

But all I can remember is Amis, scratching *Top of the Pops 1972* when he used it as a plate.

'Why don't we do it again now?' Mum says excitedly. And I don't want to, but I don't know how to say no.

And then Dad's dragging the trunk out from the back of the cupboard, while Mum flicks through albums; until she chooses Bob Dylan, 'Don't Think Twice, It's All Right', the first song I ever remember, from when she sang me to sleep as a child.

And my heart feels like the guitar strings in this song. Fast and fluttery. Even though his voice is like balm. A plaster on the hole that runs right through it.

There's a little sob in my chest. Just a tiny ache, somewhere so deep down I can't even describe it. And Mum looks at me wordlessly. The look is sad, but full of hope. Hope for the future, and this new bit of our family. And I listen to the harmonica in all its soft, acidic glory, and I think, I will learn to be OK with this. I will be happy about this, one day soon.

And then I think, where's Noel Gallagher when you need him?

'Are you OK, Mum?' I ask, noticing her stillness.

'They said . . .' she sniffs.

'What did they say?' asks Dad, concerned.

'They, they, said . . .' she continues sniffing.

'What did they say, Mum?' I ask urgently.

'Well . . .' she struggles.

'What, Nimi, what?' says Dad, his concern suddenly upgraded to full-scale panic.

'That I'm a . . .' she sniffs again.

'WHAT?' Dad and I shout in unison.

'A geriatric mother!' she wails.

'What?' I ask, looking at Dad for guidance. He shakes his head in annoyance.

'Don't be silly, Nimi, you're in great shape. You're not even forty yet! Every morning I wake up and something else has stopped working,' he grumps. And that's when the sadness, or whatever it is I'm feeling, turns to something else. I start laughing. Because it's just so ridiculous, all of this. The non-alcoholic wine, Mum being classed as geriatric when she gets ID'd for buying mulled wine, Dad deciding he's on the verge of a full-body breakdown. And suddenly Mum's laughing too.

'Harrumph. I don't know what's so funny about all this. It must be your hormones, Nimi,' says Dad, bewildered. Then that pause, followed by his gruffest possible voice. 'Ellie – who was that boy you were talking to earlier?'

And that's it, I don't think Mum and I are ever going to stop laughing.

51

Parklife Part III

Friday. The day arrives like any other lately, partly sunny, partly cloudy, cold and a little windy – a classic November, four-seasons-in-one-day day. A night built for burning piles of wood and setting off shiny fireworks, like every weekend seems to be for the whole month of November. I grab my yellow satchel and the toast out of Dad's hand as I walk past the kitchen, already late to catch the bus, and slam the door behind me, my arms half in, half out of my new *Love Story* leather jacket.

The truth is, I can't stop thinking about it. This Phantom Baby. Trying to be Amis. Trying to make me its big sister. But I'm already a big sister. Even if Amis is gone now. Should I be sad, or happy? Should I feel hopeful, or melancholy? Should I be listening to Hansen, 'MMMBop' (Mum introduced me to that one, and it is a seriously underrated pop classic) or Johnny Cash, 'Hurt'? I don't even know what music to play to soothe the feelings.

I want us all to be happy again, that's all I know.

The day passes in a blur, and I fear my lack of attention is going to start showing in my grades – even though actually I am consistently getting the best marks I've ever had in my life, as though somehow all this angst suits me. Maybe it's just the fact I'm starting to believe in myself. Maybe it's just that simple. That if you *think* you can, then you *actually* can.

I sit with Ash on the green at lunchtime, and try to believe that whatever happens, it's all going to be OK.

'Hey Ellie,' Forearms says, walking past, smirking at me. His friend sniggers as Ash stands up angrily.

'Just ignore him,' I say, pulling him back down again. Because every day since Sickgate, he smirks at me from somewhere. Trying to make me feel like an idiot. *More* of an idiot.

'You're shivering,' Ash says, sitting down and putting his arms around me.

I put my head on his shoulder.

'Mum's pregnant,' I whisper. He turns towards me, his face as close as it's been since the day we kissed.

'Are you OK?'

Up close, his eyelashes are inky black butterflies.

'I'm OK,' I say, staring back at him. And for a minute, I think I could be, if we could just stay like this forever. The world out there, and us in here. Except for the pins and needles raging through my foot, and the wind currently whipping my hair in his face.

'Hey, strangers.'

Elina appears beside us, and I sit up guiltily as she takes a seat next to us, clasping her arms around her knees: the picture of a little girl, fragile and unworldly.

'Hey,' he says adoringly. And it's easy to see why. She's cut-glass in a room of plastic cups. Not just the way she looks, but the confidence she exudes, the way she carries herself.

'Love the jacket.' She smiles. 'Very *Love Story*. What are you two up to?'

'Nothing much,' I say, thinking about Phantom Baby, and his arm, still clasped around my shoulders. 'How about you?'

'I've been in the art studio. I'm working on my final project.'

'Something about genetics, Jess said.'

'Yeah, I'm making a sort of family tree. Except no one from Mum's side will even talk to me,' she says glumly. Ash looks angry, but I can see him holding it back, his grip around my shoulders tightening.

They exchange a look, one only they can read.

'It's just weird doing the exams here,' she says. 'I know it shouldn't make a difference, not really, but I miss my old teachers, I miss my friends. I miss feeling like people actually know me. That I can be myself.'

'It must be hard,' I say, reaching out to rub her arm. 'Do you miss it too?' I ask, turning to Ash.

'Some things,' he says cryptically.

'Well,' she says sunnily, 'the people are nice – I mean, mostly. We got some grief when we were out for lunch with Mum the other day, but I guess that's to be expected sometimes, isn't it.' It's a question, but comes out a statement.

'And I do like it here,' she continues. 'It's quiet and beautiful, and most people are great. It's just different. It's not like we're going to be

317

here for long anyway.' She smiles beatifically at Ash, and it reminds me that all of this is temporary. That they'll be gone at the end of the year. That he'll be gone.

I shiver.

'Do you want my scarf?' Ash asks suddenly.

'Honestly, I'm fine,' I say, wrapping my arms around myself.

'I'll be a minute,' he says, sprinting away.

'That's my brother,' Elina says, smiling at me. 'Chivalry is alive and well.'

I stare back at her, unsure of how to respond.

'You know, Ellie,' she says, suddenly serious, 'Ash has been through a lot.'

'He told me,' I say, looking at my knees.

'So you know. He's not as strong as he looks,' she says, staring intently at me. And I'm not sure how to respond to that. Because maybe none of us is. Maybe we're all just playing the part of someone who thinks they're OK, while just trying to be OK.

'Scarf,' Ash says, appearing out of nowhere and trailing a Doctor Who-style stripy monstrosity around my neck. 'What are you two whispering about?'

'We're discussing where you've hidden your Tardis,' I say, picking up the end of the scarf and flicking it at him. And when Elina laughs, it's a bit like winning a prize. I made the beautiful girl smile. The beautiful boy has his arm around me. Am I actually awake, or is this one of my more elaborate daydreams? Is Annie Lennox, 'Walking on Broken Glass' playing? Where's Jessica?

And when I look up, I see the real thing. Walking so quickly towards the library, I'm sure she must be trying to avoid us.

'Jess!' I shout. She looks over and waves, a stilted smile like a clown's drawn across her face. I wave at her to join us, but she shakes her head.

I stand up. 'Sorry,' I say, sweeping my fringe out of my eyes and swallowing back the lump in my throat. 'I just remembered – I have to go.' Because this is exactly like my daydream, without the music, and without my best friend.

The twins look at me strangely, like I've finally turned into the aubergine I am convinced has become my natural skin colour. 'See you later.' I smile.

They exchange a look, weird and strangled.

On the bus home from school, Jess is quiet. She's staying with us for the weekend, while her dad and Barbara go to a wedding.

'Everything OK?' I ask quietly.

'Fine,' she says, turning to me and smiling. 'Just thinking.'

'I hope tonight works,' I say, trying to prompt further conversation.

'I don't think Hayley's going to enjoy being set up, Ellie. I hope you're prepared for that.'

'It'll be fine,' I say, jittery, because she's right and I know it.

'I'll never forget those chest pics James sent me,' she says, starting to giggle. I try to suppress a smile, because those *were* funny. It was more the look of pompous arrogance on his face than his actual chest that made us laugh. In fact, he was actually quite fit for a thirteen-year-old boy, not exactly Mr Green, but definitely not hideous.

'He's not so bad any more,' I say loyally. 'He's even quite nice most of the time.'

'Sugar Mice Nipples?'

'Don't be mean, Jess.'

'He tried to trip you up on the bus!' she exclaims. 'Although I suppose he did take you home the other night. But you're a much nicer person than me, Ellie.'

'That's true,' I say mock-seriously, as she swats me with her book. 'Anyway, he really likes Hayley, and I think they could be good together.'

'OK,' she says, squeezing my hand. 'So, how are Ash and Elina?' she asks, trying to appear nonchalant.

'Elina's a bit down.' I sneak a look at her, trying to work out whether or not to bring up lunchtime. 'Why didn't you come over and sit with us? Is it weird, me sitting with them? Because we can talk about it, if it is. If I'm being a terrible friend, sitting with your ex . . .'

'It's fine,' she says, interrupting my ramble. 'I told you. I'm focused on the exams. You can sit with whoever you want.'

And then even I can't ramble any more. Because tonight, the sun is breathing life into every vista, the view breathtaking as we make our way through the villages.

'I do need to tell you something, though,' I whisper.

'What's that?' she says, staring at a hay bale that seems to have turned gold in the light.

'Mum's pregnant.' She turns to stare at me. 'I wanted to tell you before, but I haven't seen you all day, and I didn't want to message it.'

'How do you feel about it?' she asks gently.

'Mum and Dad are so happy.'

'But you. How do you feel about it?' she probes.

'I want to be happy about it,' I say, looking away. Because I do, and I will be.

She holds my hand in the way that only best friends can. Like she gets it. Like she understands. And we walk home from the bus stop in silence, linking arms like we used to in Year 7.

And when we get home, we mention no more about Phantom Baby. We have dinner and get ready to go to the park. Jess, instantly gorgeous in a leather jacket, skinny jeans and gold ankle boots, and me, stood in my resolutely sensible underwear, wondering how embarrassing it would be to just wear my school clothes.

Jess flips through my hangers decisively and chooses me a black mini skirt – never worn – a green stripy polo neck, black tights, studded flat biker boots and the new brown leather jacket, all courtesy of Aunty Kitty.

'These clothes are amazing, E,' Jess says, whistling under her breath. 'I haven't seen you wear even half this stuff before.'

'It doesn't really suit me. Aunty Kitty sends it to me from New York.'

She whistles again.

'I wish I had an Aunty Kitty. And trust me, E, you definitely suit it,' she says, surveying her handiwork. And it's strange how much I recognise myself. Because this is how I look. And it isn't horrible, or invisible. It's just me.

We take the bus out to the park, and even as it rumbles along something about the evening feels laced with possibilities. And when we arrive, I can't tell whether it's the new clothes and the make-up, or whether I've just never noticed it before, but people actually do want to talk to me. Like maybe I haven't been invisible, just hiding, like one of those kids who stand behind something smaller than them during a game of hide-and-seek.

And all I can think about is Ash. About Hayley and James, and the Masterplan, and making it enough.

And when Jess is absorbed by the McQueen sisters, identically annoying in matching red bomber jackets, I hear a voice from behind me.

'Roger?' he says, as he leans down to kiss my cheek.

And I am once again the Human Aubergine.

'OK?' Ash says, looking at me quizzically, that smile of his nudging at the corners of his mouth.

'Yes,' I say, regaining my composure.

'Shall we?' he says theatrically, waving his arm as if introducing me to a circus ring.

'We shall,' I reply.

So I find Hayley and tell her I need to talk to her. Privately, straight away. And I lead her to where it's quiet, near the storage sheds further back from the pavilion.

'Are you OK, Ellie?' she asks, concerned.

'I want to talk to you about James.' The Dragon glares at me, its nostrils flaring.

'What do you mean? What is there to talk about?' I am now mere moments away from being burned down to a stump.

'I think you like him,' I breathe. 'And I know he likes you.'

'Ellie, this has got nothing to do with you. NOTHING. I don't like him, and I'm pretty sure he doesn't like me either.'

'He does like you, he has done for ages. He told me so.' She narrows her eyes, the look somewhere between thoughtful and homicidal.

'You don't get it, E. He's a footballer and I'm a . . . feminist vlogger. People like us don't go out. It would never work.'

'None of that stuff matters. Not really.'

She sighs, like a mother dealing with a small child asking 'why' repeatedly.

'Hi Hayley,' and when I look over, I see James, standing with Ash, a couple of metres away.

'James,' she says, arching her eyebrows. 'Can you tell Ellie to stop playing matchmaker? Apparently she's convinced we're made for each other.'

And that's when he does it. The bravest thing I've ever seen.

'But she's right,' he says. Hayley eyes him coolly. 'I do like you,' he goes on. 'I don't know if we're made for each other, but I like you. A lot. Other than your annoying ability to pick a fight with everything I have to say.'

I can see her softening, a hint of a smile playing at the corner of her eyes.

'Not everything,' she retorts. 'I agree we both like me.'

'You're infuriating,' he says, smiling.

'We can agree on that too,' she grins.

'Well, that's a start, isn't it?' he says, walking towards her.

And that's when Ash and I start backing away. Before his hand can reach her cheek, before her face can rest in his palm. But as we're retreating, I can feel my boots refusing to move in the mud. I wrench at them, gripping at Ash to keep myself from falling.

'Are you OK?'

'I'm falling,' I say.

'Me too,' he replies.

His smile is crooked, just a little less symmetrical than the rest of his face. Yet it's always been perfect to me, so I've never really noticed, never really cared. And that's it, isn't it? Perfection. The art of the imperfect.

As one foot releases from the mud, he pulls at me, trying to release the other, until suddenly it happens all at once, too quickly, like the pull's too much for either of us. We hurtle towards the ground, falling into each other as we land.

'I love it when a plan comes together,' he jokes. But I don't feel like laughing – I don't know why. He pushes himself up to standing and takes my hand, and every vein in it feels electric, like I can feel the pulses of his heart. And when we're finally stood up, my face upturned towards his, I keep hold of his hand and walk him towards the shelter, the strains of Lorde, 'Green Light' playing in my mind.

And those bright piano chords are pulling us together, our hands held tight. Him, and me, and all the notes that make us.

So I kiss him. Gently and urgently. Mud beneath my fingernails, and matted in his hair. The sound of green lights, and blue hearts, and all the notes that make them.

But then I hear something. Some*one*. And like a startled rabbit, I turn.

And it's Jessica, my best friend, her arms around someone's waist. Their fingers in the back of her hair.

Elina.

Elina's waist.

Jess's arms.

They're breathing hard, the two of them, caught in the act. And I look at them, and I look at Ash – none of them surprised, none of them concerned, not watching each other, just me, the one who's late to the secret, who's been in the dark. And I don't know what I feel, but I know there's anger, somewhere in there, for all these lies, all this evasion.

So I run.

I run and I run, with no care for horses, or ponies, or thoughts, or best friends, or green eyes, or green lights. I just run. Because running is still my thing.

These lights they blind you
They hurt not guide you

♡ Song 7 ♡

Intro, Verse, Chorus – Lights

It's a little bit country. A song of heartbreak and knowing. Confusion and understanding. A song of sweetness and joy, but also disappointment and disbelief. A song that hurts, even as it heals.

Cos I don't know anymore
What it is that I'm even fighting for

I want to stop running, but the notes are pushing me, driving me, the pace set by the rhythm of the music, time and distance measured only by sound. It's a song I will learn to love, but it will also be the song that reminds me of this moment. Of fear. Of lies and heartbreak and chaos. Of the mess that love can make of everything.

You need to know
That I've got to let you go

52

Clown Serial Killer Sky

I've got so good at running, it's a wonder I've not applied to be a cross-country runner. I could start a club for people looking to run away from their problems, or their lying best friends and their so-called new friends, or boyfriends, or whatever it is I should call Ash and Elina, whatever it is that they were to me. I don't know why I feel so angry, so searing, like tiny fires are erupting all over me. The November night isn't chilling me at all, not even a little bit, and as I run, I can see the firework displays, the noise of rockets and the showers of sparks that accompany them, that seem to cheer me on with their bold colours and pageantry, reflecting the fireworks that are trapped in my brain, fizzing and popping, looking for somewhere to explode.

They lied to me. Why? Why did she let me think that she'd been with him? Why did *he* let me think it? I can't understand it, why they didn't share this with me, why I had to find out like this – stupid, childish Ellie, always the last to know. It's all starting to make sense now, all the signs coming together, so obviously, right in front of my face. The notes she kept hidden from me, not *from* Ash, but delivered by him. All the

327

time she and Elina were spending together, the best friends, Ash in the background, their secrecy, pushing me away. Why didn't she talk to me? *Why does she never talk to me?*

I slow down and let my breath catch up with me. It's warm for November, and I'm overdressed for a run. I push my hair out of my eyes and look around me. I've run into the park with no obvious place to go and it's dark now, the sky swarthy and strange. A Clown Serial Killer Sky.

I follow the fireworks and head towards the lights, towards a crowd I can lose myself in.

Jessica. Jessica and her secrets. And I don't care that she loves Elina. I don't care that she loves a girl. I just care that she lied again. I care that he lied. That I was part of a game I didn't even know I was playing.

And I know I still love her, even if in this moment I don't. But him, I just can't. Because it hurts to love someone. It hurts when they don't trust you. Or when they lie. Or when you know one day they'll just be gone, even if they don't choose to be.

When I find the fireworks crowd, I run right to the middle of it. To a place I feel invisible. I let myself feel the fear of it, and I embrace it. Lost in the crowd. This is what it feels like to fall in love.

And me, I'm not invisible, and I'm not in love.

53

A Girl Called Ellie

My name is Ellie. Ellie Pillai. I used to have a best friend, and something like a boyfriend; or maybe he was just a friend who was a boy. But he meant something to me. They both did. And then I found out that they were lying to me, that I'd been lying to myself. That they were keeping things from me – big things, important things – like I was too childish or stupid to understand them. I've always thought that life was complicated, but really it shouldn't be. Why couldn't they tell me the truth? Why didn't I deserve the truth?

54

Jessica

When I finally decide to go home, the lights are on in the living room, shining down the street at me. I open the front door and heave a sigh of relief. I've been walking for hours, and all I want to do is lie down. Remove my mud-caked boots and turn off my brain, the fireworks inside still fizzing and popping.

I hang my coat on the bannister and walk quietly towards the stairs.

'Ellie?' Mum calls out from the front room.

'Yes,' I whisper, my eyes fastened on the stairs.

'Can you come here?' she asks, peering out into the hallway.

'I'm not drunk, Mum,' I hiss.

'Here please Ellie, now,' Mum says more firmly.

I follow her towards the lights, harsh and bright after the dark, comforting embrace of the hallway, fully ready to provide her with a breath test and the skill of walking in a very straight line. And that's when I see Jessica. Her mascara and eyeliner smeared across her face.

And even in this state she's beautiful, still better than me on my best day. It's annoying, like she should be in an advert for tissues.

'Why are you here?' I ask coldly.

'Jess is staying with us this weekend, Ellie. Remember,' Mum says. 'David and Barbara are away.'

'Fine,' I say. 'Sleep in the spare room. But don't expect me to talk to you.'

'Ellie, do you think we should talk about this?' Mum says, all worldly wise, looking at us like the teenagers we are.

'Talk about what?' I demand. 'Has she told you what's been going on, what happened this evening?'

'Jess has told me a little. Enough. Don't take it as an affront, Ellie. I'm sure it's not how she meant any of this to happen.'

'So she can lie?' I say angrily. 'It's fine for *her* to lie – but not me. I lie, and Dad can barely look at me, but she lies and it's all fine – because *she didn't mean for any of this to happen?*' I can feel my heart racing at a million beats a minute, my breathing shallow. I just can't. I just can't.

'Ellie,' Mum says firmly. 'This is different, and you know it.' And maybe I do know it's different. Maybe I do know it isn't the same, or anywhere near the same. Maybe I know that I'm the liar, that sometimes we're all liars. I'm just angry. Angry that Jess never shares anything with me. Anything real.

'Just listen to her,' Mum says quietly.

'I never lied,' Jess says. And I can feel my emotions explode suddenly, like a tidal wave, destructive and strong.

331

'You never LIED? You lied to me by omission, Jessica. You lied to me by not telling me the truth. You let me think Ash was your boyfriend. You let me believe I wasn't allowed to feel anything for him. And worse still, you didn't trust me. Didn't share this with me when I could have helped you. Could have been there for you. When were you going to tell me about this? WHEN? What am I, too stupid, too immature, not cool enough to understand? I bet you were all laughing at me, stupid, naive Ellie, she'll believe anything we tell her, won't she?'

She sobs quietly, not the howling heartbreak of someone in love – but timid and cracked, broken and hopeless.

'I'm sorry I didn't tell you, E. I wanted to. But you said, your aunty . . .' she says, watching the floor, the tears racking her body like she's convulsing. 'You said it would matter. If she was gay. And when I told Mum – she left. That's *why* she left. Because I told her I had a girlfriend, that I liked a girl.'

And suddenly my heart is breaking for her. Because she's just a reed; tall and thin, weak and brittle, torn from the ground, rootless.

'I didn't . . . I couldn't . . . I didn't know what I was feeling myself, for so long, and then when I did, when I tried to talk to her about it, we argued. She said it was wrong. That what I was feeling was wrong. That I was wrong.'

I want to find the hammer my dad has no idea how to use for DIY, and smash it into her mum's stupid purple walls.

'She smashed all of the photos, and she left. When she didn't come back, I didn't know what to do. I couldn't tell anyone. I knew no one would understand, that no one would accept it, so I broke up with Elina, and I came here, that night in the rain. And I wanted to tell you, Ellie. So much. But I couldn't. I couldn't face losing you too.' She looks at me then, the tears falling silently. 'I didn't mean for tonight to happen. I've been trying to avoid her, but then I saw her, and I just couldn't . . . I'm sorry, I'm so sorry.'

My heart is pounding, confused and lost, but I go to her, almost blindly, and kneel in front of her.

'No, Jess, please. That's not what I meant. I didn't mean it would matter to me, or to my family, not really. OK, Granny's a bit . . . *Granny*, but when you're a family, you just love each other, OK? For whoever you are.' I look at Mum momentarily, and she's smiling at me like I've learned some great lesson. Or maybe like she's learned some great lesson. 'I want you to be who you are – I just don't want to be lied to.' And then, 'Your mum was wrong. Your mum IS wrong. Everything about you is fine, perfect, what you're feeling is fine, it's perfect. Your mum is WRONG, OK? You can feel what you want, for whoever you want. I'm not going anywhere. Just don't lie to me, Jessica, please.' And when she looks at me, the silent sobs go from quiet convulsions to screams, to howling and heartbreak. And I am no longer angry – not with her. But at her mum, at the situation, at the stupidity of people and their rigid, awful beliefs.

I breathe deep, and look at my friend, and I love her against all of my will.

Because that's what friendship is, love, despite everything.

55

Sunday Bloody Sunday

It's a U2 kind of a day. A screeching, anthemic, 'Sunday Bloody Sunday' kind of day.

I lift my head off my pillow, and all I can hear is Bono, singing over and over in my brain, until that sudden change of tone, from not believing the news, to believing everything could be OK. And therein lies the beauty of U2. It's never really dark or oppressive. There's always something optimistic and hopeful and beautiful beneath it all.

I stand up and rub my eyes, then walk quietly to the spare room, knocking gently on the door.

We spent yesterday just talking. I wanted Jess to know she was safe. With people she could trust. But today I want to talk to her about Elina. About the fact I think she might be in love with her.

'Come in,' she says quietly.

'Good morning,' I say, sitting down next to her on the bed. 'How are you feeling?'

'Better,' she smiles.

'Are you going to talk to your dad today?'

'Yes,' she says, taking a deep breath. 'Tonight.'

'That's really good, Jess,' I say, squeezing her hand. 'I'm proud of you.' I leave a silence, trying to gauge her mood. 'You know, you never told me how you left things with Elina on Friday.'

'We've broken up,' she says firmly.

'But you still like her?' I sneak a look at her hands. Jess's hands are a total giveaway when she's lying. She taps, like she's drumming to one of those songs she likes by Lil' this or Lil' that. I must have missed so much tapping over the last three months, even if technically she claims she never lied.

'I don't know,' she says flatly. 'When we broke up she said I wasn't being honest with myself, that I wasn't being honest with you. She said if I couldn't accept myself, then she didn't want to be with me anyway. Last night was just . . . I don't know what last night was. A mistake. A one-off.' At this final statement, her hands start drumming lightly on the bed, and I can almost hear the sound of some rapper claiming the woman ain't nothing but a gold digger.

'Does she know what happened with your mum?'

She doesn't reply.

'Don't you think you owe her that? To be honest about why you broke up with her?'

'I don't know, Ellie. I don't think she'll care.' Her fingers are manic now. She's clearly moved into some kind of synth-electro pop, possibly the Human League, 'Don't You Want Me'.

'I don't think that's true, Jess. I think she would care. And if she doesn't, then she isn't worth it – and I'll karate-chop her for you.'

'Karate-chop her?'

'Like we learned in Year 7.'

'Well, technically, you didn't actually learn to do that, Ellie. You faked a stomach ache and went to lie down.'

'I got the gist,' I say, smiling. 'But you should talk to her, Jess. You know you should.'

'What about you?' she asks. 'Are you going to talk to Ash?'

'There's nothing to talk about,' I say brusquely.

'On Friday, you said you weren't allowed to feel anything for him. But we were never a couple, Ellie. So you can. You can feel something for him.'

'But I don't. And honestly, it's probably better that way.'

'Why is it better?' she says, frustrated.

'I don't like him like that. I thought I might, but I don't.' Damn, I'm a good liar. Other than when I'm spectacularly caught out by my mother.

She looks at me warily. But the truth is, I've put Ash away in a box. Because in the end, he'll just leave a hole in my heart. Like people do. Like Amis did, without even wanting to.

'She did try calling me,' she confesses.

'So talk to her,' I urge. 'Even if it's just to end things honestly.'

'Maybe,' she says. 'I don't know. But for the record, I think you should talk to him too. He was just protecting me, Ellie, protecting Elina. He always liked you, he just knew everyone assumed it was me and him who were a thing, so we sort of kept it up, so Elina and I could just be, without everyone knowing, without everyone getting involved.' She looks at her hands, no longer drumming but limp. 'It was my fault,

Ellie. My fault he couldn't just ask you out. He was protecting me, I wasn't ready to tell anyone, and Elina asked him to.'

And I know it isn't his fault, that it's not hers either. Just the circumstances. The way people are built to judge each other and tear each other down, to annihilate differences with scorn and rage. But it doesn't matter anyway. Because I've made my decision.

'It's not your fault, Jess. I just don't feel that way about him.' She looks up at me, the way she does when I let her do my make-up sometimes, focused and sharp. 'Call her,' I say, standing. She nods.

I go back to my room and stare at my phone.

Ash

8 missed calls

1 voice note

1 message

I push the voice note icon, pressing my phone against my ear.

Ellie, I know what you're thinking. Actually, I don't know what you're thinking. I never know what you're thinking. Just call me. Please.

And ten minutes later, a WhatsApp message.

'Ellie?'

'Yes,' I say, looking up at Jess stood nervously in my doorway.

'She wants to meet in person.'

'OK,' I say, sitting up. 'Can I do anything to help?'

'Come with me?' she pleads.

Anything, High School Gods. Anything but that.

'OK,' I reply.

56

Know Any Good Dry Cleaners?

We take the bus into town, and walk to the Spoke. As always, the waitress is rude and condescending when I order a peppermint tea, so I change to a flat white. Because I'm a grown-up, and apparently grown-ups love coffee.

It's horrible.

I push it around the table until Elina appears, then do everything in my power to appear as small as possible.

'Hey,' she says, sitting down opposite us. 'How are you?'

'I'm fine,' Jess says quietly, staring at her hands wrapped tightly around her cup. I nudge her. She is many things, but fine is definitely not one of them.

'I'm glad you called,' Elina says. And she's classic Audrey Hepburn today; her short dark hair tucked behind her ears. Black skinny jeans and ballet pumps. I want to ask her to sing 'Moon River'.

'Me too.'

'I'm sorry about Friday. I never meant to upset you like that.'

'You didn't,' Jess says. 'I upset myself. Because I haven't been honest with you. I haven't been honest with anyone.'

I stare at my shoes and try to pretend I'm invisible. I play *Breakfast at Tiffany's* in my head, but all I can see is Mickey Rooney, a gross, racist caricature of a Japanese man in a bath.

'What haven't you been honest about?'

'My life is complicated, Elina. My mum . . .' Jess trails off, reaching for the words. 'She's sick. She's been sick for a long time.' I nod, encouraging her to go on.

'I don't mean sick with cancer or anything like that. I mean, in her mind. She's bipolar, and she struggles with things, emotionally. Especially when she doesn't take her medication.' Elina looks at her across the table, her eyes fastened on her face.

Jessica looks down at the table, not sure how to go on. So I do it for her.

'Elina, Jess's mum doesn't take her medication quite a lot, and it means that things have been difficult at home. For a long time.' Elina stares at me, as if wondering why my brain is playing racist movie clips.

'She left home a while ago,' Jess continues. And I can hear the beginnings of a lump forming in the back of her throat. 'She walked out on me a few weeks ago. When I told her about us.'

Elina looks like she's been slapped.

'Why didn't you tell me?' she begs. 'I would have understood. I could have been there for you.'

'I didn't know how,' Jess pleads in return. 'I was confused. She was

340

gone, and I missed her. I was scared and I had no money, and no Ellie, and I just, I didn't know what to do.'

'Jess,' Elina says, reaching out over the table. 'I'm so sorry. Where are you living now?'

'I'm staying with my dad. But Ellie and her mum, they're the ones who took me in. They're the ones who have always been there for me. And what I did to Ellie, shutting her out when you and I were together, it was wrong. I've lied to a lot of people. But I'm not going to do that any more. And that's why I'm here. To tell you that.'

'I've missed you,' Elina says, stroking her hand. 'I wish you could have talked to me, that I could have helped you, but I'm here now. And I'm not going anywhere.'

'OK,' Jess replies shyly.

'OK,' says Elina, smiling.

And suddenly their hands seem fused across the table. And I'm just there, the giant brown elephant in the room. I stand up and excuse myself, taking my coffee to another table.

And that's when I see him, on the other side of the cafe – see that Elina has brought her cavalry along too. It's too late for me to run, but I try anyway. I turn quickly and gracelessly and directly into an elderly woman's chest. My coffee spills everywhere, and the woman is loud and effusive in her irritation, brushing the tiny droplets of coffee off her scarf like I've poured battery acid on it. 'Tsk,' she repeats over and over, the sound spraying fountains of saliva on to my jumper.

'I'm so sorry!' I cry to the scarf lady. But she isn't interested.

'Let me get you another drink,' the waitress smirks. Maybe it isn't a smirk. Maybe it's just her face. Set to a permanent self-satisfied scowl. I wipe myself down and pretend this isn't happening. That I haven't spilt coffee all over myself and some unsuspecting stranger, while Ash is potentially watching me, congratulating himself on his escape from Ellie the Awkward Pillai. Dear gods (any of them), please don't let him have seen me. But when I turn, he's hovering behind me.

'Are you OK?' he asks with the hint of a smile.

'I'm fine,' I say, attempting elegance in the face of disaster.

'I thought you didn't like coffee?'

'I don't,' I say curtly, trying to rub the stain off my top, and only succeeding in spreading it further.

'Can I help?'

'Know any good dry cleaners?'

'Are we ever going to talk about Friday?' he asks slowly.

'There's nothing to talk about. I'm sorry. I shouldn't have kissed you.'

'Why?' he says, hurt. 'Why shouldn't you have kissed me?'

'I don't feel that way about you. I'm sorry. I have to go,' I say firmly, putting the coffee cup down. And just like that, it's over. Whatever we were is over.

That night, even though the house is completely quiet, I still can't get to sleep. There's a symphony in my head. A cacophony of noise I can't seem to drown out. And it isn't a good noise. Not like it usually is. It's chaotic and loud and confusing. I reach under my bed and pull my headphones on, and without even thinking about it, I close my eyes and click into the first playlist I find.

I open my eyes and look out of the window; and there it is. An actual pink moon. Glowing and pearlescent. And I fall asleep to the sound of Nick Drake crooning, pink, pink, pink, moon.

♡ Song 8 ♡

Intro, Verse, Chorus – Pink Moon

I wrote this song to make sense of something. To make loss into light. Silence into sound. It's about my brother. About knowing that somewhere, we share the same pink sky.

> *And he's burning through space*
> *Lighting stars in his wake*
> *On his way to you*

It's soulful and melodic. A music box mixed in thick, heavy harmonies. It's about hope and heartbreak. Joy and loss.

Because Amis taught me this – when your heart breaks, you can't give up hope.

57

Girls, Girls, Girls

When I walk into the playground on Monday, Elina and Jess are holding hands. Gossip levels have reached fever pitch, and there's a strange buzz, like a swarm of bees surrounding them. Some stare openly, while others gather in groups. And then someone spits at Elina. 'You two make me sick,' he hisses. That's when I run to Jess, because she's about to karate-chop him, claw his face off and kill him, right here in the playground of this quiet east England school.

'Jess,' I hiss, as I reach her. 'Stop!' And actually, when I look around, people are surrounding the boy who said it, and the buzz isn't strange, it's angry and vitriolic, directed not at Jess and Elina, but at him.

'He's not worth it,' Elina says, taking Jess's hand. Then someone starts clapping, and someone else joins in, and maybe it's only half of the playground, maybe it's not every single kid, but it's a lot of them. And I think: sometimes people surprise you. Sometimes people are so much better than you have ever given them credit for.

'Have you heard about Jess and Elina?' Hayley asks when I walk into form room minutes later.

'Yes.'

'So . . . how long's it been going on?' she asks, wide-eyed.

'Does it matter?' I ask, annoyed. Girl likes boy. Girl likes girl. Why does it have to be a Big Deal, when it's basically just a person liking another person.

'I don't mean it like that . . .' she says awkwardly. 'I don't mean to gossip, or anything . . . it's just so exciting. Our first lesbian couple.'

'That we know of . . .' I say quietly. 'And she's not a lesbian, she's bisexual, not that it matters. Anyway, enough about Jessica,' and I swing my attention to her. 'What happened with you and James on Friday night?'

She blushes.

'We're going to try, OK, Miss Woodhouse?' she says, referring to one of her favourite Jane Austen characters, the matchmaker Emma Woodhouse. And I smile. There are two new couples at this school, four happy people who might not be together if it wasn't for me. I may be terrible at managing my own love life, but it turns out I'm pretty good at managing other people's.

After Mr Gorley takes the register, Hayley and I head to drama. Outside the studio, James is waiting for us. He reaches out to Hayley, pulling her into his arms from behind, and plants a dainty peck on her cheek – no doubt as instructed by Hayley, who hates any and all public displays of affection – and continues talking to his friends.

The entire class stands, mouths agape, staring at them, as Hayley blithely continues telling me about her next vlog post.

Because, Hayley Atwell and James Godfrey! Jessica King and

346

Elina Anderson! Cue REM, 'It's the End of the World as We Know It' playing at full volume in my head, as Michael Stipe assures me everything should feel fine.

Note to self. It doesn't.

I'm glad when Mrs Aachara appears and the music grinds to a halt. Because all the way through the lesson, I know it's true. Things are changing. Things have changed.

'Are you OK?' Mrs Aachara asks, as I drag behind at the end of class. 'You seem distracted.'

I turn to look at her. She's dressed in an elaborately beaded red top, the sort of thing you wear underneath a sari, but she's wearing it like a crop top, with a blazer, jeans and ballet pumps. And it's that mix of eastern and western that gets to me; the way she seamlessly embraces all the different parts of her, when I can't seem to embrace anything.

'I'm fine.'

'Really?' she asks, peering at me.

'Just thinking about the exam.'

'You're going to do fine, Ellie,' she smiles. 'A lot better than fine, if I'm honest. You've really brought that play to life. It's been wonderful seeing you come out of yourself. It's one of the things I'm most proud of about this year – watching the real Ellie Pillai emerge.'

'Thank you,' I whisper shyly. Then after a beat, 'I guess you know about Jess and Elina then?'

'Yes,' she says brusquely, turning to clear the studio up for her next class.

'Do you think it makes things harder?' I ask. 'Not being the same as everyone else?'

She turns back towards me and looks at me strangely.

'You know better than anyone what it's like to be different,' she offers. 'But different doesn't have to mean bad. We have to be true to who we are, and if that means that sometimes things are a little harder, then we fight harder for them.' She watches me carefully.

'I met my husband when I was eighteen,' she continues, looking out of the window. 'I was in my first year of university, and he was twenty, in his third year. We lived in the same halls of residence, and I used to see him around campus sometimes. He always seemed to be laughing or making a joke of something. I was alone in England, I'd been sent here to study, and it confused me, caught me off guard how different things were here, how different I felt here. One day we got talking, and I told him how lost I got in the city. So we started taking walks together. Every day, somewhere new. And that's how we fell in love. Walking around a city.' She sighs. 'He was an Englishman. White. And when I told my family, they wouldn't accept it.' She looks back at me then, a million miles away, but also right here, in this moment. 'I was supposed to marry a nice Indian boy, someone my parents picked out for me. But in the end, I couldn't, I chose him. Because he was the one place I never felt lost. Where I knew I belonged. And for fifteen years, until my father died, none of my family ever spoke to me again. Not even to my children. Even now, we aren't fully accepted, although I know my mother tries. So you see, Ellie, I've always known that being different isn't easy, that choosing love isn't always easy. But it is right.

My children know that. And I want them to fight for what they believe in. Because I wouldn't change anything, Ellie. Every day, I know I made the right choice.' She carries on tidying, and for a minute I just sit there, attempting to work out what it is she's trying to tell me.

'Thanks, miss,' I say, standing up. She smiles, like she knows more about me than I know about myself.

'Are you coming to the dance next week?' she asks.

'Maybe,' I smile.

'Well, you should. I've been making paper snowflakes all weekend, and it's going to be fabulous.'

I smile at her.

'I'll think about it,' I say. And I do think about it. I think about a lot of things, but somehow, nothing seems any clearer.

58

I Guess That's Why They Call It the Blues

I lie on my bed listening to a lot of grunge. And Elton John, 'I Guess That's Why They Call It the Blues'. Because the sound of that sad harmonica, and his backing singers *shoop*-ing and *oo*-ing, seems to pretty much sum up my existence.

And the following week passes in a blur. I busy myself with studying, preparing for the drama exam, Christmas shopping, helping Mum clean out the fridge, alphabetising Dad's bookshelf – anything that distracts from my official status as Third Wheel Extraordinaire. Don't get me wrong. I'm happy for Hayley and James, happy for Jess and Elina, but the way they look at each other now, the way their hands seem suddenly and permanently fused, it's all too much for me, sending my stomach into a sharp downward spiral.

I spend lunchtimes back in the music room, my old faithfuls, the piano and Miss Mason, never giving up on me, never turning me away. And it's not that I mind. Because I've realised I like my own company. I choose it. I just hate the idea that Ash is out there somewhere, thinking badly of me, maybe even hating me.

When we pass in the corridor, he doesn't even look at me. Even the sixties girl group don't appear any more. Just a sad brass band, playing his song over and over. I'm trying not to feel sad, but empowered that this was the right thing to do. To choose not to hurt. To choose not to lose. It's just, somehow, I feel like I've lost anyway.

'E! Why didn't you call me back last night?' I turn at the sound of Jess, stood over me in the hallway as I make my way to French. 'I left you three messages. I bought you a ticket to that new film, but I couldn't get hold of you.'

'Sorry, Jess. I promised Mum I'd help her defrost the fridge.' The absurdity of the statement only strikes me once it's fully out of my mouth.

'O-K . . .' she singsongs, unsure.

'Mum's been really stressed with work. Apparently people need extra therapy in the run-up to Christmas . . . anyway, I promised I'd help around the house a bit more.' And that bit is true; I have been helping Mum out more than usual. It's strange, this sudden need for her after all these years, but we've both welcomed it – like my mother and I are dating, and think it may lead to something more serious.

'Right,' she says, giving me a sharp look. 'I've got to run or I'll be late for geography, but I've bought you a ticket for the winter dance. You're coming with me and Elina.' I look at her and consider checking her temperature, in case she's running a fever, and has no idea she's making no sense whatsoever.

351

'You really don't need to do that, Jessica. You should just enjoy going with Elina. I don't need to tag along like some loser who needs their best friend to take them on dates. Honestly, I really don't want to go anyway, I'm happy to sit it out.'

So, maybe that bit isn't strictly true. Maybe we've been planning this for years – our first year at the winter dance. We were going to be nineties supermodels and best friends Amber Valletta and Shalom Harlow. But now she has Elina. And I have no desire to be Third Wheel Extraordinaire in public.

'Ellie, you're going. We've talked about this forever, and you are not missing it. Elina and I have talked about it, and we've agreed it's what we want to do. Not to mention the addition of an extra person might save us from being stoned the second we enter the room.' And that's something I haven't really thought about. That not everyone has wholly accepted this new state of being, that not everyone has accepted them.

'Look, please, Ellie,' she says, her voice taking on a more gentle, wheedling tone. 'I want to share this with you, and it would be great to have your support. Elina is so confident, so sure about everything. I don't know how she doesn't care what everyone else thinks, but I can't be like that.' And I glance at her and understand completely, what it is to be judged for something you fundamentally are, but have no choice in being.

'OK, fine,' I say grumpily, 'but I'm running late for French and that woman is going to force me to conjugate verbs in front of the whole class again, and I really haven't done enough revision for that.'

'Call me later.' She smiles in triumph. 'And remember, I'm not taking no for an answer.'

And I think: there's literally nothing I want to do less than attend that dance. Other than conjugate verbs, or defrost the fridge again.

I walk into French late, but thankfully, Madame Keener is distracted giving out our test scores and I slide into my seat almost unnoticed.

'E,' whispers Hayley as I take my seat next to her. 'What were you doing last night? I tried to get hold of you for ages.' I consider telling her the fridge story, but decide it's too dull to repeat.

'Didn't see my phone.'

'So, are you coming to the dance or not? James and I were thinking you could come with us. There's a guy on the football team who thinks you're really cute, but he's convinced you're a lesbian – you know, because of Jessica.'

'For starters, she's bisexual . . .' I say, irritated.

'I know that. I said that to him. Either way, he likes you, and he isn't hideous to look at or talk to, so I thought . . . maybe we could double date?' she continues, blithely unaware of the look of incredulity on my face.

'Are you serious?'

'Yes, why?' she whispers, lowering her voice as Madame Keener glares at us.

'Um, because I don't know him? And I don't exactly have the best track record with footballers . . .' I say, speaking slowly, as if she's hard of hearing, or incapable of understanding the basic tenets of life.

'James says he's nice. He's not like that horrible Adam . . .' she continues.

'Listen, I don't want to go to the dance as it is, but Jess is forcing me to go with her and Elina. She thinks a group might make it feel a bit less formal, stop everyone being quite so judgemental. Strength in numbers and all that.'

'Maybe we could all go together? A bigger group would be even better, right?'

'Why on earth would you want to do that, Hayley? You don't even like Jessica.'

'I like her better now she's gay,' she says acerbically. I look at her and raise my eyebrows. 'Bisexual. Whatever. And as a matter of fact, I think I've misjudged her. It must have been hard coming out. She's not the shallow socialite I thought she was.'

'Is everything OK, Hayley?' I ask under my breath, because she doesn't look all right. She looks sweaty and nervous, like she's about to pass out.

'I'm fine,' she whispers back, annoyed. 'I just don't want to go with him on my own, OK? Happy now? I've never been to a dance with someone like him, and I feel a bit stupid. He knows everyone, and everyone likes him. He's taken loads of girls out before, and he knows what he's doing. What if he wants to . . . you know . . .' I look at her then – this confident, smart, incredible person – and I wonder how she doesn't see it, the way he looks at her.

'Come on, Hay. You're clever and funny and brilliant, and he likes you so much. There's no reason to be nervous. Just take things at your own pace. What you feel comfortable with, and nothing more.' She looks so deflated at my advice that I can't help but relent. 'But . . . I'll talk to Jessica. A group might be fun. Like you say. Take the pressure off everyone.'

She smiles gratefully.

'Ellie Pillai,' Madame Keener announces in her perfect French accent (why does my name sound so much better in a French accent?), calling me to her desk for verb conjugation and judgement. I stand up and walk over to her, wondering how, in the space of half an hour, I've been talked into attending the dance with the two couples I've spent the last week trying to avoid. I'm no longer a third wheel, but a fifth, and when I think about it, I can't decide whether this is better or worse.

59

Definitely Maybe

It's Friday and I'm waiting for Jess and Hayley to arrive so we can get ready for the dance. I've been home from school for an hour, and Dad's back early too, skulking around my room with all the subtlety of a sledgehammer.

'Dad?' I say for the tenth time in the last sixty minutes. 'Do you want something?'

'No,' he says, pretending to inspect an imaginary crack in the wall. And this has been happening a lot since he found out about drama. The skulking around and checking on me, never quite trusting me.

'OK,' I sigh, leafing through my records.

'Do you have my *Pink Moon* album?' he asks accusingly.

'Yes,' I say, picking it up and holding it out to him.

'It's fine,' he says gruffly, waving it away. 'I was just checking.'

I put it down again.

'So . . . is anyone picking you up for this dance?'

'We're going in a group, so no.'

'With boys?' he queries, trying not to look panicked.

'Boys and girls, Dad, yes. And don't worry. No one asked me to go specifically, so you can stop looking so horrified.'

I kick the bottom of my bookshelf, as if trying to punish it for this fact. You always hurt the ones you love.

'OK,' he says, satisfied, and just when I think he's finally going to leave, he turns to me.

'Boys, girls, whoever they are, they're going to be falling over themselves for you, Ellie. Don't be in a rush. You're special, *en kathal.* They need to be special too.' And the intimacy of it, the emotion, catches me off guard for a minute. Because Dad doesn't say things like this. Dad doesn't really say things at all.

He puts his arms out, and I let him envelop me in them. Strong, and firm, and safe.

'I wish you hadn't lied to me,' he breathes.

'I know,' I sniff. 'I'm sorry, Dad.'

'Are you OK, *sina pillai?*' he asks, as I tuck my head under his chin.

'I'm trying to be,' I whisper.

'Is it the baby?' he asks wisely, and I bury my head further into his chest.

'We'll never forget your brother, Ellie. Not ever.' And I do know this. I do.

He lets go of me, his eyes a little misty, and rubs the back of my head like I'm a child who's just collided with a sharp corner. Then he kisses my forehead.

'I'll let you get ready,' he says quietly, making his way towards the stairs.

And the thought of getting ready for the dance, of being somewhere Ash might be, without him, makes me feel suddenly strange and uneasy.

I pull Oasis, *Definitely Maybe* out of its sleeve and place it on the record player. Because the tightness in my chest feels like the sound of 'Supersonic'.

'You all right, kid?'

And suddenly, Noel Gallagher is stood in the middle of my bedroom, his tall frame stooping to accommodate my low ceiling, as he stands wedged between my record player and the end of my bed.

I stare blankly into the hallway, trying to work out if I have finally and completely lost it. Whatever 'it' is.

'Hi,' I reply unsteadily. Turns out, Noel Gallagher actually is my oracle.

'Turn that up, will you?' he says, staring at my poster of *Definitely Maybe*, which is curling at its edges. 'I love that song.'

'It's *you*,' I say to Noel Gallagher.

'Tell our kid that,' he smirks. 'I'm a genius, aren't I?'

I nod.

'So how's it going?' he says, watching me.

'Why are you wearing sunglasses inside?' I ask him, transfixed. He's got this presence. Like he's just there, but he's taking up more space than everybody else.

'You're allowed to wear them indoors when you're a rock 'n' roll star. It's in the manual,' he says, looking around. I momentarily wish I could take my Blur poster down, because I'm pretty sure he hates them.

'OK . . .' I trail away, staring at the side of his face.

'No offence, love, but I'm kind of busy being a rock 'n' roll god. What exactly do you want?'

'Well, I was hoping for some advice,' I say, as he looks at me impatiently, eyebrows slightly raised.

'About that geezer?'

'Sort of.'

'Right. Well, what do you wanna know?'

'I don't know.'

'He's not good enough for you. Next.'

'You don't even know him,' I say, annoyed.

'You know what, kid – your problem is you're not very clever.'

I stare at him.

'You like him. He likes you. You're both nice, just a bit thick.'

And this isn't the way I envisaged this talk going.

'What you actually need to be doing is thinking about that,' he says, motioning towards my notebook. 'Writing.'

'Writing,' I parrot.

'Writing songs, that's what gets me going. Not the drugs or the sex or the rock 'n' roll sunglasses. It's the music. Are you listening?' he asks, pointing at me.

I nod, hypnotised.

'I love being in a band. There is no greater feeling than walking out on stage with your mates. That's a feeling. That's *the* feeling.'

'The feeling,' I say, mesmerised.

'Don't waste your time, you know what I mean?'

'Yeah,' I reply.

And then I think, no. I don't know what that means.

'Ellie!' Dad shouts from downstairs. 'Your friends are here!'

And I can't even ask him now, because Noel Gallagher, songwriter, singer and self-proclaimed genius, is gone. Just as suddenly as he appeared. Possibly the world's worst oracle. And I consider taking the Blur poster down in homage, but decide Damon Albarn may give better advice, the next time I'm facing a moral crisis.

60

Ask the World to Dance

Hayley and Jess are being weird and awkward. They've never exactly been friends, but I've always felt that was because they refused to get to know each other – mostly because Hayley assumes Jess is the reason I'm not living my best life, when truthfully, I'm the reason I'm not living my best life.

'So . . .' I say, trying to break the ice. 'Music?'

They glare in opposite directions.

'Just put on whatever,' Hayley says dismissively.

I attempt not to look horrified.

'The music we play now sets the tone for the whole evening. It's an important decision.'

Seriously, how can Hayley not understand this?

'She's right,' Jess says solemnly.

'I've never understood why you two were friends,' Hayley says, unimpressed. 'You're a lot weirder than I thought you were, Jessica.'

'I'll take that as a compliment,' Jessica replies.

'Jess and I have come to realise, over the years, that a song has the power to change an entire mood. To change the course of an entire day,' I enthuse.

'She's right.' Jess nods again, like a mindless disciple of my cult of weirdness.

'So. Motown? Indie? Pop? Rock? R&B? Jazz? Blues? Classical?'

'Jazz?' says Jess, looking perplexed. 'Classical?'

'I'm just giving her all the options,' I say imperiously.

'O-K,' Hayley says, in the manner of someone trying not to spook a horse. 'Pop?'

'Good choice,' I respond.

'I'll find a playlist,' Jess says, searching her phone.

'How about nineties?' I say, in homage to Noel.

'Yep, yep. Good.'

And I'm impressed at Jess's and my efficiency. Our shorthand.

'Found it!' Jess cries, pleased with herself. 'It isn't nineties, but . . .'

'Play it,' I say excitedly. Jess has a talent for mood music.

And it's a brilliant choice. Eighties electric guitars, drums and a whole lot of swaggering. Jess is starting to mosh a bit, while Hayley stands on the spot, pretending she isn't interested, until she just can't help it and her head starts bobbing up and down to Billy Idol, 'Dancing with Myself', until suddenly all three of us are jumping, arms around each other, heads moving in tiny blunt motions to the beat. Because Billy's right. There is nothing to lose, and nothing to prove, when you're dancing for yourself. So, I close my eyes and let go. Because there is no joy like dancing with your best friends, when no one else is watching.

And in the final crescendo, we're playing air guitar and headbanging like we're actually Idol's band.

'OK, OK, I get it . . .' says Hayley, panting, as we collapse in a heap on the floor. And Jess is grinning at her, even as she's grinning back. 'Soooo . . .' she continues, 'what are we all wearing?'

And I think, oh God. Because I didn't get that far.

I Have No Dress.

I. Have. No. Dress.

That's when I hear a knock on my door.

'Hi, girls,' Mum says. 'I brought you a little something for while you get ready.' And in her hand is a tray with three glasses of champagne on it.

'Thanks,' I say, feeling suddenly weird.

'What's wrong, Ellie?' she asks instantly, her spider senses tingling.

'I don't have anything to wear,' I lie. Because I don't. But I know that's not the real reason I feel so strange.

'That's nothing to worry about,' Mum says kindly. 'Come on.' We leave Jess and Hayley to get dressed and hear a sudden peal of laughter as we walk off down the corridor.

'We'll find you something,' Mum says, leading me to her wardrobe. 'Are you OK?' she asks, turning to me as she cradles Phantom Baby. And for a minute, I feel soothed by the idea of this baby. Because this isn't about forgetting what we were – it's about teaching someone new the stories.

'Yes.'

'Is it that boy?' she asks intuitively. 'Ash. Did you want him to ask you?'

'Something like that,' I say, because I don't even know how to describe it. What's happening between us, or not happening between us any more.

'Listen, you're going to be just fine – with or without him.' And I know, in that moment, she's right. That I'll be fine – that I am fine. Just as I am. Just me. 'But wait till he sees you,' she says rubbing her hands with glee. 'You'll knock him dead.' And just like that, she's pulling dresses off hangers, holding them up against me and throwing them down again, unsatisfied, until she finds the exact right thing. And there it is. A saffron-yellow slip dress, with delicate straps and a high, dainty cowl neck.

'Breathe in,' she commands as she fastens the zip. Like a miracle, it comes sliding up my side, a perfect fit. And when I walk back into my bedroom, I let Hayley and Jess make 'ooh' and 'ah' noises at me, without once complaining that they're paying me too much attention. Hayley braids my hair, pinning it into a crown, and Jess applies a deep-red velvet to my lips. And for the first time maybe ever, I feel beautiful. Like the most me I can be. Not because I'm wearing a lovely dress and lipstick, but because Mum helped me pick out the dress, because Hayley and Jess are getting on, because I've tried and I've been me. No hiding. And that makes me beautiful, however I look on the outside.

It's just one thing that stops me being perfectly happy. One thing I have to find a way to fix.

When Hayley and Jess finish getting ready, they too look perfect, they too look like miracles, and for once, I don't feel short and frumpy in comparison to their long, lithe frames. I just feel like me. Like *that* Ellie.

So Cinderella goes to the ball. And she doesn't care how uncomfortably high her glass slippers are, or whether the pumpkin will break down at midnight, forcing her to walk home in her bare feet. She doesn't even care if Prince Charming shows up at all.

Or.

Maybe she does.

But only a little.

A very, very little.

61

The Postman Always Rings Twice

We take an Uber and meet James and Elina at a cafe around the corner from school, planning to walk in together as a group, strength in numbers. Except the numbers are skewed, because it isn't just James and Elina at all, there's Ash too, with his ever-present earphones, all long lean legs in a cool, fitted suit, the trousers grazing his ankle to expose neat white Converse.

'Doesn't Ellie look beautiful?' Hayley says pointedly, when she notices him ignoring me. She looks beautiful herself. Like Anjelica Huston in *The Postman Always Rings Twice*, all brooding, petulant glamour. So, basically, I'm stood here with Anjelica Huston, Audrey Hepburn and Debbie Harry. Which is fine, because I'm Shalom Harlow.

Jess looks at me and shrugs her shoulders in irritation. Clearly Elina hadn't told her Ash was coming either.

'You look lovely, Pillai,' James says, smiling at me. 'And I know

366

someone who wants to meet you,' he says, taking my arm, all gentlemanlike, with Hayley on one side and me on the other.

I can feel Ash tensing, such is his discomfort at my presence. So the three of us, Hayley, James and I, accelerate our pace, leaving Elina, Jess and Ash behind.

When we arrive at school, the studio looks beautiful. It's lit up like a fairy tale; dainty white fairy lights and handmade paper snowflakes. The lights are low and music is playing from the stage, a band made up of some boys and a girl from the lower sixth. The girl, Hannah, is one of Ash's many admirers, forever liking and commenting on his Instagram. And even now I can see him nodding hello to her, her eyes following him across the room. I just don't want to see them together, that's all I ask. For the High School Gods to do me that one tiny favour, that I'm not here to see it.

The two factions of our group have split, so Hayley and I put our tiny little bags down in the makeshift cloakroom, because no formal dance ensemble is complete without a pointlessly tiny bag, and make our way to the dancefloor. I throw my arms in the air and forget I have any reason to be sad, because that's what music does for me. Drowns out all the unnecessary noise, till there's no space for anything else.

But when the music slows down, I have to admit defeat. I walk off the dancefloor and stand in a corner, waiting for the right moment to leave.

And that's when I hear them. Forearms and his band of cronies, nudging each other and pointing in my direction. And that's it. That. Is. It. Because I've thought about it. I've thought about it over and over.

367

And I've tried to make it feel OK. To tell myself that I had some kind of control. That I knew what I was doing. But I didn't. I didn't have any control, and he has no right to walk around acting like I did.

I march over to him, my fists clenched.

'What are you laughing at?' I demand.

'Nothing,' he says, looking me up and down. 'You look nice.' His friends look at me and continue elbowing each other.

'Back for more?' one of them says, laughing.

'Excuse me?' and I'm trembling at how close I am to him. Remembering how I felt the last time I was this close.

'It's always the quiet ones,' the boy says, smirking.

'Shut up, Toby,' Adam says. 'Where's Anderson? Have you two broken up?'

And I don't know what to say to that, because Ash and I haven't broken up, we were never actually together. And honestly – I don't know why. I don't know why we're not together. But that's not the reason I'm here.

'What have you been saying to people?' I demand.

'About what?' he says defensively, standing up straighter.

'About what happened in the park that night. Between you and me.'

'What do you mean?' he asks, eyes flashing.

'I was drunk. Really, really drunk. And you took me away from everybody, you scared me, Adam.'

'You were all over me. You couldn't keep your hands off me,' he replies angrily.

'I could barely stand up,' I say just as angrily. 'You were keeping me upright.'

His friends look at me nervously, stepping back a little.

'*You* came over to talk to *me*,' he states.

'Yeah, talk,' I say, faltering a little.

'And you didn't want to kiss me?' he says, staring at me.

'I . . . I didn't know what I wanted. I didn't know where I was, or what I was doing. I didn't want to be away from my friends, and not know where I was. You scared me,' I repeat.

He's starting to look sweaty and nervous now.

'What you did was wrong. And you and your little friends can laugh about it all you want – and make out like I'm some kind of – whatever you want to say I am. But I wasn't all over you, and I didn't ask you to take me anywhere. And I don't think what you did was OK – and I don't want you to think it *was* OK. Because it wasn't.'

'Whatever,' he says, turning away from me. 'You don't look that nice anyway.'

'I have never been so glad I threw up in someone's mouth,' I seethe.

'What?' Toby says, turning to Adam. 'She threw up in your mouth?'

'He *literally* made me sick.'

Adam turns to me angrily.

'Everything OK, Ellie?' and suddenly Ash is stood next to me, his hand right next to mine. And I don't need him there, but I like it. When he's close enough to touch.

'Fine,' I say. And I pretend my heart isn't racing a mile a minute. 'I was just explaining to Adam and his little friends here that a practically unconscious person doesn't really have the ability to consent.'

'Come on,' Adam says, looking suddenly frightened. 'Nothing happened.'

'You see?' I say, turning to Toby. 'Nothing happened. Pass it on. And you,' I say to Adam, 'don't you dare talk about me again. Or smirk at me again. Or tell me I don't look nice again. I look nice.'

I take a breath and try to walk away, but it's like I'm suddenly fused to the spot. It's only when I feel Ash's fingers close in around mine that I finally wake up. He's pulling me away from them, their mouths half open.

And in this moment, all I want is for him to stay with me; but his grip is loosening with every step we walk. I'm trying to hold on to him, but he's gone, leaving me alone in the middle of the dancefloor, a throng of kids swaying to the long-haired blond boy in Hannah's band singing a cover of Green Day, 'Good Riddance (Time of Your Life)'.

And it's like the blond boy is singing directly to me. His voice feels soothing and raspy and syrupy – but it isn't real. None of this is real – because I'm not facing the one thing I need to. The one person I need to. This is the turning point, I think. This is the fork stuck in the road.

I have to do something.

For one horrible second I think I've lost Ash completely – until I spot him by the door, with what seems likes a million people between him and me. Except there were never a million people between him and me. Just me. Me and my stupid me-ness.

I walk as fast as I can in my ridiculous high heels, because I've realised that running doesn't solve anything. Which is just typical. Realising I have a talent for something that is completely and utterly useless. Like cheese rolling or extreme ironing.

'Ash!' I shout, trying to catch up with him. 'Ash!'

I follow him into the corridor, his earphones emitting a melancholy hum, then catch at his shoulder just as he's about to exit the building. He turns to face me, half in, half out the door. He pulls his earphones out, the music still blaring, and stares obstinately at the wall.

'What?' he asks, pushing himself back inside as the door closes behind him. 'What do you want from me, Ellie?'

'Nothing . . .' I say. Because I hadn't really planned on getting this far. 'Nothing. I just, I just wanted to say thank you, for coming over just now.'

'You don't need to thank me.'

'And . . . I wanted to see if you were all right.'

'I'm fine,' he says softly, but there's anger in there too. Quiet and venomous. 'I have to go, Ellie.'

'Go where?' I ask gently.

'Anywhere,' he says, looking down at my hand involuntarily stroking his arm.

'Ash, please,' I say, pulling my hand back. 'I'm sorry. Please talk to me.' And I know I have no right to ask anything of him – but I need to talk to him, I need to hear his voice, even if the words come out wrong.

'What about, Ellie? What I'm listening to?'

'I don't know what you mean,' I say, confused, because yes, I want to know what he's listening to. I've always wanted to know. I want to

371

know everything about him. Where he was when he lost his first tooth, and how it felt the first time he kissed someone. And why, why it is I feel like this around him. Because underneath the fact he's so much cooler, so much more secure, so much more beautiful than me – somehow it feels like we're just the same.

'What *are* you listening to?' I ask lightly.

'Pixies, "Where Is My Mind",' he says, staring again. 'Apt, right?'

'All that angst,' I say softly. 'Isn't it time for something else?'

'I don't know. Is it?'

'It is for me,' I say desperately. 'It has to be. I want to be happy, Ash.'

'Are you happy, Ellie?' and the tone in his voice is different now. Gentle and familiar. Just like it used to be, when we were friends.

'I am,' I whisper. 'I think I am. I will be.'

'Good,' he whispers. 'Because I want you to be happy.' But then he pauses. The kind of pause that feels loaded. And I want to hold it back. Hold on to it. Pause and rewind.

'But I can't . . . I don't want to do this any more. I don't want you to ask me what I'm listening to. I don't want you to look at me like you understand me. I don't want to look at you like I'm with you. When I'm not with you, am I?'

'Can't we just be friends?' I whisper, my voice wavering.

'I don't want to be friends, Ellie. I like you. I *like* like you. You must know that.'

'I . . .' I stutter.

'But you don't feel that way about me, do you?' he challenges.

372

And we both know that's a lie. So why can't I just say it? Why can't I tell him?

'I . . . I . . .'

'Why wouldn't you let me pick you up, Ellie? Are you ashamed of me?'

'Why would I be ashamed of you?' I say, bewildered. 'You're perfect. I told you, my parents are . . .'

'Your parents are what? Like my grandmother? I'm not Indian enough for them?'

'NO!' I shout. 'They would never think that. And your grandmother doesn't deserve you if that's what she thinks.'

He turns away from me, pacing up the corridor.

'Then what are you scared of? Why are you so scared?'

'People leave,' I stutter. 'Things fall apart.'

'You can't hide from anything *real*, Ellie. Sadness and loss and happiness and all the things that make us actual human beings and not robots. Things have to happen for them to fall apart. You have to at least try.'

And I no longer have words for any of this.

'I can't chase you any more. I can't keep hanging around in the background, watching other people look at you, killing myself over the fact you won't even try – when I know, I know we could be good together. Because you're not the only person that can get hurt. Not the only person with feelings. I like you. I'm not afraid to say it, to show it. But you – you're scared of everything. So I'm done. I have to be done now, Ellie.'

I try then to take hold of his hand. To do something, anything, to make all of this stop. All this fear. All this regret. Right inside my chest, choking me.

'I'm sorry,' I whisper. 'I'm sorry.'

'What does that even mean?' he asks quietly. 'What are you sorry for?'

And I can't say anything, because I don't know. I don't know what it means.

And then the earphones are in again, and he's walking away from me, his back hunched against the cold of the night, the rain beginning to fall. And suddenly I see what I never noticed until just this moment. That over the top of his suit, he's wearing one of those yellow rain macs – the kind hipster kids wear, all Scandinavian cool.

And I want to run after him and kiss him and tell him I'm not afraid any more, and I do want him, so much. But my legs are leaden, fused to the earth, the roots digging deep and wide, holding me in place, watching him leave. And just like that, he's gone. And I know I've made a mistake. A horrible, terrible mistake.

'Won't you love me?' she cried out to the man in the yellow mac.

62

Dancing on My Own

When I walk back into the dance, the band are playing 'Dancing on My Own' – Hannah mimicking Robyn, as she sings moodily to a slick, heavy, syncopated beat. And I seriously consider screaming. Primal therapy, tearing the walls down, ending up in a 1950s asylum, screaming. Maybe Ash would be there. I'd be happy to go, if Ash was there.

Hannah's right. What she's singing is right. I am messed up and out of line. I'm the reason we're not going home together. I'm the reason I'm dancing on my own.

The words feel ironic, in the worst possible way, and for a minute, in my head, it isn't Hannah singing at all, it's me. On stage in my saffron-yellow slip dress, my red mouth parted and glowing in the darkness. My eyes shut tight, my head moving almost robotically to the beat, as I lean down into the microphone. I close my eyes, and I'm there, in that moment. Stood on stage, watching him with someone else. Anyone who isn't me. My soul flying out of my mouth.

And that image is soothing. Poetic and meaningful. When the

truth is, I'm just stood here listening to Hannah, the one with the confidence to be up there, to be sure she's heard. And I'm just a girl in a saffron-yellow slip dress and smeared lipstick, tripping over her heels, trying to reach her friends, all gathered in a corner, whispering conspiratorially.

AAAAAAAAAAAAAARRRRRRRRRRRRRGGGGGHH HHHHHHHHHHH. I try an internal scream, to see if it makes me feel any better.

'Ellie,' says Hayley, turning to face me. 'Are you OK?'

'Yeah, yeah,' I say, trying to pull a paper snowflake off my shoe. How do these things look so beautiful on the walls? Pretty and delicate and lovely, when on me they resemble toilet paper, dishevelled and misshapen.

AAAAAAAAAAAAAARRRRRRRRRRRRRGGGGGGGGGG HHHHHHHHHHH. I don't think it's working.

'What happened?' Elina asks, her tone clipped. 'Where is he?'

'He left,' I say, glancing at her momentarily. And I want to stop picking at the snowflake on my shoe and look at her again, but I'm afraid that if I do, I'll cry. All the tears. All the tears in the world.

'Left, to go where?' she asks angrily.

AAAAAAAAAAAAAAARRRRRRRRRRRRRGGGGGGG GHHHHHHHH.

'I don't know,' I say, looking up to face her.

'What the hell did you say to him?' she asks me.

AAAAAAAAAAAAAAARRRRRRRRRRRRRGGGGGGGGG HHHHHHHH.

'Calm down,' Hayley says. 'Nothing happened. Ellie hasn't done anything wrong.'

'Why are you always upsetting him?' Elina says, ignoring Hayley and looking down on me, her beautiful face distorted with rage. 'He told you what he's been through. You know how far he's come.'

'I . . .' I stutter, silent and inarticulate.

AAAAAAAAAAAAAAAARRRRRRRRRRRGGGGGG GHHHHHHHH.

'What's wrong with you, Ellie?' And that's the moment I tip from sadness into rage. Because I am bored of believing there is anything wrong with me. When there was never anything wrong with me, other than my inability to see there was never anything wrong with me.

'I'm not the one who upset him, Elina,' I counter. 'You are. Making him lie. Making him pretend.'

'No,' she says, taking a step towards me. 'You were talking to that boy. The one who was with you when you were so drunk you could barely stand. Ash was trying to protect you.' Her eyes are flashing and I can tell she's barely controlling herself, her hands shaking with the effort of it.

'I don't need him to protect me, Elina. I'm not a child.'

'Not the case the last time round, was it? Why were you even talking to that idiot?' she says disgustedly.

'As it happens,' I seethe, 'I was *telling him* he was an idiot. OK? I wanted him to know that what he did was wrong – *the last time round.*' My voice is so heavy with sarcasm, it needs a lie down.

'I don't really care who you talk to,' she hisses. 'Just don't drag my brother into it.'

'I'm not dragging anyone anywhere,' I hiss back.

'Really? Because it looks to me like you've been dragging him everywhere. He's done everything for you. And you, you've done nothing for him.'

I want to scream. Or cry. Or shout. Or possibly all three at once, in her stupid Audrey Hepburn face.

'I thought he was Jessica's boyfriend,' I state.

'But he wasn't!' she screams. 'They were never even together. You know that now. So just get over it, Ellie!'

'He lied to me!' I shout back stubbornly. 'How can I trust somebody who lies to me?' And even as I say it, I can feel the irony of lying to my parents, of lying to Jessica, of kissing Ash when I thought she still loved him.

'Stop. Please, stop!' We turn towards the voice.

'This is all my fault. All of it. I made Elina lie. So Ash had to lie too. Because I wasn't ready. I didn't want to . . .' Jess trails off.

'This isn't your fault,' Elina says angrily. And I want to hate Elina, but I can't. Not when she loves Jess and reminds me of my favourite Hepburn.

'It is,' Jess says quietly.

'It isn't,' I say, turning to her. 'You had to be ready . . . this was a big deal. I'm proud of you.'

And when I look at Elina, I can see her softening. Her stance changing, her anger evaporating. Neither of us is really angry. We just love the same person. The same people. And we want them to be happy.

'I just need to find him.' She waves her mum over, Mr Green in tow behind her.

'What's wrong?' Mrs Aachara asks, looking from Elina's face to mine, and back again.

'It's Ash,' says Elina.

'Is everything OK?' she asks quietly. 'He wasn't . . .'

'No,' Elina says, cutting her off. 'Nothing like that. We just need to find him.'

'Anything I can help with, Kyra?' Mr Green is wearing dark blue chinos and a white linen shirt. It's different to his usual jogging bottoms and T-shirts, but he suits it. Like he would probably suit a bin bag, or a prison head shot. Because pretty much everything he wears makes him look like an advert for Calvin Klein.

'It's fine, William. Thank you for asking,' says Mrs Aachara. *Kyra*. She looks like a *Kyra*. He blushes, and I've never seen him blush before.

'I'll call you later,' Elina says, kissing Jess on the cheek. Jess nods, as her mother turns to William Green and smiles the tiniest of smiles. And I watch him watch her go. And I wonder if she knows. How much he likes her.

'Should we go?' James asks Hayley, his eyes darting back and forth between my blotchy red face and Jess's pained expression.

'In a minute,' she says, pecking him on the lips. He grins inanely. 'We need to talk,' she tells Jess and me, with a strangely calm expression, before grabbing us both by our arms.

'Are you OK, Ellie?' she asks, as we enter the one place where the truth is undeniable. The toilets in the girls' changing room are weirdly empty, and I start to cry, a shrill, pathetic whine, covering myself in snot.

'I'm fine,' I snivel.

She laughs. 'You look it. So, what happened when you went after him?'

I walk into a cubicle and retrieve a roll of tissue, dabbing at my eyes.

'He told me he was sick of waiting around for me. That he liked me, but he was done. That if I was too scared to be with him, he didn't want to be with me anyway.'

'And do you?' Hayley asks directly. 'Do you want to be with him?'

I studiously ignore her.

'What is it with those two?' Jess says suddenly, her voice raised and sharp. 'Sometimes it takes a little time to figure out what you want. To tell yourself you deserve it. To put yourself out there.'

'I know,' I say, blowing my nose pitifully, the tissue now resembling a rag, my face a mess of stained make-up and snot. When Jessica cries, she looks like she's crying diamonds, the tears sliding down her face in orderly, perfectly curated lines. When I cry, I look like a pug.

'So you *do* like him?' Hayley asks, looking at me intensely.

'I can't,' I snivel, refusing to meet either of their eyes.

'Why, E?' Jess asks, wiping my tears away. 'Why can't you?'

'Because he's him, and I'm *me*, and I don't know how to do this, Jess.'

'You're the one who said those things don't mean anything,'

Hayley says matter-of-factly. And this is what eating your words actually feels like.

'So . . . ?' Jess asks gently. 'You *do* like him.'

'Yes,' I sniff. 'Obviously.'

'Obviously?' Hayley says, surprised. 'Honestly, and please don't hate me for saying this, but I never would have guessed it. I thought he might like you, but I had no idea you liked him back. I mean, I saw you spending time with him – but you never gave anything away, never gave me any reason to think it was anything more than a friendship, not for you.'

'What are you getting at, Hayley?' I ask irritably. Maybe I'm too good a liar, maybe I need to develop a tell. Like singing to myself, or hopping on one foot.

'I just mean, if you do like him, if you do want him, then go get him, E. Maybe he doesn't know how you feel about him. Maybe he doesn't realise how much you care.'

'Ellie,' Jess says softly. 'You told me to be honest about my feelings for Elina, and it was the hardest thing I've ever done – but I did it. Now you have to be honest about your feelings. Take a risk. Because whether it works out or not, if you care for someone, they're always worth putting yourself out for.'

'I . . .' I stutter, 'I . . . I do like him. So much. I always have. He's amazing. He's funny, and kind, and wise, and sweet, and he has the best taste in music, like, he can name every song on the *White Album* . . .'

'Because that's a priority,' Jess says drily.

'It is for me,' I sniff, smiling.

'So tell him. Tell him now, before you lose him. Before that singer Hannah decides to throw herself at him and he's too weak to resist.'

'God, yes,' says Hayley. 'That girl's Instagram comments are literally foreplay. I mean, seriously, have some respect for yourself.'

'It's too late,' I say, starting to cry again. 'He hates me now.'

'Seriously, Ellie,' she says, grabbing me by my shoulders. 'He hasn't taken his eyes off you all night. I've never seen anyone move as fast as he did when you went over to talk to Adam. What happened with that anyway?'

'I don't know really,' I say, shaking my head. 'I told him what he did was wrong, and he should know it.'

'I'm proud of you,' Hayley says, hugging me.

'I'll kill him if he comes anywhere near you again,' Jess says darkly.

'How did it feel?' Hayley asks admiringly.

'It felt . . . good. I felt . . . powerful.'

'Yes, queen,' Hayley says, attempting to high-five me.

Jess and I look at her.

'Don't do that again,' I say mock-seriously.

'Seriously,' Jess says, 'don't attempt it.'

'Whatever,' Hayley says, ignoring our sarcasm.

'But you can't leave it like this, E, with Ash,' Jess says firmly. 'You have to tell him how you feel. Quickly. Because you know—'

'Hannah,' they repeat in unison.

And I can't help laughing then, at the Art Girl and the Cool Girl, at my two best friends becoming friends. Finding common ground, even if it's just telling me what to do.

'I do want him,' I say simply.

'So . . .' says Hayley, looking at Jessica for confirmation, 'go get your man.'

'But how do I do this?' I ask, looking at them both to deliver me to redemption.

Because – as they say – it's not over until the fat lady sings. Or in this case, the Ellie Pillai.

♡ Song 9 ♡

Intro, Verse, Chorus - House on Fire

It's a song I wrote about him. And me. And I didn't hear it in my head this time, I wrote it. Intentionally. Sat down at the piano, with all of my feelings, and made him a song. It's about getting things wrong. Being a fool.

I'm sorry
If it took me a little time
To say you make me smile

It's all arpeggios and staccato and pleading ignorance. It makes my heart soar with triumph, and descend just as quickly in fear.

But.

I am keys and I am fire.

63

The Audition

'Can I come in please, miss?' I ask, poking my head around the doorframe. I've been knocking gently for a while now, but I don't think she can hear me. I suspect that ironically, despite being a music teacher, she's ever so slightly hard of hearing.

'Ellie! Of course, come in. In please. Shut the door. You know I hate stragglers.' Miss Mason looks at me, with those tiny, raisin-like eyes she has, the ones that seem to be receding into her head, but see everything. Notice everything. 'What do you want, dear?'

'I wanted to talk to you about something,' I say slowly.

'Quite,' she says, taking a long, slow breath. 'I imagine that's why you're here.'

'It's about the orchestra. I'd like to audition for a place.' I watch her closely.

'I'm so pleased to hear you say that. I've been waiting to hear you say that for years,' she says warmly, all wrinkled delight.

'OK, well, I'd like to do that.'

'Would you like to do it now?' she asks, putting down her pen.

'Yes. I would.'

'Go on then,' she says, pointing to the piano.

'All right . . . but there's something else too.'

'Yes, dear?' she asks, eyeing me warily. I can see she has a pile of essays to mark, and she is no longer known for her speed or lightness of hand.

'I need a favour.'

'Tell me more,' she says, pushing her papers away. She hates marking essays. Hates musical theories and academia. Just likes notes and instruments and songs and beauty, all the reasons she became a teacher in the first place.

So I tell her more. And she listens. And at the end she says, 'Hmmmm,' and picks up her pen and chews the end of it.

'Let's get started then,' she says, pushing the papers aside entirely.

And that's it.

We're off.

64

'Won't You Love Me?' She Cried Out to the Man in the Yellow Mac

When the day of the drama exam arrives, it's a week on from the dance. I feel nervous and exhausted, like I haven't slept in days. Maybe I haven't. My dreams are a symphony, thrumming and loud.

'Are you ready?' I ask, looking at the group expectantly.

'God, no,' says Hayley, looking at me in solidarity.

'You'll be fine,' says James, stroking her hand. 'It's brilliantly written and will be nothing less than a heartbreaking work of staggering genius.' She laughs. He's always making her laugh.

'It's hardly Dave Eggers, but thanks,' she says, giving him a kiss on the cheek.

Mrs Aachara is sat at the front of the stage with the examiners. She told me to imagine them in matching black wigs, the way some people imagine their audience naked. The advice made me laugh, as if she could read my mind. I don't know why she's been so kind to me. Why she seemed to understand it all, when I explained everything to her. But she did. She told me to be brave. To be brave and honest.

'It's going to be OK, isn't it, Hayley?' I whisper under my breath as one of the other groups performs.

'With which thing?' she asks, smiling.

'Both things.'

She pushes her hand inside mine and squeezes it.

'You're going to be fine, E,' she whispers back. 'And I'm here. Jessica and I are. Whatever happens.'

'Thanks,' I say emotionally. It's like Mum's hormones are catching. I found Dad crying at a shaving advert the other day.

'Are you crying?' James hisses from the other side of me. 'Because you're going to be fine, Pillai. You're going to kill it today, so just breathe.'

'Shut up, James,' Hayley hisses back. 'She is breathing. We can't all be as calm as you are.'

'It's just an exam,' he whispers, rolling his eyes.

'I don't think that's what she's nervous about, James.'

'Oh, yeah. Well, that'll be fine too,' he says, shrugging nonchalantly.

'Just shut up, will you? You're way too relaxed about all this. You're giving me anxiety,' says Hayley, jigging up and down on the spot, trying to find somewhere to put her nervous energy.

'How is me being *calm* giving you anxiety?' he hisses back, irritated. 'I will never understand you, woman.'

'Stop calling me woman. And just, you know. Stop talking,' says Hayley, equally irritated.

'OK, are you guys ready? You're up next,' says Mrs Aachara, popping her head backstage and smiling at us. 'The examiners need five minutes. I'll signal when it's time to start setting up.' We look at each other and attempt to breathe. In through the nose, out through the mouth.

'One thing, E,' says Hayley, looking at the floor. 'I've made some last-minute changes to the lighting. Just roll with it, OK?'

'What changes? What do you mean?' I ask shrilly, but there is no time for further explanation as Mrs Aachara signals us, and we take our places onstage.

We open with Katja and her friends in Sarajevo, her goodbye to her country and the only life she's ever known. She's embarking on the search for her family, one she believes will help her find herself, find her real place in the world. I watch as Hayley soars, her characterisation faultless; the perfect mix of fear and knowing, self-love and self-loathing. She's everyone I've ever known, all rolled into one. An analogy for all of us, searching, searching, searching, when all she's ever needed was right inside of her.

As I finish my monologue, I thank the High School Gods for keeping me sweat- and blonde-moustache-free. Then I descend the stage for the beginning of the music and sit at the piano, ready to begin the refrain – but as I do, building into the scene with Katja and Arthur, the spotlight shines directly on me. I breathe into it. My eyes open, staring into the light.

And as it fades, I realise this was always Hayley's plan. To take me out of the darkness and drag me into the light. I want to kill her and kiss her in equal measure, because I did it. I am doing it.

And in the last scene, as Arthur cuts a solitary figure, wondering where Katja is gone and how he's going to find her, I sing my heart out and bring the moment to life, am part and parcel of James's glory. And as Katja enters behind him and stands in his shadow, I finish.

I'm so lost that I can't see
What's right there in front of me

There's applause from the back of the room, and what sounds like whooping, until the examiners turn and look disdainfully into the shadows.

'I think there's someone here to see you,' Hayley says, nudging me.

I walk towards the back of the room, unsure of what I'll find.

It's Mum. Her eyes pouring with tears, while she and Phantom Baby absorb me wholly into their arms.

'I didn't know,' she says, crying. 'I didn't know you could do that. How didn't I know?'

And even though my heart is racing, even though every fibre in my body has been waiting to hear her say that, I just hiss, 'Mum, can you be a bit quieter?'

She ignores me.

'You were amazing up there, Ellie. Amazing.' She tucks a stray hair behind my ear. 'I should have seen it before. I should have known what you were capable of. I'm sorry, *en anbe*.'

'You can stop saying sorry now, Mum.'

'Can I?' she sniffs, locking eyes with me.

I look at Phantom Baby, swelling delicately beneath her floral midi dress, and I think – I'm glad you were here to see this. I'm glad I could share this with you too.

'Yes,' I say as she envelops me into her bosoms, and it's impossible not to notice they're at least two sizes bigger than they were last week. 'Thank you for coming. And you too,' I say, putting my hand on her stomach. 'But how did you . . .'

'Mrs Aachara, and Jessica. They said I had to see you.'

'Don't cry again, Mum,' I say, embarrassed. She cries at everything these days. Like a permanently drippy tap.

'I'm not crying. I'm . . . emoting.' She wipes her nose. 'You're so talented, Ellie,' she says, cupping my face. 'I love you, OK?'

'OK,' I say acceptingly. Because believing her feels suddenly easy. 'I love you too.' And that felt easy too.

'I have to go back to work now, but I'll pick you up after school. Celebration dinner. Bring your friends.'

'Bye, Mum.'

'Bye, Ellie.'

'We did it, Ellie,' says Hayley, as I walk backstage.

'You were amazing, Hay,' I say, beaming. 'Honestly, it was the best you've ever done it.'

391

'And me,' says James, putting his arms around both of us in an exaggerated hug. 'I was amazing too.'

'Obviously,' says Hayley, rolling her eyes.

'Obviously,' I say, rolling mine.

But relief is short-lived, because my skin is tingling like there's ice on it. Like there's fire on it. Like there's wind and rain and lightning on it. And I can't breathe any more, because there's more to this day. So much more.

'You OK?' Hayley whispers, squeezing my hand. And I'm not. But it's happening. And the real work, the work I've been building up to all week, is about to begin. The groups are starting to file outside, when Hayley announces there's another performance, and would they mind waiting another five minutes before they go for lunch. But they need to be quiet. Very, very quiet. And I want to kill her. Just kill her. No kiss this time at all.

I station myself at the piano as everything gets set up around me. There's a buzz in the air. Something electric and strange.

'Good luck,' says James, hand on my shoulder.

'Thanks,' I whisper, my throat dry, my lips sticking to my teeth.

'Ready?' says Hayley – her arms directing Ahmed, the lighting designer, to my spot at the piano. I take a deep breath and ready myself. Steady myself.

I. Am. Ellie. Pillai.

'Everyone shhhhh!' says Hayley suddenly. 'They're coming.' As the lights turn off, I fear I may be having a heart attack. I look at my shoes. Stupid Nermina and her stupid high heels. I couldn't run in these if I tried.

But it isn't them, it's Jessica, terse and out of breath.

'Good luck, E,' she says, hugging me. And I think I'm going to die. My heart is exploding into a thousand tiny pieces.

I. Am. Ellie. Pillai.

I adjust my eyes to the darkness, to the quiet, to the thrum in my heart. To the symphony in my head.

'What are you doing?' I hear Ash say. 'Mum said she's got exams all morning, we can't just walk in there.'

'They're finished,' says Elina. 'They finished before lunch. She asked us to meet her here.' I hear the door open, and out of the corner of my eye I see a sliver of light appear beyond the blackout curtains hung roughly over the entrance doors.

I take a breath.

I. Am. Ellie. Pillai.

The spotlight shines on me, so bright, so frighteningly bright, but soft and pearlescent, kind. I lay my fingers down on the keys, my home, my heart, and I play.

Eyes wide open.

Not hidden behind a costume or character, just me. I play him the song I've written, the one I hear in my dreams.

I'm just notes, and I am words

And as I play, the sound of a violin, sweet and high, begins to accompany me. Then two, then three. A viola, a cello, a guitar. A full string accompaniment, breathing life into my song, rich and full-bodied. The symphony of my dreams, thrumming and loud. And the orchestra is playing with me, playing my song, because I've auditioned for them. Won my place among them, and asked for their help. And I'm in a dream, I must be, because my song is alive in the world, a living, breathing entity, out there, real and sonorous.

And I am free, just like a bird

And I sing with all my heart, because I want his forgiveness, I want his love, I just want him.

I've overcome so much to get to this point, to admit my feelings, openly, without fear. I'm trying. I'm putting myself out there. I'm not afraid any more – well, maybe just a bit. Because it's dark, and unknown and I could turn around to realise the entire room has been murdered by a clown serial killer. But I'm trying not to be afraid. And I need him to know. I need him to know I'm trying.

And I am raw and I am hope and I'm desire
You make me sing

And as the strings ease away, it's back to the staccato of the piano.

And for you
I would do anything

I stop, I end, and I breathe out, or maybe I just breathe, for the first time in days. Then I turn to him, my mouth still dry, my lips sticking to my teeth. But he isn't there. Just an empty space where I expected him to be.

I try not to cry as the room erupts into applause. Because I'm proud of myself. I promised I would be, whatever happened, and I am. I'm proud of myself for trying.

But then I feel him next to me, his arm so suddenly around my waist, as though it was always there. Just close enough to touch.

'That was quite a statement,' he jokes softly.

'My mother always told me that if you're going to do something, you have to give it your full commitment,' I say quietly. Our inside joke, our very first one. That's when I hear James Godfrey begin a chant from the back of the room. 'Kiss, kiss, kiss,' he shouts, as the room erupts beneath his direction.

'I think they want us to kiss,' Ash whispers to me, smiling. 'What do you think we should do?'

'Full commitment,' I whisper back.

'That's what I thought,' he says, taking my face in his hands.

And so we do. He tips my head towards him, cupping my face in his hands, and he kisses me. Gently, sweetly, but urgently, like we've wasted so much time. I put my arms around his waist and kiss him back.

I. Am. Ellie. Pillai.

65

Primal Scream

As I lead Ash across the playground, I hear the sound of a guitar, loud and joyous, interspersed with piano chords, melodic and heavy. We're holding hands, my other arm pulling at him, hurrying him along.

She's waiting for us just outside the school. The little blue Mini parked in a side street, just outside the gate. Primal Scream, 'Movin' On Up' is playing at full volume, blasting out of the radio. Because I was lost – but I've been found.

She's watching us cross the road towards her, her eyes half shut against the light.

I open the door and peer inside.

'Mum – this is Ash. Ash – this is Mum. Ash is coming home for dinner.'

She looks at him and smiles.

'Well, aren't you handsome,' she says, shaking his hand.

And I think: Oh God.

66

My Happy Ending

'Won't you love me?' she cried out to the man in the yellow mac.

'Yes,' he replied.

67

A Girl Called Ellie

My name is Ellie. Ellie Pillai. And this is what I've learned. To be enough, you just have to believe it. To know it. To look at yourself and see something that no one else can see.

Because I'm extraordinary. Not perfect, but perfectly me. And when I chose to like myself, it's kind of weird, but other people chose to like me too.

My name is Ellie. Ellie Pillai. Who are you?

♡ Lyrics ♡

All lyrics by Christine Pillainayagam, except 'Rewrite the Story' by Christine Pillainayagam, Paul Cook and Julian Simmons.

Give Me a Minute

Give me a minute, just wait
right there
Give me a minute,
don't disappear
I need a minute, baby, I
need a minute
You know that, we had a minute
And I think, yes I think
You should stay right here

You know, you know, you know
You know what they say
You know I'll tell you baby
If you stay

You know, you know, you know
You know what they say
If you have a minute baby
You should stay
I saw you standing, I saw you
standing right there
And I don't know
If you saw me here
But when you look at me
I've got this feeling right here
Here, here, here
You know, you know, you know
Like you should be near

You know, you know, you know
You know what they say
If you have a minute, baby, you
should stay
You know, you know, you know
You know what they say
If you have a minute baby
You should stay

You can laugh at me
Think I'm a fool
And I won't mind if you do
Just stay
Just stay
You can laugh at me
Think I'm a fool
And I won't mind if you do
Just stay
Just stay

You saw me standing, saw me
standing right there
But I don't know if you
saw me here
But when you look at me
I got this feeling right here
Here, here, here
You know, you know, you know
You know what they say
If you have a minute, baby, you
should stay
You know, you know, you know
You know what they say
If you have a minute, baby, you
should stay
If you have a minute, baby, you
should stay
If you have a minute, baby, you
should stay

Rewrite the Story

Tell me how not to be scared
Of losing you
Tell me not to be afraid

Of making a choice
If I find my voice
Can I use it?

Tell me if you're really there
I'm not feeling you
Tell me if you really care
Don't know if I'm sure
If you're there at all
Can you prove it?
Will you prove it?

You always said that you were in
it with me
And being on my own is scary
But we can't go on just
living a memory
Time for me to rewrite this story
And learn to live

Tell me how I can be brave
I'm losing you
I don't want to be afraid
Of knowing you're not
What I need at all
And I need more
Can I be more?

You always said that you were in
it with me

And being on my own is scary
But we can't go on just
living a memory
Time for me to rewrite this story
You and me we were on a journey
And though it's unknown we're
both still learning
All I know is that we can't
repeat history
Time for me to rewrite this story

I need to be
Enough as me
I will be
Enough as just me

Tell me how not to be scared
Tell me how not to be afraid
that we're not
My story at all

You always said that you were in
it with me
And being on my own is scary
But we can't go on just
living a memory

401

Time for me to rewrite this story
And I know right now we're
on a journey
Wherever we're going we're both
still learning

And I learned that we can't
repeat history
Time for us to rewrite our story
Rewrite the story
Rewrite the story

Katja's Song

I'm not the girl you want
I'm not the girl you need
I'm not the girl that you
expect me to be

And I don't know why
Why

Tell me what I'm doing wrong
Cos I don't even know my song

Tell me what I'm doing wrong
Cos I don't even know my song
I don't even know my song
And I'm getting it wrong
More than I get it right
I don't even know my song

I don't even know my song
And I'm getting it wrong
More than I get it right

I don't even know my song
I don't even know my song

I'm not the girl you want
I'm not the girl you need
I'm not the girl that you
expect me to be
And life just passes me by

And I'm so lost
That I can't see
What's right there in front of me
The girl I need
The girl I want to be

No Fairy Tale

Did you ever feel so small
You wonder if you're really
there at all?
And nobody can see you there
So nobody can know or care
And you're shouting so loud
inside your head
But they can't hear

Just wake up
Tell yourself that it's all right
Put your arms around yourself
And say that you'll be fine

Did you know, did you know
You're brighter than this night?
Did you know, did you know
There's another way to fight?
This feeling
Just don't believe it

Please don't feel so small
Climb your own hair, slay your
own dragon, run your own course

And you know you're
so much more
Than the voices that you
can't ignore
That are shouting so loud
inside your head
So you can't hear

Did you know, did you know
You're brighter than this night?
Did you know, did you know
There's another way to fight?
This feeling
Just don't believe it

Did you know, did you know
You're stronger than you know?
Did you know, did you know
You're higher than your lows?
You know it
And you will show it

Life's no fairy tale
No prince charming to

guide your way
You've got to learn to fall
And learn to stand
And wake up with your
sword in hand
Cos you're the hero of this land

Did you know, did you know
You're brighter than this night?

Did you know, did you know
There's another way to fight?
Did you know, did you know
You're stronger than you know?
Did you know, did you know
You're higher than your lows?

You're the hero of this land

Young

You tell me that I'm young
Too young to know my mind
You tell me that I'm blind
And I can't see what's in
front of me

But you don't know me
And you don't own me
I'm too young to play
these games
But I'm not too young to run away

Run, run, you can fly

And leave this world behind
Because you're screaming inside
But they don't hear you
Fly, fly you can hide
And leave them all behind
You're in pieces inside
But they don't hear you cry

You tell me that I run
But what else can I do?
You tell me that I hide
But then, where are you?
You don't know me

And you don't own me
I'm too young to play
these games
But I'm not too young to run away

Run, run, you can fly
And leave this world behind
Because you're screaming inside
But they don't hear you
Fly, fly you can hide
And leave them all behind
You're in pieces inside
But they don't hear you cry

But they don't hear you cry

You tell me how
You tell me where
You tell me everything
You tell me who I should be
You don't know anything
Will you just see me?

You tell me that I run
But what else can I do
I'm too young to play
these games
But I'm not too young to run away

Earphones

Put your earphones in
Pretend you're somewhere else
Put your earphones in
Until it all makes sense
Because you're someone else
When you hear that sound
It turns it all around
You can feel yourself

Coming back down
To the ground
To the ground

And you can breathe
And you can see
What you're meant to be
And you can run

And you can fly
Although you're not trying to
outrun anyone
Except yourself
Accept yourself

Put your earphones in
Pretend you're somewhere else
Put your earphones in
Until it all makes sense
Because you're someone else
When you hear that sound
It turns it all around
You can feel yourself
Coming back down
To the ground
To the ground

And you can breathe
And you can see
What you're meant to be
And you can run
And you can fly
Although you're not trying to
outrun anyone
Except yourself

Accept yourself

Please tell me where you're going
When you disappear inside
yourself like that
And I'm folding in on myself
When I hear
When I hear that sound

Put your earphones in
Pretend you're somewhere else
Put your earphones in
Until it all makes sense
Because you're someone else
When you hear that sound
It turns it all around
You can feel yourself
Coming back down
To the ground
To the ground

Lights

These lights tell me to go slow
But these lights will not
guide me home
These lights are burning so low
You won't ask if I want to go
Cos I don't know anymore
What it is that I'm even
fighting for
These lights they blind you
They hurt not guide you
But these lights
You know these lights can go

You know that you can control
So much more than you know
And you've just got to believe
That you can see
What you need to see
Don't be fooled by the dark

Cos you can see
By your heart

These lights they blind you
They hurt not guide you
But these lights
You know these lights can go
If you stop and tell them so
You need to know
That I've got to let you go
Cos these lights
Got in my eyes

These lights they blind you
They hurt not guide you
But these lights
You know these lights can go
If you stop and tell them so
You need to know
That I've got to let you go
Cos these lights
They hurt my eyes
These lights
They hurt my eyes

Pink Moon

Whispered words in
white corridors
Painted smiles in white rooms
I didn't say goodbye
Wasn't by your side
When you flew away
From your pain
But now you're OK

Don't say goodbye
Don't talk about it
Look at the sky
There's a pink moon outside
It said you're gonna be all right

Pink moon
I'm watching you
And though I'm small, you
make me warm
And I know there's
something out there
That makes all this make sense
But it feels like everything's a mess

Whispered words in
white corridors
Painted smiles in white rooms
We didn't say goodbye
Just let you fly
From your pain
But now you're OK

Pink moon
I'm watching you
And though I'm small, you
make me warm
And I know there's
something out there
That makes all this make sense
But it feels like everything's a mess
Something out there
That makes all this make sense
But it feels like everything's a mess

Pink moon
Promise me, promise me
Promise he's with you
And he's burning through space

Lighting stars in his wake
On his way to you

Pink moon
Though I'm small, you
make me warm
And I know there's
something out there

That makes all this make sense
But it feels like everything's
just a mess
He left when he wanted to
He left when he was safe
He left when he wanted to
Now he's with you

House on Fire

My house is on fire
Don't try to put it out
My house is not in order
But I'm all right with that
Cos I'm just notes, and
I am words
And I am free, just like a bird
When I sing
When I sing – I can do anything

And I'm raw
And I'm scared
And I'd do anything
Not to be afraid

But you take my hand
And I can fly
You make me notes
You make me words
You make me free, just like a bird
You make me sing
When I sing
Then I am keys and I am fire
And I am raw and I am hope and
I'm desire
You make me sing
And for you
I would do anything

If it's not too late
I'd like to tell you that I've
memorised your face
Every smile sets me alight
And all I want to know
Is if you will be mine
And I'm sorry
If it took me a little time
To say you make me smile
And ask you to be mine
Will you be mine?

My house is on fire
Don't you try to put me out
My house is not in order
But I'm all right with that
Cos I'm just notes, and
I am words
And I am free, just like a bird
When I sing
You make me sing
You make me keys, you
make me fire
You make me raw, you make me
hope, make me desire
You make me sing

And for you
I would do anything